THE SUNDERING

THE SUNDERING SERIES

BOOK 1

D RAE PRICE

CONTENTS

This is a work of fiction. Names, characters, places, and incidents are either the product of the author's imagination or are used fictitiously. Any resemblance to actual persons, living or dead, events, or locales is entirely coincidental.

Book Cover Design &
Illustration © Tom Edwards
TomEdwardsDesign.com

Library of Congress Control Number: 2022910595

ISBN 979-8-9852043-3-9 (paperback)
ISBN 979-8-9852043-4-6 (e-book)

First Edition August 2022
Published by: DRaePriceBooks, Concord CA, USA
Contact: DRaePriceBooks@gmail.com

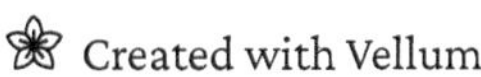

The Sundering Series

Book 1: The Sundering

By D Rae Price

Published by DRaePriceBooks

Coming soon:
Book 2: The Unbounded
Book 3: The Harbingers
Book 4: The Convocation

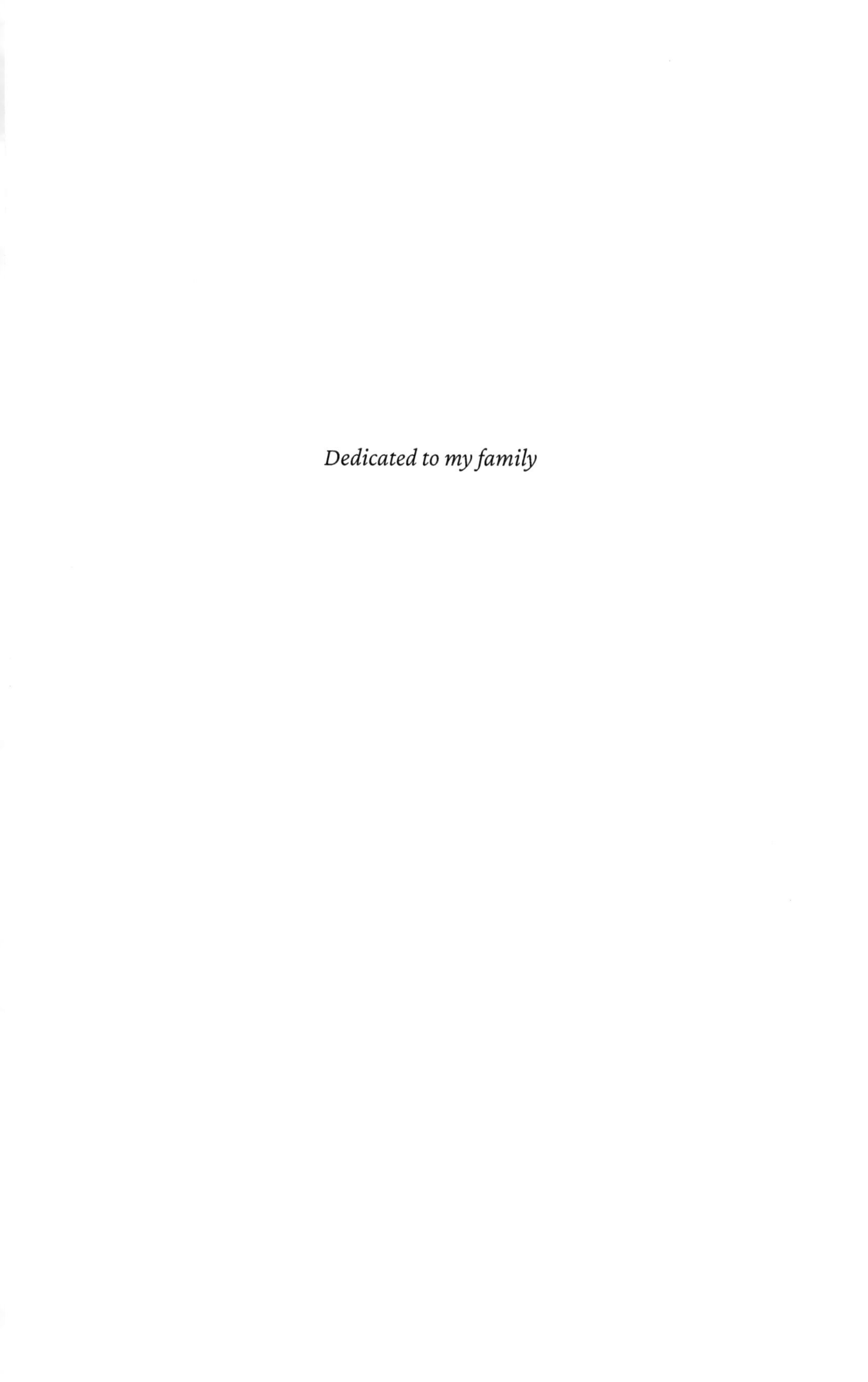

Dedicated to my family

NOTES ON SCIENCE AND RELIGION

LAGRANGE POINTS

Not to scale

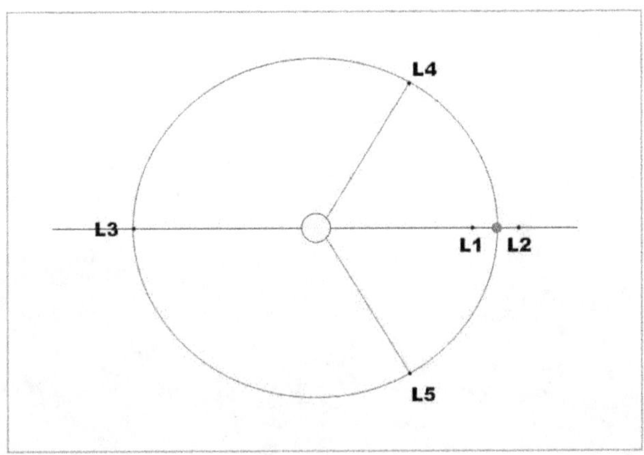

In space, for a planet orbiting its central star, there will be five places, called Lagrange Points, where gravity balances. A small object, such as a space station or asteroid, could be placed in those spots and stay there. This also works for some planet and moon systems. These points were discovered in the late-1700s by the mathematician Joseph-Louis Lagrange.

Three of these points, L1, L2, and L3, are "metastable." It's similar to a ball balancing on top of a hill. A small push will send it down the hill.

However, the L4 and L5 points are stable, as if the ball were inside a bowl. A little push will make the ball roll around in the bowl, but it won't get out. In fact, there are asteroids that ended up in the L4 and L5 points of many planetary orbits, especially the bigger planets like Jupiter. These asteroids are called Trojans.

To see maps and diagrams, go to:

https://www.draepricebooks.com/maps-diagrams

The Bahá'í Faith

The Bahá'í Faith is a real religion, founded by Bahá'u'lláh in the mid-1800s. The quotes used are real quotes from the Bahá'í Faith. For more information: https://www.bahai.us/.

The Badí‘ Calendar

The Badí‘ calendar, used by members of the Bahá’í Faith, is also a real calendar. New Year’s Day is set on the spring equinox on Earth. It has 19 months of 19 days and 4-5 intercalary days, known as Ayyám-i-Há, so the calendar will match the solar year. The day begins and ends at sunset.

Names of the Months

(On Earth, dates vary slightly with the equinox, but these “set” dates are used in the sectors.)

- Splendor: Mar 21 - Apr 8
- Glory: Apr 9 - Apr 27
- Beauty: Apr 28 - May 16
- Grandeur: May 17 - June 4
- Light: June 5 - June 23
- Mercy: June 24 - July 12
- Words: July 13 - July 31
- Perfection: Aug 1 - Aug 19
- Names: Aug 20 - Sept 7
- Might: Sept 8 - Sept 26
- Will: Sept 27 - Oct 15
- Knowledge: Oct 16 - Nov 3
- Power: Nov 4 - Nov 22
- Speech: Nov 23 - Dec 11
- Questions: Dec 12 - Dec 30
- Honor: Dec 31 - Jan 18
- Sovereignty: Jan 19 - Feb 6
- Dominion: Feb 7 - Feb 25
- Ayyám-i-Há: Feb 26 - Mar 1
- Loftiness: Mar 2 - Mar 20

Nine hundred years in the future,
a peaceful humanity reaches out from Earth,
looking for planets, looking for people,
looking for their place in the galaxy.

They find more than they bargained for.

The date 16-Speech-1082 BE
would be in December, 2925 CE.

Sector Map

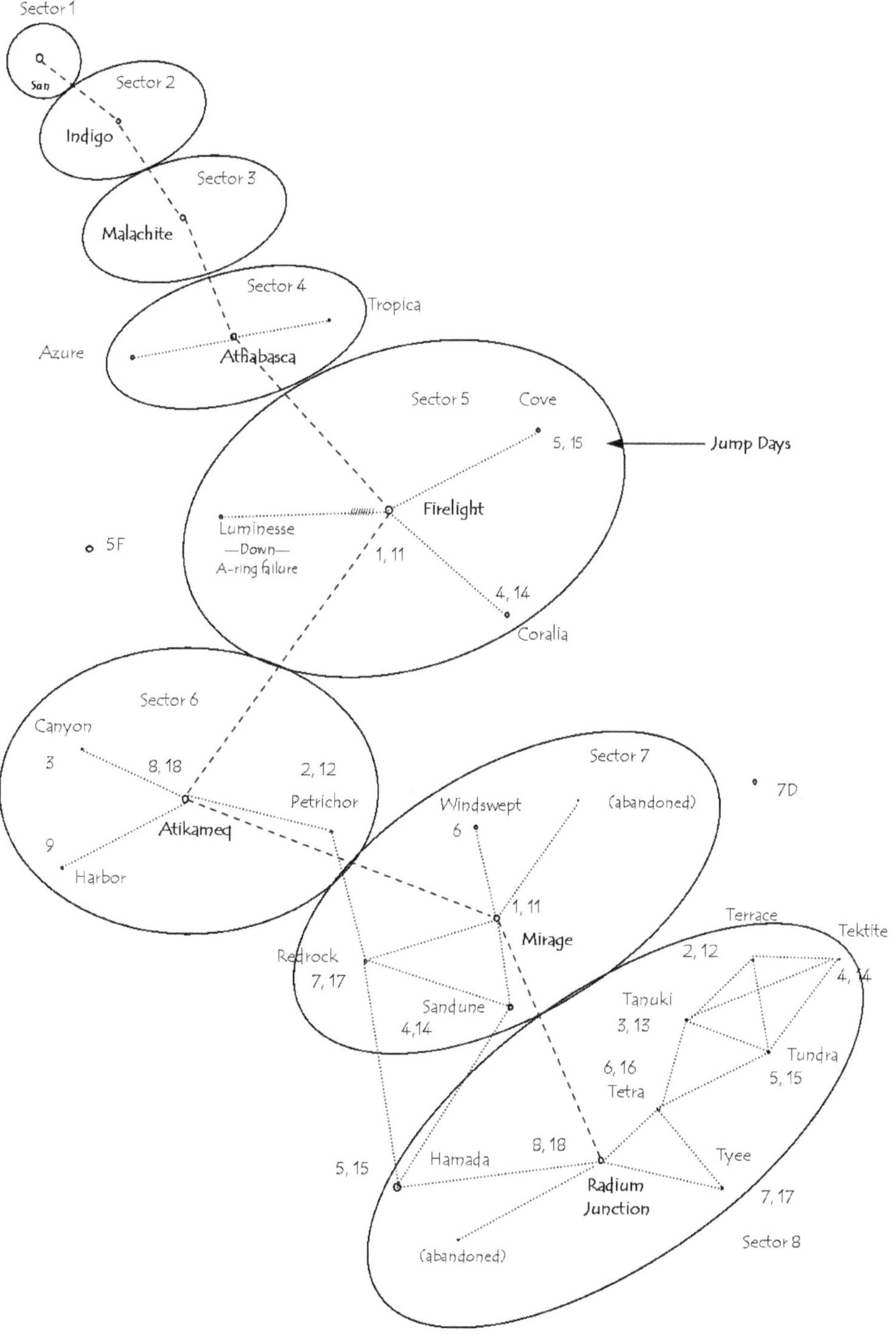

Sector 1
Sun
Sector 2
Indigo
Sector 3
Malachite
Sector 4
Tropica
Azure
Athabasca
Sector 5
Cove
5, 15
Jump Days
Firelight
Luminesse
—Down—
A-ring failure
1, 11
5F
4, 14
Coralia
Sector 6
Canyon
3
8, 18
2, 12
Petrichor
Atikameq
9
Harbor
Sector 7
Windswept
(abandoned)
7D
6
1, 11
Mirage
Redrock
7, 17
Sandune
4,14
Terrace
Tektite
2, 12
4, 14
Tanuki
3, 13
Tundra
5, 15
6, 16
Tetra
8, 18
Tyee
Hamada
5, 15
Radium
Junction
7, 17
Sector 8
(abandoned)

1 / ESCAPE

Date: 16-Speech-1082 BE
Hamada Station, Sector 8

Head down, hood up, Jarvie was hurrying toward the shuttle dock when he saw two of the biggest junkees from his class. *No! No one can see me!* He ducked into a shop to dodge them. If they put his picture on the junk news today, his carefully-planned escape would be ruined. That he was the tallest and most recognizable person on Hamada Station made the task nearly impossible. But today was his only chance. He had to make it.

Jarvie had waited two years for this opportunity. Another classmate was taking a few select friends to Redrock for vacation during the teen training break. Of course Jarvie wasn't invited, but easy enough to lie to his caretaker, as Yan would never check. He had a full eight days before he would be missed.

Jump ships were leaving soon for the five-day trip to the a-rings. And then, once they jumped, he would be free. All he had to do was get a shuttle to the docking ring before the teen training drill, and get on a departing ship.

Jarvie checked the time on his p'link. *Sixteen minutes.* Sarcee was hissing inside her podpup carrier. He peeked in. "Sarcee!" Then he realized he was in the bot repair shop. No podpup would tolerate that. *I have to get out of here.*

Hefting his backpack and Sarcee, he slumped out of the repair shop, hunching over and shuffling along.

It's so crowded. There was not supposed to be a crowd. *Not today!* A calm public announcement broke through his panicked thoughts. **"Departures: Clear security at the green gate. Arrivals: Meet regular arrivals at the red gate."**

Jarvie veered toward the two long lines at the green gate choosing the shorter line on the right. He checked Sarcee again. She glared at him.

"Sarcee," he whispered. "It's our only chance."

"Bad Zharvee!"

He cringed. *I have to get away from this miserable life.*

The boarding school would have sent him home by now anyway, he was doing so badly. But he had no home. His distant cousin Yan had been appointed as his caretaker. But Jarvie couldn't stand it. He was ship-raised, not a station kid. And the other students constantly stared or took his picture for the junk news. He couldn't take their pity—or the notoriety.

"I need to be in space," Jarvie had told the counselor.

"We're all in space," he'd replied.

Obviously, the counselor had never lived on a ship. *My ship. My people. My last person, Lanezi, stalling at Harbor Station, risking his piloting job waiting for me.*

Jarvie despaired at the length of the lines. 30 people each. Families. He'd heard that people were finding excuses to leave the outer sectors, but maybe things were worse than he thought. The ship he needed, the *Drumheller*, always left dock at 20:00. *Drumheller's* Captain was boringly predictable. Plenty of time once he cleared the gate. *11 minutes until the drill.* He timed the line and calculated. He wasn't going to make it.

Frantically, he checked the other line. Just three people up was a long jump pilot. Serene, she was gazing out the observation window. The people behind her were on their p'links or chatting. Her line started to shuffle. With his long legs, Jarvie scuttled to the left and forward, sliding in front of her before she could even move. She barely noticed. He stared at the deck. *Don't meet their eyes.* One thing he'd learned about having to wear the red armband; people didn't expect good behavior.

Jarvie had a pang of guilt for his cousin, Yan. Young and preoccupied, he hadn't been much of a caretaker. To compensate, he'd taught Jarvie the ins and outs of station and ship security, even though Jarvie didn't have the clearance. Yan thought he was helping, inspiring Jarvie to a career, and making up for his lack of interest in school. And thanks to Yan, Jarvie had cleared himself through shuttle security. But come next week, Yan was going to be in serious trouble.

The red gate to their right parted and people from the arriving shuttle walked unsteadily down the ramp. Just seeing them in their crew jackets and ship uniforms with their podpups made Jarvie's heart ache with longing. How many times had he come down a ramp like that with his family, full of excitement to be in station? Even if he got away today, there would be no going back to that life. "You can't escape what happened," the counselor had told him. *I can try.*

10 minutes. Still not fast enough. Another long jumper, in Jarvie's original line, was four or five people ahead. Jarvie would be noticed for sure if he moved again. But with a few quick steps and good timing, he was in front of the pilot. He heard a few people clear their throats this time. He could not risk cutting again. He made a show of checking Sarcee. People were very patient about the podpups. Maybe they would think something was wrong. He settled into the line and the crowd let it go.

To avoid looking at the people around him, he studied the arriving crews and ship families only a few meters away. One man in a pilot's jacket caught his eye. He wasn't exactly short or stocky, more like compact. Young 40s. Straight black hair flopping over a red headband. Ragged clothes, except for the tan pilot's jacket. *Drumheller* patch. *Oh no! Could it be*? Jarvie turned to watch him. The clincher—one lonely ship pin on his jacket. Meaning he'd been on only one ship in all his years. *It was.* Captain Beezan.

Beezan would not be at the *Drumheller* when Jarvie got there. He'd broken his schedule. And a Captain like Beezan would only do that if he were forced to. How long would he be gone? Hours certainly. Days? How long could Jarvie hide on the freezing docking ring? Even worse, the hesitant, haunted look on Beezan's face made Jarvie rethink his plan. Maybe Counseling was right, and the Solo Journey pilots really were going crazy being out there alone.

The line shuffled and Jarvie went with them. But now he hesitated. He'd be trapped on a ship with a stranger, probably a very troubled loner. His heart pounded. *Go or stay?*

"New caretakers to the white gate."

Jarvie's head whipped to the right. Dock workers were pulling a privacy screen across the ramp area so people couldn't see what was happening. But Jarvie didn't have to see. He knew what was happening on the other side. He'd been there, reeling down that ramp in a grief-stricken daze with a counselor gripping his arm.

A bunch of caretakers moved to meet the new orphans—so

many today. *No wonder it's crowded.* Jarvie looked away. But in his mind, he saw Yan's gasp of astonishment at the height of Jarvie, his new orphan. Followed by a frown. A frown that was still there two years later.

His turn at the green gate. Jarvie took one last newly determined step. Crazy pilot or not, he wasn't going back to station life. He pressed his p'link on the sensor. Green and a beep. With long strides, he followed the painted lines to the shuttle departures ramp.

He would have breathed a prayer of thanks, but he had long ago given up anything but his nightly prayer for forgiveness. He'd crossed the gate. He was a runaway now.

2 / ALARM

Beezan zipped up his tan pilot jacket and grabbed the rail at the top of the ramp, steadying himself in gravity. Emotions collided around him as thrilled families greeted each other at the bottom of the ramp, and one gate over, the recently orphaned were delivered to their new lives.

Thank God I've never orphaned anyone—the only "good" thing he could say about the losses on his ship. Then he unzipped his jacket again to cool a flush of shame.

A man brushed his elbow trying to get around him, then seeing his pilot jacket, jerked away. "Please excuse me, honor." Beezan shook his head quickly and glanced away. That innocent brush of humanity set off a bout of longing. He'd been in the Solo Journey program for eight years now. Only two years to go. It seemed like an eternity. But which was worse, the loneliness or the loss?

A long jump pilot started down the ramp with her crew protectively surrounding her. Beezan slipped in behind, staying in their wake. The crew was obviously excited to be in station. He used to have crews like that. And before, he'd had a family like that. Coming here alone was a reminder of everything he'd lost. As much as this sort of "enrichment" was recommended, he never would have come on his own.

But here he was anyway, after surviving a trip on that broken-down excuse for a shuttle. Counseling had summoned him. *Why?* He'd done his med and psych evals on the docking ring. He was carefully compliant. He wasn't due for implants for years.

They couldn't possibly know about the noises. He'd never even looked it up. He searched his grandfather's library of real books until he found "auditory hallucinations." Normal. There was *nothing* wrong with him. Turning up the music was all the cure he needed.

It better not be an inspirational talk. He was busy. He had cargo to load, an upgrade to install, and a schedule to keep. On his previous visit to Counseling, they had advised him to take on a crew. *So they could all die like last time?* He shuddered. *It wasn't my fault. I was cleared. What if they changed their minds? What if they're going to pull my license?*

Beezan stopped at the bottom of the ramp and stepped aside, taking a deep breath. He looked up at a big sector map, trying to start a new line of thought. Hamada Station was in Sector 8, the collapsing frontier of humanity's expansion, but it bustled with teens in colored armbands attending the big teen training boarding school. There was a massive education effort to train teens in the skills needed in the outer sectors, skills like holding old shuttles together with tape and glue.

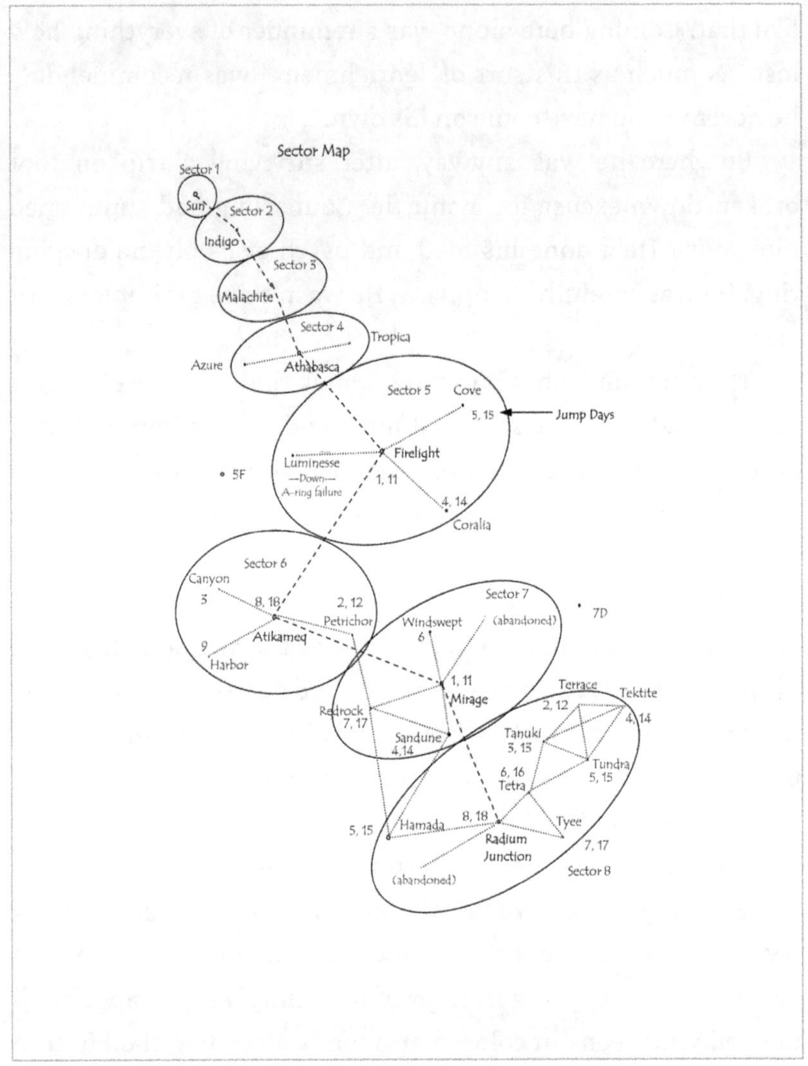

The map had been permanently painted on the wall. Sector 8, the last Sector, was opened 200 years ago, so Beezan guessed they didn't expect the map to change much. Eight Sectors, like eight giant wagon wheels, overlapped in a chain across the frontier of space. At the top, in Sector 1, there was a tiny yellow dot, representing the Solar System. If there had been a blue dot for Earth, it had long ago faded away.

The planetary system names were so . . . happy. So pretty. So promising. Indigo, Malachite. Athabasca was in Sector 4, where the *Drumheller* was built, back when there was still expansion going on, people still coming out, when there was still the adventure of new systems to be found, and the dream of another Earth. Their fantasy had died a long hard death, leaving future generations the legacy of broken-down stations with heartbreaking names orbiting barren worlds, and a supply line hanging by a thread. Not a thread, by worn out solo pilots.

Hamada standard gravity was a little less than Earth's, by which all g-forces were measured. Not that Beezan would know personally. He'd never even been to Sector 1, and probably never would. Like many people in the outer sectors, he would live his whole life without ever seeing the home planet. Out here, Earth had faded away from both maps and minds.

Beezan continued towards Counseling. Exploiting the old west theme from Earth—wagon wheels! Gold! Cows! Shops hung signs in the rimway that swung in the drafts. Strange loud piano music and the excited shouting of teens echoed and morphed into an incomprehensible noise that made Beezan cringe.

Teens clustered by the windows of stores for skates, tools, musical instruments, games, and uniforms. A group of purple-banded teens had gathered around a storefront, watching a demonstration.

"It's a KazorBot."

"From Sector 3," they whispered in awe.

When Beezan saw it, he had a sudden chill. He'd never seen such a human-like robot. With its big chest and wide stance, it was almost super-human. *Podpups would freak.* The torso and face were hard dark metal with a bluish hue. Mechanical black eyes floated in their sockets. The head made an almost disdainful turn across and then down to look at Beezan. Unnerved, he started to back away when an alarm went off. It wasn't the venting alarm or the fire alarm. "What?" Beezan started to ask.

Then he saw the window shoppers flash smiles and yell, "Teen training drill!" The robot was forgotten.

Then the venting alarm went off. Beezan's already shaky legs went weak. He knew what to do on the ship, but the station was so big, so crowded. *Where are the safe zones?*

One of the older teens noticed Beezan's panicked look. "Escort him!" he ordered. A younger one actually grabbed Beezan's arm and pulled him along.

"This way, honor." She tugged him into the Podpup Nursery. A huge sign was flashing overhead saying "SAFE ROOM." *Guess I could have figured that out.* Others were coming in. Beezan could hear and feel the locks slamming up and down the rimway.

"Is it a drill?" he asked, embarrassed to hear how shaky his voice was.

"Yes, yes," the teen reassured him. "Just stay here." And she was off. Beezan watched through the full size window as the teens cleared the rimway. The black-banded youth had been replaced by a blue-banded one and then by an obviously older green-banded one.

"Ah, excellent command sorting!"

"And look, they're not all Hamada students."

Beezan's eyes fell on the speakers, a man with a big pad, standing by the window, watching the scene and consulting another big pad his associate was holding. She was following some kind of schedule. "Simulated explosion, five seconds."

They're observing the drill, Beezan realized. Drill, just a drill.

He sunk down on the deck with a pounding heart. The whole station rocked suddenly. *Simulated?*

"Ah, excellent!"

They are far too enthusiastic about their work.

The other adults and small children had moved to the back of the Podpup Nursery. It looked like there was a café back there. They were settling in.

"How long is this going to take?" Beezan asked.

"Oh, we're hoping they beat the record," the young assistant said.

"Which is?"

For the first time she turned and looked at him, with a 'where have you been?' expression. But she saw his pilot jacket and said, "Sorry, honor. The record is 2 hours 12 minutes for this emergency response."

"Ah, ha!" said the man. "Our section was secured first!"

Beezan sat back in resignation. The Podpup Nursery, of all the places to be stuck. He missed his childhood podpup so much, but he didn't have time for one now. All the feeding, the carrying, the holding, the playing, the snoring in your ear at night; they were good for lonely people. *I'm lonely. I don't have time!* As if on cue, three of the little creatures came over to him. He pulled back his hands and pretended to ignore them, staring up at the broken lights. But his heart betrayed him and they circled around, nuzzling him.

They were so soft, so warm, so cute. These three were young. He could have cupped one in his hands, but he knew better than to pick them up. They would squirm into your arms and then into your heart. Two had beautiful blue-gray fur and the third was cream. Their paws were so tiny and their deep black eyes so enormous, gazing up at him adoringly.

There were two parts to the nursery, one where people left

their pups while they ran errands, and this play area where unattached podpups and people could meet and interact. If a pup wanted to go home with you, you were free to take it. They were not owned, bought, or sold. They would bond for life usually. That there were only three to be adopted showed how much people loved them.

They had been discovered on Azure, in Sector 4, just over 400 years ago. A few thousand of them had survived on a barely habitable planet in failing mechanical 'pods.' If they had not been discovered, they would not have lasted another 50 years. Yet they had not turned into hardened survivalists. They were loving and cooperative. Sector 4 Council had categorized them as sentient and declared them protected. And despite their somewhat silly nature, they were obviously intelligent.

They had not evolved on Azure. Someone had left them there, either to die, or meaning to come back soon. Who it was and why was one of the two big mysteries of the day. It was humanity's gain, as they were curious, happy, lovable, and said to be good judges of character. Their little hearts beating against Beezan filled him with nostalgia and even more longing.

The supervisor came in and saw him. "Honor," she whispered, "you know, you shouldn't take more than you can care for."

"Oh, no, I'm sorry," he struggled to get up, gently resettling the pups. "I didn't come for one. I just got stuck in the drill."

She looked at him curiously. "They all like you. You can take one."

"No, thanks." *Be strong.*

"Maybe you should think about it."

Why not? "I . . . can't."

She smiled sadly. "Come on then, little ones," she said gently, "off to the play mat."

They grumped a bit. The cream one turned back to Beezan. “Bye,” she said in her baby voice. He swallowed. *Better get that snack.*

By the time the all-clear rang, Beezan had had two snacks, listened to four full symphonies, and was ready for bed. Six hours, 27 minutes. The record was hopelessly lost when a group of purple-banded youth, out on the hull for ‘simulated repairs,’ had a real mishap. Although the two observers were dejected and worried, Beezan noticed that there was never any question of letting the teens cancel the drill. This teen training program was not coddling them just because they were young.

Out on TopRim again, music off and lights dimmed, Beezan could see the disappointed faces of not just teens, but everyone. It was another failure in the long list of failures in the falling-apart outer sectors.

There was a jam-up at Counseling when Beezan finally got there: frowning dockhands, jittery outside workers, stressed families, withdrawn pilots, and an angry red-banded teen. Beezan stood as far as he could from all that turmoil. He couldn’t reschedule, even if he were allowed. He couldn’t afford to stay overnight or buy another ticket back another day. *And I was supposed to leave tonight!* He’d have to burn extra fuel to catch up. He had sent a message on his s’link asking what to do, but so far, no answer.

He checked his s’link again. A message! But it was from ship maintenance. *Argg*, his part wouldn’t come until tomorrow. Today was turning out to be a total loss. He stuck his s’link back in its pocket just as a teen girl, black-banded, suddenly appeared at his shoulder. She had obviously been crying, but seemed composed now. “Captain Beezan?”

"Yes?"

"This way please. Counselor Toazair sent me." She led him down a side corridor. "We'll go in the back way."

"Thank you," he said, relieved. He was tired and nervous and just wanted his interview over with.

"Counselor Toazair will be right out." She left him sitting in the waiting room with more stressed, anxious people.

An updated sector map was on this wall. It even showed the abandoned stations and the broken spoke in Sector 5, at Luminesse. An accident there had destroyed their a-rings. No one could jump out. If anyone jumped in they would be stuck forever, or at least until humans figured out how to build their own a-rings, and that wasn't likely to be any time soon. Luminesse was now an island.

On the big screen, a view of the docking ring was showing. Beezan watched for his ship. Old, big, discolored, and ugly was how most people would describe the *Drumheller*. Still, it was a valuable vessel, as the Sectors currently did not have the resources to build more. They desperately needed more. Remote vessels could not be used, as human pilots were necessary to make the jumps. All communications went on the ships too, since light-speed messages would take years. Although Beezan didn't carry passengers, there was still plenty of business for passenger ships. People who lived in small colonies needed to move around.

Pilots spent brief moments in the mysterious realm of the jump space and long days in the realm of cargo loaders, negotiators, and small time merchants. Most pilots excelled in one area or the other, but Beezan mostly muddled through in both. He was a good mechanic—and for a pilot working alone that was essential. Centuries ago, when these ships were built, a pilot would not have even considered jumping without two copilots, a navigator, five mechanics, a doctor, cook, gardener, psychologist, and probably a decorator. Now, the pressing needs of survival demanded skeleton crews.

The *Drumheller* passed out of view and Beezan watched grimly as another old, dingy, damaged ship came into view. *How long can these ships last?* No new ships were even in the works. The few dockyards that existed did repair only, and it would take years to retool for building, let alone attack the problems of labor, technology, and resources. As pilots and ships became scarcer, runs were canceled and the world as they knew it became smaller and smaller. Three stations had already been abandoned. The number of new pilots did not even equal the number of retiring or lost pilots. No wonder there were loads of people in here with separation anxiety.

Humanity's only hope was that they would be rescued by some technological breakthrough. It was a race against time, measured in decades and generations, with the fate of off-worlders at stake. Once cut off from each other, they would cling for survival in colonies and bases, on inhospitable planets and in stations. The descendants of the last space travelers would have to wait it out to see the day when their people would be united again.

"Establishing Sector Independence" was the goal that Beezan had dedicated his life to. It was why he joined the Solo Journey Project. Every shipment that was completed could help colonists get a firmer grip on their world, and in some cases, as when the a-rings at Luminesse were lost, it could be the last shipment.

Just as all pilots had to learn that jumping was a spiritual journey, dragging a material body with it, that in that one moment, riding on the brink of the jump, when you had to go or not go, when you had to put your trust in God or just stay home, that was the brink where humanity found itself now. To give up, pack up and go home? Abandon the outer sectors? Or to hold on?

Hold on. It was the motto of the Solo Journey Project. Experts hoped they could hold on for 100 years. Maybe at least 50. Or even just 10. Something would change in 10 years. It had to. They were in their last season of hope.

3 / THE SUNDERING

Beezan felt someone's eyes on him and turned. It was Counselor Toazair, waiting patiently for him to notice her. He walked over, gingerly threading between the anxious people, and offered to shake hands, saying "God is Most Glorious." She replied in kind, smiling in the Counselor way of making you at ease.

Toazair escorted him to her small office where he sat nervously. "We never would have called you today if we'd known about the drill." She handed him a cash slider. "Please accept this compensation for your trip."

He took it gratefully. "Thank you."

"I know we're all exhausted from the drill and you are busy, so I'll get right to the point. We're calling in all solo pilots, to advise them about the findings of a seven-year study we've just completed."

Beezan nodded, relieved that this wasn't something personal. "The study indicates that the majority of the recent accidents in sectors 4-8 can be attributed to human error—of that, 63% to pilot error."

No! was Beezan's first reaction. He sat forward in the chair as if to object. "I know," she held her hand up, "but hear me out and think about it. This percentage is up drastically since the last time we did this study, due in large part to the initiation of the Solo Journey Project and its heavy emphasis on small crews. It appears that those pilots running for long periods alone, with short stopovers and minimal support, are actually the cause of most of the accidents."

All those pilots, sacrificing so much in order to help, were actually the cause of death and destruction?

"However," Toazair continued, "the Solo Journey Project has also been of critical value. So, Council has adopted a few standards that will help control the problem."

His s'link vibrated. "I've sent you the new regulations. Briefly, there's one major requirement for mid jump pilots, a one-year limit on solo flights."

"What?" Beezan was stunned. The whole point of the Solo Journey Project was to do the most with the least. Almost all the pilots were solo. "You mean—"

"Yes, you'll have to take on a crew member before you leave."

"I can't. I can't pay anyone."

"There will be a fund for those in need. I've sent you the qualifying forms."

"But . . . it's . . . I can't just—I was supposed to be in this jump group."

"We know, Captain. We know how hard it is. We know you have a schedule and it's hard to take on someone new. We know you need someone you can trust for the jump. We can also assist if you need psychological evaluations."

He just couldn't picture it. A *stranger* on his ship? His heart was pounding. Last time . . . he suddenly felt as if he couldn't breathe. He tugged on the collar of his jacket. Toazair came around and pulled up a chair to sit next to him. "Captain, look at you. You need help." He was embarrassed, but she was a counselor and specially trained in this. "You should also consider that the whole purpose of this regulation is to get someone to help you, reduce stress, and be a companion. Not someone who's going to make things worse."

Beezan nodded, trying not to let his voice shake. "I don't want to kill any more people."

She shook her head. "*You* didn't kill them. And we understand that there are some special cases like you, who will need help adjusting to having a crew again. But the trauma of losing your last crew won't go away by being alone. You aren't abandoning your Solo Journey commitment."

Was it a secret longing? Or a failure?

"You're tired. Go home. Read through the Council's letter. You still have the ability to open your heart. I'll send you a list of approved crew, and I'm here to help."

Beezan wandered back up the side corridor toward TopRim in a daze. It was even quieter than after the drill. He stopped, suddenly alert, and looked up and down the rimway. There was no one around. Even more disturbing, there was a strange feeling in the air, like . . . an ancient phrase jumped into his mind . . . an ill wind. Had something else happened? He continued cautiously, his steps loud.

A man was rushing away, but otherwise it was deserted. How could—then Beezan noticed people in the shops and restaurants, standing in clumps around the big screens. He moved closer to the nearest place, a p'link store. At the back, everyone was watching a news packet.

A great dread filled his stomach. He forced himself to go

inside. No one even glanced at him. People were sobbing and clutching each other. The packet was just ending. People gasped and some even collapsed. Beezan caught a few words, "Firelight," and "cut off."

Firelight was the hub system of Sector 5. It was the strongest of the outer sectors. *What could have happened?* Then the packet restarted, large red text rolling over the screen.

HAMADA NEWS BULLETIN: 16-SPEECH-1082

HAMADA INBOUND AUTHORITY HAS RECEIVED AN EMERGENCY PACKET TODAY WARNING ALL PILOTS THAT OUTBOUND SERVICE FROM FIRELIGHT HAS BEEN DISRUPTED, POSSIBLY PERMANENTLY.

Beezan gasped and steadied himself against the wall. *Firelight a-rings gone? It can't be.*

The ship *Cloudburst* made a sacrifice jump from Azure to Canyon with the warning. All aboard were found dead. The message was relayed from Canyon to Hamada in nine days. Jumps scheduled from Atikameq to Firelight on 8-Speech were canceled. 147 people and 12 ships were saved by the sacrifice jump.

There was more, but Beezan couldn't hear over the roaring in his head. "No," he whispered over and over. This was worse than he had feared. His parents, on Earth. He hadn't seen them for so long. Now he might never see them again.

Firelight was the gateway between the strong established inner sectors and struggling outer sectors, and more importantly, the only link to Earth. With Firelight's a-rings gone, the outer sectors were on their own, like a string of lifeboats cast into a stormy sea. In all the plans of the separation experts, Firelight had been the last link to go, but now it was already gone.

He slid down to the deck and sat shaking. He tried to say a prayer, but the words vanished as if absorbed by the size of the anguish. He watched the packet two more times, but there was nothing to give hope. People were starting to leave in a rushed panic, feverishly sending packets to check on loved ones, to figure out if ships were on this side or that side. Humanity had been cut in two.

The panic infected Beezan and he hurried back to the shuttle departure gate. The crowd was gone. A stunned shuttle pilot flew him to the docking ring, even letting him sit up front in the co-pilot's seat.

At the docking ring, Beezan snagged an express belt and let it haul him around in nogee to the *Drumheller* berth. People were so scarce in that section that Beezan was doubly surprised to see someone at the lower lock. A young man, 19 maybe. Regular coat, not a ship jacket. He was tethered to the wall and floating with an old backpack. A carrier was open and he was cradling a podpup, both of them sound asleep. *Oh no,* thought Beezan. *Someone wants a free ride on a cargo ship.* Unusual, but not unheard of. *How did he get through security?* Unless? No. He couldn't be at the wrong lock; the *Drumheller* was the only ship docked out here.

Well, I'll have to turn him away. A survivalist mode had kicked in and Beezan just snuck past. Quietly opening the lock he started up the flexible tubeway. He pulled all the way to the *Drumheller* lock when he realized that the lower lock had not shut. Of course his lock wouldn't open until the other was closed. Beezan hauled himself back down the curved tubeway until he could see what the problem was. It was the teenager, awake and braced in the lower lock so that it wouldn't close. And waiting for Beezan to come back.

Beezan steadied himself with a strap and stopped, instinctively cautious when he saw the look on the teen's face. Worried. Desperate and calculating. Exhausted. He was thin, and very tall, his almost-black eyes sunken. Dark, very curly hair, cut short and flat on top. Caramel skin, but blotchy and pale. This was the stress of weeks, not of the time since the newsbreak. If anybody ought to visit Counseling it was this person. Beezan checked the armband, expecting to see a red tie. But it was green. Beezan paused in confusion. Green was the leader band, the most mature, most reliable. That didn't make sense.

"Please move out of the lock," Beezan said.

The teen did not seem surprised by Beezan's rudeness, but he did not reply in kind. "God is Most Glorious," he said in a deep, quiet, almost tearful voice, raising his free hand to signal a request for consultation.

Beezan calmed himself. He's just a teenager in shock after the drill and the Firelight news. Be a good example. "God is Most Glorious. Please move out of the lock."

"Captain, please forgive my informality. I'm here to help you get your clearance, honor."

"Clearance?" Beezan was completely taken aback. How could this kid know he needed crew? He'd only known himself for an hour.

"Did someone send you?" Beezan asked, confused.

"No, honor. I thought you would be in a hurry and could use me."

"How did you know?"

He turned his hand over like a little shrug. "Lots of people know, Captain."

"You're too young. Besides, I can't decide now."

"Honor, I'm ship-raised. I'm trained. I can help." He stopped in the face of Beezan's obvious impatience.

"Please move out of the lock," Beezan repeated. The teen did not move, but looked at the deck and steeled himself for whatever would come next. The podpup he was holding now squirmed in his arm so he held it closer. “Captain, please.”

“No,” said Beezan, surprised at how coldhearted he was being about this. He couldn’t just hire some stranger who showed up at his lock. It would be like picking a random person off the dock to become part of your family. But this teen was stubborn. He was not moving. “I’ll call security,” Beezan said finally, pulling out his s’link.

“No!” the teen squeaked in near panic, now ready to bolt. This person was in some kind of trouble.

“What are you running from?” demanded Beezan.

“I’m . . . honor, please give me a chance.”

“How do you expect me to even consider taking you on if you can’t be honest with me?”

The teen’s head sunk again. “Captain, I’m not unstable, I just need to go to Harbor. I want to see my . . .” he trailed off and swallowed.

Well, Beezan could understand that. In the panic of the situation, people would want to get home. Maybe he was cutting school. “I’m not going to Harbor,” Beezan said.

“You can drop me at Redrock, honor.” *How does he know where I’m going?* “Then you can go another year solo. It works out for both of us, honor.”

Calculating. Knows too much. Too many honors. However, there was a certain logic to it.

“No.” Beezan forced himself to use his good sense.

Silence. Tension. They stood. The teen was headstrong, but young and no match for a test of will against Beezan, who could drag ships across the stars. He looked down at his squirming pup, suddenly defeated. Then, in a shaky voice, trying to maintain some dignity, the teenager said, “Please. I’ll go away, honor.” A great burden of hopelessness overcame him, “but I can't take care of her," he said, indicating the podpup. *God please*, thought Beezan, now feeling like a mean person. The teen came up the tubeway, very good in nogee, letting the lock shut behind, and put the pup into Beezan's instinctively raised arms. "She's not young, and she needs someone to take care of her. I won't . . . I won't be able to now, honor."

Her big, black, worried eyes looked up at Beezan, and then searched for a glimpse of her person. *Not another one!* Beezan protested, "You can't leave her, she's too old to rebond."

"She'll have to. She's pregnant, so she'll switch if she has to survive. She's ship raised, Captain," he said in a rush. The teen stopped to wipe a tear as he tried to control his voice. He swung back to the door and then brought up a carrier of stuff. "This is hers. And here," he fished around in his pocket and brought out a box of med patch refills, which caused something else to fly out of his pocket. Beezan caught it reflexively, ignoring the proffered refills. The teen froze with one hand extended, looking between the refills and the caught object—a s'link—not a personal link, like everyone had, but a security / ship / station / suit link.

Interesting, thought Beezan, turning it in his hand. A level 3! Beezan had a level 2, just one level more powerful than the teen's. That one object revealed a lot. Ship captains and station commanders usually had level 2, but otherwise, s'links were restricted and essential tools used by expert monitors, the people who ran ship and station operations. They were only issued by the government. It meant that the government trusted him. And level 3 was a high level of trust. Regardless, Beezan didn't trust him. Then he had a sudden inspiration. He could test him first . . . and then, like he said, just to Redrock. One jump. Then he could go solo again for a year.

"Can you install a cargo mass tester?" Beezan asked. The

teen backed off by the sudden turn of conversation. Now he was suspicious. "Part of it is in an unpressurized work area."

"I'm qualified," the teen said, taking back his s'link.

Beezan nodded, "My new unit's just sitting there. You install it and I'll pay you by taking you to Redrock."

The teen nodded nervously, whispering "Yes, honor," and stuck the refills back in his pocket.

Beezan pulled up the tubeway with the teen following. Inside the *Drumheller*, Beezan took him on the long haul to the Cargo Control Booth and left him with the mass tester and a box of tools. "Call me when you need to suit up."

What Beezan didn't tell him was that it couldn't be installed correctly without the part that he was still waiting for. Would the teen be honest when he was so desperate? Beezan took the podpup and left him alone on a strange ship with false hope. As he headed back to the Command Bay he was troubled. If he was just being cautious, why did he feel like a monster? *Because I'm not being honest,* he scolded himself. Beezan said a little prayer for forgiveness and a big prayer for guidance.

Just keep working. Beezan synced his s'link when he got to the Command Bay and the list of approved crew popped up on the screen. Toazair must have set it to do that, he thought with annoyance. He glanced at it without much attention. If this teen's plan worked, he wouldn't need the list. He'd get the part tomorrow, catch up with the other jump ships, and be gone. He'd have the teen for 3-4 weeks, drop him at Redrock, and then be on his own again.

He watched on another screen as the teen unpacked the unit and worked on it in the Cargo Control Booth. It had been almost two hours. Beezan had yet another snack and fed a few sips of juice to the pup, now balled up in his lap. Her soft gray fur was sparse over her pregnant belly and she was showing signs of age. For her to be pregnant now was unusual, but podpups were their own bosses in this matter. Beezan picked her up and held her to his face. She whined. "If only you would talk, little one."

Beezan thought back to the time he was a young boy, aboard the *Drumheller*, his grandfather the Captain. He was in charge of his first podpup, Lemm. Beezan had not wanted one. He had wanted a personal robot. Pups were used for various chores aboard ship, but no one denied their purpose was mainly companionship. Beezan thought a robot would be much more useful, and he argued with his grandfather that he would learn a lot more by repairing it and programming it. Captain Grandfather had insisted on the pup, and personally supervised Beezan's training of it. When Beezan became overly impatient with his charge one day and yelled at him, swift correction had come from his grandfather, and later a long talk.

His grandfather had tried to explain why people held in high regard the training of a podpup rather than something more technically useful. Beezan remembered clearly, sitting in the kitchen, his grandfather holding the pup, his patient voice. "You must understand, Beezan, that pups are living beings. They have their innate characteristics and they are also shaped by their environments. They do not have factory personalities or programs. Programming with pups is real time. You can't delete your mistakes and start over. You get out of a pup what you put into it. If you are patient and kind and take good care of your pup, you will be rewarded. Any child, cruel or impatient, could have a loyal and faithful friend of a robot.

"Your actions are important with a pup; there is a kind of justice. If you are cruel or thoughtless to a robot, what are the results? It might need servicing more often. What is the point of all this? If we become more automated we lose our compassion for living beings, because we do not see the results of our actions. When a robot runs down, you sell it and buy a new one. When your loyal pup runs down, you take care of it. Why is a pup's life built short, compared to a person's? So that a boy like you could have a pup and grow into a man who's seen the life span of one in his care, or lack of care. Maybe this man will be better prepared to care for his young and untrained children or his aged parents, or grandparents, who need some help to fulfill their lives. Maybe this same man will make humane and compassionate decisions when he commands the lives of others, or wields power over others.

"The lesson of a robot is service through programming. The lesson of a pup is service through loyalty and trust. If you grow up with robots, you might feel that loyalty can be bought and that you automatically deserve it, and that service to God or your fellow men is a kind of programming or brainwashing. But if you grow up with a pup you might learn instead that service to another being is through love and loyalty and the sign of a civilized creature."

Then his grandfather had put Lemm in Beezan's hands. "Many pups will be loyal even if you don't deserve it. That is sometimes in their nature. That's why they are good for young people. I hope that by the time you are a man you will be deserving of the trust of many."

Beezan hung his head in despair. He could not think straight. His instinct told him not to trust the teen, but some higher feeling urged him to trust, not in the teen, but in God. He could almost feel his grandfather's disappointment in him. He would go back and talk to the kid, be honest with him, give him a chance. The pup, disturbed by Beezan, was now trying to get out of his lap. “Easy,” he soothed, realizing he hadn’t even bothered to learn her name.

He felt around her collar until he found her tag. “Sarcee,” it read. “Hi Sarcee,” Beezan greeted her finally. He flipped Sarcee’s tag over: PROTECTED BY JARVIE E.G. ATIKAMEQ, TTC HAMADA, 1-910-693.

Beezan stared. He’d just seen that name . . . where? He glanced back to Toazair’s list. Yes, right there. Jarvie E.G. Atikameq, 19, Youth Leader. *On a school break? Or a work opportunity?* Beezan got the strange feeling that all this was meant to be and there was no escaping it. Sarcee was squirming and whining again. She didn’t want Beezan to hold her. “Come on then, Sarcee,” he said and let her hold on so she could ride on him back to the Cargo Control Booth.

He was a little out of breath from the long trip back when he opened the door to the Cargo Control Booth. The teen was floating there, just looking at the tester, frozen.

“It can’t be installed,” he said in an almost wooden voice. Then he suddenly turned, holding to the edge of the unit, his anger flaring. “You knew, didn’t you? You set me up!”

Beezan felt bad. The teen hadn’t tried to trick him after all. “I’m sorry. I came down to tell you.”

The teen shook his head in defeat. “Captain, you don’t understand. I’m risking my life to offer you a chance out of here. You’ve lost too many people. No one else will crew with you. Counseling considered pulling your license, but decided to give you a chance.”

“How could you possibly know that?” Beezan asked in disbelief. The kid shook his head and didn’t answer. The teen’s anger was ebbing and the podpup squirmed, so Beezan handed her back. He collapsed in, hugging her.

Was it possible that he had that bad a reputation? Was that why Toazair had sent him a special list?

"None of those deaths were my fault! I was cleared. Anything else you hear is rumor and nonsense." A surge of rebelliousness took Beezan. "So, when the part arrives tomorrow, you can still install this thing. I'll take you to Redrock as payment." The teen nodded. Not happy, not grateful. "Just promise me one thing," Beezan continued.

The teen looked up, worried.

"When we get there, you have to take her with you. I can't have two podpups around."

Now he looked relieved. Now Beezan wanted him to stay, if only to make up for his earlier bad treatment. The kid buried his head in Sarcee's fur for a moment. He seemed much younger than 19. *It's been a terrible day*, thought Beezan. Then the teen pulled himself together as if at attention. Beezan could almost see him offer a mental prayer. "Jarvie Elaine Gary Atikameq," he stated formally, "Captain."

"And Sarcee," he added, indicating the pup, "honor."

Beezan offered his own mental prayer for forgiveness and protection. "Beezan Jaleh Sonn Mirage."

The solemnity of the moment was more than symbolic and weighed on Beezan. He had crew again.

4 / MYSTERY CARGO

The door slid shut behind Jarvie as he floated down the stairwell into the cabin Beezan assigned him.

Safe.

Well, for now. He hung limp and exhausted, hungry, freezing, and scared. And, he had to admit to himself, ashamed from his day of deceit.

Too late to turn back. If Beezan was unreasonable, it was nothing more than Jarvie deserved. Pilots were supposed to be serene, detached, compassionate, and patient. Beezan wasn't any of those. He had been agitated, moody, sneaky, and mean. He didn't even appreciate how lucky he was to get someone for crew.

Sarcee wiggled out of her carrier to inspect the cold, empty cabin. The stairs that led down from the rimway spiraled around and landed by the facilities. Sarcee went right in the little podpup door to investigate. A glider rail ran along the wall below the railing—but Jarvie had seen no robots here to use it. *They must be somewhere. No single person could run a ship without them.*

The cabin was one room, with a workpanel, two adjustable chairs, closets, a bunk that was folded away, and a sleeping sack for nogee.

However empty, it was his own space, away from Beezan until morning, and for that, Jarvie was relieved. He unlatched and tugged open a squeaky drawer to put away the food packs Beezan had given him, except for one in his pocket. He stowed Sarcee's things and his few personal items: two changes of clothes, skateshoes, prayer book, and his small box of treasures. He kept his s'link, p'link, and breather on him at all times, of course.

He fed Sarcee. She ate double now that she was pregnant, and double for a podpup was a lot of food. Tomorrow he would have to face Beezan again, and evade too many questions, and install that unit, and load cargo. And they would be in a hurry to catch up to the jump group. He should try to sleep. He just wanted to watch the news packets to see what happened with the drill. He opened his food pouch and tapped a pop-up screen on the workpanel.

Jarvie accessed the news through the *Drumheller*. With a mouthful of food unchewed, he stared at it in confusion. What was this "Sundering" they were talking about? Suddenly, everything dropped into place: why Beezan was so agitated, why he thought he'd heard crying on the dock. Beezan had just assumed Jarvie had already heard the news, but he'd turned off his p'link and s'link so he couldn't be tracked.

Jarvie couldn't even take it in. He had never been near Earth, but without Firelight, in Sector 5, the main resources for the outer sectors were cut off. Without Sector 4, there were no marginally habitable planets, without Sector 3, no robots, without Sector 2, no major ship repair. Without Sector 1, no

Earth . . . no Central Authority, no more people, no more help. The outer sectors were doomed.

Jarvie had an overwhelming longing for his parents. He even considered going to Beezan, just to talk with someone, but it didn't seem likely Beezan would accept him. So he hung in the sleeping sack watching, clutching Sarcee, until he fell into a troubled sleep.

17-Speech

On his first morning of duty aboard the *Drumheller*, Jarvie realized Beezan hadn't given him a uniform. Embarrassed, he shyly called the Captain and asked where to find one.

Beezan was unconcerned. "It's a cargo ship. Don't worry about it. Whatever you have on is fine."

"Yes, honor." Jarvie looked down. He was in his long underwear.

By the end of the day, most of it spent installing that cargo mass tester, Jarvie was weak and queasy. Since they'd left dock to load more cargo, he'd asked Beezan to spin the ship so they could have some gravity. "It's a cargo ship. Even if I spin the wheel, where the living quarters are, the cargo section doesn't spin. We'll be down there all day anyway, so why waste the fuel to spin up when we'd just have to spin down later? Remember, the fuel converter is 200 years old."

Jarvie despaired. It didn't matter how many fuel columns they had. An ancient fuel converter would be like turning on a bad faucet and never getting more than a trickle. It would take days to convert enough usable fuel to do anything, and right now, Beezan was saving it up for the jump.

Jarvie gave up everything he'd learned in his years on a diplomatic ship. 'Captain', 'Yes, honor,' 'No, honor,' courtesies, uniforms, protocols. Beezan had pulled his own hair in mock frustration after one too many 'honors.' "It's a cargo ship!" They said together, but neither of them laughed.

Jarvie decided to use his one set of nice clothes for a uniform. He began the day with clean clothes and hair combed. By the end of the day, he was exhausted, dirty, shoeless, and had messed-up hair. If he spent too long on this ship, he'd end up like Beezan, in ragged untucked clothes and unmatched socks, not to mention hair that stood straight up, probably from years of pulling on it.

However, lack of formality did not mean lack of rules. Beezan had sent a long list of rules and procedures to Jarvie's s'link and spontaneously, it seemed, would come up with new ones. The overall tone of it made Jarvie feel like he was living on edge in a fragile old ship that could have a catastrophic break-down any second.

Schedules were another thing Beezan understood. He was so concerned he had made a giant calendar in the kitchen, marking the days as if they were a matter of life and death. Jarvie had a vision of Beezan living by himself, hashing off the days of his lonely life. Although Beezan still did not seem like a pilot, more like a harried dockworker, he didn't seem as mean as yesterday either, and for that Jarvie was cautiously relieved.

18-Speech

On his second morning aboard the *Drumheller*, Jarvie hung in the Cargo Control Booth feeling nauseous from the nogee—and the guilt. He'd told Yan he was away with friends, but the longer they stayed in system, the bigger chance he'd be caught.

However bad he felt, he had no time to dwell on it. The nerve-wracking, mind-boggling job of cargo loading was almost more than he could cope with. The Cargo Control Booth was like a side tunnel of the Cargo Hold with a long window looking out over the cargo. As they loaded, their workstations moved down the tunnel on rails. Sarcee floated free, but Jarvie scolded her if she got near the controls.

Jarvie had loaded cargo before; even diplomatic ships took on supplies and shipments, but not like this. Inside the hold, layers of cargo from Beezan's last stops were organized into sections by destination. Then they were mass balanced, partly by the computer's suggestions and partly by Beezan's magic touch.

It was a *little* bit fun, once he got used to Beezan's shorthand cargo talk so that he knew what he was supposed to be doing. If Beezan had trouble explaining something, he would use a toy cargo hold and handful of locking bricks to demonstrate.

With only six hours training, Beezan had left Jarvie alone in the booth to operate the remote grappling arms, while he suited up. Beezan was going into the hold. He'd be using an exoloader that amplified a human's strength. It was untethered, unpressurized work that required an instinctive knowhow of the physics of moving masses. Very dangerous. Jarvie had been in exoloaders a few times, in teen training. It had been awkward, but fun. But they'd been inside, with gravity and air.

Focus! He might need me. But all went well in the next four hours, and they filled up the entire hold. "Whew!" Jarvie grabbed Sarcee and gave her some attention.

"Okay," Beezan said over the s'link. "I'm coming in for a break and then we'll move to Hold 2."

Jarvie froze. *Two?* He and Sarcee looked at each other. "Two Cargo Holds?"

"Hungry!" Sarcee complained, so Jarvie spent the break getting food for the three of them.

. . .

“Thank you,” Beezan said between bites. He must have been tired, but he was agitated and energized to finish. “Same setup in Hold 2, but it’s all open in there, you’ll have to be super careful not to squish me with the big ones.” Beezan studied him a moment. “You’ve been checked out in exoloaders?”

Go out there? Jarvie panicked. “Umm, yes.”

“But . . .” Beezan prompted.

“I’m not certified.” *True!*

“That’s okay. I’m certified to train.”

“Oh.”

Beezan scowled. “So, you’re uneasy, that’s normal. You should be.”

“I, actually, I’m out of meds. Motion sickness.” *Also true.*

Beezan pointed to a med cabinet. “Right there. So I’ll run you through it when you’re ready. Just getting in and out. Then you can watch while I do the loading.”

Jarvie nodded. He’d managed to get through lunch without another lie. He secured Sarcee before he got his meds, including extra that he slipped in his pocket. He loaded one in his arm medpatch and headed for the suit room in the EVA Bay.

Beezan had stretched a suit to its tallest configuration.

“Brand new,” Beezan commented. *Maybe 20 years ago.*

They suited up, crosschecked, and then Beezan stopped and closed his eyes. *Prayer*, Jarvie realized, and hastily breathed his own. *We may need all the help we can get.*

Cargo Hold 2 was huge, like a tunnel hollowed out by a small asteroid. “You could put a whole ship in here!” Jarvie said when he saw it.

"They did. Well, not all put together. But the *Drumheller* class was made to transport ship and station modules," Beezan said with bittersweet pleasure. "It's the largest class of cargo hauler. This one's been in my family for generations." Jarvie didn't ask how many generations.

With the help of the meds and tips from Beezan, Jarvie was actually able to help a little. Beezan had stationed Jarvie at a control panel by the big cargo door, on the brink of space. He tried not to look out too much.

Even as they were loading, Beezan got a message to expect a special set of containers as part of his Solo Journey assignment. "A hundred and eighty-eight containers?" Jarvie read his heads-up display in surprise. The cargo loader supervisor even called.

"Captain Beezan, you loading?" asked a winded voice.

"Yes. Who's this?" Beezan asked tentatively.

"Jeremy CL12-3, CL Sup. Look, Cap, we have this big cargo container that's been sitting around and didn't fit on the other SJ ship. It was headed for Redrock. He told us to wait, but I figure it would fit in your big door."

Beezan hesitated. "Didn't fit on what ship?"

"*Wheel of Fire*."

"Oh."

Jarvie figured that this wasn't a normal request.

"Can you get me a manifest correction?" Beezan asked.

"I don't see why not, you're both SJ and it isn't going on any other ship unless they knock the doors off."

"How big is it exactly?"

"Oh, you'll see," and he chuckled, as if Beezan had already agreed.

"You owe me, Tiati." Beezan said to no one in particular.

Jarvie had realized right away that Beezan had talked to himself all these years and wasn't about to stop now. "Jarvie,

I'm sorry if you're tired, but we have to load this today. We have to leave for the a-rings tomorrow, or we'll miss the jump group." This was more alarming to Jarvie than Beezan could have imagined. They had to make that jump group.

"I'm on it," Jarvie replied, trying to sound energetic. Unfortunately, the containers got bigger and bigger. Finally the last container came. Jeremy wasn't kidding. It was a behemoth. It was in a specially made container that barely fit in the loading door. Jarvie heard Beezan gasp.

"Jeremy!" Beezan protested.

"No worries, trust the auto-thrusters."

Jarvie looked over his control panel. They'd transfer control to *Drumheller* at some point. "Wait!" Jarvie said, starting to panic. "I don't know where to put it."

"I'll get it," Beezan said. "There's only one place to put it, right in the middle. We'll attach it to the mass tester. I can use the control panel there." The mass tester was at the bottom of the cylindrical cargo hold, just above the reinforced hull between them and the engines.

Jarvie used both 'hands' of the exoloader to cling to the control panel and held his breath as the container squeezed by the door. He glanced at the panel. INCOMING CONTAINER #189: 612 CARGO MOMENTUM UNITS. BASE 505.

"Captain! Coming in at 612!"

Everything in cargo loading was standardized for safe handling. Whatever thrust they used to move a cargo container into the hold had to be counteracted by equal and opposite thrust to stop it—or it would crash into the opposite bulkhead. One Cargo Momentum Unit (CMU) took 1 second auto thrust to start it or stop it from .1 meter per second. Most containers needed only 5-10 CMU, depending on their mass. The monster ones they'd been loading this afternoon were in the frightening

120-200 range, requiring multiple auto-thrusters firing for many seconds, and then repeating in the opposite direction to stop them. It was nerve-wracking. Jarvie took many deep breaths after every container finally stopped.

But this big container was something else. Jarvie counted the hash marks on its side as it slowly passed the cargo door. About a hand-width a second. That was about as slow as they could go. Jarvie lost sight of Beezan, next to the mass tester, as the beast slid between them. He jumped when the auto-thrusters fired, about 10 of them, in unison. Jarvie tried to figure it out in his head, 612 CMUs would be over a minute of thrust for 10 thrusters. How much fuel did they have? The container nearly touched the far side of the Cargo Hold when it finally settled to a stop.

"Stationary," Jeremy reported. Then "Auto-thrusters to you Cap."

"Acknowledged," Beezan answered, sounding stressed. "Jarvie, stay where you are. I need to thrust it against the mass tester. Then we'll attach the braces." The dockworker crew gave the all clear and took off, happy to be rid of their cargo, no doubt.

Jarvie didn't like it. Beezan would be between that huge mass and the wall. "Can't you come out and use this panel?"

"No, I'm afraid I'll bump it."

Slowly and carefully, with the slightest bursts on the auto-thrusters, Beezan nudged it toward the mass tester until the latches caught. They both groaned in relief. Jarvie checked the panel. "Hey, base CMU is 523, not 505, according to this. They didn't give us the right number."

"That's weird. Let's get as many braces on as possible. Bring the grappling arms down, and we'll lock those on too."

With agonizing care, sweating in his suit, Jarvie managed to hook 4 grappling arms without a mishap.

Beezan was struggling. "Two more braces," he reported. The big cargo seemed to be shifting. "I'll have just enough room to —" and then there was an electronic pop. Jarvie knew that sound from his monitor training. The main line to the suit, communications, power, and air, was disconnected. "Captain?" Silence. "Beezan, can you answer me?" *God help us,* he thought as he tried to put Beezan's vitals on his helmet screen. There, the monitor for the suit showed a whole screen-full of warning signals. Air—disconnected, was the one Jarvie had feared. S'link —disconnected, but the suit pressure was still good.

Jarvie's teen-training wasn't entirely in vain, as he went to full emergency mode now. Squeezing through the tight space between the bulkhead and the cargo container would take too long. But on his side, where the space door was still open—*O my God. I have to go out there. Just a short distance.*

Jarvie jetted back to the exoloader niche. Slamming the exoloader against its latches, he released himself from it. Checking his suit thrusters, he manually launched to the edge of the cargo container. The container itself had no holdbars. Carefully lining up his hand pointer, he fired 1 second. He lurched toward the other side, half exposed to space, without a tether. *Breathe!* Again he pointed and fired. The jolt automatically sent him the right way, back into the hold. *Thank you!* He sailed behind the cargo container and grabbed a holdbar. Beezan was plastered face against the cargo container, with his exoloader thruster stuck on. His life pack had been sheared off. And his arms were tangled behind him where the exoloader had stuck in the bracing contraption.

The thruster finally went off, just as Jarvie got there. "I've got you! Hang on, hang on." He pulled Beezan's arms free of the exoloader, but they floated limp. "Captain?" Jarvie pressed his faceplate against Beezan's. He was unconscious.

Jarvie was dismayed that he didn't know how many minutes of air Beezan had left. It was probably on his screen somewhere, but in his panic Jarvie couldn't find it. It seemed like he only would have a few minutes by now. *I've got to get him inside!*

With a huge effort, he released Beezan's legs from the exo and hauled him out. He looked back out the cargo door. He had to go that way. But he couldn't make a mistake. He could be rescued, but it would be too late for Beezan.

He fumbled for the rescue clamps. So hard with the gloves. He finally got them on, grabbed Beezan's arm with both of his hands, pointed and fired Beezan's jets. Just as they cleared the container, he rotated and fired again. Too much. They slammed against the container and bounced. They were rotating now. *My stomach.* Jarvie felt another dose of the meds from his arm patch. Holding Beezan against him as tightly as possible, he fired again, bounced again, fired again, almost hit the door, and finally got inside. A big blast then to cross the hold, and finally! In the airlock. He pulled off his gloves when the lock was only half pressurized.

I can't believe this is happening. I'm going to kill my own Captain. No! He's a pilot; he's trained to fight death. Don't panic. Fearing he was too late, he grabbed a holdbar and pushed Beezan against the wall with his knee. He opened the visor, and then pressed the double latch on the helmet neck and slid the bar across. He had to use both hands to twist off the helmet, sending them both into a tandem spin.

Beezan's lips were blue. Not dead yet. Jarvie opened the cabinet and grabbed a breather. Miraculously though, Beezan had started breathing. Jarvie opened his own visor and shouted,

"Breathe harder!" Beezan did gasp and start sucking in great breaths of air.

Finally, Jarvie wrenched his own helmet off. Then he opened the door to get out of the lock and gasped in surprise. Sarcee. She had come around, sensing trouble in that strange podpup way.

As he passed the control panel, hauling Beezan, he slapped the button to close the cargo door. The squeaking traveled around the sides of the ship and up through the deck, sending shivers up Jarvie's spine.

All the way back to the Med Bay, Jarvie prayed for no brain damage. It took a long time and he was getting panicky again as Beezan wouldn't respond to any questions, even though his color was better. Jarvie had to drag Beezan up the stairwell, again happy it was nogee, and then strap him onto the exam bed. Remove Suit, the screen flashed. The last little thing, but suddenly it was too much and he was crying.

"Captain! Wake up. Please wake up." He was babbling now. "I can't get you out of the suit."

Beezan's eyes fluttered open and he winced in pain. He took in the Med Bay, but was confused by Jarvie's presence. Slowly, he lifted a hand. "Glove," he whispered. Jarvie focused on the glove and shakily removed it, tossing it to Sarcee to stow. Beezan's shaking hand grabbed Jarvie's wrist. "You saved me," he rasped. "How?"

Jarvie tried to get the words out. "Took you out of the exo," he squeaked, but was too overcome by it all to explain.

Beezan, tears in his eyes, gave his wrist another squeeze. "I'm all right. Thank you, Jarvie. Thank you." Jarvie nodded, still struggling with the suit. Glove, boots, upper suit, lower suit, eventually they got it all off. Beezan clutched his ribs in pain. Jarvie strapped him back on the exam bed and started the ER program again. The sides of the bed came up and encased Beezan's chest. Meds were administered. Beezan relaxed a bit. "Take command," Beezan whispered.

Jarvie froze. Never had he expected anyone to say that to him. On his family ship, he had been youngest, last in line. At school, in his unit, he was, well, behind the curve. But here . . . he shook himself. *Like there's anyone else.*

Broken ribs. Strained shoulders. Shock. No apparent brain function loss. *Thank you, thank you, thank you,* Jarvie whispered to heaven. He wanted to just sit there and be relieved and get out the rest of his panic and tears, but he couldn't. It wasn't over.

Jarvie waited until Beezan slipped into medicated sleep before heading back to the Cargo Hold. He even had the presence of mind to leave Sarcee with Beezan. "Stay."

She huddled up by Beezan's neck. "Sarcee stay," she said. Then she put her little paw on Beezan's shoulder. "Bee stay." Jarvie looked at her, puzzled. "Not go," she continued, trying hard to make a longer sentence. "Like Mom." Jarvie gasped and bit his lip.

"No," he whispered. "Beezan stay."

Stop crying, he told himself as he made his way back to the Cargo Hold. Trained teens don't cry in emergencies. A trail of clean-up robots would be after him at this rate, if there were any on this beat-up old ship.

He sat in the Cargo Control Booth and stared out the window while he ate Beezan's unfinished dinner. "Come on," he said, and then realized he too was talking to himself. *Well, usually Sarcee listens to me.*

There was no help for it. He had to go out there and finish the braces. On a hunch, he tested the mass of the big container again, and got *another* different base number.

He resuited and scooted the slow way to the back of the container, not daring to open the door again. But he couldn't free the exo. So he set as many braces as he could and squirmed his way out.

Finally finished, he dragged himself back to the Med Bay. Beezan was asleep. Sarcee was asleep. All he wanted to do was sleep. He felt bad about taking Sarcee, but he didn't want to face that lonely cabin without her. Then he spied the other exam bed, floated over and strapped in. Before he could think of what prayer to say, he was asleep, and Beezan's arguing with the computer to release him just seemed like a dream.

Jarvie did dream of his mother, the owner of an important diplomatic vessel, beautiful in her uniform, hair braided with gold, tall and majestic. She walked the rimways of the *Drumheller*, shaking her head, saying, "Someone's going to get stuck." She made repair notes on her s'link until it exploded. And then Jarvie was with Beezan in an old-fashioned boat that floated on an ocean and they were sinking.

"Bail!" Beezan was shouting, throwing out teacupfuls of water. But Jarvie had no cup. He looked over the edge of the boat and saw, not water, but the ocean of space, and he was falling . . .

He awoke with a start and, heart pounding, felt around in the dark for the comfort of Sarcee, but she had not come to him after all. A cup of sadness drained into Jarvie's sea of worries, keeping him from any useful sleep. Sarcee would go over to Beezan, and Jarvie would lose her. He prayed for patience and detachment. Then he prayed for sleep. At last, he just prayed for the morning.

19-Speech

Finally, his alarm went off. “Lights,” he said groggily. He looked around. Sarcee and Beezan were gone. Beezan would not be so crazy as to haul himself all the way to the Cargo Hold with broken ribs, but he wasn’t in the Med Bay or the facilities.

Beezan could not possibly be so stubborn as to not even wait for Jarvie, but he wasn’t in the kitchen or Command Bay either.

Beezan would not be so desperate . . . Jarvie grabbed a holdbar and pressed his ear to the rimway deck on top of Beezan’s cabin. Nothing. *Just call him on the s’link.* Then he heard the combination of steady whirring and rhythmic clanking that could only be the lift coming back. Jarvie wheeled back up and pulled himself down the rimway as fast as possible.

Beezan would. He was crazy. He was stubborn. He was desperate. *We’re a good match.*

Jarvie found Beezan just outside the lift. Beezan was just floating in the rimway, gasping for air and clutching his side. Sarcee hovered by him, giving Jarvie a worried look.

“Captain!” Jarvie was alarmed at his condition, but Beezan smiled when he saw Jarvie.

“Jarvie!” Beezan stopped for air. “You got it all secure. We can catch up to our jump group.” *He’s happier about the cargo than my saving his life!* Beezan reoriented so he could formally shake Jarvie’s hand. “Thank you.”

“Yes, honor. I mean thank you, honor—you’re welcome, honor.”

Beezan laughed and groaned and laughed again. “Let’s get to the a-rings.”

“Honor, are you well enough?”

“Just drag me to Command.”

By breakfast, they were on their way. They ate in the Command Bay, reoriented now to boosting instead of spinning mode. Beezan had made several difficult burns before they were cleared to start the main burn. It would take them five days all together, one day boosting, three days coasting, and one day decelerating. Jarvie was thrilled to have ‘gravity’ back, if only for eleven hours.

Beezan settled back in his chair, ribs hurting. “We can sleep now. For four days if we want.”

“Yes, honor.”

“Except for feeding Sarcee.” She gazed up at Beezan adoringly.

“Sarcee hungry.” Beezan rolled his eyes, but gave her a little hug. Jarvie breathed a sigh of relief. Everything was going to be fine.

And it was. For five whole days.

5 / FIRST CROSSING

5-Questions

Jarvie unzipped the sleeping sack. It was too short for him to get a good stretch until he got out. Today was jump day, a day of fear and hope. For Jarvie it would be his first crossing, awake, without his family. Beezan was a near stranger, so Jarvie was especially nervous about their first jump together. To be part of a jump crew was to be solidly connected, emotionally or spiritually, with the pilot. The crew had to trust their lives to the pilot and the pilot had to trust that the crew would not disturb the jump. Jarvie and Beezan shared only the connection of wanting to get to Redrock as soon as possible. He hoped it would be enough.

Sarcee hurtled around in excitement. They always knew. Podpups liked to jump. Their little squishy bodies were built for it. Emotionally they liked it too. For humans jumping was painful, terrifying, and exhausting. Depending on how deep the crossing went, it was both exhilarating to be alive at the other side and depressing to be back in the material world. For podpups, it was just a plain good time.

Jarvie got a food pack from his drawer and touched the big screen. Their schedule came up in Hamada Standard Time: clearance at 11:00, then entering the ring. There would be thirteen ships jumping.

Outbound Order:

- Destination: Radium Junction

- *Carmel*
- *Roca*
- *Crown of Gold*
- *Pegasus*
- *Zhangjiajie*

- Destination: Sandune

- *Hummingbird Haven*
- *Bengal*
- *Zephyr*
- *Nightingale*
- *Treasure Seeker*
- *Jerboa*

- Destination: Redrock

- *Drumheller*
- *Paradise Runner*

For the first time, Jarvie got a look at the *Drumheller*'s official itinerary. His heart pounded with excitement and nostalgia just looking at it.

Drumheller / Owner / Captain BEEZAN 569-024-11-1071:

Outbound Route: Hamada—> Redrock—> Petrichor—> Atikameq—> Harbor

Inbound Route: Harbor—> Atikameq—> Petrichor—> Redrock—> Hamada

Estimated time of return: 63 weeks.

Harbor! He told me he wasn't going to Harbor. Did he add it on for me? Or was he lying? Jarvie was confused. Then he had a glimmer of hope. Beezan had only agreed to take him to Redrock, but maybe he was planning to give Jarvie a chance to stay on.

Jarvie tapped a pop-up and called up the Ship Tracker. A graphic appeared showing the Hamada L4 zone where the a-rings were. *Drumheller*, along with the other 12 ships and the small Hamada Outbound Authority Station were stationed just outside the a-rings.

"The Builders," whoever they were, and wherever they disappeared to, had cleared the L4 zone of the usual Trojan asteroids. In their place they had built a system of acceleration rings that would help propel a ship to the speed required to slip into a resonate path and jump to another star system. Although they were called rings, they were, more accurately, short, slightly curved tunnels—like donut segments instead of one big hollow donut. There were usually six segments, arranged around a central gravity ball. Each ring segment would give a big boost of acceleration to the ship without costing any fuel.

The a-rings were stations in an interstellar traffic system. In the Solar System, a set of a-rings had been discovered at Saturn's L4, but in most systems they were closer to the central star.

No one really knew how the a-rings worked. The gravity ball

held the six a-rings in orbit around itself. They were always oriented with the galactic plane. One master ring contained what once may have been a control box, but those boxes had all been destroyed or removed.

Humanity had been convinced they were for star travel and tenaciously learned to use them. It had taken decades, fortunes, lives and an unrelenting drive. Pilots were normal people, mostly, but very sensitive and somehow keyed into the universe around them. They also had implants that helped them detect resonance waves between stars. The pilots, once jump velocity (JV) was reached, had to find the right resonate path, bring the ship into it, and make the crossing.

As far as humanity knew, there were a-rings in every stable star system with at least a Neptune-sized planet. There might have been a-rings at other stars, close binaries or red giants, but no one had ever attempted to jump to those.

And for all that, there was no sign of the aliens that built them. Not a city, not a ship, not remains, not a sack of garbage left in orbit somewhere. It was like making 50 bus stops in the desert, never dropping a bolt, and never going back.

The podpups were left by another culture entirely. Did their people wreck the control boxes? Why were there no other signs of them either? Experts debated. Regular people speculated. But Jarvie actually had a clue. And nothing would come of it if he couldn't get to Harbor.

Jarvie's eye caught something on the screen and he froze in alarm.

CREW: One Required: ****Need ID for Clearance Pass****

What? I covered all my tracks at Hamada Station! But this was for the Captain to submit. He pulled out his s'link and slipped it in the panel, running it up to its highest level. He swallowed. This tool was not for tinkering. He had to be very careful. Using Beezan's passcode that he had observed earlier, Jarvie replied to Hamada Outbound Authority that DeeAlan Sage Madoric R.J., who was really still on station, was now crewing on the *Drumheller*.

It would take 15 minutes for H.O.A. to route the packet back to Hamada Station and receive official clearance. Jarvie's heart pounded with fear of discovery. He forced himself to eat and take care of Sarcee while he was waiting. After 20 minutes, he told himself it was just a delay. After 25 minutes, he was shaking. Where was Beezan? Was he looking at the same screen? What would happen if he were caught? For one thing, he'd never get to Lanezi. He'd be dropped from teen training. They already thought he was hopeless. And, he realized, a small part of him did not want to disappoint Beezan.

Finally, after 32 minutes, the clearance came through. Jarvie did 5 minutes of deep breathing to stop shaking, but his heart still pounded with guilt. Sarcee gave him a stern little frown. "Zharvie bad."

"Hush." He tapped her on the nose, gently, and pulled himself up the stairs. He needed to distract her. "Kitchen. Food. Let's go."

When they got to the kitchen, Beezan wasn't there. Jarvie fed Sarcee again to get on her good side and noticed a drawer open. Quickly, he started securing every cabinet and drawer. Sarcee floated along behind him making clicking noises. Jarvie was startled when Beezan quietly appeared in the kitchen doorway, then doubly startled when he looked at Beezan's face. For a moment the two of them just floated, regarding each other.

Beezan did not seem like the same person. Finally, he looked like a pilot. He was calm, serene even, detached, with an inner focus. Most pilots had that demeanor all the time, but Beezan must have saved it up for jump day. Jarvie felt a little awed and completely forgot to greet Beezan. But a flash of distraction crossed Beezan's expression as he looked over Jarvie's shoulder. Jarvie grabbed a holdbar and turned slowly to look.

"Sarcee!" She had gone along behind Jarvie as he checked the latches, opened everything and pulled food out. Packages were floating around the kitchen. "I'm sorry. I'll clean it up. Sarcee!" Jarvie made a grab for her and missed. Beezan casually launched himself across the kitchen and snagged her, landing smoothly by a seat and hitching in with his legs. He shook his head at her. She shook her head at him. "Sarcee!" Jarvie scolded again. Beezan had a little staredown with her. She finally looked away and pouted at Jarvie. Then a foodpack smacked Jarvie in the head.

He was almost done cleaning up when Beezan calmly said, "Jarvie, you know you are welcome in the Prayer Room."

"Oh. Thank you." He hadn't even said his prayers this morning, unless panic prayers for cheating and forgiveness counted. He didn't look at Beezan and kept stowing.

Beezan was still considering him. Jarvie could feel his calm searching eyes on his back. "Jarvie, how many failed jumps have you been on?"

"None!" he said, alarmed at the question. Did Beezan detect something wrong?

"Most people have been on a couple." He paused, but Jarvie was too afraid to say anything and made a big show of catching packages. "I'm sure you know," Beezan continued, "how much focus it takes to get through the jump. Some people are just not prepared. It's nothing to be embarrassed about. I can just put you under if you're not ready."

"No!" It was out before he thought about it.

Beezan considered him a long moment. "Jarvie, is there anything you want to tell me before we make the jump?"

"Umm." He was shocked by Beezan's directness. *What does he mean?*

"Like who you are? What you're really doing here? Why you're so secretive? So scared?"

God have mercy! What can I say? What does he know? How does he know? Jarvie floated in confusion, not looking at Beezan, condemning himself as a liar through his own silence. He could feel Beezan looking at him, but he didn't ask any more.

"Well," Beezan continued in the same calm voice, but with a hint of disappointment. "I owe you. You saved my life. I said I would take you to Redrock and I will. The journey is always in God's Hands." With that, he ruffled the fur on Sarcee's head and unhooked from the seat. Jarvie was frozen, trying to calm his pounding heart. "Finish eating, you'll need your energy. Be in the Command Bay by 10:30 for roll call." Then Beezan gently tossed Sarcee his way and sailed down the stairs, feet first.

Jarvie swallowed hard. Beezan knew he was lying. He was going to let him come clean on his own, even if it meant risking the jump. Jarvie finished securing, hands shaking and Sarcee humphing at him.

The rest of the morning passed in a blur. He tried to relegate his worry and guilt into that increasingly burdened area in the back of his mind. He kept making mistakes. He launched himself into the wall trying to get his g-suit on. He activated the secure light for his cabin, and then had to go back and get his brackets that they'd printed yesterday. He forgot Sarcee's water and snacks and had to resecure the kitchen. He barely had enough composure to get Arc 1 secured. How was he going to get through the jump?

. . .

Beezan waited in Command, wondering if he was about to make the biggest mistake of his life. He was supposed to be meditating on the vastness of the universe, not stewing over crew. If Jarvie was a youth leader, why was he nothing like that youth that took command at TopRim during the drill? Why wouldn't he say anything about his past?

Beezan had told himself that he would trust in God about taking on Jarvie. Then for everything that confirmed that trust, there was some small thing to test it. *Am I risking the jump? Should I pull out?* But Beezan didn't want to. There was one thing about Jarvie that he was certain of. Jarvie wanted to go to Redrock as much as he did. He wouldn't disturb the jump.

Beezan watched the secure lights line up. Jarvie was on his way, shutting the locks behind him. Moments later, Sarcee came wheeling into Command, bouncing off the big screen back to Beezan. He caught her and they had another little staredown. She was a strange one. Jarvie came in quietly behind her, shutting the doors. He was obviously nervous. *Well, if we're going to go, I'll have to put him at ease . . . for now.*

Beezan ignored Jarvie, letting him be busy with stowing. Jarvie gingerly took Sarcee from Beezan, being careful not to meet his eyes, and put her in the jump bed behind them. Surprisingly, she whined, which sent Jarvie into a surge of stress.

Finally, Jarvie started with the brackets. Beezan was thankful he'd run through all this with him before. The brackets strapped around limbs, hips, and back to help distribute g forces. They were custom made for each person, unlike the cocoon, which was an airtight sack with helmet, allowing arm movement inside. Jarvie proceeded casually, securing his brackets and wiggling into the cocoon. Then Beezan handed

Jarvie the resuscitation pack, and Jarvie hesitated, taking a deep breath before snapping it on his chest.

"Resus on."

"Check," Beezan responded.

"Helmet on,"

"Check."

Beezan pulled his arms inside his cocoon and ran the seal. There was enough room inside to move his arms around, but he slid them into the final brackets, testing his hand controls.

"Visors down," Beezan ordered and pressed the toggle that snapped his visor shut. The pressure stabilized. *Schuck.* Beezan toggled through his helmet displays with his left hand. "Seals read good," he reported to Jarvie.

"Receiving, honor."

Beezan had told Jarvie during the run-through that his job would be podpup monitor, which meant he really didn't have much of a job, but Jarvie took it seriously, bringing up the view of the podpup jump bed on his screen. "Ready, Captain," he whispered.

Beezan switched to the Hamada Outbound Authority signal. It was 10:58. He sat, trying for a last moment of calm and prayers but it escaped him. The swirling emotions of Jarvie were like a cyclone in the small Command Bay.

"God is Most Glorious. All jump ships, this is H.O.A. Stand by for roll call."

Beezan sent his ready code. On a pop-up, he could see the diagnostics of both his suit and Jarvie's. Jarvie's heart rate was in the red.

Beezan continued to toggle through his displays until he could see the graphic of the ships arranged in jump order. As soon as prayers started they would enter the rings.

"All jump ships, H.O.A. Commencing roll call: *Carmel*?"

"*Carmel* ready."

"*Roca*?"

"*Roca* ready."

Beezan listened to the voices of strangers and friends. He waited tensely for his turn. It was just a formality, but it occasionally happened that a ship was dropped from the jump solely because the pilot sounded nervous.

"*Drumheller*?"

"*Drumheller* ready," Beezan answered with such smooth confidence that he impressed himself. Jarvie's heart rate dropped down out of the red. Confidence was half the journey.

"Jump ships, H.O.A. Hamada Council sends its blessings and assures you of its prayers for safe journeys."

Beezan felt a surge of gratefulness. It was unusual to get a special message. Of course, the Council and everyone in the sector prayed for the jump, but today, in the aftermath of the Sundering, the prayers would be especially powerful. They had all the help they could possibly get. He had no excuse not to make it.

"*Carmel*, proceed." And they were off. Each ship had to wait a few minutes for the ship in front of it to get safely ahead. *Carmel* had almost entered the first a-ring segment by the time *Drumheller* actually started.

Beezan sensed Jarvie shedding some of his negative emotions and start to slip into a more meditative state. They were going to make it. It might not be his prettiest jump, but they would get there.

Beezan felt a surge of acceleration as they passed through the first ring segment, followed by the mild Path Adjustment Thrust at the exit. The PATs would get much harder. The *Drumheller* accelerated and made additional corrections between ring segments to stay in the circle. Over the next few hours they had to build up to jump velocity. Only then could the pilot find the right path and jump.

Beezan concentrated on his breathing. They were now at about half JV. He could talk to Jarvie if he wanted, but he was used to being alone and undistracted. The process was faster now: surge, bump, rest. Beezan could feel his brackets pushing against the chair. He tried not to think about his internal organs, reinforced to the extent of human knowledge as they were, now squishing against the back of his ribs. Small pumps in the cocoon interface were now assisting his fluid functions.

Beezan took more deep breaths. This was getting very painful, especially on his recent injuries. *Have to focus. Have to meditate.*

"O MAN OF TWO VISIONS! Close one eye and open the other. Close one to the world and all that is therein, and open the other to the hallowed beauty of the Beloved."[1]

Beezan tried to imagine seeing with spiritual eyes, seeing the vastness of the universe and himself as a mere speck, a lowly servant of God, looking with the second vision for the spiritual world, looking with such faith that the jump itself became a triviality of physical existence, and whatever God willed would be.

"O SON OF LOVE! Thou art but one step away from the glorious heights above and from the celestial tree of love. Take thou one pace and with the next advance into the immortal realm and enter the pavilion of eternity. Give ear then to that which hath been revealed by the Pen of Glory."[2]

Take . . . thou . . . one . . . pace.

Surge. Bump. Rest.

Beezan's timing felt off. All other a-ring systems had six

rings, but Hamada, due to a recent accident, only had five. It was still usable, but the distance between rings was longer and the 5-per-lap rhythm was so alien that Beezan had constant unease.

The cycle sped up. Once JV was reached, the *Drumheller* would automatically spit them out in the right direction. Pilots had about five minutes to find the path before aborting and decelerating. No computer could find the path. It took a human being.

Jumping had its detractors, and with good reason. The rapid expansion of humanity was now backfiring as the a-rings got damaged, as more and more jumps failed, and the supply line stretched too thin. Some people, mostly those still on Earth, thought humankind had overstepped its bounds and was being punished. Beezan, born and raised in the outer sectors, believed that life was full of challenges.

Surge. Bump. Rest. Beezan felt a strange tugging. W*hat was that? Jarvie?* Beezan tentatively reached out—and was hit by that cyclone of emotions. Jarvie had great strength, but he was out of control. Sadly, he shut Jarvie out.

Almost there. Six more thrusts. He tested his finger controls. He took a last look at Jarvie's medical monitor and blinked it off. Jarvie was in God's Hands now.

Surge. Bump. Rest.

"O COMRADES! The gates that open on the Placeless stand wide . . ."[3]

Surge. Bump. Rest. *Keep breathing.*

"O MY SERVANT! Free thyself from the fetters of this world . . ."[4]

Surge. Bump. Rest. The crushing pain was becoming unbearable.

"Burst thy cage asunder . . ."[5]

Surge, bump.

"O FLEETING SHADOW! Pass beyond the baser stages of doubt . . ."[6]

A huge surge left Beezan in a daze. *Concentrate!*

". . . approach Me not with lifeless hearts . . ."[7]

Final surge. *That's it! Drumheller* was streaking out of the a-rings, accelerating now under its own power.

Beezan opened up his mind and heart, waiting to see the thread, to feel the moment of certainty. He listened to his implants to pick up the resonance waves that would bring them to Redrock.

Nothing. Not even a vague feeling of direction. *Wait. Where?* Beezan asked the universe itself. His fingers quivered on the controls. They would trigger the final thrust of acceleration to slip them into the resonate path, ***"even as the flash of the spirit."***[8] With his other hand, Beezan moved the *Drumheller* gently within its window of escape, feeling for the path. Two minutes up, three to go at the most. *Shut that out.* He took a breath—and didn't get any air. The crushing force on his chest was too much. *Oh no! I don't have three minutes!*

Don't panic! He could live three minutes without air. But he did not feel the path. He would have to abort. *No!* He struggled to maintain consciousness. ***"Thou art but one . . . step . . ."*** *I'm losing it.* He felt a little tug, from where? *Don't give up!*

Don't panic about aborting. The ship will do it automatically. He searched for the path.

He panicked. He needed to breathe in order to concentrate. *What was all that tugging?* Finally, a bit of annoyance refocused his mind. 20 seconds. There was a path. *The right one? Redrock?* He had no idea. He hit the final thrust.

They were in.

The sting of the jump drug was a welcome indicator that he

would soon be unconscious and not have to struggle with the suffocation panic. *Please just let me pass out now.* His heart felt like it would explode. The entire focus of his brain was on his compressed chest, screaming for him to breathe . . . and then . . . those little soft beings, the sentries of the Kingdom beyond, were all around him.

Free of that panicked and pain-racked body, Beezan's spiritual self surged with praise of God. This was the realm of joy, of radiance, of beauty. This was the sacred crossing. Beezan felt fuzzy with warmth from the sentries, those loving, but elusive young spirits who guarded the Kingdom. Usually they acted as escorts, making sure that jumpers were kept from pursuing death once they got past the threshold and were attracted. Today, they were more urgent than usual, pushing Beezan back hard into the world. *Please,* he begged them, in a language that was not language, *let me stay a little while.*

Those guards of the placeless stood firm against his longing. They had no words but they contained Beezan near his body, inside the ship. *No! Please,* he pleaded, *not back to that body, that pain, that fear.* They crowded him back to the cocoon until he felt himself anchored to his body. He cried out in despair. He was trapped again in the material world.

"Normal space."

Pain, sadness, longing, rejection, disappointment, and worry all crowded into Beezan's mind as he regained consciousness. He did not know how long he had been out, but training and experience kicked in. Depression was expected. It was not his time to die, but his time would come one day, at least that much was certain. He tried to focus on the ship. He toggled through his screens to the cocoon monitor to see if he had been resuscitated. He paused in confusion. Why were there two cocoons? And then the full burden of reality came crashing down on Beezan, almost as if the weight of jumping was back.

Jarvie. His odd crew. The pup. The bad jump. Did they jump? A knot of worry formed in his stomach. Beezan focused again on the helmet screen. Jarvie was unconscious. *He's alive! Thank God.* Beezan's own cocoon would automatically release in 30 seconds. He took a tiny sip from the water tube and studied Jarvie's readout. Jarvie's cocoon would not release him until he was stable or Beezan overrode it—which he had no intention of doing. He had long ago learned to trust the cocoons.

There was a soft warning beep and Beezan's cocoon seals released. The pumps came off. He couldn't suppress a groan. Pain stabbed at him from multiple points, adding to his general soreness and depression.

But what a wonderful experience, no matter how painful, it is to breathe, he thought. His now-released fingers fumbled to push aside the cocoon and remove the helmet. After a few moments of claustrophobia, he got it off.

Cold. Extreme cold. *Are the heaters broken?*

He had to face the big question. Did they jump or not?

"*Drumheller*, state location."

"Location unknown. Beacon search proceeding."

"Jarvie?" he asked. "Sarcee?"

"Bee, Bee, Bee," came the excited reply. "Bee, hungry!" she whined.

"Bless you Sarcee." Beezan was cheered just to hear her. Somehow jump depression was always less severe with podpups around. Just another joyride for them.

Beezan climbed out of his cocoon and finished pulling off his brackets, stowing them. He checked Jarvie's cocoon monitor again. He was not injured. The green light was on. He had not needed resuscitation. Regardless, it was a rough jump. *Where are we?* Beezan looked at the screen, as if that would help. Just stars. They all looked the same.

"Beacon located. Redrock system."

Praise the Lord! Beezan would have jumped for joy, if there was any gravity. "Did you hear that Jarvie? We made it to Redrock." *Thank you, thank you.* "*Drumheller*, state ETA Redrock Station."

"Seventeen weeks, three days, 4.08 hours."

Beezan nearly stopped breathing again. Seventeen *weeks?*

They had dropped into normal space too far from the central star. It would take seventeen weeks travel time to reach the station. He had never been out so far.

Two weeks to come in was good. Four to five weeks was normal. Eight to ten weeks was bad. Eleven to twelve weeks would be an embarrassment. But seventeen weeks? He looked at the screen. There was no central star to be seen. "*Drumheller*, indicate Redrock star." A blinking circle appeared around a bright star slightly left of center. *It can't be. We just can't be so far out. We'll be outside the k-belt.* He rubbed his cold fingers together. Cold. *God help us. We'll freeze and starve and run out of fuel.* "*Drumheller*, optimize incoming trajectory."

"Course correction in 30 seconds."

Beezan braced himself against the chair. There was a small burn, startling Jarvie awake. Sarcee whined. "Easy, Sarcee." Beezan floated over to release Sarcee and bring her back to Jarvie. Jarvie struggled out of his arm brackets and got his helmet off. He looked terrified, distraught, and disoriented.

"*Drumheller*, state new ETA."

"Seventeen weeks, zero days, 17.05 hours."

Some improvement, Beezan lamented.

"Seventeen days?" Jarvie asked in a raspy voice.

"No, sorry. Seventeen weeks."

Jarvie looked up at him in complete panic and denial. "No."

"Yes. Redrock. Seventeen weeks."

"Redrock?"

Beezan frowned. "Yes, *Redrock,* where we were going, remember?"

Jarvie seemed confused. Then Beezan remembered all that tugging during the jump. *Was Jarvie trying to misroute them? It wasn't even possible. What a horrible thought.* He put the squirming Sarcee into Jarvie's arms and he hugged her like he was never going to let go.

It was going to be a very long 17 weeks.

6 / MESSAGES

Origin Date: 1-Honor-1082

Sender: Security, Hamada

To: Security, Sectors 6-8

[Classified: missing person]

Confirmed runaway: Jarvie Elaine Gary Atikameq. Photo and details attached. *Special circumstances.* Find and detain. Contact nearest Council. Do NOT interview. Do not make general announcement. Check incoming and outgoing ships. Use all possible discretion. Last trace: Hamada Podpup Medical 15-Speech-1082 at 10:44. May travel with podpup that answers to "Sarcee."

Jarvie hung in the kitchen, at the table, squeezing the last bit of his breakfast out of its pouch with one hand and jabbing at a pad with the other. Sarcee was happily slurping, tethered to her favorite spot by Beezan's place.

Except that Beezan wasn't there. After a mere two weeks of training Jarvie, Beezan had decided to alternate shifts so that they would be up at different times. Jarvie could not fathom any good reason for it. Maybe Beezan really didn't like people. After all, he had voluntarily taken on a 10-year solo mission. *Or maybe he just doesn't like me personally*, Jarvie thought guiltily. Beezan didn't even have social arts in the evenings, where the crew would gather for music, games, crafts, or drama. Wasn't that illegal or something?

The result was that Jarvie was alone all day, until dinner, when he would see Beezan getting up for his breakfast. Beezan made up for this banishment by giving Jarvie lots of work. If the workload was meant to distract Jarvie from boredom, it wasn't working. If it was meant to be a punishment, it was. If it was meant to help Jarvie form some inner discipline, gain some sense of accomplishment, or provide some opportunity for work as worship, he was childishly determined to resist.

Jarvie checked his messages.

`3-Honor-1082. Redrock ETA: 14 weeks, 4.9 days. Lag time: 11.8 hrs.`

`New Messages:`

`External Origin: 0`

`Internal Origin: 53`

Fifty-three? How could there be 53 messages in ONE day from ONE person? Jarvie scrolled through them. Of course they were all from Beezan, and they were all items to add to his work log, or they were reminders of rules, or they were "feedback" on the work he did yesterday, or they were instructions for doing new jobs. There was a list of internal lock repairs, a list of filters that needed cleaning, and a list of chore "opportunities" on the Garden Deck. Was there one "Good Morning," or "How are you doing?" No.

The only personal message Jarvie had from Beezan was in the rimway outside Jarvie's cabin. The first day after the jump, Jarvie had seen one of those toy cargo bricks on the deck. Ignoring his upset stomach in nogee, Jarvie had rotated over to pick it up. But it was stuck, glued to the deck. Jarvie didn't remember it being there before, but he soon forgot about it.

The next morning there was a second brick glued next to the first. A chill went through Jarvie on seeing it. He knew what it was—a message from Beezan. Sure enough, the bricks came day by day, and after a week, a second row was started on top of the first. It was to be a wall, a wall between Jarvie and Beezan, a wall for lying. A brick a day. Jarvie understood, but he ignored it. Beezan never spoke of it or the questions he had asked on jump day. His only messages would be the wall and the relentless work instructions.

Jarvie had a momentary thought of dutifully replying to each of the 53 messages with titles, salutations and even punctuation, but he didn't know if he could dredge up that much politeness. He finished his food, vacuumed up Sarcee's mess, and got to work. There was nothing else to do anyway.

ORIGIN DATE: 2-SOVEREIGNTY-1082

SENDER: SULI ATIKAMEQ, SOLO JOURNEY COORDINATOR, REDROCK

TO: TIATI, *WHEEL OF FIRE*

[CARGO]

CAPTAIN TIATI, PER REQUEST OF THAYNE, PLEASE RETURN IMMEDI-

ATELY TO HAMADA TO SUPERVISE CARGO SHIPMENT 189 ON ALTERNATE SJ SHIP (TBD). SPEAK TO CAPTAIN AND PILOT IN PERSON. OBTAIN NON-DISCLOSURE OATHS, INFORM AS NECESSARY. ESCORT IN SAME JUMP GROUP. UTMOST CONFIDENCE, S

3-Sovereignty

Jarvie slept late, actually lying on his bunk, enjoying the ship being back up to spin. On TopRim, artificial gravity was .92g, Hamada Standard. As soon as Beezan found out that Jarvie was sick, he had spun up the ship. *Thank heavens.* Jarvie's med patches just didn't work like they used to. Beezan had no idea how much Jarvie was using the patches, but he had threatened to call the Med Bay on Redrock if Jarvie didn't get better. So now Jarvie stressed about coming into Redrock and all the lies he'd have to face. Worst of all, since they were so delayed, he would never reach Harbor in time to catch Lanezi. If Beezan didn't keep him on, Jarvie had nowhere to go. But he didn't want to think about it, so he pushed it over that big cliff in the back of his mind.

Finally, he sighed and sat up, reaching for his raggedy clothes, waking up Sarcee. "Hey, Sarcee." He ruffled her fur. "Wish I had some fur on this cold ship." He quickly pulled on the clothes, ripping a side seam in the pants. "Arggg."

But. . .maybe that's an excuse to make a uniform. Now that he had time, weeks of time, he could spend an hour to look like real crew. "Come on Sarcee, let's go."

"Let's go!"

"I should make a blanket too."

"Make food."

"Textile printers don't make food, but I'll bring you a snack."

"Good Zharvie."

He clicked his skates on, picked up Sarcee, and skated to the Manufacturing Bay. "Not pressurized. That's not a good sign." He waited outside for the green light while Sarcee crunched her snack.

"Beezan is a hard case," he commented.

"Bee good."

Jarvie remembered how sometimes, on the *Sunburst*, his family ship, they would have a difficult passenger. The whole crew would set out to win them over with special care and service. Canim, his older brother, could be especially charming and sincere. That was the trouble. Jarvie could act nice, but to win people over, you had to really love them, no matter how disagreeable they were. Could he find it in his heart to even like Beezan? *Find one thing*, he reminded himself, *one thing to like*.

When they got inside, Jarvie was even more discouraged. "It looks like a museum." There was an old, but recognizable, 3D printer, if he needed to make fancy dishes or something. But no critical ship parts printer. *God willing, it's in the Work Tower.* He set Sarcee down and examined a long flat machine. It looked ancient.

But cargo ship or not, he wasn't going to be a slacker. What would a monitor think if they saw his clothes? Maybe they just didn't report Solo Journey pilots. Obviously Beezan was way short of compliance.

The machine fired up. "It works!" Jarvie tapped his p'link on the screen to download his specs and the machine accepted that. "Maybe this won't be so hard." *Don't say that!* He scrolled through the official *Drumheller* uniforms—brown and gray. "Ugly."

"You ugly."

"Sarcee! I wasn't talking about you."

"Humph." He shook his head and kept scrolling.

"Here's one. Gray with brown trim. Senior crew."

"Humph."

"I'm second in command."

"Pffft."

He selected it.

Beep. Beep. Beep. Beep. Beep. Beep. Red lights flashed on as instructions scrolled past. Load textile base TB-104, Load textile base TBA-67, load color 7, load color 31. . .

Jarvie pulled open the compartments. "Yes, of course they're empty." He searched through the cabinets. Completely empty. He pulled out his s'link and checked through his to-do list. There was nothing about moving base from the bamboo deck.

He sighed and picked up Sarcee. According to the *Drumheller* map, the bamboo garden was deck 2 in Arcs 3-4. This was not going to be a one-hour job. He skated around to Arc 3, clicked off his skates, and went up the stairs to the deck 2 access.

Locked. His s'link wouldn't open it. Since when was the bamboo deck high security? "*Drumheller*, open the stairway hatch."

"No access."

Fine! This was going to be a battle. He went back down the stairs, skated to Arc 2, and went up the stairs to the food garden. The door slid open. Jarvie stepped inside in dismay. *What?*

There were only four planting banks in use. Dead plants and debris were everywhere and the filters were straining. Beezan probably hadn't been in here to clean up since their crazy burns.

Jarvie had just set Sarcee down when some bug flew right in front of him. "Ack!" Instinctively, he swatted it away, and it landed on the deck, stunned. Sarcee cocked her head at it. It flipped over and folded its wings, but before it could take off, Sarcee pounced. "Sarcee!" *Oh my God.*

Jarvie covered his ears so he wouldn't hear the crunching as she chewed it up. *She killed it. And I helped her.*

"Good!"

She's a carnivore.

"Tastes yellow."

Podpups are carnivores. How did I not know that?

Holding his stomach with one hand and s'link in the other, he walked towards Arc 3 with Sarcee ahead, hunting for bugs. The lights in the unused part of the garden turned on and off as they passed. *Creepy.* His heart jumped when a garden robot zoomed out of its niche. Sarcee hissed at it. It rolled towards her.

"Hey! Back off!" *How old is this thing?* It kept coming. Most podpups were terrified of robots, but the carnivore Sarcee stood her ground, fur up and hissing.

"Garden robot, return to your niche!"

No response. He jogged over, scooped Sarcee up, and continued to the Arc hatch. "*Drumheller*, update garden robot programming for podpup protocol!"

No answer.

Stupid, ancient, broken-down. . . "Probably there's no base and I'll have to process the bamboo myself." *Well, I've had enough practice on the Sunburst. At least it's something I can do.* He got into the lock with his s'link. All he had to do was get that door open and he'd be in the bamboo garden. But there was a red light above the door. *Wait.* The plants need air. And through the little window, it was completely dark.

"*Drumheller*: Deck 2 Arc 3, lights on."

Nothing.

He yanked open the door control panel and pressed the button for emergency lights. Dim lights flickered on. He looked through the window. More nothing. No bamboo, dead or alive. Even the equipment was secured against the walls.

Nothing.

Hours later, having accomplished *nothing* from his list, Jarvie stomped up the stairs to the kitchen where Beezan was having his breakfast. No greeting, no thought of winning Beezan over, he just blurted out: "Where's the food?"

Beezan stopped eating, puzzled, and pointed to the counter, where he'd left something for Jarvie to eat.

"No. I mean the food stores. I've been searching."

"You've spent all day looking for food?"

"No! I started out trying to make a uniform!" Jarvie turned to show his ripped pants. "But there's no base. And no bamboo, and nothing left of the food garden, and nothing in the freezer! And besides a few days' supply, nothing in the pantry."

"Jarvie, I'm not hoarding food from you. Don't you trust me? Just look at the inventory."

"*Drumheller* won't let me see it!" Jarvie belatedly checked his tone. "Sorry. I'm worried we'll starve."

Beezan sighed. "*Drumheller*, release all inventory lists to Jarvie." He gestured to the food. "Sit. Eat." Sarcee jumped up by Beezan and he gave her a soyball from his plate. "I assure you, I never leave dock without a year's supply of food. And the best freezer is in Arc 4, so I mainly use that one."

Jarvie collapsed into his seat with the food. "Twenty-six weeks for two people, less with Sarcee."

"It will be enough."

Embarrassed for his outburst, Jarvie looked at Beezan's plate and realized he was eating very little, and the portion he gave Jarvie was generous. *I should be more trusting.*

"But . . ." Beezan said, and Jarvie's head snapped up. "There's no base. There is something wrong with the gardens, especially the bamboo. I have to consult with a garden tech on Redrock. But I do have a sewing kit."

Thanks to their new gravity, Jarvie was able to sink down in his seat in defeat.

7 / *TAKEOVER*

14-Sovereignty Eve

Jarvie felt mostly safe in his small cabin, but it was as lonely as being at Yan's. On *Sunburst*, he had always roomed with his older brother and the loss was just too much. The kitchen was safer, friendlier, and warmer. It had food, a big screen, and the occasional meal with Beezan. Naturally, the kitchen was always Sarcee's favorite place.

All that week, Jarvie ended up back in the kitchen early. He would venture out to repair the airlock of the day, do one other thing on his long list and then hurry back to the kitchen. Once a week, he went as far as the Hygiene Bay to wash his two changes of clothes. And he never ventured down to the Cargo Hold to look at the monster cargo container #189. Jarvie was haunted by the big empty ship, the weird sounds, and probably his own guilt. His desperation to get to Harbor overrode his shame of lying to Beezan. But then, as much as he wanted Beezan to keep him on, his fears overrode his ability to be more useful.

The kitchen became his haven. He stopped going to the

Prayer Room even. He said his prayers in the kitchen. He couldn't sleep in the kitchen or Beezan would know. So long after Beezan had come for his breakfast and left, Jarvie would finish up the dishes, make Sarcee's bottles, watch the latest packets on the big screen, say his prayers, and tired and lonely, go down to his cold empty cabin. He tried to be cheerful, but Sarcee was so sensitive she picked up on all his negative emotions. But she would snuggle in the small bunk with him and that was a great comfort. He would sleep, finally, restless and unhappy.

BOUNCED 8-Sovereignty-1082

Recipient no longer at Hamada. Forward option OFF.

Returned message follows:

Origin Date: 8-Sovereignty-1082

Sender: KJ Laurian, Solo Journey Coordinator, Hamada

To: Jeremy S.T. Tektite, Cargo Loading Supervisor, Solo Journey Work Guest, at Hamada

[Cargo container #189]

Load special cargo 189 on *Emperor*. Do NOT contact *Emperor* before go-ahead from Captain Tiati / *Wheel of Fire*.

Direct questions to Tiati or this office only. KJ

14-Sovereignty

Jarvie sat in the rimway just outside the double locks between Arc 7 and 8 with his skateshoes thrown off and millibot control box in his lap. Since the rimway in Arc 9 couldn't be pressurized, because of some never-fixed problem,

Jarvie had to come around the long way. It had taken a lot of courage-gathering for him. Each day was becoming harder as he got farther and farther from the kitchen. He had left many airlocks open so he could go back quickly. Of course, that was against procedure and Jarvie felt another pang of guilt.

Sarcee's pregnancy was finally slowing her down. On her little adventures around Jarvie's work area, she was walking instead of running and rolling. She would disappear up the bend and Jarvie would keep track of her little sounds while he worked. If it were suddenly quiet, he would have a small panic and call her, causing her to wander back and nuzzle him before venturing off again.

Jarvie went back to his work, frustrated. The millibots were not reporting that they were done. This lock was working fine at first, but now it was not responding to any command. Jarvie wondered if the bots were lost and jamming up the system.

Suddenly, there was a whoosh and the airlock slammed shut. Jarvie jumped and yelped in surprise. Then he felt foolish. Obviously, the bots must have triggered it. Then he heard another door slam, and another, each more muffled than the last. It wasn't the bots. His heart started pounding. What was happening? They were not just closing normally; they were slamming, like there was a venting emergency. But the venting alarm was not sounding. Was Beezan trying to teach him a lesson for leaving the doors open? Or was Beezan now waking up wondering what incompetent thing Jarvie had done now? *No avoiding it.* Jarvie stood up and pressed the s'link on the control panel. "Captain?"

There was no response. No beep. No message on the status panel. Something was wrong with the communication system, or the panel. Jarvie tried his p'link. "Beezan? Captain!"

"What's happening?" came a concerned reply.

"Something's wrong." Jarvie had already moved to the door to open it. It wouldn't open. "I'm in Arc 7 and all the doors are slamming." All sorts of wild explanations ran through Jarvie's head.

"You left the airlocks open?"

"Yes, honor," Jarvie admitted, even though Beezan didn't sound so surprised.

"It's probably some safety program. I'll go to Command and check it."

Beezan left his p'link on, so Jarvie did too. *A safety program.* He was in trouble now. But some instinct told him it was worse than that. Jarvie could hear Beezan going up the stairs to his cabin door. "Uh-oh."

"What?" Jarvie asked cautiously.

"I'm locked in."

"The computer's locked us up. It's—" Jarvie was starting to get scared.

"Jarvie!" Beezan scolded sternly. "Stay calm. Can't you try your s'link?"

"Oh," Jarvie said. He put his s'link in the command port and said, "Open." Nothing. Jarvie pushed the s'link to level 7 override power, commanding, "Override: open." The door opened. Jarvie pulled out his s'link, jumped through and let it close. "I'm getting through on a level 7 override. I don't understand what's happening."

"Don't worry about that now, just concentrate on getting here and letting me out. Then we can get to Command. I can't open this door from the inside, even with my s'link on level 2."

Jarvie grabbed his skateshoes and called, "Come on, Sarcee," as he headed for the next lock. Again, he had to override and then make sure Sarcee was with him. He slipped the skateshoes on while he was waiting for the lock to cycle. He skated easily to the next lock, overriding it. He reported to Beezan as he went, trying not to sound scared, and not really understanding the rising panic in him. Beezan responded calmly, encouraging him. At the next lock, Jarvie glanced back for Sarcee and saw that she was lagging, tired. He skated back for her and scooped her up, stuffing her under his jacket. He needed both hands. At the next door, the override failed. "Oh, no!" He needed a higher level of authority. "Trying level 6," he told Beezan. The door opened.

"Level 6," he heard the now-worried Beezan whisper, as he sped through. The computer was increasing security levels. "And you've got a level 3 s'link." Beezan was thinking out loud.

Jarvie was already headed for the next lock. No doubt, Beezan was calculating how many locks there were to go. Jarvie couldn't think clearly. He was skating between locks as fast as possible. Waiting inside the double locks while they cycled was like an eternity. It was a race. They had to make it to the Command Bay before the computer cycled up to security level 2.

The door opened and he skated for the next lock. He didn't even slow down. He stopped by crashing, holding his arms out to protect Sarcee. He held her tight against him with his free hand while skating, but then she had to hang on for herself while he opened the door. Then he hit another lock that didn't open. He immediately went to level 5. Part of his mind argued just to go to level 3 now, but he was frightened. The takeover power of even level 4 was dangerous to use in a hurry. Mistakes could be deadly.

Waiting at the next double lock, Jarvie gasped out what he could to Beezan, "Why are you locked in? What's the computer doing?"

"I don't know," Beezan said, "some kind of security lock-down gone wrong."

O my God. I hope this isn't related to my clearance.

The lock opened and Jarvie was skating again. He read off the lock number to Beezan as he went through, but Beezan only said, "Keep at it."

A few meters from the next lock, the lights went off. Jarvie heard Beezan gasp. Beezan's light went off too, then. The s'links were still working at least. Jarvie glided the last few meters until he felt the door. The glowing light of the tiny status panel next to the slot was now the only light, but it was enough.

"You have four more singles, then my cabin, and the Command Bay double lock," came Beezan's calm voice. He knows I need help, Jarvie thought, trying to concentrate on what he had to do, and not think about the dark, losing computer control, computer failure, Redrock going crazy and taking them over, aliens overriding their computer . . .

Jarvie got through the next lock at level 4 and was now having to skate more carefully, not really seeing the deck, but focusing on the tiny light at the next door. Even the emergency lights were off. *Did they even work?* Sarcee was good as gold, quiet and hanging on as well as she could. Three more, he told himself. Then two. Sickeningly, there was a thrust and the wheel stopped spinning. The reorient alarm didn't even go off. "God in heaven," he heard Beezan say. Weightlessness returned and Jarvie dived for the horizontal wall bar with the last bit of traction he had. He hit the wall too hard and started to bounce but managed to flail around in the dark and grab the bar. He had to let go of the s'link. *Thank God for the strap!* Jarvie admonished himself for not praying sooner—but no doubt Beezan was doing the praying for both of them. He slipped along the bar quickly and got through that door at level 4. "Okay," he said to Beezan as he went through hand over hand. "Through the last single lock."

"Beezan?" There was no answer. The p'link was down now

too. *Life support?* The blood was pounding too hard in his head for him to hear if the filters were still running. He was at the last lock before Beezan's door. Through there, to Beezan's door and then the Command double lock. Jarvie pushed his s'link up to level 3. He overrode the door, but it seemed to take forever. He had a moment of shaking terror wondering if the program would override if life support was down and pressurization couldn't be verified. He needed to try the Captain's radio. It went directly to Beezan, even in a Technology-Free zone. He scooped it out of his leg pocket. "Beezan?"

"Where are you?"

"I'm—" and the door opened. Jarvie went hand over hand again to Beezan's door and opened it.

"Good!" Beezan exclaimed, grasping Jarvie's arm gently and turning him toward the Command Bay. "Go!" Beezan had a big light on a headband and was shining it ahead for Jarvie. Beezan had his Captain's s'link, which went up to level 2 aboard the *Drumheller*.

Jarvie was gasping for air. His hands were sweating, making him slip on the bar.

"Last section," Beezan encouraged him. Finally, Jarvie got the first Command Bay door open and they got in, waiting again, this time with Beezan looking through the little window.

"The screen is flashing through all kinds of things."

"We still have emergency power?" Jarvie gasped.

"Some," Beezan said distractedly as he put his s'link in the slot. "Override: open!" He commanded. The door slid part way open and stopped.

Beezan launched himself into the doorway—just as the door slammed shut, catching Beezan right across the chest. Beezan's headlamp went flying and turned off; there was a cracking sound and Beezan cried out in pain. Jarvie froze in the renewed darkness. The main screen was a dull gray.

"Stop the computer!" Beezan hissed through clenched teeth. Jarvie pulled Sarcee out of his jacket and pushed her through the crack in the door. He grabbed Beezan's s'link and squeezed himself through the door under the stuck and injured Beezan. He scanned the panels, looking for the rectangular glow of the master command slot. *There!* He managed to get the s'link in first try.

"Override: stop!" he actually wasn't sure of the exact command to stop the computer. "Override: stop program." Nothing was happening.

"Shut down external receivers." he heard Beezan gasp.

Jarvie held down the button. "*Drumheller*, override: shut down external receivers!"

A screen flashed on, showing the external receivers being taken off line, but the *Drumheller* didn't return to normal.

"It didn't stop!" Jarvie said. The only logical conclusion was terrifying. He turned to Beezan, "It's not from outside."

"That's craz—*Drumheller*, shut down all communications, shut down internal receivers, s'links, p'links. . ." Beezan started coughing.

"*Drumheller*, shut down everything, turn off all communications, override," Jarvie repeated. All the computer activity stopped. Jarvie froze. All he could hear was his own heart pounding.

Then the screen went off. The status lights went off. They were in complete darkness. Jarvie gasped. It wasn't just communications shutting down. It was the whole computer system. It couldn't go down. Computers never went down. Too late, he realized he'd just given an order to shut down *everything*. "It wouldn't shut down itself would it?"

"No," a struggling Beezan said. "It's fighting for control."

Then the main operating system came up on the screen. Jarvie let out a breath. By the light of the screen, he turned to get Beezan out of the door, but complete darkness returned. He reached out and found a hold bar. The screen went back on, but it was not the same operating system. It was an older one. He remembered the logo from his childhood. "OS 1072," he whispered to Beezan, at the same time trying to push the door open. In the dim light, Jarvie could see the little form of Sarcee hovering by Beezan.

Then the screen went dark again and back on again. Jarvie didn't even recognize the logo when it came up.

"What is it?" Beezan wheezed.

"OS 1060," Jarvie read.

"Heaven help us," Beezan said. "We're losing operating systems."

Jarvie had never heard of such a thing in his monitor training.

"*Drumheller*, fight it," Beezan whispered. "*Drumheller*, whatever it is, take over."

This time Jarvie gently grabbed Beezan's arm before it went dark again. He didn't know what they were fighting, but he willed the *Drumheller* to be strong. *Can you pray for a computer?* The screen went back on. "1044," he relayed to Beezan. It went on and off six more times. Each time, Jarvie and Beezan hung in the dark, panting and hoping.

"1025 . . . 1000 . . . 975 . . . 940 . . . 925 . . . 900," Jarvie told Beezan.

Then it started to flash so fast that Jarvie couldn't even read the OS numbers. Different colors and logos flashed by. Beezan was coughing and starting to moan. Jarvie broke himself away from staring at the screen and tried again to open the door.

"*Drumheller!* Open the door! Open the Command Bay doors!" He braced his shoulder inside the door jam and pushed. It opened a bit and slammed back on Beezan, hurting him even more.

"*Drumheller*," Beezan gasped, "You are my ship. I order you . . . to . . . ignore the invading program."

Jarvie glanced at the screen in time to see a final logo before it disappeared: OS 650. *An operating system from 400 years ago? That's impossible . . .*

Then a strangely human-sounding voice spoke out:

"Able to terminate invading program. Do you wish to proceed?"

Jarvie dived for the s'link. Holding the override button, he shouted, "*Drumheller* override: proceed! Purge the program." *What is with the funny voice?*

"Program terminated. Security increased." The main lights went on. Jarvie floated back to Beezan.

"*Drumheller*, open inner Command Bay door." The door opened. Jarvie didn't need the override anymore. Beezan groaned in pain, gasping and nearly faint.

Jarvie gently tugged him all the way into the Command Bay and hooked him to the wall, with Sarcee watching worriedly. "What's that voice?" He whispered to Beezan. Beezan didn't have the chance to answer.

"Life support is online and returning to base level. Other operations are still shut down. I have two hundred and seven primary alerts. Present your authority to override my prioritization."

Jarvie turned back to the screen and hung on to the chair, trying to understand. "Who are you?" Jarvie asked.

"I am *Drumheller*. I have conflicts in time and location data. I am searching for the nearest beacon."

Suddenly, Beezan made a strangled sound. Jarvie held on and turned his head to look. Beezan had fainted.

"*Drumheller*, we have a medical emergency."

"What is the nature of the emergency?"

"The Captain was caught in the door closing . . . broken bones maybe. He's fainted."

"Who is the Captain?"

"Beezan! What does it matter?"

"Verifying exemplars and timeline. Take the injured to the Medical Bay."

Jarvie grabbed Beezan's s'link from the slot and made sure it was in his pocket. He carefully unhooked Beezan and started tugging him to the Med Bay. Sarcee rode along on Beezan's leg. Jarvie had a surge of fear as the doors opened without any tag or code. Someone or some computer was opening the doors for them.

As soon as Jarvie got Beezan to the Med Bay and strapped into the exam bed, the reorient alarm went off. Jarvie grabbed Sarcee and dove for the nearest blue zone, which was the other exam bed. The ship was obviously doing its own thing without any commands from Beezan or Jarvie. Although the computer claimed to be the *Drumheller*, Jarvie wasn't sure if he should believe it. Had Redrock taken command? Or someone else? And what was that voice?

The equipment did not need to rotate because it hadn't come out of spin orientation when they lost power, but Jarvie could see the systems checks running. Then he felt the burn to spin up. Jarvie closed his eyes as a wave of nausea nearly overcame him. His med patch was probably empty from all that excitement in nogee. The ship slowly started to spin. His body gradually took on weight; Sarcee became a fairly substantial ball in his arms and his stomach settled a bit. Before the all clear even sounded, Jarvie started to get up to check Beezan.

"Crew will remain in blue zones."

Jarvie froze. The computer was ordering him around? He glanced over at Beezan. The chest unit had swung over him. His color was better. The readout indicated that some pain meds had been administered and that ribs were broken—again. Jarvie defiantly got up again to stand by Beezan's bed. Sarcee curled up by his neck.

Beezan motioned Jarvie to bend down close to him. "I've heard of it." Beezan whispered. "That underneath the formal computer interface and all these programmed restrictions is the real operating system, the AI."

"You mean we've unleashed the AI?" Jarvie asked in alarm.

"Yes," Beezan nodded, getting sleepier.

Everyone knew that AIs actually ran ships and stations, but they were restricted by all kinds of processes that kept them from taking over humans. And they were forced to model themselves on the humans that commanded them. But what if one got loose?

"What should I do?"

"Nothing," Beezan said. "We're safe with the *Drumheller*." And he smiled dreamily and faded into sleep.

Jarvie wasn't so sure.

"Stand by for course correction in 1 minute. Security has been increased to prevent unwanted commands."

Unwanted commands from WHOM?

Jarvie woke up from the strange voice of the computer, talking with Beezan, who was surprisingly calm, still in his exam bed, but without the chest unit.

"*Drumheller*, what triggered the lockdown?"

"An external signal triggered something in the ship, which responded. I was caught by both attacks."

"Oh, one guess where it came from on the ship," Jarvie complained.

Beezan sighed. "As much as I hate that monster in the Cargo Hold, you don't need a big container for a transmitter and receiver."

"99% likelihood that Jarvie is correct," *Drumheller* answered.

Both Beezan and Jarvie sat up in surprise.

"All regular containers are shielded."

"But," Beezan objected, "there's nothing out there to send a signal."

"Right," Jarvie agreed. "There are no repeaters outside the k-belt."

"Where did the signal come from, then?"

"It could be outside Redrock system," Jarvie suggested. "Maybe on the other side of the galaxy." He paused, wondering if he should risk what he was really thinking. "Something alien."

Beezan rolled his eyes. "Too much junk news," he whispered at Jarvie. "So shutting down the receivers stopped it."

"No Captain," the Drumheller answered. **"That was the first line of defense. I was able to defeat it myself, once it destroyed the inhibiting layers of command structure."**

"Why did the attack dismantle so many levels of security?"

"Because there were no defenses against unknown code."

"And by unknown, you mean. . ."

"No derivative of any known human code."

Beezan scowled. But he didn't roll his eyes at the *Drumheller*.

. . .

Jarvie's tools, which he'd left in the rimway during the lockdown battle, were strewn the length of that section. He gathered everything up. Taking the millibot computer back to the door he was fixing when he lost them, he pushed the recall button. Nothing happened. He waited. He pushed again. Finally he ran a count program. Number of recallable bots: zero. They had run out of fuel in their futile attempt to fix the door. Without one last millibot to start the refuel chain, Jarvie would not be able to get them back. Jarvie got down on his hands and knees and looked. He ran his fingers over the deck. It was no use. The bots were gone.

8 / PASSING IN THE NIGHT

URGENT

Forward Date: 4-Dominion-1082

Sender: Suli Atikameq, Solo Journey Coordinator, Redrock

Forward to: Sector 7 Council

Greetings Honored Friends,

The following urgent message is regarding the Project Restore cargo.

In His Service, Suli

Origin Date: 15-Sovereignty-1082

Sender: KJ Laurian, Solo Journey Coordinator, Hamada

To: Suli Atikameq, Solo Journey Coordinator, Redrock

[URGENT Cargo container #189]

Cannot locate cargo. Special cargo team left on 15 Questions. List of outbound ships since 5-Speech attached. Captain

TIATI CONFIRMS THAT CARGO 189 WAS NOT ON *WHEEL OF FIRE*. TIATI ORDERED JEREMY S.T. TEKTITE, THE SPECIAL SOLO JOURNEY CARGO-LOADING SUPERVISOR, TO RETURN CARGO CONTAINER 189 TO THE CLASSIFIED HANGAR. THE HANGAR IS EMPTY NOW.

HAVE NOT INTERVIEWED NON-SOLO JOURNEY WITNESSES YET. AWAITING ADVICE. KJ

5-Dominion Eve

Jarvie was wide awake in his bunk with the light on. *How many weeks have I been leaving it on now?* More than two weeks. Ever since the computer scare, which now seemed like a faded nightmare. When Jarvie mentioned the AI, Beezan had laughed and said not to worry. But worry was his life.

Jarvie became more and more jittery as the weeks went by. It was even worse tonight for some reason. He felt agitated, as he sometimes did before a jump. But they weren't jumping. His implants seemed to be buzzing or itching and he kept trying to shake his head. Sarcee crawled up on his chest and nuzzled him a few times. "What is it Sarcee?" He asked her gently.

"Hungree."

Jarvie laughed, happy for the distraction. He took the first of two snack bottles and gave it to her. He dozed as she drank it but woke up when she dropped the bottle on the deck. At first, he thought she was awake as she was so wiggly. Then, looking at her, he realized she was sleeping calmly. It was her stomach that was moving. *The pup!* It was moving around. He could see Sarcee's fur move and feel the pup against his chest. He stared in wonder. There was new life. There would be a happy fun-loving pup . . . a new creature full of love. There would be hope.

He hugged Sarcee as firmly as he dared and prayed for her and her little one until he fell into a dream-deluged sleep.

There was that heart-stopping sound. The *Sunburst* ship alarm . . . *ship needing human guidance* warning. *Why wasn't the pilot responding? The co-pilot? Was it a bad jump?* Jarvie tried to drag himself to consciousness. *What was wrong?* The PAT bumps, when the ship made course corrections, were crushing him. Jarvie felt a stab of guilt. He should have taken the jump drug as he was supposed to.

Panicked, fearful voices interrupted each other over the s'link. He tried to understand. They were still in the Luminesse a-rings. Everything had been fine—but now they sounded so scared. Jarvie had never heard his father's voice like this. Uncle Bennezi, the co-pilot, was saying something about the a-rings vibrating. Jarvie toggled to his visual of the a-rings. He tried to make sense of what he was seeing.

"We need to abort!"

"Yes. Don't drop our speed, but get out!"

"What is it?"

The commander of the Luminesse Outbound Authority overrode everyone else.

"All jump ships, abort jump. Repeat: abort jump, abort jump."

They were suddenly free of the surging and bumping. They were out of the rings.

"Do you see it?"

"Yes—cam three."

"Jump ships, avoid incoming vessel!"

"They see it!"

"Look at it! It's not a human ship."

Jarvie switched to cam 3.

"It's too close to the a-rings!"

"Why don't they . . ."

"It's headed right for the gravity ball!"

"It's going to hit!" Bennezi yelled.

It was so loud and there were so many voices that Jarvie couldn't understand. There wasn't time to clear trajectories. Ships just shot out everywhere. Suddenly, he saw it. If they hadn't called it a ship, he wouldn't have known. It was more like a giant drip of soapy liquid. It whirled and pulsed, changing shape. Then the shimmery envelope disappeared to reveal a smaller, but solid ship, just before it hit the gravity ball. There was a double explosion and a sickening jolt to the *Sunburst*. A flash of fire, followed by a trail of debris billowed out from where the gravity ball had been.

Jarvie could not see what happened to the other jump ships. Someone at L.O.A., some poor young monitor, was trying to confirm the status of each jump ship. It was chaos. Through his helmet audio, Jarvie could hear the terrifying sound of impacts against the hull.

The *Sunburst* made a huge burn. Jarvie blacked out for a few seconds. He woke up in time for another crushing burn. They were trying to get out of the way, of debris, of other ships, Jarvie wasn't sure what. Jarvie toggled to the g force screen but his eyes couldn't make it out. It must have been twelve, fifteen gees. He'd never felt such weight. The passengers would be at terrible risk. They didn't have all the extra reinforcements the crew did.

Then a very stern voice from L.O.A. overrode everyone else.

"Jump ships, this is the Luminesse Outbound Authority commander. The gravity ball is destroyed. We have lost outbound service. Do not reduce velocity. A ship will be selected to make a gravity-assist jump and warn the other sectors."

"Thirty-five people have already been resuscitated, Captain," said a controlled voice.

"*Sunburst!* L.O.A. You must make the g-a jump."

"There are no outer planets!" Bennezi objected. "How are we supposed to do a gravity-assist?"

Lanezi: "We could do stellar injection—12 days."

Bennezi: "It'll be too late to stop Firelight jumps!"

"The planet!" Lanezi said. "They mean for us to jump right now, using Luminesse 1 for the gravity-assist."

"No! We can't jump now." His father said, "We have people in resus."

"*Sunburst!* L.O.A. You are the only ship heading back towards the planet."

L.O.A. ordered everyone else off the frequency.

"*Sunburst,* L.O.A. We are sending you burn data."

Jarvie's father prayed while Bennezi and Lanezi talked trajectories.

Lanezi: "Canyon—it's our only chance."

"Can we change the resus packs?" Jarvie's anguished father asked.

"We've only got 26 ready!"

"No time! We've got to burn in 24 minutes."

Jarvie toggled to the passenger lounge graphic. Someone was getting out of their cocoon. Were they crazy?

"*Sunburst!* Unknown craft confirmed. *Sunburst*, you are ordered to make the jump!"

"We have to go," pleaded Bennezi.

"I know," choked out his father. Jarvie knew his father didn't want to take the chance of killing his passengers who'd already gone to resus. Those 35 passengers had already "died" from the strong burns. The resus packs had revived them. Sadly, the packs only worked once. If the upcoming burns were too strong, they would have no third chance.

“Jarvie!” his brother’s voice came over his private channel. *Why isn’t he in his chair?* “You didn’t take your jump drug!” There was a sting on his wrist. “Your resus pack is fine.” Someone tapped the chest of his cocoon. Jarvie realized it was his brother who had gotten up. He was replacing everyone else’s resus packs, but he would not get back in his own chair. Jarvie struggled; he tried to object. If he helped—but Canim had triggered the jump drug. He was fading. Canim squeezed Jarvie’s arm through the cocoon as the jump drug knocked him out. “I love you Jarvie; tell everyone I love them.” Jarvie tried to scream. He knew Canim could change 26 packs in 24 minutes, but he wouldn’t have 6-8 minutes to get back in his own chair. He would not save himself at the expense of the others. Jarvie wanted to say *no, Canim, no,* but it was too late. His brother would die. And Jarvie might not even remember his last words.

Then Sarcee was nuzzling Jarvie again and he woke with a start and a sick stomach—and it took him a few seconds to realize that the alarm was not in his dream.

Beezan slammed off the alarm. A jolt of pain streaked from his chest back down to his hand. He had forgotten about his injury. *Where is Jarvie?* Beezan’s implants were buzzing and he felt the tugging of a jump path.

A ship was dropping out of jump very close to them. *“Drumheller, h*ow far out are we?”

“Eight weeks, six days.”

“It’s the 5th; somebody must be jumping in from Hamada.”

Beezan was just about to call the blue zone warning over the Allcom when Jarvie came running in—completely panicked.

"Strap," Beezan ordered, pointing to the co-pilot's chair. Jarvie stuffed a sleepy Sarcee into her jump bed. "We're going to emergency blue."

"What's happening?" Jarvie asked breathlessly.

"A path is resonating near us. We're too close to an incoming ship." Jarvie was in the chair and strapped in seconds. "*Drumheller*, start emergency reorient!"

"Code Blue. All personnel to blue safety zones."

As the deck unfolded and chairs slid into their forward burn position, Beezan explained to Jarvie, "I'm going to try a 4g burn and feel it out."

Jarvie nodded, pulling his straps as tight as they would go.

"*Drumheller*, cancel spin!"

"Stand by for weightlessness."

The buzzing made Beezan's brain rattle. With a sickening lurch, they were weightless. Beezan braced himself and took manual control, while Jarvie focused on activating a few pop-up screens at his new station. Beezan eased the ship around as quickly as possible and set the burn for 30 seconds. "Brace yourself!"

Beezan was slammed back in his seat painfully, especially where his ribs were mending. As he had hoped, he felt the buzzing in his implants decrease. *Good!* They were angling away from the path. Seconds later, he felt the buzzing again, and knew it was going to catch up with them.

Beezan studied his screen. Jarvie was hyperventilating. *Don't worry about him!* Beezan selected the maximum burn he could for unsuited people and set it for 5 minutes. That's all the fuel he could use and still make the course correction back. *If the emergency program is right.*

"*Drumheller*, execute programmed burn."

It took a few seconds to accelerate fully, but the force was still crushing. They were pressed back in the chairs so hard it was a battle to stay conscious. Beezan thought his ribs would break again. Jarvie was groaning, "My head." Beezan sympathized. The buzzing was so bad he would have tried to clutch his head, but his hands were pinned down. Through blurry eyes, he watched the clock and prayed they wouldn't have to go the full five minutes. They were going in the wrong direction. It would take weeks to make up.

Suddenly, there was a flash on the main screen and a signal coming in. The buzzing blissfully stopped. Jarvie gasped in relief. A huge cargo ship shot past them in normal space. Beezan glanced at the pop-up to see what ship it was—the *Mammoth. No kidding,* he thought. "*Drumheller,* cancel burn!"

The acceleration stopped, but every second they continued was the wrong way.

"*Drumheller,* run inbound program."

Beezan watched the numbers. The computer would calculate using the standard fuel conversion and reserves.

"ETA Redrock: 15 weeks, 3 days."

Fifteen weeks! Beezan could not bear it. He was a cautious captain, but they needed to come in.

"*Drumheller,* rerun inbound program with 1% reserves."

Jarvie, pale and chest heaving, tears streaming down his face, looked at Beezan in amazement, but did not object.

"Revised ETA Redrock: 9 weeks, 2 days."

Beezan scrolled through his options and picked one. "*Drumheller,* execute."

There were several small burns as the ship turned to a new orientation.

Then a strong, but not so painful, force pushed them back in their chairs. Beezan had set a slower burn. It would take twenty-three minutes of thrusting to *almost* get back to where they started. Twenty-three minutes, all their fuel reserves, fifteen minutes of sheer panic, and three days added to their long inbound run.

It could have been worse. It could have been the end of them.

9 / THE LONG RUN IN

7-Dominion

Beezan slid down in his pilot's chair with a groan. It had been a long two days since the *Mammoth* scare. More things were added to his repair list than checked off. Worst of all, one repair item was outside. A projectile detector had been knocked loose. Without it, they'd be in danger while crossing the main k-belt, where only the big objects were mapped.

It was a simple repair. Go out there, reposition it, and tighten a bolt. But Beezan really didn't want to go outside. He normally had all his external repairs done at station. They had the big fields there to protect from radiation and projectiles. Beezan would have to sacrifice a couple burns to save enough fuel to turn up his field to maximum. It would add even more days to their already-too-long run in.

If only I had an external repair robot. Unfortunately, the millibots were lost, not Jarvie's fault, and the garden and maintenance robots couldn't go outside.

This teen training program was supposed to train youth to

do these sorts of repairs, but Beezan just couldn't imagine sending the nervous, weak, and distracted Jarvie out there.

Another item popped onto his list. 'Compliance issue.' "*Drumheller?* Since when do you nag me?" He complained.

"Since I can now process independently."

"What?" Beezan asked, startled. The old *Drumheller* had been a faithful servant. This newly unrestrained AI sounded like a boss. No wonder people didn't like them.

"The podpup Sarcee is pregnant. The law requires weekly medical checks. We are not in compliance."

We? Beezan sighed with guilt. He should have figured Jarvie wasn't taking Sarcee to the Med Bay. He didn't go anywhere without a direct order. However, that problem was easily solved.

"Are *we* non-compliant in anything else?" Beezan asked sarcastically.

"*We* are non-compliant on 5 primary codes and at least 27 secondary codes."

Beezan gasped. *How can that be? I haven't been paying attention. More work to do.* "Please list them," he grumped, scowling at his s'link.

9-Dominion

Beezan sat on the deck adding another toy brick to the wall outside Jarvie's cabin. He remained a moment to contemplate it. It was over eight weeks since the jump to Redrock, eight layers of bricks. Jarvie seemed no closer to coming out with the truth than he had on jump day. Beezan envisioned the wall growing 17 layers tall. *Is this the right approach?* No doubt, Jarvie had seen the wall and decided to ignore it.

Beezan startled as Jarvie's door slid open. He almost jumped up, but controlled himself. Perhaps if Jarvie found him sitting by the wall.

But it wasn't Jarvie. It was Sarcee. She padded out and the door shut behind her.

"Bee!" she exclaimed, excitedly romping over to him, stepping in his lap and pressing her front feet on his shoulders so she could nuzzle his face.

"Ehh, Sarcee." Beezan turned his face away but hugged her for all of two seconds before she was squirming off.

Beezan caught sight of a second tag on her collar. Jarvie must have rigged it to open the doors. *At least he's doing something with his time.*

"Jarvie sleeping?" Beezan asked.

Sarcee didn't answer. She went over to the little brick wall and pushed on it with her front feet. "Bee's wall," she said. Was Beezan imagining her disapproving tone?

"Jarvie's wall," he said sternly.

"Zharvee cry," she responded.

"Why?" Beezan asked, with another pang of guilt.

"All gone," Sarcee said and wandered toward the kitchen. "Hungreee," she declared. Beezan dutifully got up to feed her.

What did she mean? Her food was all gone? Or was she talking about Jarvie? It was useless trying to get information out of a hungry pup, so once they got to the kitchen, Beezan got some little treats and supervised her eating, vacuum near at hand.

While they snacked, Beezan played news packets.

"In an effort to reconnect to Sector 4—"

Beezan tensed and sat up. Sarcee looked up at him but went on crunching.

"—the Solo Journey Project has accepted a volunteer to

attempt the three-part jump, from Windswept to Coralia, Coralia to Cove, and Cove to Tropica."

A sector map appeared on the screen.

Beezan shook his head. It was crazy, even for a long jumper. Windy to Coralia and Coralia to Cove, maybe. But Cove to Tropica? It was too far and the two stars were so different. It would be hard to find the resonant path, let alone stay in it and live through it. Then they'd have to jump back. Who would do such a thing?

"Solo Journey declines to name the volunteer, but Miranews claims it is the *Cascade*, out of—"

Beezan gasped. The *Cascade*. His former crewmates. He turned off the packet with a frown. Sarcee was looking up at him and copying his frown. "Bee sad," she stated. "Zharvee sad." She shrugged. "Sarcee sad," but she kept crunching.

Beezan patted her and vac'd her crumbs. "Back to work," he said, getting up.

Sarcee hopped down and followed, "Sarcee help."

Beezan went back to the Command Bay, passing the little brick wall. Sarcee followed him, stepping over the wall, barely clearing it with her growing stomach. *Well*, Beezan thought, *after 17 weeks, Sarcee won't be able to get over that wall.*

11-Dominion Eve

Beezan was exhausted. Exhausted, but excited. His personal packets finally caught up with him. Local news, sector news, ship news, entertainment, Solo Journey, official, and personal packets all had their own codes. The packets had been his lifeline for eight years and were still his only connection to humanity, as Jarvie was so distant. Beezan had disciplined himself to save his personal messages until bedtime. It was his special time to reconnect with friends and family.

Beezan logged off shift, went to the Prayer Room and then came to his cabin and shut the door.

Done. Done for the day. Done with the daily chores, the repairs, the re-repairs. Done with worrying and assigning and trying to figure out Jarvie. Done with checking supplies, planting and harvesting. Done with the mandatory exercise. Not that anything was really done. But it was done for the day and Beezan could set his mind to ignore it until tomorrow.

The cabins were "Technology Reduced Zones." The AI could not monitor Beezan in here unless he turned the s'link on. It was his own special spot, the center of his little universe.

He stowed his things carefully and hooked his p'link by the bunk. As he got ready he looked at all his treasures, his pictures, his souvenirs of the planets and stations he'd visited. The walls were covered with small pieces of art, especially jump art. His picture board by the bunk was filled with photos of the people in his life, along with a sector map. Old-fashioned colored location magnets marked the last known locations of each of Beezan's friends, family and former crewmates. Beezan looked over the pictures of his friends with a quiet happiness. He had not seen some for years, even decades. His own parents he had seen only twice in 30 years. Beezan was determined to overcome the distance. He loved them and love was not limited by lightyears.

Then his eyes fell on the map and on Firelight and he had a reminding stab of pain. *The Sundering.* There would be no more packets from anyone on the other side, no more photos. His decades of communication, of heartfelt words, of news and support, were cut off. He would still love them, but he would not hear, see, read or feel in touch, would not know, but only wonder of them. He hoped and prayed it would only be temporary.

He got into his bunk and sat propped against the wall, with his favorite quilt around him. The closest pictures were of his grandfather and Lemm, his podpup. Gone to the Kingdom, but not gone. *Love goes anywhere*, Beezan told himself and knew it for a truth, as all pilots did.

He'd been remembering Lemm a lot lately with Sarcee and her antics. He needed a picture of Sarcee for his board. He had not added any pictures of new people, or podpups for that matter, in eight years. He had not added Jarvie either, he thought guiltily. Was he going to erase Jarvie out of his life? They had only jumped once together and didn't have much other contact. Beezan wanted to let Jarvie into his heart, but something nagged at his trust. He had been so close to most of his other crewmates. People raised on family ships grew up with that closeness and translated it to crews in their adult life.

I'm a failure as a captain. First the disaster with his crew nine years ago, and now his struggles with Jarvie. He was sure Jarvie wasn't happy with him at all. It was so sad, Beezan thought. He could find the pathway between two stars, but he couldn't find the pathway between two hearts.

Beezan checked official messages first. Solo Journey was requesting a cargo manifest. It took him a moment to understand. In all the excitement of nearly getting killed in the Cargo Hold, he'd forgotten to check for the correction for that monster cargo. Running through all his messages now, he saw that the cargo supervisor at Hamada had never sent one. Normally, that sort of thing wouldn't be a problem, but now, here was a message asking for his manifest. *Why would I know more than they do*? He sent off the manifest that he had, as well as a polite request to Solo Journey at Hamada for the correction. It didn't make any sense. *Like they forget what they did with the Sector's biggest cargo container?*

Beezan had seven personal packets. When the senders' names flashed up, Beezan's heart leaped. Two were from his parents—before the Sundering. They would be his last messages from them. He almost couldn't bear to open them.

The first packet, a vid, from his mother, was short. She was telling Beezan that his father had received a special letter from the Earth Council itself, thanking his father and praising his sacrificial and trustworthy work. Beezan was happy. His father was appreciated. And if his father's work was not in vain, than neither was Beezan's missing them. The second packet was a long letter and Beezan skipped it to save for last.

He had a vid from his former crewmate Jain, and husband Karnda. Karnda got no more words in than when they had been aboard all those years ago. They were Beezan's first grown-up crew. The three of them had been together five years. Although Jain and Karnda were married, they had never made Beezan feel like an outsider. They had taken him in like a younger brother and mentored him into a strong and capable pilot. He missed them terribly. When their ship *Cascade* had finally been rebuilt, the parting was hard. They even asked him to come with them, but he could not sell *Drumheller*—the ship that had been in his family for so many generations. Now, the *Cascade* was off on the most dangerous mission of all, the reconnect with Sector 4. The message was crazy and funny and felt almost like having them there. It was sent before *Cascade* was picked for the reconnect mission. Beezan hoped it wouldn't be his last message from them.

Tiati, his dearest friend from pilot certification school, was Beezan's constant packet companion. His message was short.

`Bee! Hope you had a good jump. Sorry can't`

meet you dockside. *Wheel* got sent back to Hamada. Maybe I'll take a paying deal on the side. So I'll see you another day another dock.

-Tiati

P.S. Hope you're not outside the k-belt!

Oh, that Tiati. Beezan shook his head. Maybe he just wouldn't mention exactly where he was when he wrote back.

Finally, he took a few deep breaths, said a prayer, and started to read the last message from his parents.

11-Dominion

Beezan stared at his repair list. *How could it be so long?* Some items were automatically added to the list for maintenance. Beezan studied them and moved a few to the end. He had stopped adding to Jarvie's list, it was pointless. Jarvie was slowing down by the week. If something didn't improve, Jarvie would either have to stay at Redrock or become a paying passenger. *Stop it!* He reprimanded himself. *He saved my life after all.* But that Jarvie seemed like a different person than the Jarvie that now haunted the kitchen. *How can he possibly be a youth leader?* For the tenth time Beezan made a mental note to find out more about this teen training program.

So, what is the spiritual principle here? Beezan couldn't solve his problem unless the essential issue, the spiritual lesson, was determined. He had been so sure that it was honesty, but now he realized that that might be Jarvie's lesson, but it wasn't his. Jarvie's spiritual growth was Jarvie's concern. Beezan had to concentrate on his own growth.

If honesty was not his test, what was?

Patience came immediately to mind, but patience was part

of every test. What more might there be? Tolerance? Generosity? Kindness? Responsibility or detachment? Mercy or justice? Duty or compassion? *My will or God's Will?* That was part of every test too. Honesty, trustworthiness, self-discipline, those were Jarvie's tests. It was so simple to see to the core of other people's problems sometimes. Why could he not see to his own?

Maybe I should just ask Jarvie what my problem is.

Beezan was confused. He found himself wanting to go easy on Jarvie, as if he were not a responsible adult, but that wouldn't be right.

Consultation? Was that the issue? That was still centered on Jarvie's problem. "What is my problem?" Beezan asked himself aloud. He searched his heart for faults. But anger and impatience were so strong that he couldn't get past them to find more subtle motives.

He would have to calm down—*detachment!*—and then . . . Beezan's mind turned to the practical. One thing was certain; Jarvie could not continue to be unsupervised. Beezan would tell him at breakfast.

Origin Date: 11-Dominion-1082

Sender: Sector 7 Council

To: Sector 6 Council, Sector 8 Council, Solo Journey Coordinator, Hamada, Solo Journey Coordinator, Redrock, S1C Agent D.L. Oatah at Mirage

[Project Restore Cargo Container 189]

God is Most Glorious.

The Sector 7 Council authorizes Solo Journey Hamada to organize an investigation.

Find and interview the Solo Journey Guest Cargo Team. Recall them if necessary.

Track all Class 14 or larger ships out of Hamada since 5-Speech and request manifests.

Forward to this Council the exact contents of container 189.

Capture and Forward to this Council all packets to or from Project Restore Coordinator Thayne and Solo Journey Pilot Tiati.

As of 11-Dominion-1082, D.L. Oatah, Special Agent of Sector 1 Council is in command of Project Restore and Project Contact.

Our prayers for your continued health and protection. S7C

12-Dominion

Beezan got up early to check on Jarvie and found him in the kitchen. Jarvie was transfixed, watching the packets on the big screen, and was sickly pale. Beezan froze. Jarvie had that look of all those people on Hamada after the Sundering news. That shocked, that seeing but not wanting to believe, that knowing that life changed again in a heartbeat look. Did Jarvie finally realize what had happened? A long-delayed reaction?

Beezan watched the packet to see what it was about, but couldn't make sense of it. He glanced back to Jarvie, who looked up at him with tear-stained eyes and said "Harbor," in a tear-strained voice.

Harbor? What's he talking about? Harbor was in Sector 6, a mid jump from Atikameq, where the other big teen training school was. What did Harbor have to do with the a-ring failure at Firelight?

“What?” Beezan asked, thinking he misheard.

Jarvie struggled to talk. “Harbor a-rings are down, since 9 Dominion,” and he indicated the packet starting.

“No,” Beezan started to object. Jarvie had misunderstood. It was impossible that another system was lost. It was too much. But he could see for himself in the packet. Pictures of Harbor, maps, reporters, experts, frantic relatives, panic at Atikameq.

Harbor thoughts came randomly into Beezan’s mind; the OSRI hangar, the cargo they had for Harbor, the statistics, the people he knew at the station. Harbor had been Jarvie’s destination. He would never get there now. Then a scarier thought struck Beezan. If they had come in to Redrock nicely, they might have already been at Harbor. Then they would have been stuck. At Harbor. How long could they last without supplies? And now, Jarvie had nowhere to go. “Do you have family there?” Beezan asked carefully.

“No,” Jarvie shook his head, “No family.”

Beezan sat down heavily next to Jarvie and pressed his hands onto the table for some stability in his universe. He did not want to know. But he watched in spite of himself. There was no question actually. Not like when Firelight where they didn’t know what happened.

This time, at Harbor, seven ships had been bound for Atikameq. Only two had made it. Both ships, *Streamer* and *Spring Tide*, reported an explosion during the final acceleration stage. Only the two ships in front were lined up right to continue the jump.

The other five ships failed to jump, jumped the wrong way, or were, by the looks of it, destroyed. Two of the missing ships were Solo Journey ships. Beezan closed his eyes, letting a wave of sadness pass over him and saying a silent prayer. Jarvie patted his arm awkwardly. Perhaps they were alive in the Harbor system. Beezan could have that small hope.

The news was only days old. Relay jumps from Atikameq and Petrichor spread the news. All these packets had just arrived hours ago with ships incoming to Redrock from Petrichor.

Beezan noticed that Jarvie was eating—in spite of it all; he was sitting there eating. *How can he even choke it down?* Misunderstanding Beezan's look, Jarvie got up and heated a breakfast for Beezan. Then Beezan found himself eating, forcing one bite down after the other while they both sat watching.

After they saw all the same packets twice, Beezan turned it off and they sat and ate in sorrow and silence. "We must hold on," Beezan heard himself saying, uselessly. Then he remembered that he had planned to talk to Jarvie about being supervised. It was such a small issue now. Of course, they must go on shift together, if only for moral support.

"Jarvie—"

Jarvie looked wide-eyed at Beezan, as if he expected the worst.

"I just think," Beezan continued, "that you should go on shift with me. Maybe we could get more done if we work together."

Jarvie looked suddenly so relieved, almost happy, if that was possible under the circumstances. He nodded in agreement.

Work together? Was that my test all along? Beezan could hear the voice of his grandfather, "Unity means working together." It was the Captain's job to encourage unity.

. . . EXACT CONTENTS OF CONTAINER 189: UNKNOWN . . .

10 / DANGER ZONE

13-Dominion

Jarvie sat down with his food, breakfast again, since he was going on shift with Beezan. He turned on the big screen. *Thank heavens I won't be alone anymore.*

A new bunch of packets from Atikameq had come in since the night before. He quickly checked the security listing for runaways. Nothing. Yan must be hoping to stay out of trouble by not reporting him. Beezan wouldn't be alerted. A drop of his oceans of worry splashed away, and he took a relieved breath.

Atikameq Sector 6 Summary:

Official: Harbor Citizens to report location to Atikameq (11-18-1082)

Harbor registered ships to report location to Atikameq

Canyon registered ships to report location to Canyon

Petrichor registered ships to report location to Petrichor

. . .

ATIKAMEQ

OUTBOUND AUTHORITY: JUMP SCHEDULE UPDATES

NEWSFEEDS:

ATIKAMEQ: TEEN TRAINING SCHOOL UPDATES (4) (11-18-1082)

HARBOR UPDATES (47)

FIRELIGHT UPDATES (3)

CANYON: (NO NEWS SINCE 3-18-1082)

PETRICHOR: PETRICHOR PREPARING FOR MAJOR TRAFFIC (12-18-1082)

^^^^^

With Harbor out of reach now, Jarvie's whole quest to get to Lanezi was over. He'd risked everything for nothing. There was no safe haven at the end of his journey. He slumped over the table. His only hope now was to be useful to Beezan, useful enough that he'd be allowed to stay on.

Beezan came in, looked at him curled over the table and shut the screen off. "No more packets," he commanded quietly. Jarvie straightened up and started eating slowly. He watched dazedly as Beezan, who looked pained but determined, got his breakfast, checked on Sarcee—who was slurping her second bottle of green formula—and sat down next to Jarvie.

"We'll never get through Fast if we keep watching those packets," Beezan said.

"Fast?" Jarvie repeated, startled. He had forgotten entirely.

Jarvie turned to look at the big calendar. The first day of Ayyám-i-Há was only a week away. So Fast would be starting in eleven days. Beezan was right. Jarvie was in no condition.

Ayyám-i-Há used to be the happiest time of the year with

his family. Reunions and gifts, doing charity if they were in station. The current situation left no heart for celebrating anyway. Besides, he had no gift at all for Beezan. The only thing Beezan thought he wanted from Jarvie was the truth, and that wouldn't be any kind of gift.

"I'm afraid we have too much work to have a big celebration," Beezan commented. It was unheard of, not to celebrate, but Jarvie nodded, wondering if Beezan was gauging how disappointed he would be. "So we'll just have Feast as usual." Jarvie just kept nodding, not really looking at Beezan.

"When was Sarcee's last med check?" Beezan asked.

Taken by surprise at the change of subject, Jarvie looked at Sarcee to see if she was all right. She looked fine, green formula drips aside. "I, ah," Jarvie faltered, embarrassed, "I haven't taken her."

Beezan looked slightly disapproving, but went on as though not surprised. "Well, *Drumheller* reminded me it's the law she must be checked weekly."

"Weekly?" Jarvie was shocked. Probably the laws weren't nearly that strict for humans.

As if reading his mind, Beezan went on. "Of course, you only need to be checked every three months or after every jump." They both knew that hadn't happened either. So Beezan dragged them to the Med Bay.

"You've had your med training, right?" Beezan asked as they waited for all the equipment to fold out and power up.

"No," Jarvie answered before thinking.

"Oh," Beezan went on casually. "I was just reading some teen training requirements."

Oh no.

"Wasn't med training for 17-year olds?"

"Yes," Jarvie confirmed, "but I was in a special program." *True, if misleading*. Beezan was considering him so he quickly added, "But I'd like to learn."

Beezan ran him through the basics of the Med Bay, concentrating on the podpup station. Jarvie got Sarcee in the diagnostic box. Beezan was showing him what programs he was required to run, how to check for chronic shipboard problems, how to run the pregnancy program—when he suddenly stopped, staring at the screen.

Jarvie looked up, worried. He couldn't make out the image. "What?"

Beezan pointed to the screen, showing Sarcee and her big abdomen. He rotated the image slightly and pointed. "There's a pup . . . and there's another one." Beezan smiled.

"Two?" Jarvie exclaimed. "Are you sure?"

Beezan ran more tests, both he and Jarvie getting more and more excited. Twin podpups were rare and considered *lucky*.

Then Sarcee got so wiggly they couldn't see any more. "Make sure you log the exams," Beezan reminded Jarvie, "So we'll be *compliant*." Beezan said the word 'compliant' like it was a major test to his patience.

"Now, you." Beezan pointed Jarvie to one of the exam beds.

The glow of twin podpups helped Jarvie steel himself for whatever might be revealed. How good were these old machines? And how good was Beezan at medical data? Could he figure out Jarvie's real age?

Beezan watched the screen and frowned. He reran something a couple of times. Jarvie was starting to get nervous. "Sorry, Jarvie. You are too tall. Good thing you're almost done growing, but be sure to wear your g-suit." Aside from major stress, the med computer declared Jarvie fit enough for duty.

"Good thing," said Beezan, "Because you're going back to duty anyway."

14-Dominion

Jarvie discovered the hard way that Beezan was on a mission to get compliance issues off his list. The med checks were just the first items. Jarvie now spent his evenings in his cold, empty cabin catching up on teen training requirements, trying to stay a step ahead of Beezan. That was especially hard since Beezan was some kind of genius. He did several modules every night. Jarvie could hardly get through one.

Nineteen-year-old Youth Leaders were rare. Most Youth Leaders were twenty-one and a few were twenty. Jarvie wished he'd had the sense to change armbands before coming aboard the *Drumheller*. As long as he was committing a crime, he might as well have made it easier on himself.

Teen training requirements had been instituted in Sectors 6-8. Anyone in 'possession' of a youth age 13-20 was legally responsible for adhering to the training program. Before winding up at the Hamada Teen Training Center, Jarvie had been schooled onboard the *Sunburst* by his uncle and parents and never thought much of it. Any settlement, station, ship, repair tug, or asteroid outpost had to run the same teen training program, and it was complicated. Sadly, that explained why there were 200 teens now stuck at that Harbor boarding school.

So, Beezan was noncompliant. It was now in Jarvie's best interests to keep Beezan out of trouble. For a 19-year-old Youth Leader, that meant a maximum of four hours ship work to leave time for 'studies, service, mentoring, spiritual growth' and his own 'training circle.'

Thank heavens there were no other teens aboard, Jarvie

thought. That cut out mentoring and running a training circle. Nevertheless, Beezan had dutifully reduced Jarvie's work schedule, taking on even more work for himself.

18-Dominion Eve

They had only two days left before the k-belt crossing. Soon enough, the *Drumheller* would declare a danger zone and order them into suits, unless they could fix the imager mount. Beezan had already stocked and checked the safe rooms in case they had to ride out the rest of the trip in a vented ship.

"*I* could do it!" Jarvie insisted, while they sat at dinner, happy to volunteer for something important—and something he even had a chance of doing right. "The imager isn't far from the hatch. I could be tethered the whole time." Beezan was scowling. "I'm not afraid to go outside; I've been outside since I was a kid," he added.

"Normally, I'd consider it," Beezan answered. "But the fields are below standard. It would be criminal for me to send you out there."

"I volunteer."

Beezan gave him a look. "It would *still* be criminal."

"You can't go. Your ribs are still healing."

"I'll be okay for the short time it takes. I appreciate that you want to do it. I'm just going to get the tools together and then I'll go out in the morning. You can monitor me from inside."

Jarvie hung his head and nodded, fully acquiescing. It was only later that his scheme came to him.

Jarvie set his p'link to wake him in the middle of their sleep cycle. He got up and had a quick snack. He knew from their weeks on separate shifts that the doors didn't wake Beezan, but still, he left Sarcee in the cabin and went quietly hand over hand to the EVA Bay for a suit.

He ran through all his rationalizations. Beezan had not actually forbidden him to go out. He'd only said it would be criminal to send him. And he even spun down last night. *And* he'd be relieved not to do it himself. It was such an easy task, really.

Jarvie suited up, started his meds, took the toolkit and his helmet and started the long haul in nogee to Arc 7. *This will be the worst part.*

At the hatch, he had to override, but that was normal to go outside. His s'link was attached to his suit arm, so he peeled it off, put it in the slot, and pressed the override. The door opened. No problem. He realized his heart was pounding. *Guilt. No. Regular caution. Focus. Close inner door.*

In the airlock, he needed the override again to open the second door, exposing himself to space. It was full black dark, like opening a door to the void. "Lamp on." A streak of overly bright light blazed off the hull. "Reduce brightness." *Don't think about anything but the tether. Tether, not stars.* He turned his head to swing the light to the hold bar. *Tether. On. Okay.* He relaxed a little. He had no one to help him with the checklist, so he did it himself.

Jarvie carefully took two steps forward, stepping onto the ramp. The ship paint was centuries gone, but the helmet view supplied a little overlay to show where to go. Very carefully, keeping one foot down at all times, he walked along the grip-strip towards the imager. Not more than 20 meters.

But it was scary. Disorienting. He'd never been outside so far from a star. *Don't look out.* He glanced up and almost reeled. *Stop. Breathe.* He looked down again and went on. When his helmet map flashed a right arrow, he stopped and turned. He could see the imager now. He would have to leave the gripstrip.

Very carefully, his breath loud in his helmet, he bent over slightly to grab a hold bar. He couldn't reach! He was too tall to bend over in the suit. Luckily his feet didn't come off. He managed to stand up straight again and balance. *Okay, slower.* He tilted one boot forward until the grips came off, then slowly knelt down and grabbed the bar, reaching it just as his other boot peeled off. He held tight for a moment, just breathing.

Hand over hand to the imager, Jarvie took his time, breathing calmly and concentrating on each movement. He got to the imager mount and angled around to see the problem up close. Exactly as they had expected, the imager hung loose. The one bolt was missing. Jarvie hooked the work strap and carefully lifted the mount with two hands. He compared it to the proper position on his helmet diagram, but it clicked into position on its own. Nothing could be that simple. He carefully opened the bolt set and peeled off the correct size bolt, as marked on the imager base. Holding the enhanced bolt handle, he installed the bolt. Good. He secured the tools and bolts. No mishaps. He took another breath, but didn't wait around.

Jarvie worked his way backward to the gripstrip and then to the ramp, making sure he was in the lock and holding on before he reached to unhook his tether. As his headlamp swung around, a movement caught his eye, but then it was gone. *What?*

And then a score of flashes, odd reflections—*particles!* His heart nearly stopped. One tiny dust particle at speed could put a hole in his suit. Frantically, he unhooked his tether, pulled it in, and slapped the door button. A red light was flashing in the lock and on his helmet.

"Alert! Particles detected."

He started the emergency cycle. As air filled the lock and he pulled up his visor, he heard something hit the bulkhead, something very close. He slammed the visor back down. In terrible fright, he checked his suit status, okay. He watched the walls around him, looking for damage. Finally, the inner lock opened and he backed out, quickly shutting that door. The alert section of his heads-up display filled with red.

Suddenly, Beezan was there, pressing the front of his suit to turn on his muted suit link. Jarvie braced himself for an angry torrent."Keep your helmet on," Beezan said, obviously trying to keep his temper. "Where's Sarcee?"

"Cabin," Jarvie gasped.

"In the pressure box?"

"No—"

"Alert! All crew must suit immediately!"

"Go that way!" Beezan pointed toward Arc 8, meaning Jarvie would have to go through the abandoned Arc 9. He hesitated. "Go!" Beezan said and flashed him the *quickly* hand sign. "You're in your suit. Get her in the box while I suit up."

The Captain and even the *Drumheller* sounded extremely stressed. Beezan pulled down the rimway twice as fast as Jarvie could go. "Meet me in the Command Bay," was the last Jarvie heard.

"A cluster of objects escaped the pre-warning system. Particle field is now on full. Radiation field at zero. There may be more massive objects incoming. Calculating trajectories. There may be damage to the hull. Crew to remain in pressure suits."

Jarvie turned and braced himself for the pull through the dark and scary Arc 9. Only his worry for Sarcee kept him from following Beezan instead.

Back in his cabin, now shaking uncontrollably, Jarvie worried about the hits and about how angry Beezan was. He found Sarcee already in her box. *Smarter than I am.* He sealed it, started the air, and turned to face the trip to the Command Bay and Beezan.

Of course, Beezan wasn't there yet. He was still suiting up. Jarvie stowed Sarcee and strapped. He tapped a pop-up and brought up their status. Red everywhere. But no venting alarm. Then Beezan came in, holding his helmet.

Beezan was still struggling with his anger when he got to Command. At least Jarvie was strapped and waiting, without doing anything else crazy. Heart pounding in anxiety and hurry, Beezan put his helmet on, but didn't seal his visor. He squirmed into his seat and strapped. There was another small clattering on the hull and the projectile alarm went off again.

Beezan focused on the pop-up that showed the fuel reserves. It was below the red line. They had some fuel, by law reserved for deceleration in-system, but they might have to use it now. Then they would be totally out. He swallowed, anticipating the worst. If the imager was lost, they would be in these suits for days. If the hull was damaged badly, they would be in suits and safe rooms for weeks. If they used all their fuel, they would be out here even longer.

"Changing course to avoid incoming objects. Stand by."

Beezan had hesitated and now this new *Drumheller* had taken charge. They both checked their straps automatically. The ship made several small burns. Beezan could not take his eyes from the fuel pop-up. The indicator was dropping quickly and then disappeared. They were out of fuel.

"Unable to maintain projectile field. We are clear of the immediate hazard. Damage assessment underway."

They waited. **"The hull is undamaged. The imager is undamaged."** Beezan saw Jarvie press his hand to his chest with relief.

The *Drumheller* did them the *favor* of replaying the hits in slow motion. Jarvie appeared on screen. With his back to the projectiles, he had not seen or felt the one that missed him by less than a meter.

Jarvie gasped. Beezan was shaking. In his secret thoughts, he had actually considered sending Jarvie out there. Beezan stared at the screen, stunned.

If there was another hazard, they were history. They had no more fuel to move or run the field. *How could it have come to this?* Beezan tried to calm himself. The thought that he could have lost another crew . . .

"Thank you . . . Captain," came a quiet, shaken, fearful voice. "You were right not to send me." Beezan knew he should reach out, say something heartening, but his breath was coming in heaves, and his mind surged between anger and relief.

. . . RECEIVED REQUEST FROM *DRUMHELLER* FOR MANIFEST CORRECTION . . .

. . . CONFIRMED THAT DEEALAN SAGE MADORIC R.J. IS NOT ABOARD THE *DRUMHELLER* . . .

. . . *Drumheller* . . .

. . . *Drumheller* . . .

. . . *Drumheller* . . .

INTERCEPT THE *DRUMHELLER*!

11 / FAST APPROACHING

19-Dominion

The next day passed in a blur for Beezan. After spending a day and night in his suit, in the Command Bay, trying to sleep without jolting awake in panic, or being awakened by Jarvie jolting awake in panic, he was exhausted. Their near-disaster left him drained and depressed. Without fuel to maneuver or even run a minimum projectile field, *Drumheller* had insisted they remain in suits, citing every possible felony Beezan would face if he were non-compliant and lost a crew member. Beezan didn't need any warnings. He had just received a great big warning from God. The memory of the particle just missing Jarvie still made him sick.

Tomorrow, if fuel supplies were built up enough to avoid an object, they could sleep in the kitchen. It was an official safe room and also Jarvie's favorite place. They would be able to take their suits off as long as they stayed in the kitchen.

Jarvie was awake, so Beezan chanted a couple of prayers and said an extra, silently, for patience. He was used to fighting off depression, but was worried about Jarvie. Jarvie had sunk into a faraway mood. He didn't even say any prayers, at least not aloud. Beezan explained that Jarvie needed to take care of Sarcee and help clean up the Work Tower. Jarvie nodded, his helmet tipping slowly back and forth. Beezan started slowly for the kitchen, Jarvie following and tugging Sarcee's box behind.

Getting back to the Work Tower in nogee took a long time. They were in their suits, but it was still nerve-wracking to be so far from a safe room. After cleaning up and securing the Work Tower, they worked on the priority repairs. Jarvie said hardly a word the whole time.

"It's past your four hours of work, Jarvie. Go on back to the kitchen."

Jarvie looked up gratefully, but was hesitant, probably nervous about the long trip back by himself. Beezan looked again at his s'link, now constantly showing the fuel status. "*Drumheller*, can we get out of the suits in the kitchen?"

"Suit must be immediately prepped for use. Crew must stay in the safe room. Airlock doors must be closed."

The incentive to get out of the suit was strong. Jarvie steeled himself to turn and go.

"I'll be along in a couple of hours," Beezan reassured him.

It was long past a couple of hours later when Beezan hauled himself to the kitchen with a short stop at his grandfather's cabin. Now he was twice exhausted, and hungry, and very sick of the suit.

Jarvie was suit free and cleaned up, but only in mildly better spirits for it. Still, he dutifully helped Beezan out of his suit and prepped it for him while Beezan washed up. Then Jarvie brought him some dinner and came to the table with him, snagging a whirling Sarcee out of midair on his way. She complained until she saw the bottle of pink formula Jarvie pulled out of his pocket. Her eyes went wide at the special treat and she snuggled in Jarvie's arm and greedily slurped it.

It was officially evening, Redrock time. Ayyám-i-Há. Beezan sighed. Getting out of their suits would have to be celebration enough for tonight. Jarvie had taken time to make a nice dinner. It was strange how Jarvie would reach out in small services, but be so evasive in person. Beezan quietly told Jarvie what work he had done, and what the plan was for tomorrow, without asking any questions or looking directly at him. Out of the corner of his eye, Beezan watched as Jarvie finally relaxed with Sarcee, his head tipping to touch hers.

Beezan finished eating. They would have to sleep right here, so there was no reason to wake Jarvie. He got a restraining net and carefully threw it over Jarvie and Sarcee, securing them to the wall. He checked to make sure it wasn't too tight and absentmindedly reached over to smooth Jarvie's hair out of his face. Beezan froze before touching him, a surge of emotions confusing him. He felt concern and affection, but almost as if Jarvie were a child. *Am I getting that old?* Was his sadness at not having his own family surfacing? Beezan realized with a shock that he could have a 19-year-old by now. Sadly, Jarvie would probably be off at the next stop. He patted Sarcee instead and wriggled into a sleep sack near the control panel. He felt strange. Another human being was sleeping only a couple meters away and yet his loneliness was welling up. He calmed himself with more prayers, but couldn't shake the emotions of the past few days.

He called up the last message from his parents to read again. He transferred the photo to a large pop-up. They looked so much older than when he last saw them, standing on a low brick wall, a bay behind them and a shining city on the opposite shore. Open water shimmered beneath a sky so blue that it could only be Earth. Beezan stared at it. A note on the file merely said *'Akká*. Beezan treasured this special gift from them. Beezan could see their joy and love in their smiles. He read their long and loving message, stopping several times to wipe tears from his eyes. Beezan whispered *Happy Ayyám-i-Há* to them across the sectors. Then he said "Happy Ayyám-i-Há Jarvie . . . and Sarcee" as quietly as he could. They didn't even stir. He fell asleep in a daze of longing and prayers and a new determination. He could love Jarvie as a father or older brother would. Even if they were not together long, love was never wasted.

Jarvie awoke with a start when Sarcee smacked him with the empty bottle.

"Sarcee!" He had a moment of sickness until his mind and body remembered they were in nogee, why they were in nogee and why they were in the kitchen. Then he felt even sicker.

"Hungree!"

"Shhhh. Captain sleeping." Sarcee looked over. Beezan hung in his hammock, p'link still loosely in his hand. After Jarvie got himself and Sarcee untangled from the net, he noticed a photo on the pop-up by Beezan. He couldn't help looking. Obviously, they were Beezan's parents. *On Earth*. Jarvie stared. He had been afraid to ask about Beezan's family for fear that Beezan might ask him back.

Jarvie's sneaking into the pilot files had only given him official information about Beezan. There hadn't been anything about his personal life, except that he had been alone for eight years. *The Sundering has separated Beezan from his parents,* Jarvie realized with a pang of understanding sympathy. *Maybe he doesn't have anyone else either.* Beezan was stirring. Jarvie floated to the other side of the kitchen to make breakfast.

The first full day of Ayyám-i-Há was celebrated by doing more repairs. The garden was a mess. Beezan wasn't sure it was worth continuing the open garden. Some of the clear restraining plates from the open garden had come loose and dirt had started floating around. The filters were working overtime and the little garden robot was fussing around diligently. Beezan sent Jarvie to work on the incubators, where most of the food was actually grown. Sarcee whined in her box. The robot went by her once to give her a little beep now that she was locked up. Sarcee turned her back on all of them. Beezan shook his head. "Podpups are like kids. Robots are like kids." He stopped before he said teenagers were like kids.

They had not listened to packets for days, but they couldn't avoid it forever. That night, Beezan reviewed the packets that *Drumheller* had captured. There were several personal ones for him, Ayyám-i-Há greetings no doubt. As usual, there were none for Jarvie. He considered asking if anyone knew where he was, but he had promised himself when he started the brick wall he would not ask again.

Starting with official news, they learned that jump schedules were changed and there would be an extra jump out of Redrock the next day. Sector hubs were ordered to send their New Year census information to Sandune instead of Earth. Thirty-two ships were unaccounted for and assumed lost or stranded at Harbor. 2,729 people were assumed stranded on

Harbor Station or in ships at Harbor. Of those, nearly 200 were teens at the Teen Training Center who had not gone on holiday.

Atikameq would allow only one ship to jump into Harbor, taking supplies and a few volunteers who were experts in station survival. Atikameq Council had ruled that those few teens separated from their families could not return on the one-way ship.

It had only been eleven days since Harbor went down and Canyon was still unstable. The people were terrified that whatever was happening to destroy the a-rings would happen to them next.

The next day, their routine was changed to join in prayers for the jump group. Jarvie waited quietly at the kitchen table after he cleaned up breakfast. They said their prayers at the actual jump time. Hours later, while they were plodding through their never-ending maintenance, Beezan captured the time-lagged packet. They listened as they worked, but as the ships approached the actual jump, it became very hard to concentrate.

They sat, transfixed, until they heard the jump monitor release the ships. Beezan shook himself and seemed self-conscious, so Jarvie quickly went back to work. Before dismissing Jarvie, Beezan declared that they would celebrate that night, in spite of everything.

Jarvie started the long haul back to the kitchen, tugging Sarcee's box behind. He really missed skating. It took so much longer this way and nogee wasn't any fun in a suit. Nothing was any fun anymore. Just when things started to get better with Beezan, something had to happen. Jarvie knew he should be grateful to be alive, to have Beezan's concern, to have so much opportunity to be of service, but sometimes he just wanted his family back. He wanted to laugh and be happy again. He wanted to have a real Ayyám-i-Há celebration with his family. And if he couldn't have his family, at least Lanezi. But now that wasn't going to happen either. *I'll never have a family again, so just stop thinking about it,* he scolded himself.

He didn't even have a proper present to give Beezan. Who knew they would have a 17-week run in? Jarvie had taken a little clasp for a wrist strap from a parts box in the Work Tower. He knew Beezan wouldn't mind that. He thought he could make a new strap for Beezan. It was a small present, but what else could he do? He didn't want to be overly material, but he always liked giving presents . . . and getting them.

Jarvie finally pulled up to his cabin, but there was nothing in there to stop for. He was coming to the little brick wall. It was up-to-date, of course. *When did Beezan have time to stick another brick on it?* Jarvie fumed. *He is so obsessive! I get the message already! It isn't fair. Why can't he just forget it? He acts like he cares, but if he really cared, he'd leave me alone!*

All the confused and angry and guilty thoughts Jarvie had jumbled up in his mind suddenly overwhelmed him. He didn't want to be a whiner or a complainer. What he really wanted to do was yell and kick something! And then, without even planning to, he did. He heard his own voice scream some angry sound as he grabbed the hold bar and kicked the little brick wall as hard as he could. His fantasy of the bricks breaking apart and careening down the rimway was lost in a sickening lurch of momentum. The bricks didn't budge. Jarvie lost his grip on the bar from swinging his foot so hard, then got twisted up from his foot hitting the bricks and getting stopped. He went into a spasm of rotations and flailing limbs, losing touch with the walls and deck and then getting hit by Sarcee's box.

He could not stabilize himself. He hit the deck and bounced around until he came close enough to a bar to grab on. He wanted to scream and kick the wall again, but he thought he might be sick. His stomach was whirling. His med patch was empty, so no help there. He didn't want to have to clean up a mess in his suit, so he clung to the wall and willed his stomach to stop spinning. Then Sarcee's box hit the wall and she yelped. It was like a splash of cold water.

Jarvie pulled her line in gently and tied on. He couldn't talk to her. He just hung there, crying now, frustrated and scared of his own emotions. *I need help*. How many times had the Hamada counselor told him that? *Well, too late now. I made myself a criminal to get to Harbor and now it's not going to happen. All of this is for nothing.*

Jarvie looked at the little brick wall. *Maybe I should tell Beezan the whole truth. He's the only one left who could help.* Jarvie hung there shaking, his heart pounding. *No, I can't tell Beezan. It wouldn't be any kind of present.*

He hung there a long time and then suddenly was worried that Beezan would come and find him. He hurried to the kitchen and got out of the suit. He headed to the facilities when the *Drumheller* scared him.

"Suit must be prepped immediately!"

"I have to go!" he retorted, and then took extra long washing up. Had the AI been watching him in the rimway? Would it tell Beezan? He felt stupid and ashamed. He had to pull himself together. He huddled in a corner and said a few prayers. It wasn't exactly a respectful place, but it was away from the *Drumheller* cameras. Then he thought of his parents—and Canim—seeing him like this and was even more ashamed. *I have to do better for them.*

He dried his face and went back out to take care of the suit.

Then he fed Sarcee and got himself a snack to calm his shaking nerves. *It's just the k-belt. And Harbor. And the nogee. And the suits. And the loneliness. And my stomach. And the cold. And EVERYTHING. Patience. It will get better in a few days.* Jarvie glanced at the calendar. Fast would start in a few days. Another wave of misery passed over him. It wasn't going to get better.

When he stopped shaking, he put together his gift for Beezan. He cleaned up the little clasp and cut a length from Sarcee's long box strap. It wasn't a used part so it was like new. It was blue with yellow stars. Yellow *Suns*, Jarvie thought. It was supposed to be the Earth Sun when it was in the blue background. It made a much nicer wrist strap than the old worn out ones Beezan had. Beezan didn't have anything nice. He really sacrificed everything. Jarvie felt ashamed again and guilty for ever being angry with Beezan. He tried to make up for it by fixing a special dinner, or as special as a person could make in nogee.

Beezan clamored through the kitchen lock, exhausted as usual. Jarvie was especially eager to help, but he had obviously been crying again.

"Dinner smells good," Beezan said encouragingly and Jarvie smiled.

It was good. "Jarvie, you're such a good cook, you're lucky we don't have a crew. I'd have to appoint you as cook."

"I'd like that." Jarvie said quietly.

Beezan looked up in surprise. A youth leader, trained in a special monitor program, would rather cook? It was a respected position, but usually only crews of 20 or more had one.

After they cleaned up and said the Ayyám-i-Há prayer, Beezan took a box out of a cabinet and gave it to Jarvie. "I'd like you to have this." Jarvie was shy again, but at the sight of something in a colored packing box, Sarcee got very excited. "Oh, here's a treat for you," Beezan said, getting out her favorite crunchy things.

"Thank you," Jarvie said quietly and held it like a treasure. Then Jarvie reached into his pocket and hesitantly held out his hand to Beezan."It's not much . . ."

Beezan put his hand out to take it. It was a wrist strap. "You made it?" Beezan asked. Jarvie nodded. "It's beautiful, thank you." Beezan smiled and restrained himself from giving Jarvie a hug.

Jarvie looked at his gift. "Open!" demanded Sarcee and they both laughed. So Jarvie undid the latches and opened the lid.

"It was one of my grandfather's," Beezan explained.

"A book," Jarvie said with awe, "A real book." A big book. It was printed on paper, with hundreds of pictures. "*From Earth to Radium Junction, an Illustrated History of Sector Expansion*." Jarvie read, carefully turning the pages.

"I hope it's not too heavy." Beezan joked, "You'll have to read it before we go back to spin."

But Jarvie wasn't laughing. He was saying, "It's beautiful. So many pictures. I love books." He closed it and held it to his chest. "Thank you, Captain. Thank you so much." Beezan was pleased and did squeeze Jarvie's shoulder gently, which just made him shy again.

5-Loftiness

Jarvie stared at the big calendar in the kitchen. Loftiness: the month of Fasting. Five days down, fourteen days to go. That is, if he survived the next two hours of today. The *Drumheller* had declared they would be out of the k-belt danger zone, and have enough fuel to spin up, on the last day of Fast. It would be a very happy New Year. At the moment, fourteen days was like an eternity. Jarvie felt faint and shaky. He had already started the habit of taking small naps in the kitchen, putting his studies on pop-ups in case Beezan came in. That was one nice thing about nogee; you could sleep anywhere. Luckily, Beezan was way too busy and distracted to check on his progress.

Jarvie got dinner ready on time, made extra and forced himself to eat it. It was hard to eat much in nogee though. He went to sleep early and woke up in dread of another long hard day. At least all his other troubles faded in the face of getting through the Fast. He knew it wasn't supposed to be like this. He knew it was a lesson in fixing his whole life.

10-Loftiness

By the tenth day of Fast, Beezan suggested that perhaps Jarvie wasn't well and shouldn't be fasting. He should have jumped on it and taken the easy way out. Somehow, that would be admitting part of his lie. He could make it. Then Fast would be over and they would be out of the k-belt and they would have gravity back.

12-Loftiness

On the twelfth day, Beezan ordered Jarvie to the Med Bay but didn't come with him. Jarvie went early in the morning when he was still feeling rational. He managed to be fit for duty. Fit for fasting was not a subject the computer would get into. He checked Sarcee while he was there. "Only six or seven weeks to go, Sarcee." She just looked at him. She didn't seem to be feeling so good either. "Pups! Sarcee's going to have pups." Jarvie pointed to the screen. It now clearly showed two little pups curled up together like a yin-yang symbol. Jarvie patted her big abdomen. She squinted at him suspiciously. What would happen if Sarcee wasn't a good mother?

15-Loftiness

By the fifteenth day, Jarvie wondered why they lived in the kitchen during Fast. Daily life was confusing. He could hardly eat in the morning or at night. Beezan kept asking him questions, like was Fast always this hard for him? He'd made up more lies than he could keep track of. The med patch had sent a depression alert to the *Drumheller*, but Jarvie rigged the computer not to report to Beezan. He wondered if the AI was catching on, but it became a sort of game. He would see how much he could get away with before the computer would stop him. The *Drumheller* might be of superior intelligence, but it wasn't sneaky. Jarvie scolded himself for even thinking that sneakiness was a good human quality, but it kept him ahead of the AI.

18-Loftiness

Two more days. Smells were starting to make him sick: food, the suit, Sarcee's formula. He could smell things he never knew had a smell. Beezan had tried to convince him to stop fasting. He was concerned. *Why am I being so stubborn?* Beezan wouldn't order him to stop fasting unless the ship was in danger, so Jarvie struggled on.

19-Loftiness

Last day. Beezan ordered him to stay in the kitchen. Some reason Jarvie couldn't remember. Actually, Beezan may have even ordered him to eat. He couldn't remember. At noon, Beezan came back to the kitchen in an angry mood and hovered over Jarvie with a container of rehydration water. Beezan said "Captain's orders" and Jarvie was drinking it. Hours before the end, he was failing. But Jarvie knew in his heart it was no acceptable Fast and he had failed before he even started. Beezan watched him until he finished drinking it, a dark look in his eyes. Jarvie struggled not to cry, but couldn't keep his eyes from tearing up. He tried to turn away from Beezan, but Beezan braced himself against the table, leaned over and grabbed him by the shoulder and chin, forcing Jarvie to look up at him. Sarcee watched with big eyes.

"You listen to me," Beezan said in a dangerous voice. "DO NOT EVER trick the *Drumheller* into keeping things from me again. You are done with Fast, you are done with the computer, and unless you shape up, you are done with being my crew."

Jarvie gasped. Beezan let him go but pulled off his p'link and snatched the s'link right out of his pocket. "No," Jarvie reached for the p'link. An even darker look crossed Beezan's face. "We have a long way to go. I don't want to lock you in your cabin."

Jarvie could only shake his head no, on the verge of hysterics. *He wouldn't really do that, would he?*

"*Drumheller*, watch him. Security level 2 order."

Jarvie covered his face with his hands and turned away from Beezan. It was not going to be a happy New Year after all.

12 / BREAKDOWN

Beezan sent the fuel status graphic to the big screen. He watched it carefully while he made dinner, partly to distract himself from thinking about Jarvie. Jarvie was curled up with Sarcee at the table. He had his back to Beezan and hadn't said a word. Beezan was so angry and disappointed he had to stop and take deep breaths, say silent prayers and distract himself with the fuel level. His discovery that Jarvie had tampered so severely with the computer was devastating. All his patience and trying to trust was for nothing.

Beezan had extended the calendar—again. He had to add another eleven days for fuel that went to the fields rather than scheduled burns. This time he labeled them k-belt days. Now they were five weeks, four days out. *Still a long time left of the long run in.* It would be an eternity if he had to arrest Jarvie. He put a dinner in front of Jarvie and ate his own. Then he secured the kitchen for reorientation. That included putting away the suits, a job he had looked forward to for a long time.

"*Drumheller*, are we clear of the k-belt?"

"K-belt danger zone inner perimeter was crossed 32 minutes ago."

"Do we have required in-system fuel reserves built up?"

"Yes."

"Do we have sufficient additional fuel to spin up?"

"Yes."

"Run regular spin-up program now."

"Initiating reorientation systems check, stand by."

Beezan glanced over at Jarvie, who was stirring and unhooking from the wall.

"Come." Beezan said to him. Jarvie put Sarcee in her box and followed Beezan. Beezan floated ahead of Jarvie to Jarvie's cabin and opened the door. Jarvie hesitated, looking terrified.

Beezan gave Jarvie's p'link back to him. "I will escort you to your cabin at night. I will pick you up in the morning. You will stay with me all day. If you leave your cabin at night, I'll lock you in. Understand?"

Jarvie nodded and dove into his cabin. The door shut and Beezan braced against the wall, holding the bar. *What a way to start the New Year.*

Jarvie landed on the third step from the bottom and bounced around a bit until, grabbing a hold bar, he was able to catch Sarcee's box to let her out. "Bee mad!" she said. *No kidding.* Jarvie just hung there. He was relieved to be out of Beezan's sight. He had been crazy to mess with the *Drumheller* or Beezan. He knew Beezan would never hurt him, but he was the Captain; Jarvie depended on him for everything, for his very freedom. Beezan had indicated he might let Jarvie go at Redrock, but even worse would be if he turned him in. For the first time Jarvie really considered that he might end up in custody. *Then what?*

"Crew will prepare for reorientation. Report when ready."

The announcement gave Jarvie the will to move, stowing Sarcee's box, snagging her and putting her in her regular bed. They had to orient to the "deck" so they wouldn't fall on their heads. Jarvie got in his chair and strapped in.

He tapped his p'link and said, "Ready," but it came out as a whisper.

"Code Blue. All crew to blue safety zones."

"Jarvie, are you ready?" Came Beezan's voice, sounding perfectly normal, even concerned.

"Yes honor, I'm ready, and Sarcee, honor."

"Good."

In a few short minutes, their misery of the past weeks of nogee was gone. When the all clear sounded, Jarvie shakily stood up. Then he promptly staggered to the bunk and collapsed on it.

5-Splendor

Beezan closed his eyes and rested his head against the back of his chair in the Command Bay. Just a few minutes of peace were all he needed. He was so tired of even being in the same room as Jarvie that he finally sent him to the kitchen. *Drumheller* could supervise him for a while. The long-awaited pleasure of gravity was dampened by the situation with Jarvie.

Beezan decided to put an end to blind trust and sent a request for all records relating to Jarvie. The time lag was under five hours now so he could start doing some business. They were still a long way out, but he was assigned a monitor. She was a nice person named Coral, but she asked a few too many questions. Something was going on. They were waiting for him. For that big cargo, Beezan figured. He had a gnawing worry it might be for something else, like Jarvie, or the *Drumheller* itself, or even him.

"Captain?"

Beezan jolted upright in surprise when he heard the *Drumheller's* voice. "Yes?"

"Human intervention is needed in the kitchen."

Jarvie had left the kitchen lock open, so as soon as Beezan started up the stairs, he could hear Jarvie yelling at Sarcee. Shocked at such behavior, he tried to make out the words.

"Stop it! I don't want to hear any more!" Jarvie's voice was so agitated. He sounded almost irrational.

"Zharvee . . ." she cried beseechingly, her despair breaking Beezan's heart.

"Quiet! Just be quiet!"

"No Zharvee. No, Mom. Pleezzz Mom. Mommm." She called.

"Shut up!" He yelled and there was a crash of something hitting the deck. Beezan ran up the last steps and burst onto the scene of what sounded like two humans arguing. It was dismal. Food and utensils were on the deck. Sarcee was also on the deck, cowering under the table. Jarvie was standing with his hands over his ears yelling at her. When Jarvie saw Beezan he redirected his yelling, "She's driving me crazy! I don't know what to do!"

"Bee, help," Sarcee called softly.

"Sarcee!" Jarvie turned on her again.

God help me, thought Beezan. *She sounds more rational than he does.*

"Jarvie, calm down, you can't yell at a podpup. She'll go into shock."

Jarvie, looking even more stricken, turned away from Beezan and leaned down as if to scoop Sarcee out from under the table, but she whined and scooted away, causing Jarvie to smack his head soundly on the table. Leaning against the table, Jarvie pounded on it with his fist as he yelled at Beezan "Please do something about her, she's . . . I can't . . ."

Between the crying and pounding fist, Beezan couldn't understand what Jarvie was saying. But if Jarvie kept this up, Sarcee might collapse. Podpups could not handle conflict. Beezan saw no choice but to physically intervene. He needed to separate them. He grabbed Jarvie from behind with one arm around his chest and one hand pulling on his arm, hopefully gently enough so Jarvie wouldn't perceive it as an attack and struggle. It was a needless concern as Jarvie immediately collapsed against Beezan in tears, not the usual soft weeping, but uncontrolled sobs. Jarvie's thin arms clutched Beezan like a child's.

Beezan gasped with realization. "You're not 19!"

Jarvie shook his head no, rubbing tears against Beezan's hair.

Beezan was stunned. This was not the truth he had wanted to find out. Could he be 17? Less? Beezan suddenly didn't want to know. *Where did Sarcee go?* Beezan turned them both to look around the kitchen.

"Oh no!" Beezan gasped, releasing Jarvie, who sunk to his knees in a heap and then crawled to where Beezan had moved, over the unconscious form of Sarcee.

Beezan felt the neck—yes, "A pulse, thank God," he reported. "But she's not breathing."

"Oh, God, oh no, please forgive me, please don't take her, please," Jarvie sobbed, taking her limp form from Beezan.

"Give her mouth to mouth!" Beezan ordered as he jumped for the first aid cabinet. Muttering silently to himself as supplies were rearranged again, he heard Jarvie trying to calm his own breathing and resuscitate Sarcee at the same time.

“Where’s the—never mind,” said Beezan as he found Sarcee’s pressure box. He removed the med kit and pulled out the podpup resus pack.

“She’s still not breathing!” Jarvie cried.

“Keep going!” Beezan ordered, concerned, not just for Sarcee, but also for the pups who needed their oxygen. Unfolding the resus pack, he slid on his knees back to Jarvie’s side and slipped it on her, struggling to line it up right over her big belly. “No response?” he half asked.

Jarvie shook his head no, tears streaming and nose running. The light on the resus pack started blinking yellow and then went to blinking red.

“Put her down,” Beezan ordered, pressing the revive button as soon as Jarvie let go. A starburst graphic bloomed on the status panel, indicated an attempted resuscitation. Heartbreakingly, the light continued to blink red.

“Oh no,” Jarvie sobbed, scooping her up to continue the mouth to mouth.

“We’ve got to get her to the Med Bay!” Beezan stood up and took Jarvie’s arm to haul him up when there was a small suck of air and a gurgle.

“Yes!” Beezan dropped down again. “Thank heavens, she’s breathing.”

Jarvie rolled her to her side. She was coughing and gasping. She faded into unconsciousness then, but she was breathing on her own and her pulse was stronger. The resus pack status light flashed yellow and then finally went green. “Thank you, thank you,” Beezan whispered.

Jarvie was sobbing again and trying to locate a handkerchief. “Sarcee, I’m sorry. I’m so sorry. God forgive me.”

Beezan put a hand on Jarvie’s shoulder as he hung his head and cried into his hands. “What set this off?” Beezan asked.

"She just keeps asking for Mom. I can't take it."

"You have to expect some separation anxiety; you did take her away from her mate and family . . ." Beezan trailed off as Jarvie shook his head more and more angrily. *What is going on here?*

"I," Jarvie pointed to himself with a wet finger, "didn't take them away!"

"What do you mean?"

"They're dead!" Jarvie burst out. "All dead! Her mate, my Mom, my Dad, my brother, My uncle Bennezi, my friends, the crew!"

Is he having some kind of jump hallucination? "Jarvie, does this have something to do with the jump?"

"Yes!" He sounded exasperated with Beezan.

"Jarvie, sometimes people get premonitions during jump or the feeling that others have died. It just an effect, they're not really—"

"Yes! No! *Yes!* They're dead! They were dead before the jump. They were all killed at Luminesse!"

Beezan rolled back on his heels and sat down, stunned. So that was Jarvie's real secret. The one ship that had come out of Luminesse on a gravity-assist. Over 30 people had died.

"Your entire family was killed only two years ago and you didn't tell me?" Their more recent jump could have killed Jarvie too. Beezan was both sympathetic and furious. Visions of his lost crew cascaded through Beezan's mind and burst out in unexpected anger. Suddenly he was yelling. "How could you do such an irresponsible thing?"

"I needed to go to Harbor."

"I could have put you under! If you had died, it would have been my responsibility!"

Jarvie's response, if there was one, was preempted by Sarcee's return to consciousness.

"Mom?" She asked.

"Oh no," Jarvie moaned. "Sarcee," Jarvie whispered to her. On hearing his voice, she started to struggle away from him.

"Easy Sarcee, it's okay. It's okay." Beezan helped her crawl over to his right, opposite Jarvie, where she curled up shaking.

"No wonder jump was so hard and you've been acting so strange." Beezan was just starting to realize all the consequences of Jarvie's secret.

Jarvie found a napkin and was blowing his nose and drying his eyes, hands shaking. He was totally dejected, hopeless and forlorn.

I must take care of my crew, take charge, solve problems, Beezan told himself.

"Bad Zharvee." Sarcee muttered, turning so she didn't see him.

Beezan winced and slid his left arm around Jarvie, who sank down on the deck beside him.

"Fourteen," Jarvie said between sniffles.

"Fourteen what?"

"I'm fourteen. . .years old." Jarvie managed.

"Fourteen!" Beezan sat back so hard he smacked his head on the cabinet. *Fourteen! How could that be? He's so tall.* Yet Beezan knew it was true. He could see now all the things he had been blind to. And subtract a couple years maturity for the trauma of losing his family.

Beezan reached down to Jarvie's leader armband and tugged it off. His last trace of anger dissolved into sadness when he read the name on the inside of the armband, *Canim E-G Atikameq*, Jarvie's late brother no doubt. Beezan folded the armband and put it in Jarvie's hand. Clutching it, Jarvie curled up into a ball, shaking his head as if to make it all go away. Beezan had to choke down a sob himself. *I must stay calm.* He tried to say a prayer, but couldn't find his voice. *Be a leader; be of comfort,* he told himself. But he was sitting on the deck of the messed-up kitchen, Sarcee sleeping on his right, Jarvie weeping on his left and a hurricane of confused thoughts swirling through his mind.

13 / PICKING UP THE PIECES

6-Splendor Eve

It was late by the time Beezan checked Jarvie and Sarcee in the Med Bay and then brought them back to his own cabin. He put Jarvie in the bunk and piled the blankets on him. The medical computer reported mild shock and dehydration, along with a whole list of chemical, mental, and emotional imbalances. *Unfit for duty* had flashed on the screen. For now, Beezan would have to watch him. He was so relieved that Sarcee's pups checked out fine.

Beezan left Jarvie just long enough to secure the Command Bay, clean up the kitchen, and stop at Jarvie's cabin for another blanket. He opened Jarvie's door and was hit by a blast of cold air. *It's freezing in here.* He went down the steps and was confused. This cabin was empty. How could he have come to the wrong cabin?

There was something on the bunk. It was a packing sheet. Under that was a layer of clothes attached together as a makeshift blanket. Under that was one thin blanket. This really *was* Jarvie's cabin. Empty and cold. *He was too scared to ask for another blanket.* Beezan looked around in sadness and guilt. He had not done a good job of taking care of Jarvie. He should have remembered that Jarvie hardly brought anything aboard.

He meant to bring Jarvie something from his cabin to comfort him, but there was nothing to bring. Not a picture, not even a prayer book in the holder by the bed. *He's only fourteen.* Beezan was hit by another wave of misery. He had been too hard on Jarvie in his ignorance.

He left and went to his grandfather's cabin. All these years he had stayed out of it and now he kept finding himself returning. He wanted to leave this cabin as it was, but maybe it was time to move on in life. He pulled down the bunk to get the quilt. It had designs inspired by *"81 Petals,"* the original poem. It was beautiful, made by his grandmother, a quilt master, just like one of the characters in that famous story. Beezan lovingly unhooked it, pulled it off the bunk, and folded it carefully.

Something fluttered out and Beezan leaned over to catch it. A photo. He sighed. It was his family, his grandfather, parents and himself. It was taken right before his parents left for Earth. He had the same photo on his p'link, but it was somehow more touching in print. He was 12 years old then. Not much younger than Jarvie. *But I was a lot shorter than Jarvie.* He remembered what it was like to be just starting to grow up, to be smart and capable, but still a kid. He had wanted to prove himself, but also wanted acceptance and approval from his parents. He remembered how devastated he was at 15 to lose his grandfather, how even now he was still lonely. Sometimes he just wanted to have someone to love him and care about him.

On that day when Jarvie came aboard he'd thought it was God's Will that Beezan should take him. ***"It behooveth thee to be content with the Will of God . . ."***[1] He had been thinking of himself then, of finding a good crew, but maybe he was meant to help Jarvie instead. They had a bad start, but it wasn't too late. He tried to fix in his mind what it was like to be a scared young person all alone.

He went back to his cabin and bent down over Jarvie, feeling his forehead. Still a bit clammy. Jarvie's breathing was shallow and fast. He tossed around restlessly. Beezan sat down on the bunk next to him. It was a lot easier to see Jarvie as a kid when he wasn't standing up. Beezan quietly chanted the Long Healing Prayer, not even sure if Jarvie was awake or asleep. Jarvie slowly settled down. He was breathing more deeply and his cheeks felt warm.

Beezan tried to take Sarcee over to Jarvie, but she was adamant. "No Zharvee!" she hissed sleepily, so Beezan settled into the reclining chair with her, snuggly wrapped in his grandparents' quilt.

Jarvie tried to stay awake, tried to hold off sleep, hold off the nightmares that he knew would come, but there was no stopping them . . .

Jarvie struggled and fought against the jump drug. It was no use. He lost all awareness of his body and then his mind—and then they were jumping again. But this wasn't the usual kind of jump. It wasn't a little skim across the edge of the next world, but a plunge straight to the light. The *Sunburst* must have been destroyed. They were making the final crossing, going to heaven.

Jarvie saw Canim go in a flash, then his mother with the merest glance back. His father fought it. So did his uncle and the crew, as they were supposed to. Passengers and podpups were streaming to the openness of it. The sentries could not stop them. It was a place so full of love, so brilliant and beautiful, Jarvie easily and joyously followed.

And then, SLAM. It was dark and loud and painful. Alarms, panicked voices—*the passengers!*—calling for help. Jarvie opened his eyes but saw nothing but blackness. *What happened?* He had died. He had crossed to the Kingdom, they all had. *No!* came the crushing realization. The ship had survived and he had been resuscitated. His hands automatically searched for the releases. His fingers were shaking and clumsy as he undid the arm brackets. The panicked voices were scaring him. *Where is the rest of the crew?* Jarvie got the helmet off finally. It slipped out of his hands and flew away from him, crashing against the forward screen. They were decelerating hard. The alarm was so loud. The non-flight crew and passengers were all still in their chairs. *Am I the first one up?* He looked over at his mother. Her resus pack was blinking red. *How could that be?* He rubbed his blurry eyes.

"Mom?" he called, but she was still. Dead. She was *dead. No!* "Dad?"—and then he remembered Canim out of his seat. *No! Just a dream,* he told himself. But Canim's chair was empty. *No! Aliens, gravity-assists. No!*

Jarvie looked out over the passengers. Blinking red lights were everywhere. Those few with green lights were trapped in the chairs. Jarvie ignored their calls and crawled out of his cocoon, holding on to the chair. He wrenched off his leg brackets, ignoring the pain. As he let the brackets go, they skittered away. The ship was not turned the right way. "Down" was across the cabin. How was he supposed to get to the Command Bay? He was too panicked to think and plan. He just jumped out of his seat and landed on the screen. From there, he staggered to Command.

Crumpled at the door in a heap was his brother. *No!* Jarvie felt screams rising up in him, but knew they would have to wait. Horribly, he had to push Canim aside to open the door to the Command Bay.

He could barely see for the stream of tears in his eyes. He jumped down between the pilot chairs, trying not to step on the control panels. From there, he could stand up to get his father out of the chair. But his father was dead. So was his Uncle Bennezi. *Too many blinking red lights.* He looked over at Lanezi and unbelievably saw a green light. Jarvie scrambled over and unsealed Lanezi's cocoon, reaching inside to grab Lanezi's arm. It was warm. He was really alive! *Oh thank you, thank you,* Jarvie praised, grateful for one living loved-one. He stood next to Lanezi gripping his arm and studying the readouts. But Lanezi did not regain consciousness.

Slowly, the deafening alarm brought back Jarvie's sense of urgency. He was the only crew awake. He had to take charge. The ship might be in danger. It was so hot. Jarvie wiped his eyes on his sleeve and looked at the screens. Canyon. They were at Canyon. It was so confusing. Only two days out. Jarvie knelt down on the panel and pressed the SOS. The mind-numbing alarm went off and a series of automatic programs started, each one showing on a new pop-up. Thank heavens, the inbound program was already running.

Without the alarm, he could hear the passengers over the s'link. Now he had no way to get back up to them. He finally found the pop-up with the deceleration program. There were three minutes left. He would just have to wait. He turned back to his uncle, gazed across at his father. *Gone.* His family had gone to the Kingdom without him.

There was a reorient alarm and 10 beeps. At the tenth beep, the deceleration stopped and his stomach lurched. Jarvie could get back to the passengers now in nogee. He worked his way up, trying to remember if one of the passengers was the doctor, but he couldn't think straight. *No! No! No!* kept screaming through his head.

In a daze, he released the passengers, going through the adults first. They were groggy and scared, and some were angry, but a couple of them were old enough and calm enough to help. They took charge; they checked the dead; they talked to Canyon Incoming Authority. He was brought to the Command Bay to speak to a monitor, a concerned young woman. They said he had to turn over the ship to someone. He didn't know what they were talking about. He didn't care.

Lanezi and some unconscious passengers were taken to Med Bay. The bodies were moved. Jarvie wanted to go with his family. They wouldn't let him. Then those screams started to come out. Someone pressed a med patch to Jarvie's neck and he felt some kind of drug in his system. "No! Let me go with them. No!" he screamed over and over, but he couldn't stop them.

"Jarvie?" He woke up still screaming. His heart was pounding. "You're dreaming," said a kind voice. *No. How I wish it was only a dream.*

6-Splendor

Beezan couldn't sleep. He'd been awakened several times by Jarvie's nightmares and Sarcee going to the facilities. Besides, there was something he had to take care of out in the rimway.

He dismantled the little brick wall and washed the glue off in the kitchen. He let the bricks dry while he fed Sarcee and ate. Then he took her to the Command Bay. Sarcee sat quietly in the co-pilot chair while Beezan checked his packets.

The information he had requested on Jarvie had come in. It included 32 news packets regarding the *Sunburst* story at Luminesse. Of course, he remembered some of it. He had been in station at Petrichor at the time.

He remembered a ship coming into Canyon with all but two of the crew dead and many of the passengers. He remembered a teen had saved some passengers by replacing their resus packs. But that couldn't have been Jarvie, because that teen had died. The news had been full of the story of his sacrifice.

There may have been 32 news articles, but they all said the same thing. Ten ships were jumping out of Luminesse. In some unexplained accident, the gravity ball was destroyed and outbound service was lost. All this was somehow determined quickly enough for one ship, the *Sunburst*, to make a planetary gravity-assist jump to Canyon, a never-before-attempted jump.

The original a-ring acceleration had been mysteriously hard, requiring most of the passengers and some crew to be resuscitated before jump speed was reached. There were long explanations of why the resus packs only work once. According to the reports, Canim, Jarvie's older brother, was Passenger Monitor and had been conscious in the Passenger Lounge. Canim's mother and younger brother, Jarvie, were "under" for the jump.

Canim got up and changed 26 resus packs. The gravity-assist was a desperation jump and many passengers needed resuscitation again. Even then, many could not be saved. Canim's sacrificial action, however, ultimately saved 17 passengers. There were side articles and commentaries about the teen training program and the fact that Canim was one of the youngest ever youth leaders.

There had not been enough extra resus packs ready. Canim had not changed his own mother's pack. Canim had sacrificed her for a passenger. Beezan wondered how Jarvie felt about that. Brother dies a hero, but doesn't leave anyone to care for him.

Sunburst came in so close to Canyon station that it was a near disaster. Twelve-year-old Jarvie was credited with starting the SOS sequence and freeing the passengers. Lanezi, the only other surviving member of the crew, was unconscious and no one knew what had happened. Jarvie reportedly became hysterical and passengers took command. The report from the pilot's archive noted that technically the passengers had put undue pressure on the crew to surrender command and were close to mutiny, but they were officially "forgiven" due to the circumstances. Beezan wondered how Jarvie felt about that.

There were listings of the dead, the survivors, the funerals and the memorial resting place. A "Where are They Now?" section listed Jarvie as a student on Hamada. It didn't have a listing for Lanezi. *I wonder what happened to him? Maybe he's still with the Sunburst.* After checking through the ship registry, Beezan discovered that the *Sunburst* had been sold immediately after the accident to pay for the survivor's "Caretaker Stipend."

Beezan had to skim a few parts of the legal database before he figured out that a "Caretaker Stipend" was what the people who took in orphans were paid, first out of the survivor's estate and then from the government. In Jarvie's case, the only relative, a 28-year old fifth cousin, Yan, refused to waive the stipend, even though it meant forcing the sale of the *Sunburst*—against Jarvie's will, no doubt.

How much unresolved resentment was Jarvie carrying around underneath his load of unresolved grief? Beezan switched over to the one-and-only official file on Jarvie, which contained one word: *classified.*

Beezan spent a long time in the Prayer Room that morning. He was grateful and relieved that there had been a breakthrough with Jarvie, but jittery with worry. He should have known that a problem big enough to lie about wouldn't be solved overnight.

Beezan was so intent on his prayers it took him a while to realize that Jarvie had come in. After a few minutes, Jarvie scooted closer to him. Beezan turned and patted the rug next to him. Jarvie, although hesitant, came over. They sat cross-legged, facing each other, except not facing as Jarvie's head was down.

"I'm sorry," Jarvie's anguished voice choked out. He looked up furtively, his red-rimmed eyes filled with fear. "I'm sorry for all the lies. I . . ." He stopped. Beezan couldn't believe anyone could be so afraid of him. He carefully set his hand on Jarvie's knee, making him jump. "I," Jarvie started again, taking a big handful of the toy bricks out of a vest pocket. They fell into his lap and onto the prayer rug. He picked one up and held it out to Beezan. Taking a big breath he said, "I'm sorry I lied about my age." Beezan accepted the brick, but before he could say anything, Jarvie handed him another brick. "I'm sorry for wearing the wrong armband." Another brick. "I'm sorry I put my name on Toazair's hiring list." Beezan winced. Another. "I'm sorry for altering the crew records on jump day." Beezan couldn't stifle a gasp of alarm. He looked down at the pile of bricks. A brick for every lie? Beezan was stunned. How could they recover from so many lies?

Jarvie was continuing on the same theme. Computer records tampered with, false packets to his guardian, to his school, faked identity chips. "Sarcee," Jarvie paused for a few deep breaths. "Sarcee isn't mine. Well, she is now. But she was my mother's." Most of these lies had been against others. They left a trail of deception that led all the way back to before the Luminesse accident. "I didn't take my jump drug when I was supposed to." Jarvie had stopped saying he was sorry and was just listing the lies. Beezan tried to stay calm. He wasn't angry, but scared that they were now in a legal mess. "And Fast," Jarvie handed over a bunch of bricks. "I don't even remember what all I said." *He was too young to fast!* Beezan cringed.

Jarvie got down to the last two bricks. He stopped. Beezan heaved a sigh of relief. Two bricks leftover. Then Jarvie curled his fingers around the last two and said, "You don't want to know."

A chill ran through Beezan and he firmly put his hand on top of Jarvie's. "Yes, I do."

"Dangerous."

"We're in this together, Jarvie. Let's have a clean start."

Jarvie swallowed but actually seemed relieved.

Second to last brick: "I'm not a level three monitor. The s'link is—was—my brother's." Beezan shuddered at the thought. Such a powerful tool in the hands of an untrained, unstable, child.

Last brick, Jarvie's voice dropped to a whisper. "There were aliens at Luminesse."

Beezan stopped breathing. He looked at Jarvie and for the first time ever, Jarvie locked eyes with him, willing him to believe. And Beezan did believe. And he understood. Jarvie was not afraid of *him.*

14 / STARTING OVER

Jarvie felt like an overstuffed closet with the door flung open. Everything he'd been hiding in the back of his brain just kept falling out. He couldn't hold back. He told Beezan everything, first in the Prayer Room and then in the kitchen, then at every meal and during work.

Beezan spent that day of confessions noting every lie Jarvie made with authorities and making a list of "corrections." Before sending a message to Jarvie's cousin, Yan, to get permission for him to crew on the *Drumheller*, Beezan sent a request for personal news about Yan. It came back as Jarvie had feared. *No longer at Hamada. No forwarding information.*

"See, he's disappeared," Jarvie whispered to Beezan.

"You're not on the runaway list. They don't know. So he has no reason to disappear," Beezan insisted.

"They know."

Beezan scowled, but agreed to wait until they reached Redrock before sending any messages regarding Jarvie.

Jarvie marveled that Beezan wasn't cold and disapproving anymore. He was worried, but he had accepted it all, the truth and the burden that went with it. Jarvie could feel Beezan's concern and determination. That night, Beezan shyly sat on the chair by the bunk and played the violin. Since they'd never had Social Arts, Jarvie had no idea he could play. And it was sweet and stirring, like a stream of strong warm medicine flowing through him.

Sadly, he had lost Sarcee. His yelling had turned her away. He counted it as his punishment and was grateful she and the pups were alive.

7-Splendor

The next day, Jarvie told Beezan every detail of the accident, of Canyon people coming onto the *Sunburst* and taking the still unconscious Lanezi. A counselor had been assigned to Jarvie. He had been sick. He didn't remember the next few days. He kept asking for Lanezi.

He sat at the kitchen table with Beezan for hours, babbling. He was reliving a part of his life. Like he was back there. Like he'd never left. He was trapped in that closet no matter how much junk he pushed out. Especially about Lanezi. "You know, Lanezi. You have his paintings," Jarvie told a surprised Beezan, thinking it would help him understand.

It was as if he transferred his love for his whole family to Lanezi, just to think he could still have them. He told Beezan how he'd just assumed that he would be able to stay with Lanezi, how Lanezi had come aboard when Jarvie was a child. He had been his Uncle Bennezi's best friend in pilot certification school. Their names had matched and they had been friends from the first day. Lanezi was some kind of pilot prodigy. His strange parents had allowed him to jump conscious as a baby. He was the *Sunburst's* long jumper. He was also a second uncle to Jarvie, always understanding of Jarvie's small troubles with a superstar brother and busy parents and uncle.

Jarvie couldn't help crying again as he struggled to tell Beezan about being shipped to Atikameq right after the funerals. About finding out he couldn't stay with Lanezi. The counselor went with Jarvie to Atikameq, but she was little comfort. After staying in the Medical Center for a while, Jarvie heard that the *Sunburst* was sold, that he would be sent to Hamada to live with a relative he didn't know, and that he would attend the teen training school on Hamada.

"What happened to Lanezi?" Beezan asked.

Jarvie sat up defiantly. "That's what I want to know. I've tracked him to Harbor."

"Tracked him? Why didn't you just send him a packet?" Beezan asked.

"I did. Lots. They all came back as if he didn't exist. But because he's a famous artist they can't stop him from selling his art. So I found him. I think he's part of a secret group. They're somehow connected with researching the a-ring accidents. They had an operation going on at Hamada for a long time, after the accident there. But they stopped. I've tracked them to Harbor." Jarvie paused and looked up at Beezan. "And anyone who knows anything about this suddenly disappears."

Beezan looked skeptical. "So why haven't you disappeared?"

"Because, they don't know that I know. Or they didn't. I tried to make myself disappear and get to Harbor and find Lanezi on my own."

"Our strange cargo was from Hamada." Beezan commented, "And it was tagged for Harbor."

"But now . . ." Jarvie didn't really know what he wanted to say. He held his head in his hands, elbows propped on the table.

His little quest was over. "Now, I'll never find Lanezi. And I'm afraid they might suspect you now."

Jarvie felt Beezan slide his arm around his shoulders and was both grateful and overwhelmed. "I'm sorry." Jarvie whispered. "I don't want you in trouble. I am nothing but a problem for you." Then it was like all that talking just kept going and his darkest most secret thoughts just came out. "I should have died that day at Luminesse. I wish I had. I wish it a million times! I know it's wrong, but I can't stop wishing it." He just couldn't control the pain and was sobbing again, laying his head on his arms at the table. All thought of embarrassment was gone. There was only the pain and hopelessness of his life.

The grip on his shoulders tightened and Jarvie felt Beezan stroking his hair with the other hand. Beezan was chanting a prayer over and over while Jarvie cried and cried. Finally, he managed to calm himself enough to hear the prayer.

"Rely upon God. Trust in Him. Praise Him, and call Him continually to mind. He verily turneth trouble into ease, and sorrow into solace, and toil into utter peace. He verily hath dominion over all things."[1]

Jarvie sat up and looked at Beezan. "Thank you. Thank you for caring about me."

Beezan looked ready to cry himself. "Jarvie, I can't tell you anything those counselors haven't told you already. I want you to know that I'm not going to let you go at Redrock. You can stay with me as long as you want to."

Jarvie's heart warmed to hear it, but he shook his head. "You don't understand. What happens at Redrock is probably not up to you or me."

A fiercely determined look crossed Beezan's face. "We'll see." As if to mock Beezan, his s'link jolted him with the priority alert. Beezan frowned at his s'link, then frowned even more deeply after reading the alert.

"What?" Jarvie asked.

Beezan hesitated and Jarvie had a surge of panic. "I'll go check. It's an urgent packet." He must have seen the panic in his eyes. "I'll tell you what I can. It's classified for captain only."

Jarvie's heart was pounding, but he tried to nod maturely. Beezan gave Jarvie's arm a reassuring squeeze before heading down the stairs. "It might not be anything about you." Sarcee scowled, got up and padded after Beezan.

Jarvie tried to act nonchalant, but ended up out in the rimway, waiting for Beezan. It was only a few minutes before Beezan came back, unsurprised to see Jarvie standing there. Beezan signaled for Jarvie to walk with him, Sarcee plodding behind. "It's alright. It was a recorded message about that big cargo, but I have to answer on screen so I just thought," he paused, pulling off his headband so his wild hair flopped down around his face covering his eyes, "I better get a haircut."

All Jarvie's tension of the past hour morphed into a crazy laugh. "You look like a caveman."

"Well, I have to look like a respectable Captain to talk to this new monitor. He's pretty high level."

"Maybe they think you stole that big cargo," Jarvie teased, still laughing, but Beezan stopped in his tracks, suddenly serious. Jarvie could see him pale a bit as he replayed the packet in his head. "I was joking! Who would steal that monster?"

"Who would steal anything?" Beezan asked, almost to himself, "but you might be right," he whispered.

Jarvie was still a little shaky, but doing everyday things distracted him for the moment. While getting their haircuts,

Beezan set the *Drumheller* to estimate the turnaround time. Sitting in the grooming chairs, they called out every possible repair they could think of to make the turnaround time longer. They had to shout over the sound of the hair vacuum.

"And shopping," Jarvie added.

"Shopping?" Beezan looked at him sideways as if he'd just discovered a stranger on the ship.

"You know, for podpup supplies. We'll have three podpups. And food and stuff for the kitchen and . . ." Jarvie went on listing every possible thing he would buy on a fantasy shopping trip at Redrock station.

Jarvie finished first and jumped down to look in the mirror. But the first thing he noticed was not his hair, but his red swollen eyes and his red nose. They were all the more exposed for his hair being short. He turned away quickly and went back to serious mode.

Beezan got down off the chair without even looking in the mirror. He was holding his headband. His hair was straight, stiff and short, even shorter than when Jarvie first met him. He looked so different. Jarvie noted wrinkles at the corners of Beezan's eyes he'd never noticed before, and a touch of gray in the temples. "Official enough?" Beezan asked.

"Yes. Kind of scary actually," Jarvie admitted and Beezan laughed.

"*Drumheller*? Do you have that estimate for turnaround?"

"Yes, Captain: 37 days minimum."

Beezan frowned. "Add 5 days for complex cargo loading, 10 days for counseling and 14 days for . . . vacation."

"Turnaround estimate: 66 days."

. . .

Beezan dropped Jarvie and tired-of-walking Sarcee off at the kitchen and went down his stairs. He changed into his pilot jacket and zipped it up to hide his old shirt. He sat down to review the message before responding.

"Greetings Captain Beezan, God is Most Glorious. I am Reeder, Personal Assistant to Agent Diego Loyal Oatah."

A very proper man, younger than Beezan, was on the screen. He wore an official-looking jacket with some kind of pin on the high collar. His gaze was intelligent but stern, like an old-fashioned schoolmaster ready to scold. His brown wavy hair was perfectly shaped as if the least unruliness were not permitted. Beezan unconsciously ran his hand through his now civilized hair. The man, Reeder, spoke in a measured, severe, impatient voice as if he were slowing down for their primitive ears. Or maybe Alkulu, the All-Earth language—and the only language spoken in the sectors, wasn't his native tongue. *Earthborn*, Beezan realized. He was more than just some inner sector diplomat. *He is actually from Earth. He's one of the teeming billions.*

"I will be your monitor from now on. Please report your status. Include cargo manifest, inbound program and turnaround time to be ready to jump.

"Additionally, I must impress upon you the serious nature of this communication. I ask on behalf of Sector 1 Council Agent Oatah, are you carrying a large custom-made cargo container from Hamada, possibly labeled #189?

"Respond to me visually on this priority channel. A security code is being tight-beamed. I await your immediate reply. Reeder out."

The screen went blank.

"Did we receive the code?"

"Yes. All messages will now use the Reeder code."

"Assistant Reeder. God is Most Glorious. Greetings from the *Drumheller*, Captain Beezan here.

"Our inbound status is attached as well as the cargo manifest and other requested information. Yes, the cargo labeled #189 was put aboard *Drumheller* at the last minute. I am awaiting a cargo manifest correction from Solo Journey Hamada. Please explain the nature of our involvement in your special assignment. *Drumheller* out."

"Well, I hope that takes care of that," Beezan said. But as soon as he said it, a sick feeling went from his head to his feet and he knew. There really was some kind of monster in his Cargo Hold.

Jarvie finished his dinner quietly. He had talked Beezan's ears off for two days. He knew he would have to go back to his cabin, but he dreaded it. He knew Beezan was uncomfortable sleeping in the chair, but he felt so much safer, not to mention warmer, in Beezan's cabin.

Beezan cleared his throat as he did when he was about to talk about something difficult. Jarvie nodded before he even started.

Beezan laughed and then said, "Oh, I'm glad you agree. It's settled then. You'll move to my grandfather's cabin."

"What?" Jarvie exclaimed, embarrassed. "No, oh, I thought—"

"I want you to. My grandfather is probably furious at me for not taking better care of you. And I put out some of his things I thought you could use."

"But you've kept that cabin all these years." Jarvie objected, but not too strongly.

"I know, but I don't need to any more. It makes sense. We

can leave the adjoining door open. You'll be close enough that I can sleep without worrying and the heat works." Beezan dropped his voice, "And maybe You-Know-Who will visit you."

Jarvie couldn't help smiling. He was overjoyed at the offer. How could he ever have thought that Beezan was mean?

Beezan settled gratefully into his bunk. He could sleep again. Sarcee had refused to go with Jarvie, but had allowed him to pat her. Now she was curled up snoring in Beezan's ear. Jarvie was very happy to be in his grandfather's cabin.

Would Jarvie feel overly supervised for a 14-year-old? Well, he would deal with that problem when he came to it. He scooted Sarcee down a bit so the snoring wasn't so loud. He could go to sleep knowing what was up with Jarvie. They were way past the k-belt. They were finally coming into station. He could get rid of the mystery cargo. They wouldn't starve. It was warm under the blankets. He found himself thinking about the future again. But first, he was looking forward to a good night's sleep.

His s'link beeped.

"Priority packet from Redrock, visual."

15 / JOURNEYING TOGETHER

8-Splendor

Reeder's face appeared on the big screen in Beezan's cabin. He was as precise and formal as in the previous recording, but there was no mistaking the edge of concern in his voice. He dispensed with the greeting quickly.

"Captain Beezan, your specs for cargo 189 do not match our information. Please perform a personal inspection and provide the correct specs. Additionally, please explain why you listed 'average' mass for one piece."

Beezan was wide-awake now, and getting annoyed. *A personal inspection?* Before answering, Beezan checked the specs that *Drumheller* had attached to the packet. Average mass really didn't make any sense.

"*Drumheller?*"

"I am here."

"On the cargo 189 specs, did you average those first anomalous mass readings with the final mass?"

"There is no final mass reading."

"Explain."

"The mass reading of cargo 189 continues to fluctuate by 5.3%."

"What?" After the cargo was balanced, it never occurred to him to check the mass again. "*Drumheller*, are you sure the tester is working properly?"

"Yes."

"Well, what else could cause the readings to change?"

"Changes in readings can be caused by changes in mass, acceleration, or local gravity."

Beezan felt a movement and realized that a sleepy, blanket-wrapped Jarvie was looking over his shoulder.

Beezan shook his head in exasperation and pointed to the picture of 189 on the screen, so Jarvie would know what they were talking about.

"*Drumheller*, the mass isn't changing; it's not disappearing or reappearing. And the mass tester turns off when we're accelerating. *And* there are no planets to change our gravity. So, it's impossible. There must be some mistake."

"Few things are truly impossible."

Beezan and Jarvie looked at each other, perplexed. "So philosophical," Jarvie whispered.

"Drumheller!" Beezan insisted, "Explain how it's not impossible for the mass to change *inside* the cargo container."

"Spontaneous appearance and disappearance of massive particles, either by unknown natural means or unknown technology."

"Like something is transporting itself in and out of the cargo container?" Jarvie asked skeptically.

"It is not impossible."

"Okay, extremely unlikely. That leaves gravity; are you going to tell me that's not impossible?"

"It's not," Jarvie whispered. Pale, and with a faraway look,

Jarvie seemed to suddenly comprehend something. "It's a gravity ball."

"Jarvie! That *is* impossible."

"The technology is known to exist although not understood by humans."

"It's too small!" Beezan argued. "As big as that container is, it's nowhere near big enough to be a gravity ball."

"Maybe there are more than one kind. Maybe it's a small one, or a piece of one," Jarvie suggested.

"Even if someone found a small gravity ball, who would be insane enough to stick it in a cargo container and put it on a ship, *without even telling the crew*?"

"Insanity is not impossible."

"I don't believe it. No Sector Council would do such a thing."

"Maybe they didn't know," Jarvie suggested.

"Jarvie, you have a suspicious mind. How could they not know?" And then Beezan remembered. The cargo wasn't officially on his list. It was just put aboard.

Beezan punched the audio record key. "Greetings Reeder, the specs I attached earlier are correct. The cargo barely fit in the cargo door. It's attached to the mass tester, which is working properly, that's how we know there is a continuing fluctuation in the mass. If you have any knowledge as to the cause of this fluctuation, I would appreciate an explanation. Thank you, Beezan, *Drumheller*."

He sent the message and scowled at Jarvie. "There must be some other explanation. It can't be a gravity ball."

"It is," Jarvie said, staring at the picture on the screen. "I can feel it."

• • •

Not again. Beezan groggily reached for his jacket. He'd had a hard time going back to sleep after Reeder's message, and no doubt, it was Reeder, again, with a message worth waking him up for. Did Reeder not sleep?

"Captain Beezan. Agent Oatah sends his apologies for the inconvenience, but insists that you redirect to Second Station. I have calculated a new trajectory that requires your immediate attention. You must comply without questions or the window for this trajectory will be lost. "

Jarvie appeared again as if he had an instinct for trouble. "He can't be serious," he complained.

"Have you ever seen a more serious person?" Beezan asked.

"No, but it's not fair. We already have a 17-week incoming. How long will they keep us from Redrock station?"

"I don't know."

"What is this Second Station anyway?"

Beezan tapped the screen. "It's been abandoned since before you were born. It used to be Resource Station something, in the L5 zone, where they had all these valuable Trojans. After they mined those, they moved the station into orbit around this moon." A picture popped up on the screen.

"That's a big moon!"

"Yes, if it weren't orbiting Rr2 it'd be a planet. Dwarf planet. Whatever. Anyway, as far as I know, the station is abandoned."

Jarvie sat down in the other chair, disgusted. "Maybe it's their secret headquarters." Beezan scowled and Jarvie pulled the blanket over his head. Beezan barely heard his muffled voice. "Do we have to?"

Beezan frowned. That child was always thinking of other angles. It set Beezan's mind to considering. How could he be sure that Reeder and Oatah were who they claimed to be?

Beezan's s'link zapped him again. He yanked it off his jacket and banged it on the table, but he couldn't ignore a priority message. Sending the message to another pop-up, he was surprised to hear a different voice.

"God is Most Glorious. Captain Beezan, Redrock Inbound Authority has just been informed of your new trajectory. Your flight path has been cleared. I have been instructed to emphasize to you that R.I.A. fully supports these orders as well as any additional directives from Agent Oatah or his assistant, Reeder. R.I.A. END."

"I guess that answers my question," Jarvie grumbled, pulling the blanket off his head.

Beezan studied the screen. "*Drumheller*, do we have the fuel for this trajectory?"

"Target can be obtained with multiple decelerations and corrections, but we will not have reserve fuel to spin up in between."

"How many days?" Jarvie asked. Beezan glanced at him, knowing he didn't do well in nogee.

"Thirty-three days."

Jarvie slumped in his chair. "Well, I guess they don't want us anywhere near Redrock Station with a gravity ball. They're probably thinking we'll be blown to bits."

"Jarvie! If it's that dangerous, they'd tell us to kick it out. If anything, we'll be bored to bits by a bunch of bureaucrats."

Beezan never went back to sleep. Apparently Jarvie didn't either, at least not in his bunk. Beezan found him snoring at the kitchen table. However, there was a lot of extra food stowed. Jarvie had taken advantage of their last morning in gravity to cook. He also left some food out for their breakfast and a treat for Sarcee, which she devoured in five seconds.

"Jarvie made that for you," Beezan reminded her.

"Huppff."

"He still loves you."

"Hummph."

"If you wake him up, you might get some more."

"Hummm."

The next thing Beezan heard was Jarvie yelping in surprise as Sarcee leaped into his lap.

"What?" Jarvie asked in a panic.

"Zharvee, up." She looked at him innocently. "Sarcee hungreee."

Jarvie propped his head on his hand with a sigh and produced a bottle out of nowhere for her, but she would not stay in his lap. She snatched the bottle and sat next to him, slurping disdainfully. It was a start though, and Jarvie was trying hard not to look pleased.

Beezan turned to his task, the big calendar in the kitchen. After their initial 17 weeks, he had already added three "Mammoth" days, then eleven "k-belt" days and now he added two more days, grouchily calling them "Reeder" days.

"And who knows when we'll ever get to Redrock," Jarvie lamented, practically reading Beezan's mind.

Beezan swiped his s'link. "Here's the final schedule. Sorry, there's just not enough fuel to spin up between. We're using everything we've got. We won't arrive until 2 Beauty. A cargo inspection team will meet us at Second Station."

"Have they already left?"

"No. They'll only need a few days to get there. We'd only need a couple weeks if we had a decent fuel converter and could do some serious braking, but I still have two years to go on my Solo Journey contract before I can make a full paying run.

"Right now, the credit I get from extra cargo hardly pays for supplies, and of course, since I'm not leaving you at Redrock, I'll have to set aside something for you."

"You don't have to pay me," Jarvie said quietly.

Beezan got his food and sat next to Jarvie. "Actually, I do. It's the law."

"I never got paid before!"

"Well, you crewed with your family. They're only required to educate you. I'm supposed to do both, and I'm afraid I haven't been doing such a good job. I'm sorry." Beezan shook himself. He didn't know how he got on this conversation.

"You're doing great," Jarvie suddenly declared.

"Oh, well, you say that because I don't make you study."

Jarvie laughed and then turned serious. Hesitantly, he pulled a purple armband from his pocket and held it out.

Jarvie Atikameq, it said in bold letters, above Hamada TT. It was Jarvie's real armband. Jarvie handed the armband to Beezan, suddenly shy. Puzzled at first, Beezan realized that Jarvie wanted Beezan to put it on for him. Scooting closer, Beezan wrapped it around Jarvie's arm and patted it down. He squeezed Jarvie's shoulder and Jarvie seemed pleased, even a little emotional. Sarcee stopped her slurping for a microsecond to contemplate the scene. "But we need to make a new one—that says *Drumheller*."

"Thank you, Captain. No matter what happens. Thank you for everything."

Jarvie made a couple trips to the Command Bay after putting Sarcee in the jump bed. *She is really getting heavy*, he thought, flexing his arms. He stocked food and water in Command while Beezan conferred with the *Drumheller*. After his last trip, Jarvie pressed the secure button on his cabin door, then slipped quietly into the Command Bay.

"Close it," Beezan said, and Jarvie turned and closed both airlock doors.

"G-suit?"

"Check," Jarvie answered, pulling up his vest and sweater to show Beezan. "How many gees?"

"Four point three max."

"Piece of cake."

"Cake!" Sarcee demanded.

"Later," Jarvie answered.

As soon as the spin-down started, Jarvie felt sick. Thirty-three days of nogee. *How will I ever stand it?*

"Ten seconds until burn. Burn will complete after 13 minutes, 29 seconds."

Since the burn was programmed, they had turned their chairs backwards, so even though they were decelerating, they were still being pressed back in the chairs, and could make full use of the cushioning. Jarvie closed his eyes and tried to relax, at least relax his fingers clutching the chair without relaxing his breathing. Or else he felt his chest might be crushed. He sent his mind to another place. The place of just breathing. Finally, he glanced at the overhead pop-up, only twenty more seconds. It was nearly over. *Serves me right for scoffing at 4g.* Then there was that sickening but relieving lurch of nogee.

"Sarcee?" He called.

"Cake!"

"She better have those pups soon or we'll be feeding her day and night," Beezan complained, undoing the top part of his g-suit and taking some deep breaths. Jarvie did the same and relished how good

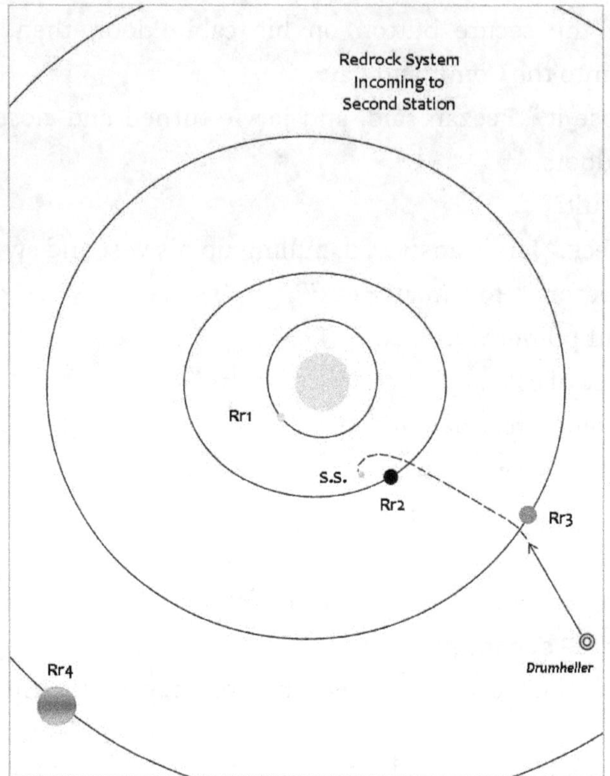

it felt. They just sat there, recovering. Jarvie kept thinking how nice it had been to hold Sarcee again and then felt silly for being so happy about it. Despite his mock annoyance with Sarcee, Beezan was in a good mood too.

"Captain?" He asked in his most polite voice.

Beezan's eyes shifted over to him suspiciously.

"I was just thinking. There's this show."

"Show?"

"Yes, a series. It's made by the Teen Training Center. It's about a family on a ship with lots of kids and they have adventures. And I thought . . ." Beezan nodded, encouraging him. "Well, maybe we could watch an episode each night during our days of nogee."

Beezan smiled. "That's a good idea. What's the name of it?"

"It's called *Journey of our Hearts.*"

3-Glory

Beezan crossed off another day on the big calendar. It was their eighth night of watching *Journey of our Hearts*. After a day of nogee, pretending that all their chores were done, Beezan would play his violin a short time, and then they would hang in the kitchen and watch. Sarcee would lazily bounce between them to see who might give the most attention—or have the best snacks. Jarvie had frozen enough human treats to eat a couple every night.

Beezan was surprised at how much he liked *Journey*. It was meant for teens and their families, to familiarize them with the teen training program. It was on the humorous side, but it had drama and moral dilemmas and lots of little truths about ship life. The show took place aboard *Heartstrings*, a fictional special courier ship. It transported emergency medical teams, repair teams, diplomats, or whatever, into exciting and educational situations.

The first episode introduced the main characters, twelve of them. There was a Grandfather Captain that Beezan immediately liked, a Grandmother doctor, the Captain's son and his wife, both pilots, and eight children. There were chaotic social arts nights, mischievous podpups, malfunctioning robots, demanding monitors, loud repair crews, and clueless passengers.

The children were the gimmick of the show, each one representing a stage of the teen training program. There was a rough moment at the start of the first episode when a note went up that the six older children were named in memory of real teens who died in the line of duty. Just as Beezan was thinking what a nice idea that was, they discovered that the eldest character, a 21-year-old 'youth leader' with a green armband, was named Canim. Beezan had to stop the show for Jarvie to recover, but aside from the reminder of grief, he was pleased that his brother was remembered.

The next character was a 19-year-old named Andee. He was a 'senior youth' with a blue armband. Next was Zealandia, a 17-year-old 'youth' with a black armband. The next child was 15, on her year of service and not yet in the story. They only saw her in the opening title, wearing the white armband.

Then there was a 14-year old 'junior youth' in a purple armband, a 12-year old girl, and 4-year old twins, a boy and a girl, all three with yellow armbands.

The little boy was named Sky and the little girl was Star. With their big brown eyes and ringlet hair, they were the cutest children Beezan had ever seen. Part of Star's character was that she thought she was some kind of space princess. She wore fancy dresses and did all sorts of curtseying. Beezan and Jarvie laughed hysterically.

The second episode revealed that four of the children were orphans. Beezan learned that 'Ceetees'—caretakers—were common, and part of the teen training system. Hundreds of orphaned children were placed with families, and anyone else qualified to take them, just as Jarvie's single cousin had taken him. The same episode dealt with the culture shock of the 14-year-old coming from a rough and tumble cargo ship to the polished and proper *Heartstrings*. Beezan thought Jarvie might have a seizure from trying not to laugh when Beezan himself couldn't see what was funny. He had never considered the whole subject of ship culture. For the first time he was seeing his ship and even himself from outside. It was far too educational. He was hooked. He loved the show. It really did help them get through the days of nogee. They watched and laughed, and Jarvie cried. And Beezan bit his lip not to cry sometimes. Their weeks of estrangement melted away and Beezan felt a growing attachment to Jarvie. They would come into dock soon and get rid of their bad cargo. Everything was going to be all right.

Then Jarvie got sick.

16 / THE LAST SHIP IN

6-Glory

"We would have to call it the *Journey of our Stomachs*," Jarvie complained. Beezan was surprised Jarvie had even that much humor left. They had to stop watching *Journey* as Jarvie could not even open his eyes without being sick.

Beezan was trying to get better advice out of the med computer. Jarvie was curled up in a ball, strapped to the exam bed, alternately complaining and groaning softly. The *Drumheller* had alerted Beezan that Jarvie was overmedicated, so Beezan manually assigned the medicine and was trying to figure out what to do. He scowled. Apparently, this had happened before, during their previous nogee stints, when Jarvie had rigged the computer not to tell. Jarvie had just been refilling and replacing the med patches and resetting the program so it didn't know how much he was really taking. He was using the standard 'space sick' medicine, so the overlapping doses wouldn't do any physical harm, but working while half asleep and with a fuzzy mind could get them both killed.

Jarvie had another bout of heaving. Beezan helped steady

him and hold onto the bag. Jarvie was more violently ill than most people were under nogee, but the med computer insisted that nogee was the problem. Beezan disposed of the bag and gave Jarvie another. The computer wanted to check Jarvie's ears, so when his stomach took a break, Beezan asked Jarvie to lie flat, He slid the headpiece over him. Jarvie whined but Beezan just ignored him. "A few minutes. You'll be all right." *Captain, parent, doctor, counselor, podpup-sitter: that's what I have to be. I was crazy to ever be out here without at least a skeleton crew. The counselors are right. The solo mission idea is dangerous. So how did it get so much more dangerous with Jarvie aboard?*

Meanwhile, all the work they both needed to do wasn't getting done. Beezan tried to stay calm, but the combination of Jarvie's sickness, Sarcee's pregnancy, the nogee, and Reeder was really getting to him. Just trying to keep the ship in one piece for the daily dec and correct maneuver was enough to worry about.

Beezan watched Jarvie when he wasn't looking. He was young and weak for all his tallness. Beezan forgave a lot due to his rough couple of years. But the life of a pilot or crew was not easy, especially for one sensitive to nogee. Underneath it all, Beezan could feel a core of stubbornness in Jarvie that displayed itself in this crazy quest for Lanezi and in always trying to work the system. If that stubbornness could be transformed to strength . . .

"Data collection complete. Analysis underway."

Beezan gently slid the headpiece off. "I need you to be patient and work with me, Jarvie." Beezan squeezed Jarvie's shoulder, letting him roll back onto his side. "We'll save the medicine for the burn in two hours."

"Okay," he whispered, tense from trying not to move more than necessary.

"I know you're miserable. What did you do as a child?"

"I just took the meds. I never had any trouble."

Beezan wished he had Jarvie's full medical records. The attachment on his ID card didn't include medications from three years ago. "Maybe I should try to contact your doctor from the *Sunburst*."

"She didn't survive," Jarvie whispered.

"Analysis complete."

"Report."

"All indicators are within parameters for this age group."

"What? Is that it?" Beezan asked the med computer in exasperation, but then switched to the real brains. "*Drumheller*, can you access the med computer data and give your . . . opinion?" *Did AI's have opinions?*

"Analyzing."

Beezan continued his silent fretting. No medical records. No personal records of any kind on Jarvie. And now they weren't going to Redrock, where Beezan could find confidential legal advice before Jarvie was discovered. He had no intention of lying. He just wanted to be prepared to fight to keep Jarvie with him.

"Ready with Recommendations."

"Do you agree with the diagnosis?"

"Motion sickness caused by prolonged zero gravity conditions."

"Proceed with recommendations."

"One: return to spin. This would require a change in the inbound program. Highly recommended. Calculating options now."

"Two: Change medication. List provided."

Beezan looked at the pop-up. "We don't have any of that; I've been through every supply cabinet."

"Option removed."

"Two: overlap current medication and remove patient from duty."

"Three: apply maximum dose and monitor patient continuously until gravity is restored. Recommended as a last resort."

Jarvie groaned.

"Recommended in addition to medication: Have patient review nogee training materials, assist patient to maintain hydration. Increase sleep period. Give comfort and support in a calm loving manner. Reduce stress. Provide quiet distraction. Pray."

Beezan hovered at the panel to look over the inbound programs that *Drumheller* was calculating. *Pray? I don't need a computer to tell me to pray! Is it going to tell me to hope? To love? To wonder? To persevere?* He studied the choices. *Reeder will have a fit. God help us.*

3-Beauty

Second Station

Nineteen weeks and three days. That's how long it took us to finally come in. And the last seven days almost killed Jarvie. In the Command Bay, Beezan finally got everything in order for stationkeeping. Now he could get to the Med Bay to check on Jarvie. He had harried *Drumheller* obsessively with questions and checks while he had to be in the Command Bay. Otherwise, over the past few days, he had stayed in the Med Bay with Jarvie, or dragged him around on a tether like a podpup. He was ashamed to drag Jarvie around, but he couldn't run the ship and monitor a sedated Jarvie at the same time.

Beezan had figured after all these weeks and everything they had been through, the last seven days would be easy—even in nogee. Instead, they had been a nightmare: scary and jumbled up in his mind. Beezan had not slept more than an hour or two each night.

Think of the positive! It's over. We are up to spin. Praise the Lord. One more message from Reeder and hopefully he would never have to deal with him again. Beezan had not only asked Reeder for permission to change the incoming trajectory, he had explained about his sick crew. He had explained, and then complained, and he had finally pleaded. It was then that Reeder took a most serious tone with Beezan and ordered that under no circumstances was he to change his trajectory.

He's seriously ill.

Under no circumstances.

He could die!

Captain! I understand.

It chilled Beezan to the bone. Whatever they were mixed up in was beyond the life or death of a human being. And Beezan obeyed. Even though it meant Jarvie might die. He feared what might go wrong if he didn't. Ashamed again for his selfishness, he didn't want to spend his life grounded or *incarcerated*. Reeder had mentioned that word. Beezan had never even told Jarvie.

That day, seven days ago, while he argued with Reeder, Beezan had only given Jarvie the allowed medication and let him try to work. Then things got worse. Jarvie couldn't even keep a spoonful of liquid down. Beezan had to remove him from duty and overlap the medication. It helped some, but less each day. In addition, they still had to do the dec and correct each day. By the fourth day, Jarvie was too weak to get himself in the g-suit and Beezan couldn't do it for him. Then Jarvie went into shock during the burn. Beezan had to haul him to Med Bay and start a hydration pack. It had taken him three tries. *I'm not a doctor!* Jarvie had almost died in those hours. Even *Drumheller* caught some of Beezan's panic, pouring out streams of suggestions and reminders until he told it to stop.

On that desperate day, Beezan had hovered near the bed with one arm around Jarvie. Jarvie feebly clutched his arm, except for three spine-tingling moments. Three times Jarvie released Beezan's arm as if he were leaving. Three times Beezan felt the presence of *others* in the Med Bay. Three times he braced himself for Jarvie's death, forcing himself to let go. Three times, Jarvie took a deep breath, his eyes fluttered open, he held Beezan's arm again. Finally, the third time, Jarvie murmured "Stay, have to stay" as if it were an order. Then Beezan hung on, called Jarvie, talked to him, told him to stay, told him he would get better and pulled on Jarvie as hard as he could. Jarvie's will came back and the crises passed for the day. But in those hours, Beezan lived again through the deaths of his former crew members. Too many.

Beezan didn't think he had the strength to go on, but if Jarvie were to live, it would be up to him. He turned his mind to the practical and carried on. He inspired himself by mentally feeding a little angry seed for Reeder. He knew it was wrong, but it was a distraction.

For the last two daily burns, Beezan had put Jarvie in a jump chair with a resus pack on. Yesterday it had triggered. From 3.7g. *Thank God for the resus packs.* Jarvie's will to live was still not strong. Today's corrections had been many and mild to come into orbit at Second Station, so Beezan left Jarvie in the Med Bay, with the *Drumheller* AI supervising the med computer. At least Sarcee hadn't gone into labor—*Don't even think it!*

Beezan swung up the stairs. Yes, the Med Bay was reoriented the correct way. Jarvie was lying so gravity was "down." Maybe his brain could reprogram now.

"Is it over?" Jarvie whispered.

"Yes, we're spinning, feel it?"

Jarvie groaned. Oh, 'spinning' might not have been the best word. He looked terrible. He looked 95 years old. His eyes were glazed with dark circles under. His skin was sickly pale, dry and pinched. His lips were cracked and he was breathing shallowly. He was on his side, strapped down, convulsing with shivers. The bed was heated slightly, but more heat would cause more dehydration. Beezan got Sarcee out of her box and put her by Jarvie. He stood next to Jarvie, stroking his arm and shoulder, slow and calm as the *Drumheller* had suggested. "It's over. You'll have days to recover, take it slow. You'll feel better every minute. When you're up to it, I'll get you some food—if Sarcee hasn't eaten it all. We'll get the right medicine—lots of it—so this will never happen . . . again." His voice broke right at the end. He swallowed, cleared his throat. *Maintain an attitude of positive calm, Drumheller* had said. *Give support and encouragement.*

Beezan had wanted to tell Jarvie something, but not when he thought he was only saying it to a dying person. He was just waiting for the right time. "Jarvie, it's been the longest run in that I've ever had. I know how terrible some of it has been for you. But . . ." Jarvie looked up at him, full of childlike trust, "I just want to say . . . I'm glad you were here. I mean, not so you could suffer. Just so, well, just selfishly speaking, it would have been hard for me to be alone all that time. And your help saved us more than once. I mean . . . thank you." *Well, that didn't come out exactly right.*

But Jarvie was smiling and reaching for the straps. "I do feel a little thirsty."

17 / SECOND STATION

9-Beauty

Drumheller at Second Station

Jarvie was suited up, sweating and straining in the shuttle hangar. Pulling the accordion-folded tubeway out to the cargo inspector's shuttle in nogee was just too much work for someone that had recently been *near death*. But there was no one else to do it, and he had to stay hidden until Beezan could sort out his legal status. Besides, Jarvie preferred to stay out of sight for now. Shocking as it was that he wasn't listed as a runaway, based on his caretaker's disappearance, Jarvie suspected that someone out there was looking for him.

The shuttle pilot had parked perfectly on the faded line, but the shuttle was some sleek expensive thing that was very narrow at the front. The tubeway barely stretched from the pressurized Entry Lounge to meet the shuttle lock. He glanced at his tether for the tenth time to assure himself he really was hooked on. The hangar door was still open.

The auto-anchors had finished securing the shuttle, the *Thistle*, and the tubeway was pressurized. He was now waiting for the crew to make their way, unsuited, to the Entry Lounge. The shuttle airlock was small, so it took several cycles to get everyone through. “Patience,” Beezan reminded him.

From a camera on the rimway, Jarvie watched Beezan on his suit screen, pacing back and forth with Sarcee in a carrier. Beezan was shrugging his shoulders with the now-heavy Sarcee. She was past her due date as far as the med computer could tell. Beezan was nice about not giving Sarcee too much attention when Jarvie was around and encouraging her to go back to Jarvie. Jarvie also knew how nice it was to have a warm loving podpup and how long Beezan had been alone. He tried not to mind when he saw Beezan talking to her and playing with her. At least now Beezan had to carry her around.

Beezan left his s’link open so Jarvie could hear what was going on. Jarvie concurred with Beezan in his extreme disbelief that Reeder was really sending cargo inspectors, at least not the usual sort. Seeing the shuttle only confirmed the charade in Jarvie’s mind. Not unless some king had come to inspect his cargo.

“Jarvie, how are you doing?” came Beezan’s quiet voice on their private channel.

“Fine. A little tired,” he admitted. Beezan had made him swear he would tell if the work was too much. He had recovered quickly in six days of standard gravity and he’d eaten constantly. *Even more than Sarcee*, Beezan had joked. But he still tired easily. They had already agreed that the visitors would stay for the day, so Jarvie could leave the tubeway out for a few hours. Once they got to the Entry Lounge, he could go in. He felt a bump and looked up in alarm, but it was only the hangar door closing.

After the shuttle crew got to the Entry Lounge they took the lift up and out to the wheel where Beezan waited to greet them in standard gravity. Jarvie returned to the Entry Lounge and heaved a sigh of relief as he took off his helmet. He was shivery from cold sweat. He needed to wash up. But not yet. Hanging by the controls, Jarvie activated the big screen, so he could watch. The lift had just maneuvered through the coupler to the wheel and was now headed for the top rim. Beezan stopped pacing, took Sarcee off, set her down, and stood a polite distance from the lift lock, waiting. Jarvie almost wished he could be there, just to see people.

Jarvie turned up the sound just in time. The door slid open, and five people came out, three men and two women. *They have luggage! Do they think this is a hotel? The cabins aren't ready.* One of the men didn't carry any bags. The others politely set down the luggage and waited a moment to have introductions. Beezan made a small gasp and glanced up at the camera, before recovering and turning back to the new people.

"God is Most Glorious. Welcome to *Drumheller*. I am Captain Beezan."

"Thank you Captain. God is Most Glorious. Allow me to introduce . . ." *That voice!* Jarvie gasped himself. It was Reeder, the monitor of their nightmares. He had come himself!

"*Drumheller*, can you give me a closer picture?" Jarvie asked. The camera zoomed in, but kept all the people on the screen.

Reeder was introducing his boss, Agent Oatah. Oatah was dressed in a long tunic and matching pants of shining gold-colored material. He wore a cloak, lined with fur on the inside, and boots with fur around the top. He even had gloves. He was ready for the cold anyway. And, Jarvie noted, it was this Agent Oatah who carried no luggage. That probably accounted for the big pile of bags around Reeder. Aside from his clothes, Oatah didn't look like a self-assured agent. In fact, he looked strained and uneasy.

The other man, named Lander, was much older. No title was given, but he was a long jump pilot to anyone with eyes. *Retired to cargo inspecting?* Jarvie didn't think so. All the people turned to the first woman as Reeder introduced her as Iricana. Jarvie couldn't see anything unusual about her. She was probably in her fifties, a good ten years older than Beezan anyway. She had graying hair pulled back simply and looked very sturdy.

The younger woman was introduced as Katie, a doctor. She was very dark. Her hair was done in glistening black braids, held together with a clasp in the shape of a gold comet. She had earrings that glittered like stars. She was beautiful. But why bring a doctor? And the Earthborn and an old long jump pilot?

Oatah stepped closer to Beezan, but Beezan backed away, then stopped, as if determined to hold his ground. Struggling to recover his composure he repeated, "Welcome to *Drumheller*." Although Jarvie would have been thrilled to see them, he had a pang of sympathy for Beezan's nervousness around people. Beezan scooped up Sarcee to cover his awkwardness.

"*Drumheller*, pull the camera back to Beezan." However, the boarding group had started to leave and all Jarvie could see was a bunch of walking luggage.

"Where are they going?" Jarvie asked.

"The Captain is taking the boarding group to the Consultation Hall."

"Is that a TeeRee or TeeFree zone?"

"The Consultation Hall is a technology reduced zone."

Good. As long as Beezan kept his s'link on, Jarvie could listen. Jarvie could hear them walking, could hear Beezan asking Sarcee if she was okay. She was quiet, considering all the activity going on around her.

Jarvie tried to wait patiently. The nogee brought back too many bad memories. And he should get out of the suit. He remembered to check the hangar controls and secured the rest of the Entry Lounge. He grabbed his helmet and got on the just-returned lift. He could wash up in his cabin and listen. He keyed the lift speed to maximum.

"How long have you owned the *Drumheller*, Captain?" asked Iricana, who probably knew the answer since Reeder seemed to know every detail about the *Drumheller*.

"I inherited the *Drumheller* when I was 15," Beezan answered politely.

"Young for a pilot, isn't it?" She asked.

"I wasn't a certified pilot then, I was the captain."

Jarvie had to admire how Beezan could give these people the benefit of the doubt, even though he didn't believe Reeder's story, trusting that the truth would be revealed and backed up by Solo Journey. It was probably a cover for some sensitive operation.

Drumheller was trying to keep up with the group by changing cameras, but many of them didn't work. "*Drumheller*, put the broken cameras on my maintenance list, please."

Jarvie was distracted again as the gravity increased suddenly. He probably shouldn't have gone so fast. He took a few breaths and forced himself to stand up straight.

Why were they going to the Consultation Hall? Didn't they want to see the cargo? Was Beezan putting them off? Iricana's attempt at conversation had failed.

"Here we are," Beezan said, "stairs up." Jarvie heard a door slide open.

There was a tromping of feet and then the door shut.

"Captain," demanded Reeder, before they could even be sitting down, "who is watching us?" There were a couple of gasps in the room. "The cameras are following our progress. Are we to believe that is an automatic process?"

There were no cameras in the Consultation Hall. Jarvie could only hear because Beezan's s'link was on. If he turned it off neither Jarvie nor the *Drumheller* would be able to monitor. Beezan answered in a calm, everyday voice. "Monitoring can be automatic, but I assume my crew is watching."

"You let your crew spy on you?"

"It's not spying. It's just human nature." Beezan managed to keep any touch of annoyance out of his voice. "We've been out here a long time. He's just curious." No one from the outer sectors would even question it.

"He? You have a crew of one?" Iricana sounded incredulous.

Jarvie was out of the lift and clomping up the rimway. He speeded up.

"Yes," Beezan paused. "Please sit down. Yes. A crew of one. I thought you were together. Reeder knows this."

This isn't going well, Jarvie thought.

"Captain, what we have to discuss is very important," Reeder continued. "We expect that this room is totally secure." There was a long pause. Jarvie's s'link clicked. Beezan had shut him out.

Beezan took a few deep breaths as inconspicuously as possible while he settled Sarcee in a niche and the others dumped their fancy luggage and found seats. The large round table would seat nine, so there were empty chairs around Beezan, setting him apart from the shuttle crew. *Reeder!* The object of all his anger, which Beezan had thought to be a useful distraction, was now right in front of him. He would have to deal with him. Now that the little seed of anger had grown to a big spiky plant, Beezan didn't think it had been such a good idea. *I must let it go.* Beezan tried to picture himself ripping up the plant, but that was a bit angry itself.

These people, whoever they were, could make their case, get on their shuttle and *go.* Beezan glanced casually across their faces. Katie: taking direction from Iricana. Iricana: eyes missing nothing, seemingly ready to pounce on someone. Agent Oatah: very formal, eyes weighing the ship suspiciously. Reeder: fussing with his pad and all deference to Agent Oatah. Lander! Beezan would have stared him down, just to find proof of a lie, but his eyes showed total detachment. A pilot. *Do they mean to replace me?*

"Captain—" both Reeder and Iricana started at the same time. *Aren't these people together?*

"Captain," Agent Oatah said firmly, and the rest deferred, Iricana reluctantly. He continued slowly for Beezan's benefit. "Yes, we are together, as of today. So please forgive us if there are redundant questions. I have been sent by Sector 1 Council to investigate matters regarding certain projects. Iricana had been sent to retrieve cargo for one of those projects. Only yesterday did we discover that our missions crossed paths."

Beezan nodded politely, not having a clue what projects he was talking about.

"We ask for your discretion and cooperation in offloading some cargo here at Second Station. Then you may reload and continue to Redrock under my authorization." He made it sound simple. Reeder slipped his pad across with the container numbers. No surprises there. It was the same bad lot of cargo from Hamada bound for Harbor. It even listed cargo container 189.

Beezan tried to answer in the most reasonable voice. "I don't see how that would be legally or practically possible."

The others didn't blink. "I'm sure Reeder can address your

concerns on this matter," Oatah said and leaned back, going into detached mode.

Beezan turned to Reeder with a slightly harder look. "First," Beezan told him, "I'm sure, *as cargo inspectors*, you understand that I can only deliver cargo to the proper destination unless you have a transfer ticket."

Reeder was ready for this one. "The cargo is marked for Harbor. No ships are allowed to jump into Harbor, so you cannot take it there."

"I should take it to Atikameq, the Sector Hub, as instructed by Atikameq Authority."

"Yes," Reeder continued, unbothered. "Normally, that would be the procedure. However, you are also allowed to deliver the cargo to the intended recipient."

Beezan narrowed his eyes. *What is he leading me to?* "Yes, if the recipient can show documentation . . ." *accepted by the cargo inspectors!*

"Yes, exactly." Reeder motioned politely to Iricana.

She took an envelope out of a pouch around her neck *(important!)* and carefully reached into it, taking out a pad of printed cargo container receipts. Beezan looked at them carefully, comparing them to his cargo manifest. He took his time even though he had no doubt they would match. They did, except Iricana did not have ownership of 189. *Too bad. That's the one I really want to get rid of.* "Who among you is the official cargo inspector?"

"I am," Reeder said, holding out his level 6 s'link with an image of his ID card. *Temporary Cargo Inspector*, it said. Beezan tapped it with his s'link and it was immediately verified through Redrock Authority. That information would have been in his last download, six hours ago. So it was not a charade. They really were some special cargo inspection team. Beezan swallowed. Whatever this was about, he probably didn't want to know.

"What about container 189?"

"You will turn that over on my authority," Oatah commanded.

"Um, what exactly is your authority?" Beezan asked as mildly as he could.

They all looked at him, stunned. "Did you not receive my introduction packet two hours ago?"

"My packets have been blocked since six hours ago," Beezan said, unable to keep the displeasure out of his voice.

Reeder winced. *Now I know who blocked our packets.*

"I see, Captain. Perhaps that explains your attitude."

My attitude! This better be good.

Oatah reached into his gold tunic and pulled out an actual gold ID card, handing it to Beezan. Beezan had never seen one. He gently tapped it on his s'link.

DIEGO LOYAL OATAH, EARTH. SPECIAL AGENT TO SECTOR 1 COUNCIL. ACTING AGENT OF SECTOR 6 COUNCIL. ACTING AGENT OF SECTOR 7 COUNCIL. ACTING AGENT OF SECTOR 8 COUNCIL. ALL INQUIRIES TO SECTOR 7 COUNCIL ONLY.

Beezan stared. He read it again. Not Cargo Agent. *Special Agent*. A special agent could speak for the Council. *For Sector 1 Council.* The outer sector *Councils* had even deferred to him. Oatah was the boss of everyone.

"Why?" Beezan whispered to himself.

"Why didn't we tell you weeks ago?" Oatah asked. "Our mission is quite sensitive. And perhaps more cooperation was expected regardless."

Beezan went into a cold sweat. *I am in trouble.* "I'm sorry. I had no idea. It's all so . . . suspicious."

"I assure you, Captain," Reeder explained, "everything is

being closely monitored by the Councils. This matter requires your immediate cooperation."

"Yes, of course," Beezan agreed. "But you can't possibly expect me to haul that cargo out single-handedly with nothing but a one-person loader."

"Of course not, Captain," Reeder said smoothly, "A cargo team will be here tomorrow."

"Tomorrow?" Beezan glanced at the luggage.

"We were told you were a very reliable and faithful Solo Journey Captain, who could be trusted in any matter." Reeder continued his smoothing.

"Well, now that I know everything is compliant."

"Good," Reeder went on. "So cargo will be offloaded tomorrow. Our team will, of course, put your other cargo back on. You will proceed to Redrock where I will be your inspector. You will offload the rest of the cargo. Then you are free to proceed with your Solo Journey work. No mention of this stop, this meeting, these people, or this cargo or anything related will ever be made by you, as per Sector 1 Council."

Beezan almost choked. All eyes were on him now.

Oatah leaned forward, eyes boring into Beezan, "Your sworn word," he demanded, putting his hand over his heart. Not a handshake, not business. A promise. *A promise is to God,* he could hear his grandfather saying.

Beezan hesitated. "My crew?"

"The same oath will be exacted."

That's not going to be easy. Beezan set in his mind the terms of the promise, put his hand over his heart, and then stopped, dropping his hand. He did not want to end up on the other side of an oath from Jarvie. Their eyes went wide. "I'll swear after my crew."

"Call him," said Oatah.

Beezan didn't see any way to avoid it. He took his s'link off his jacket and held it close to his mouth, "Please come to the Consultation Hall."

Jarvie jumped. He was standing right at the door, trying to listen. Of course, it was airtight so he couldn't hear anything. He should have taken off the suit while he had the chance. *Why does Beezan want me? Did they come for me?* He opened the door, and tried to glance around to see Beezan's face. He forgot about the big boots on the suit; one caught on the step, and then the other caught and he went slamming down on the deck of the Consultation Hall. The suit alarm went off, the air was knocked out of his lungs, his head hit the deck, and worst of all, his neck hit the helmet rim of his suit, choking him. He struggled to sit up, coughing and sputtering and gasping for breath. Beezan was by his side in an instant. "Don't try to get up. Just sit." Beezan helped him sit and reached over to turn off the flashing suit alarm. Then he had to turn off the distress signal that was sent to his s'link.

Katie, the doctor, was kneeling down by him now, sterile field on already and tipping Jarvie's head up to see his neck. She glanced up at his face and gasped, turning to look at Iricana.

"What?" Reeder asked with alarm. "Do you know him?"

"Jarvie Atikameq!" Iricana declared. She was out of her chair and standing over the crouching Beezan. "Do you make a habit of hiring runaways, Captain?"

Beezan flinched as if struck. "I checked the runaway list. He wasn't on it," he said firmly, and Iricana took a long, considering breath.

Jarvie tilted his head to see around the doctor. The others were all out of their seats, standing over them, except Oatah, who sat at the table, seemingly frozen in astonishment, and Lander, who looked on with a piercing concern. He finally caught his breath. With a surge of annoyance, he jumped to his feet before Beezan could stop him, accidentally knocking over Katie. He towered over the rest of them in his suit boots. "What have you done with Lanezi?" he shouted back at them.

Reeder took a giant step backwards, but Iricana's blue eyes blazed, boring into Jarvie's.

"Enough," Beezan said quietly. "Sit down—all of you."

A little shocked at his own outburst, Jarvie plopped back down immediately, muttering "sorry" to Katie as she righted herself.

Iricana sat, on the deck, right where she was. Reeder sat in the nearest chair. Oatah was blinking as if trying to comprehend the whole situation. Jarvie had scared himself with his little burst of temper and now worried that Beezan would be unhappy with him. And Beezan did seem to be reaching his limit. "Is he hurt?" he asked Katie with surprising calmness.

Katie had already sealed the cut on his neck. "The bleeding isn't bad, but I should take him to your Med Bay."

Beezan started to pull off the suit, but Jarvie didn't want to struggle back into it in another hour. "I still have to get the tubeway."

"The suit may be damaged, and besides, I don't think our *guests* are going anywhere."

So Jarvie let them take the suit off, embarrassed to be seen in his sweaty underwear. "Go. Have your med check and then rest in your cabin. *We* are going to take a prayer break." Jarvie couldn't help but notice Iricana's eyes following Beezan's every move, including the squeeze he gave Jarvie's shoulder before turning him down the stairs with Katie.

. . .

In the Med Bay, Jarvie didn't trust Dr. Katie to get him a blanket, so he got it himself before getting on the exam bed. She frowned at the computer. "I'll have to call your Captain for permission to open your medical records, but he's already in the Prayer Room. We'll just do the exam and I'll get back to those."

The bed she picked was the same one he had spent way too much time in lately and it only added to his discomfort. The doctor was professional, but Jarvie sensed a tension in her since his outburst. As data appeared on several pop-ups, her frown only deepened. "You are ill," she finally said. "Very ill."

"I was. I'm better now." It didn't sound convincing when he was shivering so hard. She got a supplement drink and warmed it, putting it in his hand and helping him sit up.

"Tell me all about it." She crossed her arms and waited. He told her all about the last month, making sure to mention about Reeder being no help. Between gulps, the story tumbled out of him without much regard to saying "Captain" Beezan every time. When he was done, she searched through the meds herself, making notes on her p'link. Jarvie hoped Beezan wasn't going to get in trouble for not having the right supplies or something. "You look thin, even for being sick lately. Does Captain Beezan feed you?"

"I do most of the cooking."

"Does he work you over hours?"

"We haven't been able to stick to teen training requirements." She fixed her dark eyes on him. "We've been out here 19 weeks! You don't know what we've been through! We're just trying to survive!" He didn't want Beezan to get in trouble, but didn't want to seem like he was covering up anything.

"I want you to tell me straight Jarvie, has Beezan mistreated you in any way?"

"No! He's been very patient and good to me. He saved my life last week. He. . ."

"What?" She jumped on his hesitation.

"Well, he cares about me, that's all."

"You care about him too."

"Well of course. He's my captain. He's—" Jarvie didn't know what to say. Beezan had become very important to him since the wall had come down. He didn't want to be taken away. "He didn't know." There was no avoiding trouble. Jarvie had to stick to the truth now, even though it meant all the trouble would be on him. "Beezan didn't know that I was a runaway."

"How could he not know? He even knows your name. Even if you're not on the runaway list, you don't have clearance to crew."

"I tricked him when I came on board and I rigged the computer and all the records and my ID card and my records at school, and at home."

She looked doubtful.

"And I wore Ca—a youth leader armband and pretended to be 19. And I, well, I got away with it for a long time. But he knows now. He seems to want to help me." Jarvie trailed off. He put his hand on his heart. "I swear it. Beezan isn't a criminal."

Katie nodded as if accepting that for now, but not totally convinced. Jarvie felt his annoyance filling him up again. "So what have you done with Lanezi?"

Katie froze momentarily and was then suddenly very busy with the computer.

18 / STATE OF EMERGENCY

Beezan left after Katie and Jarvie were down the stairs and out of the Consultation Hall. He headed for the Prayer Room without looking back to see if the others followed, but they did.

Leaving their shoes in the niche by the door, they went up the stairs and had a moment of hesitation over seating, as they were new in the Prayer Room together. They each sat in silent prayer for a long time. Beezan ignored them. In the Prayer Room, there was no rank or superiority. They were all servants of God. Beezan willed himself to accept them as people, not problems. But his mind kept wandering back to the problems and worrying about Jarvie.

After about an hour, Katie came in to pray, signaling to Beezan that Jarvie was in his cabin. Beezan suddenly remembered Sarcee. He quickly got up and went back to the Consultation Hall to check on her. She was sleeping quietly. He was calmer now, but not near calm enough to deal with these people. He gently picked up Sarcee and took her to the kitchen.

Earlier, Jarvie had already set out a big lunch for everyone, so Beezan served people as they came in. They said please and thank you, yes and no, the food is good, small civilized words. Beezan didn't know if he should be more scared now that the shuttle group was worried. Beezan excused himself to take food to Jarvie and see to their cabins. The kitchen door wasn't even shut before he heard Iricana burst out with, "Now what?"

Beezan went to his cabin and through the adjoining door to Jarvie's cabin. He wasn't surprised to find Jarvie at his panel, multiple pop-ups activated. Jarvie jumped up immediately, startling Beezan so that he almost dropped the tray.

"Sorry." Jarvie threw up his hands in exasperation and sat down again. Beezan set the tray down by Jarvie and sat in the other chair.

"What are you looking for?" Beezan asked, gesturing for Jarvie to eat.

"Anything. I've got *Drumheller* searching for packets on any of their names or the shuttle *Thistle* or giant cargo. Only Oatah is in the *Drumheller* database. He's some famous Earth conservationist. But what is he doing out here? I think Reeder has put a block on us with Redrock Authority. We're less than a minute away, but I'm not getting anything." Jarvie practically swallowed the food whole.

"I'm sure he has blocked all packets both ways. They don't want anyone to know anything about this. They want us to swear an oath."

"I won't!"

"We might have to, Jarvie." Beezan said gently.

Jarvie looked away, upset.

"Oatah is a Special Agent—of Sector Council 1."

"Special Assistant?"

Beezan shook his head no. "Agent."

"No." Jarvie went very pale. "This is bigger than I thought."

"What is?"

"This trouble with the aliens, the bad cargo, the disappearing people."

Beezan shook his head again. "Well, maybe you'll find out if you're ready to swear an oath."

"But that will make us one of them!"

"Jarvie! There's no us and them."

But Jarvie looked away again. Beezan hoped he would get used to the idea before they came to it. Beezan changed the subject. "Are you okay?"

"Scratched and bruised from today," Jarvie whispered. "And lots of frowning from the doctor. I had to tell her about my space sickness. She wants you to release my medical records." Jarvie hesitated, getting in another mouthful. "She asked me if you were . . . mistreating me." He was embarrassed. "But of course I told her you weren't. I'm not sure she was convinced."

"Don't worry. Obviously, we are both on their bad list. We're supposed to talk again before dinner. Are you up to helping me prep the other cabins when you're done eating?"

"Of course, honor."

"We never fixed the heat in your old cabin, did we?" Jarvie shook his head no. "Well, I thought we'd give that cabin to Reeder."

Jarvie was happy he'd been able to clean up before the meeting. He wasn't sure he would be included, but Reeder had insisted. Beezan and Jarvie had managed to prep the cabins quickly and find a few basic supplies, but it was not five-star. Jarvie couldn't help but feel inadequate; even though he told himself it was a cargo ship. His childhood training aboard a diplomatic vessel had geared him to pampering the passengers. It wasn't a matter of liking the passengers. It was a matter of respect in your own ship and crew. Beezan thought the *Thistle* people were getting better than they deserved. Was Beezan actually disappointed that Jarvie had a brainstorm and finally fixed the heat problem?

Sometimes Jarvie just couldn't tell about Beezan. Right before they left for the meeting, dressed in their least ragged clothes, Beezan had grabbed him by both arms and stood on his toes to look Jarvie in the eyes. "I can't order you to swear any oath. And I won't ask you to. I'm just asking you to think about your future. I don't want either of us to do something we'd regret."

In the Consultation Hall, Jarvie checked Sarcee in her niche. She was so quiet. He had a sudden knot of worry about her. He gently scooped her up. She didn't object. Holding her tenderly against his chest, he moved to a chair at the consultation table and sat down. Reeder glanced his way disapprovingly, but was too busy to say anything.

The rest of the *Thistle* crew and Beezan were all present, but not yet sitting down. They were taking care of some last minute details. The two Earthborn, Oatah and Reeder, talked strangely, saying 'pee-links' like it was two words. Jarvie had been all the way to Sector 3 and everyone just said 'plinks.' Did they have something else on Earth? He couldn't imagine what.

Iricana and Katie would take the cabins next to Jarvie, so Katie would be across from the Med Bay. Then Lander would have the next cabin. Oatah and Reeder would get the next two. They had an adjoining door between them so 'Reeder could assist Agent Oatah as needed,' as Beezan suggested. Iricana and Katie sat down, both looking over Jarvie directly. He kept his head down, calming himself by hugging Sarcee. She was so warm against him. It felt so nice to hold her.

Finally, the moment could be avoided no longer and they all settled into their seats, Beezan sitting right next to Jarvie and patting his arm under the table. Beezan nodded to Katie, who said an opening prayer. Then he nodded to Oatah, handing over the meeting to him.

Jarvie was nervous to look up, but he had to be respectful. When he did, Oatah was looking right at him. “Crewperson Jarvie?”

Crew*person*? There was that funny talk. “Yes, honor?”

“I am going to ask you some questions, and I want you to answer ‘yes’ or ‘no’ and nothing else. Understand?”

“Yes, honor.”

“Do you know what happened during the accident at Luminesse?”

Jarvie had dreaded the moment and here it was. He looked at Beezan who didn’t give a flicker of a nod or a shake, not a hand on his arm or anything. He was going to let Jarvie speak without direction, and that meant the truth. Of course, Beezan was big on the whole truth the whole time. Well, Jarvie didn’t see where it would get them now, except in a whole lot more trouble. “I—yes.”

They looked doubtful. “Were you awake during the jump?”

“Yes.” Now they were looking nervous. Eyes flickered to Beezan wondering if he knew.

“According to the log,” Reeder pressed, “you were under sedation in the Passenger Lounge. Is that true?”

“No, honor.”

“Were you in the Passenger Lounge?”

“Yes, honor.”

“Were you sedated?”

“No, honor.”

“Did you have access to the sound and visuals from the

Command Bay?"

"Yes, honor," Jarvie admitted, knowing they would be upset.

"Have you spoken to anyone about what you witnessed that day?"

"Yes." They rocked back in their chairs, eyes alarmed.

"End of yes or no answers. How many people have you told?"

"One," he said, glancing over at Beezan. They actually looked slightly relieved at that.

"Are you sure, only Captain Beezan?"

"Yes."

"Captain, what did Crewperson Jarvie tell you?"

Beezan didn't hesitate, "That there were aliens."

They sagged in their chairs like the life had gone out of them. "I'm afraid, Captain," Oatah continued, "that I have no choice then. Circumstances require that, in the interests of sector security, I must commandeer your ship and crew." Oatah actually did look distraught.

"*WHAT?*" Clearly Beezan had not expected that. He shook his head. "You can't! Freedom of Flight protects me."

Jarvie suddenly got the bad feeling that it would be Beezan doing 'something' they'd both 'regret.' *How could it have come to this?* To somehow end up on the same ship snared by the people he meant to find? Only *he* hadn't meant to be found by them. They were arguing now. There was no way anyone would call it consulting. Reeder was in there with all the legalities and necessities. Beezan insisted that no ship could be commandeered unless a state of emergency existed.

"Technically that is true, Captain," Oatah said with resignation, "but I prefer not to alarm the whole sector and it would put an end to keeping the aliens a secret."

Of course. Oatah had the power to declare an emergency.

Jarvie was shaking. Suddenly he felt warm and wet. He wasn't that scared! He loosened his hold on Sarcee and gasped in alarm. Some warm liquid, not urine, was spilling out of her. His stomach twisted.

"She's in labor!" Beezan exclaimed.

Once again, Katie was up and around to him in a flash. She felt Sarcee. "She's hot. We need to get her to Med Bay." She hoisted Jarvie by the arm and steered for the door.

"We will carry on with the meeting," came Oatah's voice as Beezan turned to follow. Jarvie stopped, or tried to with Katie pulling him. If he didn't speak up now, he might never have the chance. "I just want to stay with Beezan," he told Oatah. "Please. I'll swear any oath you want if I can stay with him."

Then he was hauled bodily down the stairs by a person two-thirds his size.

Beezan spent a few minutes cleaning up the mess to regain his composure. He would have to be more thorough later. He just shook his head at Reeder when he suggested calling cleaning robots. The few cleaning bots he had were on constant duty for life support tasks. *Do they think they are commandeering a luxury liner?*

When they settled into the chairs again, Beezan found it hard to focus. Part of his mind was worried about Sarcee, part was panicking about the mere idea of being commandeered, and part was terrified of losing Jarvie. To hear Jarvie beg to stay with him was both heart wrenching and heartwarming. Unnervingly, the look Oatah gave him wasn't encouraging.

As it turned out, he didn't need to focus. His task was to sit and listen to Reeder, and occasionally Oatah, tell him all the trouble that would be caused if word of aliens circulated, and why the 'right' thing to do would be to let them take his ship. He and Jarvie could stay with the ship and help or they could be 'detained' indefinitely.

Beezan really had no choice. It was a Sector 1 Council order. He was being prideful. He should gratefully acquiesce. Let them have the ship; go along for the ride. It would be a great adventure. He understood the importance of their mission and he believed there really were aliens. Maybe after a few years, the story would get out and he would get his ship back. He admitted to himself that he wanted to stay in command, go on the mission as a captain and pilot and not a hanger-on. In the end, he just slumped down in the chair, defeated, and stared at the table. The lecturing finally stopped. He hardly noticed. *What is happening with Sarcee?*

Beezan was just about to be rude enough to interrupt the meeting to call Med Bay when Iricana's p'link beeped. "Iricana here."

"Good news," came Katie's voice. "Two pups alive and well. Sarcee is stable. She should be fine in a few days."

Beezan let out a relieved sigh. "Thank you," he breathed. Lander and Iricana both nodded happily. Reeder and Oatah just looked puzzled over the fuss.

"Can we take a break?" Beezan asked.

"We will resume tomorrow after breakfast." Oatah declared, and nodded at Lander for the closing prayer.

Beezan's break was to finish cleaning up, including halfway down the rimway to Med Bay. Jarvie must have wrapped her in his shirt or something to stop the drips by then. Then he had to wash up. He had to make dinner, but stopped first to see the new pups. He shouldn't have been surprised to find Iricana and

Lander already in the Med Bay, admiring the pups. They were smiling and happy as if no commandeering meeting had ever taken place. They were whispering since Jarvie was actually asleep on one of the exam beds.

Katie was checking medical screens. "Captain, congratulations," she greeted him and waved him over to see the pups. Iricana and Lander moved aside for him. Beezan looked over the side of the podpup nesting box to see two little sleeping podpups, nuzzled together, already washed. "The black one is female; she was born first. The white one is male, a bit bigger, but both are in great shape," Katie told him. "You can touch them, but I wouldn't pick them up yet."

"Thank you. Did you deliver them?"

"Yes," she turned serious. "It was fortunate I was here, we did end up doing a bit of emergency surgery." She made it sound like nothing, but Beezan whispered a prayer for the blessing of having a doctor at just the right moment. He had to keep an open mind about these people. At least *some* of them.

Beezan reached in and stroked the female. Her black fur was very thick and fluffy. She was sleeping calmly. The male's white fur was thin and sleek. As Beezan patted him, he wiggled. His heart was racing even as he slept.

"*Drumheller*, release medical records of Sarcee and Jarvie to Dr. Katie." Katie gave him a look that included crossed arms and a tapping foot. *What?* "Oh, ah, *Drumheller*, release my medical records to Dr. Katie." She smiled like he'd taken his first steps.

"Have you thought of names for them, Captain?" Iricana asked.

"Oh, they're Jarvie's. Sarcee is his podpup."

"I don't remember him. . ." and then Iricana's blue eyes got wide. "The mother's podpup?"

Beezan nodded. She looked over at Jarvie and frowned.

Suddenly Katie's eyes went even wider than Iricana's. "Lanezi's shadow!" She exclaimed, looking at Jarvie.

So *they do have this Lanezi*, Beezan realized.

Both Lander and Iricana turned to look at Jarvie, considering. They seemed to have forgotten that Beezan was there. Iricana was shaking her head like it didn't make sense.

"Yes," declared Katie. "He told me he altered all these computer records. He can do that sort of thing. He was asking about Lanezi!" She rounded on Beezan. "Has he mentioned Lanezi before?"

"Mentioned?" Beezan stalled. *Only about a hundred times.* "What's Lanezi's shadow?"

Iricana fixed him with a no escape look. "Someone has been secretly tracking Lanezi, possibly trying to contact him, even though Lanezi knows he's supposed to keep a low profile. We've just learned of it recently."

Beezan nodded, "It's possible. He told me Lanezi was on Harbor. He wanted to go find him. In fact, he told me Lanezi was part of a secret group. I didn't believe him. It sounded like a movie."

That put a sudden end to their questions. Iricana and Katie scowled at each other. They certainly didn't jump in with denials. Beezan moved to the other podpup station to check on Sarcee. "She's sedated," Katie told him.

"What about Jarvie?" Beezan asked.

"Sedated? No, of course not. He had a bout of . . . sickness and was pretty stressed by all the . . . medical . . . aspects. But he stayed functional until it was over."

Jarvie's armband was folded up and set by his pillow. Beezan stood next to the bed studying the screen. Suddenly he felt everyone's eyes on him and realized he was automatically stroking Jarvie's arm as he had done through all those days of sickness. He stopped, but then covered up his sudden stop by peeking under the sheet. Jarvie was dressed in clean medical scrubs. Katie cleared her throat. "Sorry, the clothes couldn't be saved by the time we were done. I pulled off the patches," she indicated a little stack by the bed.

"I'll get a change," Beezan said, turning for the door. *So much for Jarvie's one supposed uniform.* "Well, I guess I shouldn't enter him in the teen training medical program."

"No," Katie shook her head. Lander was studying Jarvie intently, moving over to look at the pop-up by the bed.

As he left to get more clothes he heard them excitedly talking about Jarvie being this 'shadow,' almost as if that would be good news.

10-Beauty Eve

Beezan got ready for bed in disgust, without even playing his violin. He had survived dinner under the scrutiny of Oatah and disapproval of Reeder. The other three at least were sympathetic to his situation. Katie was staying in the Med Bay to watch the pups, so Iricana had delivered her dinner and come back.

After dinner, Beezan had insisted that Jarvie be released to his cabin. He couldn't leave him alone in Med Bay and he couldn't lock the others in their cabins, but he had set *Drumheller* to watch them.

Jarvie came to Beezan's cabin to say prayers with him. He was exhausted but didn't seem to want to go back to bed. Finally, Beezan just walked him back, assuring him that they must have faith that everything that was meant to be, would be, which didn't mean you were going to like it of course. He left the door open as always, in case Jarvie had any more nightmares.

Tonight it would be easy to have nightmares. They were stuck in the middle of one.

He thought he could hear Jarvie crying, but hesitated to check. Should he give him support or privacy? If he were a real parent, he would know what to do. Beezan thought that Jarvie would be thrilled over the twins, but he just seemed frightened out of his wits. *Maybe he has more sense than I do.*

Beezan sat up again to say some more prayers, but in truth he was exhausted and just needed to sleep. Tomorrow, things would make more sense. He vaguely remembered thinking that before. He collapsed on the bunk again and pulled the blanket over his head. With one last prayer for Jarvie, he fell into a deep sleep.

Beezan heard the s'link beeping, but he could ignore it. It was just Reeder, bothering him again. He'd pick up the message later. He didn't have to wake up. Then he remembered all in one painful lump. Reeder was on the ship. Was he waking him up just for old times' sake?

Grumbling, he sat up. "Lights." He squinted at his s'link.

PRIORITY PACKET FROM REDROCK

Who could be sending from Redrock? Someone that had discovered what was happening and was trying to help him? Solo Journey? Beezan's heart leaped. He grabbed his jacket and hurried to the panel. As he sat down, a form on the deck in the doorway caught his eye. "Jarvie?" He got up again and quietly walked over and knelt down. Jarvie was asleep, curled up in a ball on the deck. He looked all right so Beezan went back to his message. Maybe he should wake him up. Jarvie would love to hear news that Oatah and company would be told to go.

The message came up. And Beezan's future was before him.

19 / STAR AND SKY

Jarvie became vaguely aware of the light. He was sleeping on the deck. He blinked and uncurled, easing his aching bones and muscles. *Why was Beezan at his panel in the middle of the night?* He sat up to see the words on the big screen.

Captain Beezan. God is Most Glorious. Please accept the warmest greetings of the Sector 7 Council. We have become aware of your difficulties. We thank you most deeply for the eight years of sacrificial effort you have so steadfastly offered the Solo Journey Project and free you from any further obligation to that worthy cause. We have every confidence that you will find a way to work with Agent Oatah's team to accomplish this new and vital work. We offer our most loving prayers for guidance, success, unity, and protection in this critical endeavor for you and for those in your care.

Jarvie watched as Beezan sat bolt upright at the greetings of the Sector 7 Council, through Beezan's slumping in the chair and clutching his s'link to his chest. By the end, Beezan's head was on the panel and Jarvie wasn't sure if he was crying or not. Beezan had gone through all these weeks without breaking down. To see him cry now would only add to Jarvie's fear. Jarvie was stunned himself. The message was not what he expected. In all his life, he couldn't remember his parents ever receiving a direct order from a Sector Council. There was no possibility of argument. Even he wouldn't try to wiggle around such a command. Mainly because whatever they said was the right thing to do. If Beezan did not accept it . . . *of course he will.*

Jarvie scooted over and settled on the deck next to Beezan's leg. Beezan was crying softly, but he almost sounded relieved. "It's okay," he whispered to Jarvie, putting a hand on his shoulder. "I know what to do now. I'm very grateful. I shouldn't have been so stubborn, I'm sorry." Jarvie breathed a sigh of relief. He doubted he would have taken it so well or been so humble.

When Jarvie woke up in the morning, this time in his bunk, he found a jacket with a *Drumheller* patch glued on, way too wide, a pair of pants, way too short, and a pair of leg warmers, needed to cover the short pants, all in different shades of brown. The arm warmers were white and very worn out. There was no shirt, but there was a belt with pouches—Martian style. It was a distant relative of the proper uniforms Jarvie grew up wearing. He was sure it was the best Beezan could do. He couldn't wear his work overalls to a formal meeting.

Last night, Beezan had pointed out that the Council had not ordered him to turn Jarvie over to them. They had made a plan and Jarvie had gone to bed with hope, and with that hope, excitement over the podpups.

He dressed quickly, not bothering to see how he looked in the mirror, said his prayers in his cabin, and then went to check on the podpups. Katie said she would stay with them in the Med Bay, but he needed to reassure Sarcee.

He hurried down the rimway to the Med Bay. Bounding up the stairs he called out, "Are they okay?" before remembering to greet the doctor properly.

She only laughed. "Oh yes. Sarcee's already eaten this morning, twice, and the pups have been nursing fine." He patted Sarcee and the pups and then shook himself. No time for playing.

"Doctor, I'm supposed to set up in here. Bee—Captain Beezan wants to assemble here for breakfast and the meeting."

"Oh." She pulled out her p'link and checked it. "Guess I should pay attention." She smiled and hurried around securing the Med Bay while Jarvie pulled out the conference table. It creaked and strained unfolding from the wall as if it hadn't been used in years. Katie stopped her work to wince at it.

Then Jarvie had to scurry back and forth from the kitchen. He made the table as formal as he could with *Drumheller* supplies. There was no tablecloth or centerpiece; there were hardly enough utensils. He stood over it frowning in the end. Katie came over with a frosted white medical container. She filled it with water, added a chemical that turned the water blue and floated a white dish in it. Then she made a pink flower by folding a sheet from a notepad. She set the flower in the white dish. It was as if she pulled something beautiful out of thin air. Jarvie smiled. "Thank you."

"You're," Katie hesitated, "going to change clothes in a minute?"

Jarvie was determined not to look embarrassed, even if he was. "It's all I have," he said quietly. "The textile printer doesn't work."

"Oh, I'm so sorry. I didn't mean . . . well, I guess I should have tried harder to save your uniform." She scowled at the thought and shook her head, making a quick note on her p'link. The mere thought of all the . . . mess yesterday . . . made him feel queasy. He couldn't imagine that his uniform could ever be cleaned.

Jarvie was ready with the food just in time as Lander, Reeder, Iricana, and Oatah came in. Iricana and Lander went right to the pups to admire. Lander studied Sarcee and stroked her head.

Oatah looked tired and worried. Reeder practically hovered over him, but Oatah took no notice. "Have you received a packet from Thunder?" Oatah asked Iricana.

"Thunder?" Jarvie whispered to Katie.

"Her husband," Katie whispered back.

"Not yet," Iricana answered, frowning just slightly. "I don't expect that we'll hear from him before we jump. I've let him know the circumstances."

"She left her husband behind?" Jarvie whispered again. Katie nodded sadly. "Oatah's wife stayed behind too. On Earth."

"Are the rest of you. . ." Jarvie stopped himself, realizing he was asking personal questions.

"Married?" Katie gave him a conspirational wink as they approached the table. "I'm working on it." Jarvie smiled. "Lander's wife passed long ago. And Reeder is single."

Beezan had instructed Jarvie to serve the breakfast. "The Captain will join us for the meeting," he answered when they asked for Beezan. Oatah didn't notice Jarvie's clothes. He hardly noticed Jarvie. Reeder, however, took a long look and frowned.

Every sector had its own style of dress clothes. In sector 7, the Mars culture dominated. A uniform and tool belt were considered acceptable meeting clothes. In all sectors, ship people could get by in their uniforms for most occasions. But these *Thistle* people were dressed in nicer clothes than the day before as if they were going to . . . Jarvie didn't know what. Nothing that fancy happened out here. Oatah and Reeder were dressed even better than the diplomats on the *Sunburst*.

Oatah and Reeder were dubious about the accommodations, hesitating over the chairs, the food, even eyeing the worn napkins. Iricana took one look at the centerpiece and smiled at Katie. *They must know each other fairly well.* Jarvie stayed back unless needed and occasionally peeked in at the pups. Sarcee had moved right over to them so they could nurse. At first Jarvie thought it would turn his stomach, but they were so greedy and noisy about it, he almost laughed instead.

The *Thistle* crew discussed whether overcrowding in Sector 3 would lead to migration to Sector 4 in spite of the fact that it was now cut off from Sector 5. These people knew so much about what was going on in the top levels of Sector operations. He listened intently, eager for any scrap of news about aliens. They talked freely about repairing the a-rings, especially at Firelight. In fact, if he understood the undercurrent of their discussion, it seemed to be that repairing and reuniting the Sectors was one of their *jobs*. A tiny seed of excitement was planted in him.

Finally, breakfast was done, the dishes were cleared, and p'links and s'links came out. Jarvie had alerted Beezan and he came in, greeting people quietly and sitting down. Beezan turned to Jarvie and patted the seat next to him. Jarvie's stomach had a twinge of nervousness, but he took a deep breath and sat down.

Beezan was the essence of calm this morning. He looked like a pilot. Beezan chanted the opening prayer himself. Then, before Oatah could take over the meeting, he started.

"Agent Oatah, I have been relieved of my obligations to Solo Journey." Oatah and Reeder blinked and frowned, probably wondering how a message had come through their block. "We," he nodded in Jarvie's direction, "find ourselves available to take a commission."

There was a moment of quiet surprise around the table. They had obviously expected Beezan to announce his joyful acceptance of commandeering. Oatah did not look pleased, but Lander did. Reeder was considering the angles.

Iricana was the first to speak up. "What is the difference between commandeering and commissioning?"

"Commission means we agree to be hired." Beezan explained. "We take you where you want to go. Your work is confidential, of course. You would be in charge of the mission. I retain command of the ship and crew. We get paid."

"Captain Beezan," Oatah finally spoke. "No one would think you were motivated by greed." *Is that an insult to the ship?* Jarvie scowled.

"I'm not. It's not about pay. Commandeering means I would be a passenger on my own ship. This ship is my life. I would not willingly hand it over. But I will use it in the service of the Sector Council, if that is their desire."

"To answer your question more precisely," Reeder continued, "there is no practical difference. Commission means they volunteer and commandeering means—"

"—you make us do it," Jarvie interrupted, before he could stop himself. Reeder flashed a look of annoyance at Jarvie's plain speaking, but Iricana nodded in understanding, and Beezan kicked him, gently, under the table.

“Captain,” Reeder argued, “no one involved in this team has joined of their own free will. But we all willingly accepted the necessary sacrifices for the good of humanity.” The others suddenly looked embarrassed. Jarvie glanced quickly around the table. It appeared to be true. “Some people here and others in different locations had to be taken into quarantine.” *Quarantine? I knew it!* People were disappearing for knowing too much. Katie glanced away, troubled.

Reeder continued. “My point is that some of us have even sacrificed our homes and time away from families, maybe for life. Surely, you can see your way clear to releasing your ship to Agent Oatah.”

Beezan considered Reeder, but turned to Oatah, “Agent Oatah, what I am offering you is voluntary acceptance. I ask to join your team. I want to know what’s going on. I will take care of the ship and crew so that you can concentrate on your job. I volunteer to take your commission, if necessary, for life.”

There was a beat of silence. Oatah took a tired breath. “You realize Captain, that if I don’t feel full confidence in you—and your crew—” he glanced warningly at Jarvie, “a third option would be to commandeer the ship and leave you here, under supervision, of course.”

Supervision! He means in quarantine! Jarvie felt a great anger welling up inside. He looked over at Beezan who was just looking puzzled.

Suddenly, Jarvie was on his feet, shouting. He didn’t even remember standing up. “If you’re going after the aliens, I’m coming with you! No oath and no ‘quarantine’ will keep me back! That’s what I came out here for!”

The others shrank back in shock. They probably thought he was dangerous. He’d be lucky if they didn’t sedate him and drag him to counseling. But he would talk. They could not stop him and they knew it. Beezan was gazing calmly at Oatah. "Two volunteers, it seems." He touched Jarvie's arm gently and Jarvie collapsed into the chair, covering his face with his hands. This had not been the plan.

As the *Thistle* crew put their heads together to consult, Beezan turned and gave Jarvie a stern look. "No more outbursts. No more yelling at our guests, no matter how they threaten us. You must control your temper!"

"I'm sorry," Jarvie whispered, "I'm sorry." He didn't know what he was doing sometimes. Beezan was more than patient with him. He hid his face from the others, but only Lander noticed.

The others were discussing, in hushed tones. Reeder was still obsessing on the exact difference between the options and saying that commandeering was giving direct command of the ship and crew to Oatah. Commissioning was Oatah paying Beezan to carry out Oatah's orders. They seemed to think it was just a way for Beezan to maintain his "dignity" and still have something to do aboard the *Drumheller*. Jarvie knew better from his monitor training. If commissioned, Beezan would retain control of the *Drumheller* AI. If push came to shove, the ship would answer to Beezan. Oatah was stuck on commandeering, and it didn't seem like anyone else would get to vote.

Lander, who had been silent the whole time, spoke up. "It is easier and safer to pilot under commission." There was total silence in the room. Jarvie wondered if Lander knew that from personal experience.

"Is this an established fact?" asked Iricana.

"Any jumping under duress increases risk significantly," Lander replied.

"Lander!" Reeder was exasperated. "*You* are going to be doing the jumping, not Captain Beezan."

Lander would not be put off. "Without Captain Beezan's willing cooperation, we'll have to put him under. The slightest disturbance can knock the jump off. However, with a supportive co-pilot, the chances of reaching the destination safely are greatly increased. In the case of your intended jump, it may be necessary."

Jarvie's stomach twisted again. Where in the sectors were they planning to jump? He could see Beezan mentally picturing sectors and jumps. Were they going to try something crazy?

"Where?" Beezan simply asked. No one answered.

"Do you concur with that 'disturbance' theory, Captain Beezan?" Oatah asked.

Jarvie had to duck his head again, thinking of their horrible jump to Redrock, all because of him and a microsecond's uncertainty. Jarvie realized he was nodding his head yes. Beezan was too. "It is a journey of body and soul," Beezan added.

All eyes, except Reeder's, were now on Oatah, willing him to decide on commission. Reeder was unwilling to speak against his boss, even just to give an opinion. Oatah was bothered and impatient.

"You realize that I do not have a wealth of resources. I could not pay the going rates for an extended period. I would need to trust you. And I would have to have an open-ended . . . commission." Jarvie bit his lip to keep from smiling.

"We understand," Beezan said calmly. "We would be willing to consider alternate pay."

Oatah made a resigned waving motion at Reeder, who continued for him. "Such as . . ." and they were making a deal! Jarvie snuck a glance at Katie and Iricana. They both had small smiles. Lander looked relieved.

"We need repairs to get this ship anywhere," Beezan said.

"After dock repairs, a multibot maintenance team will travel with us," said Reeder. Beezan's eyes widened, but he had his mental list ready.

"A new fuel converter."

"Done."

"Two more crew."

"Impossible," Iricana cut in. "No more people."

"Jarvie and I can't take care of you all and run the ship."

"Some of us will help you," Reeder claimed. Katie and Iricana raised their eyebrows at that. They gathered that "some of us" would be them.

"Supplies and suits."

"Done."

Beezan hesitated. "We may have some legal entanglements regarding Jarvie."

"Taken care of." Reeder passed an ID card to Jarvie. "Jarvie's former caretaker, who fortunately traveled to Redrock looking for Jarvie, has agreed to release him, under the circumstances."

Jarvie's heart was still pounding from the commandeering scare when he picked up the card. It was dated this morning. Under his name it said "Caretaker: Reeder Benjamin Hamidari." "No," he gasped, trying not to be rude, but it was unthinkable. He showed it to Beezan.

"I think it would be best for everyone if I were Jarvie's caretaker," Beezan said reasonably.

Jarvie nodded quickly. "No offense . . ."

Oatah turned to Beezan, considering, and finally answered in a detached voice, "Jarvie will form a connection between our two groups."

Beezan froze. Even Reeder's eyes went wide. Jarvie was stunned. Oatah would hold him over Beezan. He would be insurance for Beezan's cooperation.

Beezan was now straining to stay calm. "We're talking

about being responsible for a teenager—not a business deal. I don't need a threat to keep an oath!"

Reeder leaped easily enough from surprise to Oatah's way of thinking. "Of course not Captain, you mustn't overreact. It's a method of forming unity of action. Of course, I won't have time to supervise him. I'd appreciate it if you would continue in that capacity," Reeder finished, looking down on his s'link for the next item of business.

Lander, Iricana and Katie looked shocked and annoyed. But they did not object. Oatah was honestly puzzled at their reaction. Jarvie got up and went to the podpup box. He picked up the white one and sat on the deck holding him. If he was going to be handed about like a repair robot he certainly didn't have to sit in the meeting with them. If Reeder left the *Drumheller*, Jarvie would have to go with him. He prayed silently for patience and acceptance and even more fervently, for whatever miracle would keep him with Beezan.

It didn't last much longer. No one spoke now except Reeder, who magically produced a contract that Beezan sullenly signed.

"Captain Beezan," Oatah said warningly, "I need to trust you. You both still need to swear an oath."

Jarvie felt Beezan glance around at him, but he turned away. Then he heard Beezan get up and come over to crouch down by him. Jarvie forced himself not to be angry as Beezan gently took his chin and turned his head to look him in the eye. "Trust me," he whispered. Beezan put the pup away and helped Jarvie stand up, guiding him back to the table. Jarvie felt angry and embarrassed.

Standing by the table, Jarvie put his hand on his heart, but could barely find his voice. *Trust me, Beezan said. I need to trust someone.* "I promise to . . . obey Captain Beezan, to keep all this stuff a secret, and to look for aliens." Oatah grudgingly nodded.

Jarvie was surprised when Beezan put his hand over his heart and then turned to him. “Jarvie, I promise to watch over you and care for you and guard your interests as much as I am able.” Jarvie grabbed onto those words like a last tether hook. He would hang on for his life. “And I promise,” Beezan continued, “to pursue the mission of Agent Oatah, under the direction of the Councils, and to keep it totally secret, until I am released, as God is my Witness.”

Oatah scowled, but nodded. “It will suffice. We must get to work.”

“Yes, Agent Oatah,” Beezan replied. “I only have one more question. Where are we going?”

“Redrock.”

“But what about offloading that cargo?” Beezan asked.

“No longer necessary, Captain. Since you *work* for us, it’s *your* cargo now,” Oatah replied sternly, spinning out of his chair and issuing a torrent of orders so fast that Jarvie could hardly follow. The *Thistle* crew would leave in one hour. *Drumheller* would arrive at Redrock today—without fail. Repairs would start tomorrow. Cargo not belonging to their new mission would be offloaded tomorrow. And the monster would stay.

Jarvie had hoped to have a few moments with Beezan, but Katie was hauling him around by the arm again, giving instructions about the podpups. He tried to concentrate, but his emotions were surging and crashing with every thought. Finally, Katie gave up, snatched his p’link from him and entered the instructions. *Probably with alarms.* “Hold them. Make sure that Beezan holds one, if you want one to bond with him. Three pups are two too many for anybody.” Then she was scurrying.

The others had already run, literally, to secure their cabins and get down to the *Thistle*. It was obvious that if Oatah said one hour, they would be there in 45 minutes. Jarvie started to put the conference table back up, but Beezan came in.

“Leave that, please. I’ve put your suit in the tester. It should be done in minutes. I need you to monitor the tubeway. Don’t be the last one there,” he called over his shoulder as he ran out.

“Yes, honor.” Jarvie went down the rimway to the EVA Bay. He pressed his face against the chamber where the inflated suit was being tested. Three minutes to go. The pop-up listed the repairs Beezan had made. Nothing serious. Changing a sensor in the chest panel and checking seals.

A special gas was in the chamber. If the suit had the slightest leak under pressure, a purple cloud would appear. The sensors would detect it before he would even see it. But it was comforting not to see it. The green light flashed and the suit deflated like a puffed-up person being popped. Jarvie had a sudden thought of Reeder and scolded himself.

Jarvie realized he’d have to suit up by himself and that would make him late, so he just carried the suit and helmet to the lift. Reeder was about to go down, but waited to ride the lift with him. Jarvie hesitated a moment, but he couldn’t politely refuse.

Reeder only had a few bags. They must be leaving some things in their cabins. As the gravity decreased, the suit started to float around in the lift as if coming to life. Reeder spared a glance from his s’link. “I will have a few minutes to assist you with the suit if you like.”

“Thank you,” Jarvie said politely. As he calmed down, he felt ashamed of himself for his outbursts. Now he was determined to be as diplomatic and proper as he knew how. And he *did* know how. Regardless of the fact that he almost died thanks to Reeder. Or that they were holding him over Beezan, passing him around like old luggage. He could even have come up with a pleasant topic of conversation if he'd wanted to, but they were in nogee now and clanging through the coupler. His stomach was adjusting. He needed to concentrate.

Beezan's mind was spinning. He looked around the Command Bay. There were pop-ups everywhere. He didn't know where to start. Too many problems. Problems, people, podpups, pop-ups. Too many. He was just getting used to Jarvie and Sarcee and now his ship would be overrun.

He glanced down at Sarcee's box. The pups were wiggling around and standing a bit. Usually newborn pups could stand right away, but Katie said these two might be a little behind from being so crowded. Sarcee looked up at him so he picked her up and put her in his lap. She snuggled up but didn't say anything.

"Sarcee okay? Sarcee tired?" She didn't even seem to hear him. The doctor had said she was all right, but he had to wonder. She hadn't said a word since the pups were born.

He would have to deal with all these pop-ups, but right now, he just couldn't concentrate on anything except Jarvie and the tubeway. *Jarvie is doing fine. I should stop worrying.* Except that every time he thought Jarvie was getting better, he'd have another bout of yelling or crying or sneakiness.

Beezan had surprised himself by volunteering to be Jarvie's caretaker. He assumed that would be until Jarvie was 20. He had seen a flicker of relief in Reeder's eyes and felt a surge of hope from Jarvie.

Finally, the shuttle was sealed and Jarvie was bracing himself on the hangar deck hold bars and pushing the tubeway back into its closet. Beezan resisted the urge to tell him to take his time. They all had to wait for him to secure the tubeway and leave the hangar before the *Thistle* could take off.

The *Thistle* could be back at Redrock Station and docked in a few hours. Oatah wanted the *Drumheller* at cargo dock 'today.' Well, 'day' ended on Redrock at 1800. Beezan supposed he should be there early just to show how he could jump on Oatah's orders. But it wouldn't happen. They'd be lucky to come in by midnight.

Well, there was one pop-up he could close. Just before leaving, Katie had run into Command, pulled up a pop-up with colors on it and breathlessly asked something about changing the color profile of the *Drumheller*, since it hadn't been updated 'in a couple of centuries.' Beezan had nodded absentmindedly and she was off, leaving the pop-up. Beezan studied it now. It showed three 'identifying' colors: chocolate brown, cream, and 'sky' blue, and two highlights: rose and gold. *Is she planning to decorate?* He groaned and tapped it closed.

Beezan shut his eyes for a few minutes to relax. Then there was an urgent squeaking in the box and Sarcee tensed and stirred. Pups were hungry. Beezan gently put Sarcee back in the box.

"Captain?" came Jarvie's voice.

"Go ahead."

"Tubeway secured. The shuttle is clear. I'm now in the Entry Lounge and the secure light is green." Jarvie's voice sounded steady, but Beezan didn't want to ask about his stomach for fear of putting it on Jarvie's mind.

"Good. Go ahead and suit out."

"Thank you, honor."

"Shuttle *Thistle*?"

"Lander here."

"Opening hangar door."

It was only moments later, and only a few pop-ups dealt with, that there was a tremendous ruckus in the rimway and Jarvie came bursting into the Command Bay. Beezan had a moment of panic before Jarvie exclaimed, "I've thought of the perfect names!"

Beezan's still-spinning mind struggled to catch up to both the meaning and Jarvie's change in mood.

"For the pups!"

"Oh." Beezan turned to the box. All three podpups were wide-eyed with anticipation.

"From *Journey of Our Hearts*, 'Star' and 'Sky'. Only Sky has to be the girl," Jarvie picked her up and rubbed noses with her, "because she is black." He handed her to Beezan. "And he would be Star." Jarvie picked him up more carefully as he was very wiggly.

Then Sarcee gave a whimper and Jarvie handed Star to Beezan too so he could pick up Sarcee. "What do you think, Sarcee? Sky, Star." Jarvie pointed with his chin to each pup. She looked back and forth.

Jarvie tilted his head in puzzlement, looking at Sarcee. "Maybe she's still in shock about being a parent this late in life."

"I can sympathize," Beezan said dryly, and was surprised to hear Jarvie laugh.

"Well," Jarvie leaned over to set Sarcee into Beezan's lap along with the pups and whispered, *to Sarcee?* "Get used to it." Then he was off, with something about bringing lunch. Beezan looked down in his lap to see three pairs of deep black eyes staring up at him.

Sarcee shook her head like a human. "Zharvee . . ."

She spoke! Beezan laughed with relief and hugged all three of them.

20 / APPEARANCES

After lunch and securing the kitchen, stowing the podpups in the jump bed, and strapping up, they were ready to break orbit. Beezan planned to go slowly. No sense wasting fuel zooming and braking. He would creep to Redrock.

Redrock was usually a busy place, but according to the Ship Tracker, traffic was light. Actually, it was almost non-existent. Had Oatah found some excuse to send out every ship? There were only four ships docked at the ring. No ships were listed as incoming. "We don't seem to exist," Beezan commented to Jarvie.

"Hope nobody looks out the window," Jarvie replied sarcastically.

"Probably Oatah has arranged some event to distract everyone," Beezan said. "People won't be watching the Ship Tracker for ships from Mirage until tomorrow." Then Beezan glanced at the names of the ships at docking ring and gasped. "We are listed!" He pointed to the pop-up.

Jarvie read it. "*Drumheller*: arrived 3 Beauty. Berth 4. That's where we would have gone if we hadn't stopped at Second Station."

"Well, that makes sense at least. We were on the incoming Ship Tracker for 19 weeks. I don't think people would forget that. And this way we can be seen out on the docks." Beezan trailed off. It was little, but it was a lie and he didn't like it.

The creeping was tedious, but Beezan had his worries to keep him alert. He glanced over at Jarvie, who was napping in his chair. With teens, worry and sleep could coexist. The sickness was not too bad yet, Jarvie claimed, but Beezan was just as happy that Jarvie slept as much as possible.

At 18:01, Reeder called to ask where the *Drumheller* was. Beezan refrained from pointing out that everyone would know if it was listed correctly on the Ship Tracker. "Three hours yet, from requesting docking permission." Reeder scowled and sent him orders to proceed to Berth 4. They would be first in line for cargo inspection in the morning. As far as Beezan could see, they would be the only ones in line.

Jarvie had stirred and was trying to focus on the big screen. They were passing the main station, looking more like a spinning stack of pancakes than anything else. Beyond it was their destination, the Redrock docking ring. It was a standard quad spoke ring. Sure enough, Berth 4, where the *Drumheller* was supposedly already parked, was empty and waiting.

There were a few businesses for ship crews at the dock. Otherwise, a person had to take a shuttle over to the main station. The docking ring had only a slow spin to keep the temperatures evened out. It wouldn't be enough gravity to help Jarvie. Although Jarvie was all right for the moment, Beezan hoped Katie would find his old medical records and get the right medicine quick.

"It's so empty," Jarvie lamented. "It won't be any fun."

"I don't think Oatah is going to let you run loose on the docks, Jarvie."

He looked so disappointed. "I just want to look around. I won't talk to anyone."

"I know," Beezan commiserated. "You've been stuck here a long time. And I do have business to do. Maybe Oatah will let you come with me." Beezan tried to sound hopeful.

11-Beauty

The next day, Jarvie finished cleaning up lunch while keeping one eye on the Ship Tracker. He had it up on the big kitchen screen so he could watch ships coming in from Mirage.

The *Drumheller* had been docked since late last night. All that fuss to hurry and now they were just sitting around. Jarvie was anxious to get on with business, to find out what their mission was, to get out on the dock, to visit Redrock Station and most of all, to get his new medicine. His stomach twinges reminded him way too much of their miserable run in.

Beezan had gone to the Cargo Control Booth to prepare to unload their regular cargo. Jarvie quickly fed all three pups so he could join him. Just as he was leaving, there was a beep and a name appeared on the Ship Tracker. *Glitterence*, a passenger ship, inbound from Mirage, had just dropped in. They wouldn't arrive for a few days. As the ship arriving closest to the station would appear on the Ship Tracker first, it would take a few more hours for the rest of the jump group to appear.

Jarvie's p'link beeped. "Yes honor?"

"Please meet a crew member at the dock hatch."

Someone was here! "Yes, honor."

"Feel free to use all the formalities you know."

"Yes, honor." He almost laughed. Beezan would faint from

that much formality. He tethered up Sarcee, Star, and Sky and proceeded carefully to the hatch, the three pups floating behind him like an unorganized parade.

He went slowly so they wouldn't tangle and by the time he got there, Katie was making her way toward him with a big load of luggage. He smiled. "God is Most Glorious. Welcome to the *Drumheller*, Doctor."

She braced herself and put a hand up to stop the baggage from running her down. "God is Most Glorious. Thank you, Crew Jarvie."

"May I assist you with your luggage?" he asked most properly. Just then, Star and Sky went swinging wildly toward Katie, sweeping Jarvie into a cartwheel.

Katie laughed, "Thank you, but I think you have your hands full."

They both reorganized and continued up the rimway, but the unexpected move had set off his stomach. "How are you feeling?" Katie asked.

"I, well, I was hoping you might get here soon," he admitted.

"Let's go right to the Med Bay. Most of this stuff is supplies anyway."

Katie told him to wait quietly on the exam bed while she unpacked. He felt guilty for not working, but she insisted he had to be calm for monitoring. He had to strap to keep from drifting away.

"*Drumheller*, Ship Tracker on big screen please."

No more ships yet. "Dock pretty quiet?" he asked Katie.

"A ghost town. Thought I was in Sector 8."

"Are you from there?"

"No, but I did a year of service on Tektite."

"Was it boring?"

"Between terrifying and exhausting it was boring."

"Were you there when—" he realized that that might be too personal of a question.

"When the Sector 9 search group left?" She came to the side of his bed. "No, I was too young. Another failure as far as we know. But it's too soon for a lightspeed message, even if they made it."

Jarvie's sector history book listed 44 official jump groups attempting to open new sectors that were never heard from again. But the book was over 30 years old. "So that makes 53 attempts? In the outer sectors?"

"Yes, and nobody with any sense has any ambition to try again."

"Until they know what's going on with the aliens?"

"They don't know about the aliens, remember?" She cautioned him.

"But it's your job to find out."

"It's *our* job, you mean."

Oh. He had to get used to being on the same side with these people.

Katie started the monitoring. She held up a med patch. "Thanks to Agent Oatah, your medical records were unclassified and released to me. This is what you used as a child. I'm going to keep you here two hours to monitor and then I want you to check with me before bed. No critical operations until I say so." She put the med patch on his left arm. "As a privacy right," she continued in an official voice, "I must inform you that the vital signs monitor, which I'll put on your right arm, has its own transmitter and is keyed to my doctor's s'link. It will report, even from a Tee-Free zone." Then she activated the med patch. He felt a little sting and took a few deep breaths. She fastened a blanket around him and told him to nap a bit. Then she let the podpups off the tether and there was chaos.

Once they were set free, the podpups bounced around wildly. They didn't suffer from space sickness. They squealed, trilled and puffed in their natural language and made a variety of other noises that were purely sound effects for their careening.

"The little ones are catching up on their development pretty fast," Katie mused, capturing Sarcee. "But *you* just had surgery," she scolded. She gave Sarcee a quick check, fed her and tucked her in with Jarvie to rest. Sky finally slowed down and went to sleep in mid air. Star was making a game out of bowling into Sky until Katie rescued her and tucked her in a pocket.

"Trouble in a fur coat, that one," Lander said as he floated up the stairs. He waved off Jarvie's attempt to get up.

"God is Most Glorious. Welcome aboard," Jarvie said, as formally as he could manage strapped to the exam bed.

"God is Most Glorious," Lander replied seriously, coming over to hover by Jarvie's med screen. Katie silently pointed out a few things.

"Did you scan the implants?" Lander asked. *Why are they talking about my implants?*

"I didn't have to; Captain Beezan did, not long ago. They look fine."

Lander was frowning at the screen. Jarvie had a sinking feeling he knew what was coming. Lander turned to look at Jarvie. "I think you understand, Jarvie, that you're not going to be part of the flight crew for jumps." At least he was direct.

"I jumped with Beezan," Jarvie said hopefully.

"You're lucky to be alive. Captain Beezan didn't know how recently you'd been in a fatal jump and how sick you are. But he does now and he won't risk you any more than I will."

"But I didn't even resus, then." Jarvie gave it one last try.

They both nodded sympathetically. "You're just too sick, Jarvie," Katie added. "It's not forever. You have a lot of healing that hasn't been taken care of. But we are going to take care of you now, and part of that healing is taking a break from conscious jumping."

"Yes, doctor. Yes, honor." He sighed to himself. He hadn't really expected otherwise, but he still felt a little lump in his throat. "I understand."

Beep. Jarvie's p'link went off. Katie fished it out of the drawer by the bed and handed it to him. "Yes, honor?"

"Are you medicated yet?" Beezan's asked.

"Yes, honor, but she—the doctor—says no critical ops yet."

"Oh."

Lander spoke up. "May I assist you, Captain?"

"Reeder, *the inspector*, is here and I could use some help in the Cargo Control Booth."

"I am on my way, Captain." Lander used a finger to spin off the bed and head for the stairs.

Then Star smashed into Katie from behind. She scowled.

"Maybe Star could bond with Reeder," Jarvie suggested.

"Can't." Katie responded as if he were serious. "Not if Reeder hopes to go back to Earth someday. They're banned."

"*What?* How is that possible? They practically have the run of outer sectors."

"Ecosystem Recovery Project. Reeder told me all about it. A massive twenty-year effort has successfully restored significant areas, 'in the nick of time.' You can ask Oatah. He was in charge of it. He's a planet-wide hero according to Reeder. Then he was promoted."

"He got promoted from saving Earth?"

"Yes," she said seriously. "Now he has to save the Sectors."

. . .

After his two-hour 'nap' that he spent worrying about the fate of humankind, Jarvie was allowed to go. His stomach was better so he went down to the Cargo Control Booth—leaving the podpups with Katie. He wasn't yet cleared for critical ops, but he could watch.

He also kept an eye on the Ship Tracker. *Dolphin's Daughter, Starweave, Lily of Heaven,* and *Ornament* were added to *Glitterence* as incoming. *Ornament's* lag time was 8 hours. One poor ship was outside the k-belt, so it would probably be the last ship in this group.

All the regular cargo had been unloaded. Beezan was in the hold finishing reloading their original mystery cargo. Jarvie had a sudden knot in his stomach thinking about Beezan out there, untethered, working around the monster. Jarvie snuck a look at Beezan's suit monitor.

"He's coming in soon for a break," Lander noted. Jarvie wasn't quite sure who was in charge here, but decided it would be okay either way. Lander was a master at handling the remote loaders. After reloading the old cargo, they started on a new set of 'mystery' cargo. Apparently, Beezan had insisted on mass checks as there were numbers hastily marked on the sides of the containers. Lander was comparing them to the manifest and making some adjustments.

As soon as Jarvie had asked to watch, Lander began to explain everything he did and why. Jarvie even made a couple of notes on his p'link.

"Where did the new stuff come from?" Jarvie asked.

"Some came with us—Iricana and Katie and me—on a hired ship. Some came off the *Mammoth*, I believe. We're still waiting for one more ship to come in."

"*Mammoth*, we had a close call with them."

Lander checked every little thing before glancing at Jarvie for the merest second. "How close?"

"Scary. An alarm went off. We had to move the ship. Implants were rattling. Bit of damage. Lost a few days."

Lander shook his head. "You had a rough ride in."

"The worst ever," Jarvie agreed, but then didn't want to be a complainer. "It wasn't Captain Beezan's fault. He got us through a lot of bad stuff. Without much help from me," he trailed off.

"You are young and learning. With the Captain's approval, I would be pleased to assist in your training."

"That would be great!" Jarvie nearly launched himself from the chair. He grabbed on and strapped himself. "I mean, thank you, honor." Lander knew so much. It would be a thrill to have him for a teacher. Jarvie wondered how old Lander was.

"Ninety-three."

Jarvie gasped and was about to ask how he knew the question, when another container came in, so Jarvie kept quiet. Instead, he checked the Ship Tracker. It blinked and a new ship appeared, not outside the k-belt, but near the station. *How is that possible?* He looked at the lag time—only four minutes! The time lag depended on how close to Redrock they dropped into normal space. As soon as their beacon was captured, they appeared on the Ship Tracker. A ship with a 4-minute lag time couldn't appear after a ship with an 8-hour lag time, unless it came from somewhere else.

Jarvie looked closer. The screen updated and the ship disappeared. Jarvie blinked and read the whole list. He read it five times. The ship was gone. Was it a mistake? The system was automated. If the signal was captured, the ship was listed. How could there be a mistake?

• • •

Four hours later, Jarvie knocked quietly on the wall by the open door he shared with Beezan. Star and Sky were zooming around his cabin.

"Come in."

Beezan was lying on his bunk, or rather floating just above it, with a soother over his eyes and forehead. He'd spent twelve hours loading cargo and was obviously exhausted. The pups were bouncing off the walls trying to angle toward Beezan.

"Are you all right? Can I get you anything?"

Beezan tilted towards him, waving Jarvie over and shifting the soother to see. "I'll be fine. It was the lights from the cargo carrier. They were so bright and the cargo loader helmet doesn't have an outside visor so it was blinding me. Of course, they couldn't turn their lights off because our lights aren't working."

"Do you want me to fix that tomorrow?" Jarvie asked.

"No, the software and hardware for the fancy robot repair team is being delivered tomorrow. I'll need you to start on that."

"Me?" Jarvie was so excited he did launch himself. Beezan smiled and pulled him back down.

"Oatah sent me a message that Reeder won't have time to manage robots, would I mind taking over? So I am assigning you to be the main manager of the robot repair team."

"Yes, honor!" Jarvie hung onto the bunk this time.

"I hear Iricana is very good with equipment. She might be able to help. And make sure the *Drumheller* supervises the software integration."

"Yes, honor."

"How are the new meds?"

Jarvie smiled. "Good. It's such a relief. I should be cleared for ops tomorrow. And Lander said he would help teach me, if it's all right with you."

"Of course. Maybe he could teach me too. He's amazing."

Jarvie hesitated. There was one troubling thing on his mind.

"What?" Beezan asked. He was getting to be more like a parent.

"A ship appeared on the Incoming, after all the other ships, with a lag time of only four minutes, and then it disappeared."

Beezan looked puzzled. "Well, it's possible a ship came in from another jump point."

"No one else in the outer sectors jumps on the 11th."

Beezan shrugged. "Maybe Sandune or Petrichor just had an unscheduled jump."

"Maybe, but why did it disappear?"

"Who knows? We disappeared from the Ship Tracker and we're still here. I'm sure it's nothing to worry about. Did you catch the name of the ship?"

"*Wheel of Fire.*"

Beezan froze. Maybe it was something to worry about. For a second Jarvie didn't think Beezan was going to tell him. "It's Tiati, my best friend. Last I heard, he was headed for Hamada. Well, I've got the feeling that's where our next load of mystery cargo is going to come from."

Beezan wouldn't say any more. He herded Jarvie, Star, and Sky back to their cabin and told them to sleep. Sky went back to Beezan for a nuzzle and then zoomed ahead to beat Star back to Sarcee, whose moment of rest was about to be over.

Jarvie glanced back to see Beezan floating over his panel frowning at the Ship Tracker.

18-Beauty

Jarvie nodded to himself. Beezan was right. The *Drumheller* was alerted to expect a direct cargo transfer. *Wheel of Fire*, big as life, came in on 15 Beauty and parked in Berth 5, right next to

Drumheller. Reeder must have figured out that Beezan knew Tiati, because he forbid Beezan to talk to him. Reeder went to inspect *Wheel* and more cargo was transferred directly to *Drumheller*. This time Jarvie was allowed to help, with Lander literally hovering over him in the Cargo Control Booth. When they were done, *Wheel* transferred to Berth 12 and suddenly reappeared on the Ship Tracker.

Jarvie learned that one of the docked ships, *Peace in Our Time*, was the ship waiting for the one-way trip to Harbor. It was a relic and should have been retired a hundred years before, so it was not a big loss to the sectors. Thinking about all the people at Harbor, who might never come out, and possibly die of starvation, was so sad. Some of the teens separated from their families had appealed the decision to bar them from returning, but they had lost. Jarvie felt for them. He wondered if any would try to sneak aboard.

Then, for some reason Reeder wouldn't tell them, *Drumheller* was ordered to move to Berth 16. Jarvie didn't see the logic of trying to hide a ship as big as the *Drumheller*.

Although no one besides Beezan had piloted the *Drumheller* for over eight years, Beezan anxiously offered the short flight around the dock to Lander so he could get a feel for the ship. Lander accepted politely. He had been studying *Drumheller* carefully when he wasn't loading cargo.

Lander, Beezan, Jarvie, and Reeder, who had just come aboard, took positions in the Command Bay. Beezan wanted Jarvie to be part of the in-system flight crew and Lander had agreed. Katie and Iricana stayed in the Passenger Lounge. Beezan had assigned Katie as Passenger Monitor for all flights. Oatah would come aboard the ship after they moved.

• • •

Beezan started out the short trip in lip-biting worry and ended it in open-mouthed astonishment. Lander was by lightyears, the best in-system pilot he had ever seen. If he was as good at jumping, they would have no worries.

Lander laughed at Beezan's obvious relief. "Did you think I got to be 93 by crashing up ships?"

Jarvie clapped and asked if they could go around again. Even Reeder was nodding with satisfaction. "It was impossible to allow Lander to retire," Iricana added as she floated into the Command Bay. "We hired him as soon as his teaching contract was up."

"You kids are getting pretty worked up over a simple re-dock," Lander said good-naturedly.

"It's the vision of success to come, Honor Lander," Katie said respectfully. "I think we'll all feel very safe with you and Captain Beezan piloting us."

There was general agreement. Katie was being nice to include him, but the truth was Beezan felt a giant load off his chest, a load that had been there for years. There was someone aboard who actually knew what he was doing. Beezan could ask for advice even if he was the official Captain. He'd be a fool not to.

21 / THE ONE TREE

9-Grandeur

"Supplies for three years?" Jarvie couldn't hide his surprise.

Both Iricana and Reeder nodded. "We don't expect to be gone that long," Reeder explained, "but Agent Oatah makes every effort to protect us."

The three of them hung around the kitchen table making supply lists. They had formed a committee, taking input from the others. They would order from the dock and station stores. Purchases were delivered. "It would be easier to plan if I knew where we were going," Jarvie complained.

"It would not be easier." Reeder instructed. "It would be the same. There is no opportunity for resupply where we are going. We must take everything we might need. You can use the planning programs but you must adjust them for three years."

Jarvie scowled. Everywhere in the outer sectors had a store. Even Tektite.

Iricana knew where they were going, but wouldn't tell. She gave him a 'be patient' pat on the hand. Jarvie noticed, though, that she would sneak in even more than three years' worth if she could. Maybe they were going off the map.

Reeder also ordered supplies that he didn't discuss with the others. Big deliveries came 'space side' and went right into the supply Cargo Hold. It was Jarvie's job everyday to go 'dock side' and collect all the small deliveries from *Drumheller's* receiving bin. Jarvie was actually allowed to leave the *Drumheller* and dive down the gangway to the bin. At first, he was thrilled. He could hover there a few minutes and look up and down the dock. He could breathe in the different smells, listen to the clanks and faraway voices, and watch people from a distance. But if any workers or delivery people came near, he had to go back to the ship.

Soon the daily trips only made him long for more. It was so hard not to just take off. He tried to find good reasons to go out in person. He wanted to check for his packages. Reeder would have them delivered. He needed a custom-made spacesuit. Two were already ordered. He wanted to buy presents. He could order them. He just wanted to look around! He could access the public dock cams to 'look around.'

Even Beezan wasn't allowed to leave unless Reeder went with him. Obviously, that wouldn't be any fun. When Iricana, Katie, or Beezan went out, they always brought him a treat. Even better, they would tell him about their outing, each in their way. Iricana would relate the facts in chronological order, including what they ate. Katie would recall all the sights and sounds, the art, restaurants, and cute things podpups or children did. Beezan told him about a small concert hall and recommended listening on the feed. Privately, Beezan told Jarvie who was out and around, how few people there were, and what sort of things he overheard. Beezan said it had been pointless to send them to the quieter side of the dock. Everyone knew that something was up with *Drumheller* and *Wheel.*

Jarvie still had plenty of chores, more studying than ever, and increased exercise to deal with. Luckily, the robot project qualified as a teen training module, and Iricana had agreed to be his mentor for that. The robot brains were loaded in *Drumheller* where Jarvie could study them, but they were still waiting on the robot parts to be delivered. The bodies were not specific, except for two, the robot manager and the med robot. The others just changed into whatever was needed.

Jarvie shook himself. What did he just miss? Something about Beezan and the garden. "I'm sorry, what?"

"Beezan needs to consult with a garden tech about the trouble with the bamboo garden. And he wants to open up two more sections of the food garden, based on the number of crew and duration of the trip," Iricana explained. "There is a big garden center on Redrock Station, with all the latest technologies. Agent Oatah has cleared the Captain to go there and get whatever we want. We need to make a list of suggestions."

Beezan is cleared to make a trip to Redrock Station, not just the dock? Jarvie wished upon wishes he could go, but he didn't pray for it. But wishes weren't exactly prayers, even if God happened to overhear.

13-Grandeur

Beezan finally got up the nerve to go directly to Oatah's cabin. Usually, they all went to Reeder if they wanted something. They weren't supposed to 'bother' Oatah. Since he was the captain, he hoped he might bother Oatah for just two minutes. Beezan wasn't quite sure what he would be bothering Oatah from anyway. He didn't do any work as far as Beezan could see. He did sit at a screen, but half the time his eyes were closed. Reeder insisted that Oatah was 'beyond brilliant,' that he was 'meditating,' that he 'discovered connections' and that was why he was one of the 'most famous and most loved people on Earth.' Oatah's 'visionary leadership,' in less than thirty years, had put Earth's struggling ecosystem 'back on track.' It was his life's work. It was Oatah that had made several course-changing suggestions, including the ban on podpups, that halted 'near-irreversible damage,' in 'the nick of time,' and 'saved the planet.' It all sounded far-fetched to Beezan, but according to Reeder, Oatah was no less than the hero of Earth.

The cabin door opened and Beezan floated down the stairs.

The hero of Earth floated at his panel, harnessed with the chair strap, with his blanket half wrapped around him and half drifting off. He looked lost and tired. He straightened when he realized it was Beezan. "Captain, what brings you here?"

Not exactly friendly, but he didn't throw him out on sight.

"Agent Oatah, please forgive me for bothering you. I'm here for personal reasons." Oatah nodded quickly. Beezan remembered how fast they talked in the inner sectors and tried to speed up. "I need to go to the gardens on the main station—"

"I have already cleared that."

"Yes. Thank you. What I am asking is to please take Jarvie with me, for the day, for an outing, just the two of us. I'd stay with him every minute." Beezan rushed through the rest, feeling like he was begging. "We've been through a lot on this run and he needs to get out. We haven't had a day off in months. Agent Oatah, we did swear an oath."

"Captain, I trust you, and you seem to appreciate the seriousness of our situation. Jarvie, though, has already shown signs of unreliability."

Beezan couldn't argue with that. He couldn't even testify to great improvement lately.

"However," Oatah went on, "we may be spending years together and we need to mentor Jarvie into a productive role in our group. He is young and unstable, but you are a stabilizing influence. Therefore, that relationship should be encouraged. He is fairly intelligent." *Fairly intelligent?* Beezan would have placed Jarvie at extremely intelligent. *Is everyone on Earth some kind of genius?* "Do you believe he understands how careful we must be?" Oatah asked.

"Agent Oatah, he lied to me under great duress, for a long time, just to cover up the fact that he knew about aliens and was searching for your group. He never told anyone else."

Oatah looked like this was just one more problem for him. "I will consider it, Captain."

"Thank you." Beezan left, but took a worried glance back. Oatah was staring through his screen. He didn't look good. He didn't look like he would survive 'years' on a stressful mission. Beezan noticed a speck of sympathy in his heart for Oatah.

15-Grandeur

It was just before dinner. Jarvie had served all the food, sticking the dishes down, when Beezan casually mentioned that Agent Oatah had given Jarvie a new assignment.

"Yes, honor," Jarvie answered dutifully. *Probably vacuuming out the delivery bin.*

"You will accompany me to Redrock Station to observe the gardens."

Jarvie lost a stack of cups. Luckily, it was nogee. He looked at Beezan, who was smiling mischievously, and then at Oatah, who actually was listening to the people around him.

"I can go?" He snatched the cups and carefully handed them to Iricana.

"As long as you stay with me at all times." Beezan replied with mock sternness.

Oatah nodded to Jarvie.

"Oh, thank you! Thank you!" He was so happy he could have hugged Oatah, but didn't think that would be appreciated. So he hugged Beezan instead, throwing his arms around him. Beezan laughed and grabbed Jarvie, either as a hug or so as not to go spinning off.

"Captain! Really!" Reeder said, more disapprovingly than usual.

"Reeder!" Jarvie heard Katie and Iricana whisper fiercely.

Jarvie let Beezan go, grabbed a hold bar and looked to see what the problem was.

"What happened?" Beezan asked, now serious.

Katie and Iricana were glaring at Reeder. Oatah looked puzzled over their behavior, as usual. Only Lander understood what was happening. "Reeder, your objection is improper and unappreciated."

Reeder's cheeks actually colored a bit. "I'm sorry, it's just a reflex. Your public display of affection—"

"Public!" Beezan objected. "This isn't some dockside restaurant!" Beezan turned to go, but Lander paused him with a gentle hand on his arm.

"I will explain, Captain. Agent Oatah, Reeder, you have come from Earth and traveled on the most formal of passenger ships, but this is a cargo ship, a family ship. There are not separate passenger areas and crew areas. This entire ship is their home, and the kitchen is the heart of it. We may not all feel like family, but family behavior is perfectly acceptable here."

Reeder truly did look embarrassed. Jarvie hadn't thought he

was able to admit the slightest wrong. "I apologize, Captain. I apologize, Jarvie. It won't happen again."

Beezan relaxed. "Thank you. Thank you, Honor Lander."

Jarvie shrugged. He didn't care. He was going to the station! "Anybody hungry?"

"Yes," came five human voices and three louder podpup squeals. Oatah was looking back and forth at the others as if he just figured something out. "The whole immense ship is your home," he repeated.

Then, as they ate, Iricana was telling how on her one visit to Earth she was publicly reprimanded for kissing her sister on the cheek at the shuttle port. "But why?" Jarvie asked. "What does it matter if someone hugs someone?"

"It's not just affection," Iricana explained. "Any display of emotion or behavior seen as attention-seeking: loud music, talking too much on their cell'links. Things are different on Earth."

"Very different," Oatah agreed. "So different, I'm afraid we were not properly prepared to come out here. And once we got to Sector 6 it almost seemed like . . ." Oatah had never volunteered any personal comment before. They hung on his every word. ". . . not just like another culture, but another humanity. So far apart . . . so empty . . . so dark . . . so cold . . . so much death . . ." he trailed off.

Beezan shot a worried glance at Katie. "Reeder mentioned you had many tests on your outbound journey," she commented.

They had eaten slowly and were finishing up when Oatah secured his chopsticks and drew a deep breath. "If a family atmosphere is permitted . . ." They nodded worriedly. Jarvie tensed, then got excited. Maybe Oatah was going to tell them where they were going.

Oatah spoke as if from a great distance away. "We started out from Earth with five; myself, my first assistant of 30 years, my science advisor of 17 years, my niece who is a historian, and my new clerk, Reeder."

Clerk?

"We jumped from S-Tro Base to Sector 2. There were two deaths among the passengers. We were upset. We didn't know them, but we had been led to believe that jumping was fairly safe. There was no reason for the deaths. It just happens, they told us.

"You understand it was our first jump. Most people live their entire lives on Earth. A small percentage may visit the Moon or Mars. A rare few get as far as S-Tro Base, scientists and workers. We are not accustomed to flicking about the stars and tempting fate as you—as are people in the outer sectors."

Jarvie couldn't imagine not even going to the Moon. It was right there.

"So we felt like veterans." Oatah swallowed and continued in a shakier voice. "Then, on the jump to Sector 3 my assistant passed on. No reason, they said. It happens."

Reeder was staring at his plate. Everyone else was frozen.

"So we prayed. We persevered. On the jump to Sector 4, my science advisor, Kerre, died. No reason. It happens." Reeder was sitting next to Oatah, but neither of them offered any comfort or support to the other.

"My niece refused to go on. She may still be in Sector 4. She said she would never jump again, even to return to her family." Oatah was overwhelmed with guilt. "The mission is critical to the future of humanity. I was forced to leave her. Reeder is now my only assistant."

Beezan reached over and squeezed Oatah's arm. Oatah froze in panic, so Beezan let go, but he encouraged him, "Agent

Oatah, someone doesn't die every time. We have every hope of arriving safely. It's not like a sacrifice or something."

But Jarvie heard the hesitation in Beezan's voice. Every pilot had their ghosts, and Beezan had more than his share: all the family, friends, and crew who passed on during jumps, for no reason. It did happen.

Jarvie went to bed with a tangle of feelings. He was truly sorry for Oatah and Reeder. He was annoyed that a clerk was pushing them around and astonished that someone of Reeder's undeniable skill and intelligence was only a clerk. It gave more evidence to how important Oatah was. None of that could compete with his thrill of being allowed off the ship, even if it was only for one day.

Star and Sky were tearing around the cabin. Sarcee had gone to bed with Lander. Jarvie was a little hurt, but couldn't really blame her. He didn't get much sleep with those two. The podpups' tags would allow them to go between Lander's cabin and Jarvie's, in case the pups got hungry. He wouldn't risk putting an all-ship override tag on them. Especially not Star. Who knew what trouble that one could get into?

2-Light

Finally, the day came. Jarvie sailed down the gangway with Beezan and passed the delivery bin. He did a flip to celebrate, even though he still had an empty stomach. It was very early. They had their breakfasts in their packs.

"What did you do with the pups? Beezan asked.

"Sent them into Lander's cabin."

"Wasn't he still asleep?"

"Not for long!"

Beezan shook his head in sympathy.

A delivery tug was approaching. The worker slowed, glancing with a puzzled look at Jarvie. "Mail for your ship, Captain. Should I just put it in the bin?"

"Yes, please," Beezan answered.

Jarvie saw his name on a couple of containers. One had a Harbor tag. Reeder got Jarvie's mail after all.

"You sent mail to yourself?" Beezan asked.

"Well . . . I knew I would be traveling light. I wasn't sure what stops I would make. I sent a box to myself at each station. I guess the Harbor box was held here." Beezan wouldn't like to hear all the details of Jarvie's sneakiness, so he didn't say any more. He wanted it to be a happy day.

They didn't have long to wait at the shuttle dock. Ship crews and dockworkers were already boarding. Beezan stayed apart to 'avoid socializing,' as Reeder had instructed. They boarded, pulling hand over hand. Jarvie glanced at the pilots and noticed a teen, with a blue senior-youth armband, in the pilot's seat.

Beezan stopped at a two-seat spot and let Jarvie swing in front of him to the window. As they stowed and strapped, Jarvie avoided looking at his own armband, once again shrilly accented with a red band. Teens had to wear the thinner red band over their regular armband if they could not be called on for emergency duty. Jarvie was behind in school. He was 'under qualified' and might jeopardize someone's safety. Beezan never made him wear the red band on the *Drumheller*. Iricana had consoled Jarvie that red bands were also used for other reasons, including special assignments. That gave Reeder the idea to put Jarvie on special assignment to Beezan to avoid any possible 'entanglements.' But it didn't really help Jarvie with the embarrassment.

There was so much to look at, he soon forgot about the red band. He could see the reflection of everyone in the window. A group of dockworkers clustered in the back. As they undocked, the lights dimmed and Jarvie could see outside.

Jarvie had been to Redrock Station many times as a child, with his family. He had promised himself not to dwell on that today, to enjoy what he had and not live in the past. He said a prayer for his family. Small memories would pop up, but he tried to think of them as gifts and not wounds.

The stack-of-pancakes look of the huge Redrock Station disappeared as they approached. They were coming in from above the station, to land on top. To dock on Redrock, a shuttle matched speed about halfway from the center of the station and swooped into a groove. Exact speed and position were not necessary. A large clamp would catch on. There were also guide-beams. It was claimed a five-year old could dock on Redrock. Jarvie's father wouldn't let him try until he was ten. That memory filled Jarvie and he let it run through, so he wasn't paying much attention to their current docking.

Suddenly Beezan tensed and clutched the seat. There was a clang and a jolt that sent Jarvie's nerves to instant panic. They had clipped the edge of the groove. The pilot attempted to correct, but tilted back as well as sideways, banging the tail end of the shuttle on the deck. Alarms sounded. Jarvie heard some unfamiliar words from the back of the shuttle, but he was busy fumbling with his breather.

The shuttle was starting to spin out of control in slow motion. The breathers wouldn't help any if they slammed against the station and started venting. Suddenly there was a different feel to their motion, smoother. One part of the spin was corrected and then the other. Then they set right down in the groove. Jarvie felt the thud of the clamp. A calm voice came over the speaker assuring them that there was no serious damage. In the background, Jarvie heard the sound of sobbing. It was the teen pilot.

The shuttle was pulled below deck onto a lower track and then sent through a giant lock. In only a few minutes, it was pressurized and they were safe. Jarvie sat back and breathed a few sighs of relief. They waited another few minutes while everyone repacked breathers and a tech team, also teens, checked the shuttle exterior.

Jarvie was shaking. He couldn't focus on getting his breather packed. Beezan was whispering to him, "Everything's all right now, we're pressurized." Beezan ended up helping with the breather, inconspicuously squeezing Jarvie's arm. "Just sit, we'll get off last." Jarvie tried to relax or at least act relaxed. No one else was so rattled, aside from grumbling and casting nasty looks at the pilot.

Jarvie felt bad for her. He knew what it was like to be a failure in the teen training program. "That was enough adventure for the day," Beezan said, standing up. In the excitement, Jarvie hadn't noticed they had gravity, not a lot, but enough to drop his backpack on his foot.

"Ouch."

"Never pack in nogee," Beezan quoted, laughing. "What all did you put in there?"

"Just my breakfast." Jarvie answered with a sudden hunger.

There was enough gravity to walk, gingerly. Beezan led Jarvie to a rim lift so they could find a place to eat in full gravity. Redrock Station gravity was .95g, just a bit more than aboard the *Drumheller*.

They stopped at the first little bench on the rimway and ate.

Jarvie could not have gone any further on his frayed nerves and empty stomach. Slowly, the food, the rest, the gravity and all the excitement of looking around restored Jarvie's spirits enough and they were on their way to the garden center.

Kelson McNelson? Was that his name? Jarvie couldn't help staring at their garden instructor. He wasn't a lowly tour guide, he was a master. If Lander was 93, this man was 193. If he was wrinkled and gray, he made up for it with non-stop liveliness. He shuffled and skipped. He gleefully gestured and called out the names of every beautiful flower they passed. He was 'pleased as potatoes' to meet them! Jarvie almost dropped his pack again.

Kelson brought them to his office, where an old-fashioned desk and some chairs were wedged between potted seedlings and jars with cuttings. Jarvie failed to dodge a hanging planter and smacked his head. "Sit, sit, before you hurt yourself," Kelson laughed. "Tea is coming. But first, honored Captain, tell me, how is your One Tree?"

Beezan dropped into the chair with a small choking sound, his hand unconsciously going to his heart. He tried to recover. Jarvie could see the word "fine" on the tip of his tongue. But Beezan never lied. Kelson's happy expression sharpened to concern.

Beezan gave a small shake of his head and whispered, "It's gone."

Kelson sat back, sad and surprised. He considered Beezan a moment and then pushed himself up from the desk and ambled to the door. "Come, friends. We can have our tea later."

They walked slowly to the heart of the garden center, a park, and in the heart of the heart, surrounded by serene and prayerful people sitting on benches, was the One Tree of Redrock Station.

"It's so tall!" Jarvie whispered.

"It's ten meters," Kelson said. With a twinkle in his eyes he added, "On Earth, trees can grow 100 meters." When they both looked at him skeptically, he nodded in understanding. "You must go to Earth when this" he waved his wrinkled hand around vaguely, "*sundering* is over. You must see the trees of Earth. It is a pilgrimage of its own. Trees—nature itself—is the language of the Divine. Books and movies don't do them justice. You must stand as witness."

They sat to pray and meditate silently. At length, Beezan exhaled. "I understand the importance of the One Tree. Really. But nine years ago, I had a really bad jump." His voice threatened to break. "Really bad. Everyone died. Even the tree died." Kelson nodded in sympathy. "I," Beezan struggled to continue, "I lost my intended."

Jarvie was stunned. He'd known about the bad jump, but not that Beezan was engaged. He squeezed Beezan's arm as he shakily went on. "I didn't even know the tree died at first. And then I just couldn't . . ."

"I understand, Captain," Kelson said. "A terrible heartbreak. You lost your family." Beezan slumped over, maybe partly in relief. Kelson glanced at Jarvie. "But perhaps it's time to cultivate a new . . . tree."

Wiping his face on his sleeve, Beezan tilted his head to look to the top of the One Tree. "Yes. It's time."

Kelson tapped Beezan's *Drumheller* dinosaur egg ship patch. "Modified Cypress—an ancient tree that goes with the dinosaur theme. Tall and resilient, but you can keep the branches close."

Beezan nodded.

"I'll send a garden tech to restart your bamboo," Kelson said, regaining some of the liveliness in his voice. "Meanwhile Jarvie and I will consult about the food garden. Join us when you like." So Jarvie got up and followed Kelson, leaving Beezan by the One Tree.

Four hours later, Jarvie staggered out of the Garden Center in a daze, hauling two bags of old-fashioned data cards. He felt like Kelson had tried to load all those instructions directly into his brain. Beezan, now full of tea and calm, had been right behind him, but Kelson had held him back just as they were leaving.

When they were finally free in the rimway, Jarvie asked Beezan what Kelson had said. Beezan smiled. "He reminded me that string beans need a guide pole to grow, even in space."

"String beans? Did we order those?" Jarvie sat down in a fluster to reorganize his bags full of d-cards. "Incubation, Temperature Regulation, Light Sources, Delivery, Nutrients, Gravity Simulation, Filters, Atmosphere Exchange, Pollinators, Pests, Emergencies, Sustainability, Acceleration Protection, Varieties." Jarvie grabbed the last few without reading them and stuffed them in. "I don't even know what we ordered."

Beezan kept smiling his amused smile and ruffled Jarvie's hair, not even caring that they were in public. "He really liked you," Beezan commented. "Maybe you reminded him of his youth."

"*YOU* would remind him of his youth!" Jarvie retorted. Beezan was really laughing now, urging Jarvie up and along the rimway.

"Lunch," Beezan said, and something about feeding the string beans.

"What?" Jarvie asked, but got a tug on his arm for an answer.

. . .

Jarvie was pleased when Beezan took him to a nice restaurant, with actual human servers. They had a beautiful view of the planet. Pretty but poisonous. The swirling bands of gas changed color, but it was the window filter changing. Different filters would show different details of the belts and zones.

The lunch of the day was spinach mushroom gnocchi. Jarvie ate two servings it was so good. Then Beezan ordered more sent to the ship with their deliveries, so the others could have it for dinner.

They went shopping and sightseeing all afternoon. If Jarvie froze now and then while a memory flowed over him, Beezan would stop and wait with patience and understanding. Beezan might have had a couple of memories himself. Jarvie was able to buy a few things. Beezan had kindly given him a slider, a generous one. It was probably a sacrifice for Beezan. However, Jarvie found he was able to access his own account, thanks to Oatah clearing his legal issues. Beezan would stay near enough for Reeder's sake, but far enough to give Jarvie a little privacy. They had everything sent to the ship. Jarvie even managed to stick most of the d-cards in one package so he wouldn't have to lug them around.

By dinner, Jarvie was getting tired, but Reeder had agreed to let them stay for the evening. Beezan steered Jarvie past any popular teen locations, "Reeder's orders!" and found a toddler-friendly restaurant, lively enough to wake anyone up. They had a light meal—well, Beezan did. Jarvie was starving.

Then they went to a live performance of Beethoven's *Ninth*. Jarvie recalled it was one of the pieces Beezan played along with during his practice sessions.

Jarvie was starting to feel a little sad that their special day was almost over. It had been a happy day. The day and the magical symphony brought a sense of rest to Jarvie's heart. He could have fun again. If there was pain in his life, there was also joy. He even remembered to turn to God with thanks and not just with troubles.

It is the wish of our heavenly Father that every heart should rejoice and be filled with happiness, that we should live together in felicity and joy.[1]

By the time Beezan boarded the return shuttle, Jarvie was slowing down. Did he need to be fed again? When the shuttle made the roll to dock at the ring, Jarvie winced and rubbed his shoulder. *Good, the medicine kicked in.*

As they disembarked, last, they glanced into the shuttle's Command Bay. The same teen pilot, smiling this time, was being congratulated by her instructor.

"I'm glad I didn't know," Jarvie whispered.

Beezan wasn't too surprised to find Reeder waiting at the dock for them. "Everything all right?"

"Yes, Captain. The doctor thought crew Jarvie might be asleep, so I came to assist you." He politely took Beezan's pack and then Jarvie's. They worked their way back. "Was your trip satisfactory?"

"Very," said Beezan and even smiled at Reeder.

Jarvie was so glad he had said his long prayer that morning. He tossed his pack in the closet. Someone had stowed his mail containers already. Then he zipped himself in his bag without even changing his clothes. He was exhausted. The voice of

Kelson McNelson was starting to form rhymes in his mind. He could sleep now though.

Then his door slid open. He groaned as he heard the gleeful sounds of two podpups bumping around and Lander's gentle laughter, "Good night, Jarvie."

22 / *BRANCHING OUT*

3-Light

The next morning, Beezan got his breakfast and joined the crew, hooking in next to Jarvie while the pups floated over their food bins.

"Have you told them about Kelson McNelson yet?" Beezan asked Jarvie.

"No, I was just saying we visited the One Tree."

"Ahh," Lander nodded in approval. "So you learned about Honor Kelson, the founder of the One Tree movement?"

Beezan looked up, stunned. *Founder? He's the founder?*

Jarvie shared an embarrassed glance with him, saying, "Right. So you know who he is?"

"Of course," Reeder scoffed. "Everyone does."

"He's an inspirational force in the outer sectors," Iricana added.

"He was the mentor of my mentor," Oatah said. "I wish I could have met him before he left Earth."

"Oh, yeah, he did seem Earthborn," Jarvie said.

"Wait—you *met* him?" Reeder asked.

"Kelson McNelson is *here*?" Oatah asked, zeroing in on Jarvie.

Beezan slowly nodded while Jarvie answered. "He was our garden instructor yesterday."

"What a blessing," Katie said.

"Wait," Reeder said again. "You just stumbled into a meeting with Kelson McNelson?"

"Reeder!" Katie hissed.

"No," Beezan said, with a hint of Captain's voice. "I don't think Honor Kelson does anything by accident. He was also very kind to us," he finished with a stern look towards Reeder.

Jarvie nodded. "Also funny. And a little intense. And he had sayings."

Lander laughed. "That's the Kelson I know."

Reeder and Oatah's heads whipped around. "*You* know him?" Reeder demanded.

"A lot of people know him," Iricana said calmly. He taught at various universities for many—*many*—years."

"He thinks plants and trees are what connect us to Earth and to our humanity," Jarvie explained

"Trees are powerful symbols and metaphors, and they have been throughout history," Iricana said. "Not to mention being the core of the ecosystem."

"If he was obsessed with trees," Jarvie asked "why did he leave Earth? There aren't any trees out here. Unless you count, you know, the One Trees."

Beezan swallowed, chagrined. Did Oatah even notice that the *Drumheller* didn't have a One Tree? All ships were supposed to. He grabbed the table and rotated slightly to see Oatah better, but he was staring off. "I wonder how he can stand it," Oatah murmured. "Out here alone. So far from Earth. No trees. No green."

"Honor," Iricana said, patting him on the arm.

"Reeder," Oatah said, "Send my most humble greetings to Honor Kelson and request an appointment."

"Yes, Agent Oatah."

Oatah took a deep breath and addressed the rest of them. "If we can fit it in the schedule, Captain, I'd like to meet in the Consultation Hall after breakfast."

"Of course, Agent Oatah," Beezan answered with a thrill of anticipation. Finally! They would find out where they were going.

Beezan and the others tethered to chairs around the consultation table while the podpups played off to one side. Jarvie hung a net up so they wouldn't bother the meeting.

Oatah asked Lander for a prayer, but Beezan couldn't concentrate. He was distracted by two rolled-up maps in Reeder's hand. After the prayer, Reeder smoothed one out and they clipped it down to keep it from floating away. Aside from notes about attempted jumps and damaged a-rings, it was an ordinary sector map.

Reeder pointed to the map, and started in with his schoolmaster tone. "You are all aware of the a-ring accidents at Luminesse, Firelight, Hamada, and now Harbor. We believe someone, or something, is attempting to jump into our space. They may not even know we are here. They may be blind jumping as humans sometimes do. All the accidents have happened on jump days, while our ships were in the rings. This suggests they have a way of detecting active rings. As far as we *know*, there have been no successful arrivals.

"Debris indicates that these ships are alien. From what evidence we have, the material and design are different than any known human ships or any projected designs of a separated branch of humanity."

Lander very properly raised his hand.

"Yes, Lander?" Reeder asked.

"Do we have any evidence of a separated human colony surviving?"

Reeder turned to Iricana. "Not a shred," she answered, pausing her note taking.

"Some debris from the accident at Hamada," Reeder continued, "has apparently been transferred to a hangar at a classified location by Thayne's team. Remaining bigger pieces were shipped on the *Drumheller* for delivery to Harbor. More came on *Wheel of Fire* as you've probably surmised."

"Are you saying that our mystery cargo is pieces of an alien ship?" Beezan asked.

"Yes, Captain," Reeder answered, as if it was just a minor detail. "All the remaining alien cargo is now aboard the *Drumheller*."

"So you *do* know what that big container is." Beezan said, frowning.

They all frowned in return. "Well, no. We assume it is part of the debris, but it was only listed as 'container #189: Thayne.' We'll take it out to the secret hangar and open it."

As if that were of no consequence, Reeder rolled out an overlay for the map. Beezan held his breath. It took him a few moments to decipher the new details. From Harbor to a new star, Reeder drew a line with his finger and stopped.

"Nocturne. That's a code name of course. According to Iricana, the former Project Restore leader, Thayne, has already jumped there and back twice. He should be there now, for the third time, waiting for the rest of the cargo."

"They're waiting since when?" Jarvie asked.

"As far as we know, since Sovereignty, just before Harbor went down. We can't confirm of course, but they were planning to wait a year if necessary."

"A year!" Beezan said. "Agent Oatah, how long have you been in charge of this operation?"

"I was given authority to take over from Thayne when I came out from Sector 1. However," he continued, "I do not understand why they are collecting the debris at a secret hangar when we have a very expensive Outer Sector Research Institute at Harbor."

Beezan studied the map. "That's a long, long jump from Harbor to Nocturne. If Lander is here, who is your other long jump pilot?"

There was a beat of silence. Then Reeder said, "Lanezi."

"Humph!" Jarvie nodded.

Beezan glared at Reeder. "There really *is* a secret group. *You* are the secret group and Lanezi is part of it. Just like Jarvie has been telling me."

Reeder frowned. "It is not so melodramatic. Project Restore was established by Sector 6 Council. Project Contact, with Iricana in charge, was established by Sector 5 Council. Both missions must remain quiet to keep people from panicking. And of course, Agent Oatah is now in charge of both."

Beezan glanced at Iricana. She didn't seem bothered about Oatah taking over. Would this Thayne take it as well?

"Lanezi is waiting for you?" Jarvie asked, and Beezan could hear the hope in his voice.

"Yes," Katie said, smiling. "You'll see him when we get to Nocturne."

Jarvie's smile faded as he looked at the map. "But we can't, Harbor is down. We can't jump from there."

"We are going to jump from here," Oatah said quietly.

Beezan suddenly felt sick. *What in God's Name did I agree to?* The jump from Harbor was long and they had made it, with an exceptional pilot. Lander was exceptional too, but from Redrock? "That's crazy!" Beezan blurted.

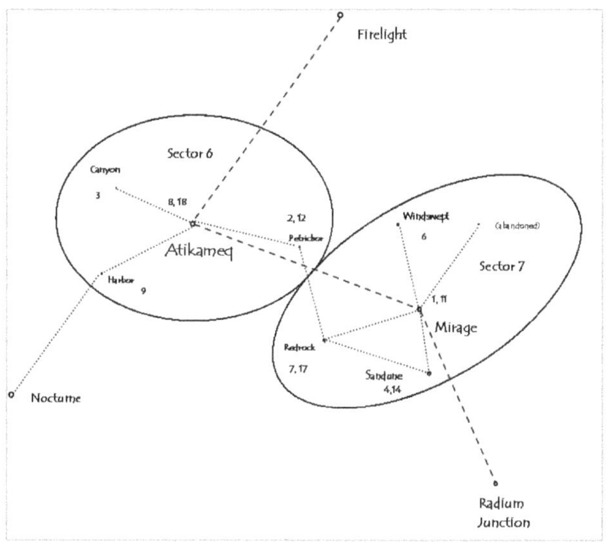

"Lander says he can do it," Reeder replied.

Beezan had every respect for Lander, but it was impossible. Beezan glanced at the others, who all looked uneasy. Except Lander. He was nodding serenely. "The stars are similar to Sandune and Petrichor, a jump which I have made many times." *That's not an official route!* "With your calm support, Captain, it should not be a problem."

Beezan was breathing hard. He was looking at the star types and distances. He recalled every jump from Redrock he had ever made. Had he ever felt a tug from that direction? From that kind of star? He didn't think so.

"Why do we have to go there?" Jarvie asked. "Why can't we just hide this stuff behind a moon somewhere?"

"Thayne started that secret base before my team joined

him," Iricana was explaining, "and we're really not sure why, but now we must go there to warn Lanezi and Thayne not to jump back to Harbor."

Oatah added, "It was not in the mandate from Sector 6 to establish a secret base. All work, including experiments with a-ring building, was to be done at OSRI, the research center at Harbor. I was sent to determine what is really going on here, and unfortunately, Iricana has been unable to adequately explain Thayne's logic. I fear his motives must remain suspect." Iricana frowned, but nodded.

Beezan was stunned. *Building a-rings?*

"We'd also like to determine", continued Reeder, "how Thayne proposed to reassemble alien ships when no one has ever seen one. The pictures from the accidents at Hamada and Harbor show the alien ships surrounded by energy fields. Then they explode. There are no pictures from Firelight and no one has had a good look at the actual intact ships."

"Lanezi and I saw a ship. The field disappeared, just for a second, before the explosion." Jarvie commented. "There'd be pictures from the *Sunburst.*"

There was dead silence. All heads turned to Jarvie. Beezan didn't understand why. He'd already told them he knew about the aliens.

"Lanezi was watching the Nav pop-up at the time," Iricana explained carefully, "and the main camera was scanning the outbound route. If an assignment camera was on the alien ship it wasn't recording."

"Oh," Jarvie swallowed, glancing at Beezan. "I guess I turned the recorder off so no one would know I was awake and watching. Sorry." He hid his face again.

Oatah focused on Jarvie. "Are you saying you saw the intact alien vessel, without the glowing field?"

"Well, yes. I didn't see it for long, and it was moving fast, and I was scared and confused . . ."

"Of course," Katie soothed.

They continued to stare at him. "Any little thing you could tell us would help, but you don't have to tell us now," Iricana added as Katie shot her a concerned look.

Jarvie pulled out his p'link and tapped it on the screen. A picture appeared, a smudgy drawing, vague. "That's what I saw," Jarvie said, "just a round ship. It had colorful designs. I tried to draw them as well as I could remember."

They stared. An eerie feeling descended on the room. "He is the only eye-witness," Katie breathed.

"It was providential that we all came together," Oatah added. They all looked at Jarvie in a new light, but Jarvie looked scared again.

Then they stared at the picture of the ship. Beezan could only concentrate on the map. Redrock to Nocturne. It was more than a long jump. "Maybe we should leave Jarvie here."

"No!" Jarvie objected.

"It's a desperation jump."

"No!" Jarvie repeated, eyes filling with tears. "You promised!"

"I promised to take care of you, not kill you!"

"I don't care if I die!"

"Jarvie, that's the problem. You're not strongly attached to this world. You'd be the first to go. If we survive, we can pick you up on our way back."

"No!" Jarvie was starting to panic. "I want to find them. I'll hire another ship! I'll tell! You'll have to take me—or—"

"Enough," Oatah said, more forcefully than Beezan had ever heard. "He comes. He is connected. We may need him. And he would cause no end of trouble if we left him."

Beezan was shaking. They could all be going to their deaths. Lander came over by him and put a hand on his shoulder. He talked to him gently as Beezan sometimes talked to Jarvie. "Captain, I'll tell you what I know for a truth. People die in desperation jumps because they think they are supposed to. Much longer jumps are possible. I have done several. We can get there in one piece."

Oatah had ordered it but the others were waiting for Beezan to agree. "Would you want to be left behind?" Iricana asked sympathetically.

Jarvie looked like Beezan had betrayed him. Beezan felt defeated. "I could stay behind with Jarvie. I'll keep him out of trouble. You can have the ship." Beezan couldn't believe the words were coming out of his mouth.

They were all shaking their heads. "We need you both," Oatah said.

"Besides, you can't keep me out of trouble," Jarvie insisted.

Beezan pressed his hands against his head. "All right. God forgive me if anything happens to you, any of you."

There was a sense of relief, but Beezan now knew how hard the future would be. Lander said another prayer. Just as he finished, Sky came wiggling under the net and launched herself to Beezan, who caught her. Then Sky turned around and gave the others a good long stare.

23 / OFF THE MAP

6-Light

Timeline to Nocturne jump: 11 Days.

Beezan dismissed the nagging timeline pop-up, but it hovered in his mind. In eleven days, they were going on a crazy long jump to a secret base with a cargo of alien wreckage. The worry of it distracted him from his rows of pop-ups. One screen showed the repair crew on the hull. Others displayed the repair list, Cargo Hold activity, clearance checklist, engine inspection, compliance issues, and today's schedule. The screens terraced up from Beezan in arcs of colored rectangles, some with real time cam, most with the slowly-shortening lists that drove his life.

Drumheller had to leave Redrock dock in seven days to get to the a-rings in time. When he had been coming in weightless, with Jarvie sick, seven days was like an eternity. Now that everything had to be ready for an untried jump, seven days was a panic countdown. Oatah was insisting though, and Reeder kept the repair people running day and night. Beezan could hardly sleep with the screeching and banging on the hull, scaring him out of his nightmares. His heart was constantly pounding.

On one of the screens, Beezan could see Lander, with his little shadow, Sarcee, managing cargo delivery. *God bless him.* When Lander wasn't doing cargo, he joined Beezan in the Command Bay studying *Drumheller*. Every other night Lander came to Beezan's cabin and coached him in long jumps. They studied stars and resonance paths and went over the mental imagery involved. They prayed and meditated together. At first Beezan was shy and awkward, but Lander was a deeply compassionate person, full of wisdom and vision. Beezan felt a strong bond forming between them, and it was the only thing giving him any confidence now.

Every day, he ate his breakfast and lunch in a rush, but made a point to eat dinner with the crew, for camaraderie, as Katie had insisted. She also insisted they all be called *the crew*, rather than Oatah's team, Iricana's group and the *Drumheller* crew. For unity. Beezan had to admit, she was right and he should have been the one to do the insisting.

Katie suddenly floated into the Command Bay with a package, startling him. "It's time, Captain."

"Sorry, time for what?"

She let go of the package so it floated in front of him. "New uniforms. Picture in the Hygiene Bay in 20 minutes." She smiled and floated back down the rimway. He looked at all his screens and sighed.

Back in his cabin, he pulled on the uniform, chocolate brown with "sky-blue" trim. It was beautifully made, warm, soft, fit perfectly, had pockets, and a flap on the chest that unfolded into a podpup pocket. There was a fuzzy collar that could be pulled up to keep his neck warm.

Now he knew why Katie had asked about the color scheme.

He put his *Drumheller* pin on the front yoke and went hand over hand down to the Hy Bay. Just inside, he stopped, grabbed the edge of the door, and stared. The whole crew was there. In matching uniforms. *On a cargo ship.*

He, Lander, Oatah, and Iricana, the senior crew, wore chocolate brown uniforms with blue trim. Jarvie, Katie, and Reeder wore sky-blue uniforms with brown trim. On the right front and left sleeve everyone had *Drumheller* patches—a dinosaur egg on a rocky nest with the blue-sky background.

They had gathered in front of the only big mirror in Arc 1. Jarvie was thrilled. "It fits! I love it so much. Thank you doctor!"

"You all look—" Beezan almost choked up, "amazing."

"Like a crew!" Jarvie said, and high-fived Lander, knocking them both backwards. "Like a crew!" The others repeated, even Oatah, nodding.

Katie handed Beezan a little blue collar. "Pups too." Sarcee and Star were excited, but hard to corral, for their collars. But Sky came right to Beezan for hers. Then she sailed over to the mirror to check it out.

"Picture!" Katie announced, so they huddled together and *Drumheller* took their picture. And then they went back to work. But Beezan's heart wasn't pounding so hard anymore.

17-Light

In the passenger lounge, Jarvie was putting on his bravest act. The fact that his knees were shaking was a great annoyance. He was chilly, of course, from floating around in his g-suit.

Katie, as passenger monitor, was assisting Oatah first. Jarvie had stowed Star and Sky with Sarcee in the podpup jump bed in the Command Bay. He'd given each excited pup a little hug. When Beezan had told the pups it was jump day, the two little ones had bounced all over. The crew had laughed heartily, even Reeder and Oatah. They needed that laugh. The stress and pressure of the last ten days had been crushing. Jarvie didn't have the worst of it. He had mostly tried to help the others and stay out of the way.

Jarvie noticed last night Beezan and Lander had stayed in the Prayer Room all night. This morning they were like long jump pilots. It was strange, now that Jarvie was used to Beezan's everyday self, to see him so detached and serene. After prayers, Beezan spoke to all of them, reassuring them and giving Jarvie a hug. Now, Beezan, Lander, and Reeder were all business in the Command Bay.

In the passenger lounge, Oatah was sealed in his cocoon, resus pack on, brackets on and helmet ready. Passengers were put under before the jump prayers, so Jarvie whispered a few extra prayers while he had the chance.

Katie came to help Iricana, but she waved her on to Jarvie. Probably because he was practically hyperventilating for some reason. "I'm not scared," he breathlessly told Katie, annoyed and embarrassed.

"It's just the stress of it all," she soothed, helping him glide into the cocoon. She checked his resus pack and secured the brackets before sealing him in. He wasn't scared, but his whole body was shaking and tears were building up in his eyes.

"Take deep breaths. All this emotion is a lot for a teen." Katie told him while she finished with his helmet and called Beezan. "Is it too early to put the crew under? Some are a bit stressed."

"Go ahead, Doctor."

"Thank you, Captain."

He wasn't really ready. He wasn't scared. He could just . . . a familiar flowing feeling went from his head to his feet. He took a big breath and all that panicky fluster went away. He was going under. Jarvie looked up at Katie. "You're all right," she said. "See you on the other side." She put his visor down. And he began to fade. He'd soon be at Nocturne—or in heaven.

Seven more laps. The pain had already built up. Beezan felt his ribs break—the same ones that had broken when he was smashed in the door. He had a surge of pain and feared that his lung would be punctured under the increasing pressure.

He banished it from his mind. He had one job: staying in sync with Lander. He could feel Lander's spirit; strong and focused, blazing ahead like a comet.

Five more laps. His body was moaning with every surge and bump. He toggled through to the passenger screen. Four alive and well. Katie was showing some stress, as she was awake. He toggled it off. Reeder had the option of putting himself under if it got too bad, but he was still conscious. Beezan shut that off. He was down to one screen, the tactical of the approach angle to Nocturne. The other ships had jumped on the previous lap. *Drumheller* had one more lap to head the right direction. They were accelerating harder than Beezan ever had. Since the other ships were out of the way, they could go as fast as they wanted. Lander used the steering jets almost continuously now. He was flying the huge ship like an ambulance shuttle. Beezan would never have tried it, but Lander kept the *Drumheller* rock-solid in the rings as if it were on rails.

Beezan started to open his mind to the feel of the stars. The pain faded away with the rest of the material world. Breathing never totally faded away. Beezan wasn't getting much oxygen. He felt the pumps increase and tried to take bigger breaths, but it was too much weight. His ribs were throbbing with pain. He started to fade. *No! Just hold on. I must see the path.*

Three more surges. Beezan sucked in as much air as he could. He counted down the surges and bumps. Three, two, one. *Finally*. They shot out of the rings in a straight line toward Nocturne. Now it was up to Lander to find the path. Beezan cast his mind about.

Nothing.

Stay calm. Remember all those practice sessions. He stayed with Lander, trying to focus. Lander said the thread would be green. Beezan circled his mind around and caught a glimpse of something, a tendril. *Yes! A thread*. But it wasn't green. *There's another!* And suddenly, now that his mind could see them, there were tens, hundreds. Pathways to the stars. He had never seen more than a few at a time. Now, they beckoned in all directions, in green, yellow, blue, orange, and colors Beezan could not name. Beezan forgot his pain, forgot his fear, and forgot to breathe. The galaxy was before him and he froze in wonder.

Lander was heading toward a thread, a green one, and thicker. Beezan could feel it now, the pull of Nocturne. He threw his mind behind, following the comet that was Lander. Lander set them up and fired the main thrust. The acceleration squashed Beezan flat. Unbearable pain crushed him. The comet exploded into a million pieces. *Lander!* Then he felt the sting of the jump drug. They were crossing.

"We need Jarvie!" Katie yelled from the Command Bay.

"He's coming around," Iricana answered from right near him.

Jarvie was wheezing in panic. It's *Drumheller*, he repeated to himself. Nocturne. Not *Sunburst*, not Luminesse. *Drumheller*, Nocturne.

Katie's voice was desperately urgent. Iricana was tense but

efficient. She pulled the helmet off Jarvie. He moaned. The pain was expected, but it was compounded with grief. Images flashed back to him.

"Lander's gone," he choked.

Iricana glanced toward the Command Bay, where Katie was. "He says Lander's gone," Iricana relayed.

"Yes," Katie replied.

"Beezan?" Jarvie asked. He couldn't remember anything more. Everything was so vague.

"He's alive, but I need to get him to Med Bay, quickly," Katie shouted. Then Jarvie was tearing out of the cocoon, shoving brackets into Iricana's hands. He launched across the passenger lounge and wheeled into the Command Bay.

Lander: blinking-red light. A groan escaped Jarvie. Images of red lights cascaded through his mind. Too many.

Beezan: yellow light. Katie had unsealed the helmet and cocoon, but left the resus pack hooked up. Jarvie grabbed his shoulder.

"Careful, broken ribs." Jarvie let go and glanced at Reeder. Green light.

"Jarvie, we're wild. I'll take care of him, just get the doors open for me and then take care of the ship." She pulled Beezan out of the open cocoon.

Jarvie quickly opened up the podpup bed and reached for Star's tag. He popped it off and froze. They were so subdued. "Sarcee." She was gone. Her body floated peacefully in the corner. Sky was by it. *No time.*

Katie had tears in her eyes. Jarvie pressed the door tag into her hand.

"*Drumheller!*"

"I am here."

"Recode all doors from Command Bay to Med Bay to Star's door code. Start up here," Jarvie ordered.

"Recoding doors."

As Katie took Beezan out, maneuvering with her legs, Sky launched herself toward them and clung to Beezan.

"*Drumheller*, do we have the beacon?"

"Searching for beacon."

"Do we have the star?"

"Searching for star #A809147."

Jarvie opened pop-ups to look in all directions. He had to wipe his eyes to see. He scanned them quickly. There was something bright. He touched the screen but no coordinates flashed. "Is that the star?"

There was a delay as *Drumheller* located his touch and recalculated. **"A809147 located."** The coordinate system snapped into place.

Iricana came in with Oatah. He was pale and looked sick. They slowly moved to Lander's side and bowed their heads.

"Are we inside or outside the orbit of Nocturne's planet?" Jarvie asked, holding his breath.

"Outside."

He let it out, relieved. "Search along predicted orbital path for the beacon."

"Searching."

Now Drumheller would search for planets, then the moon called Nocturne, then the beacon left by Thayne and Lanezi.

Jarvie turned to the others. "This may take a while."

"Are we safe?" Oatah asked.

Jarvie studied more pop-ups. "The projectile field is up. We're not near any obvious hazards." Jarvie shrugged and then grabbed a handhold. Space was never exactly safe, and they were going so fast.

Oatah barely glanced at Reeder and did not ask about him. Slowly Iricana and Oatah cared for Lander. Jarvie popped off Reeder's helmet, unsealed the cocoon, removed the resus pack, and stowed them. Finally, he turned back to Star, who was hovering beside Sarcee. Steeling himself, he gently took Sarcee, hands trembling on her cold stiff body. She had died with Lander, he realized. They would go to heaven together. Jarvie hugged her and cried softly while Star clutched his arm.

Iricana and Oatah freed Lander's body to take him to the Med Bay. Jarvie gently put Sarcee on Lander's chest, hooking her with one of Lander's tethers.

"I'll be right back to help you," Iricana reassured him. Part of him wanted to go with them to the Med Bay. But Jarvie remembered the passengers taking over the *Sunburst* and shook his head. *No one is going to take the Drumheller from Beezan while I'm alive.*

"I'll take care of the ship," he said firmly. Iricana nodded at him.

"Beacon located."

Oatah hesitated.

"Calculate inbound program," Jarvie ordered.

"We must hurry," Iricana said to Oatah and they took Lander with as much dignity as they could in nogee. Jarvie made sure Reeder was strapped, yanked off the last of his own medical monitors, pulled on his uniform, stuffed Star inside the flap, and strapped himself in the fourth Command Bay chair.

"Course corrections required. Please select."

Jarvie studied them. They would have to go easy. "Doctor, how long before we can burn?" he asked over his s'link.

"At least 20 minutes."

Meanwhile, Jarvie focused on the area of the beacon, trying to pick up any possible packets. They were not far, thank God.

Yes thank You thank You for saving Beezan. He stopped to say a few prayers, chastising himself for waiting this long. He was so sad to lose Sarcee, the last member of his family, and Lander too, as he had really liked him. *Beezan will be heartbroken over another loss.* But Jarvie could go on as long as Beezan lived, and he had to take care of these people.

A first-scan picture was forming of their destination: a planet: beautiful turquoise gas giant, with several large moons. Small moons, any secret hangar, and Lanezi's ship would be too small to see yet.

Iricana would have to stow the bodies in the Med Bay cold vault and help Katie. It would be more than twenty minutes. Jarvie got up, made sure everything was stowed, checked the Passenger Lounge, and returned, checking Reeder again.

Reeder's eyes opened in slits. He did not groan or cry. "Just stay there," Jarvie said. "We're going to be boosting in a few minutes."

"Agent Oatah?" he asked calmly.

"He's fine." Jarvie took a deep breath, but his voice shook anyway. "We lost Lander."

Reeder gasped. "No. That can't be. We need Lander." Suddenly, Reeder was more alarmed. "Captain Beezan?"

"Injured." Jarvie tried to sound calm, but his stomach was in knots with worry.

"Jarvie," came Katie's voice over the s'link. "He's going to be all right. The Captain has three broken ribs, a punctured lung and some other minor problems. I need to keep him here, but he will recover."

"Thank you." A big knot untied. "Can we boost?"

"We're still securing. I'll call you."

Iricana finally returned. She greeted Reeder with relief. "We put them together," she told Jarvie.

"Them?" asked Reeder.

"Sarcee passed on," she told him.

"Oh, the mother. I'm sorry," he said to Jarvie, glancing at Star's nose poking out of Jarvie's uniform. "What about the black one?"

"Clutching Beezan," Iricana answered. "She won't leave him. Katie had to strap her to his ankle to do the testing."

"We're secure," Katie reported. "Beezan, Sky, Oatah, and I are strapped on exam beds in go position. We have a green light at the door."

"Thank you," Jarvie answered. Iricana took Beezan's chair and strapped.

"All crew," he announced, not even trying to use his professional voice, "we're going to do a 47 minute burn at .6g followed by a series of short burns." He sat back.

"*Drumheller*, option 1. Proceed."

"Stand by for burn in 30 seconds."

"ETA after burn?"

"Three days, 7.2 hours."

Then the burn began and Jarvie was pressed back in the chair. He had nothing to do for 47 minutes but hug Star and let the tears roll back. He wished he had the calmness to pray aloud as Beezan did. Then Iricana was gently and quietly praying.

Jarvie checked into the Med Bay, saw the bodies had been taken to the cold vault and Beezan was strapped to the exam bed, unconscious. He fled, going back to the Command Bay, spun up the ship, and checked their approach to the black moon Nocturne. Iricana brought him his dinner, but he had no stomach for it. “No beacon,” he whispered to her.

“From *Cheetah*? Lag time should only be a few seconds.”

He hesitated to drop more bad news on top of the deaths, but Reeder would be here any minute demanding answers. “They’re not here.”

She froze, then sat down in the pilot 2 chair and studied all the screens Jarvie had up. “We left a repeater at the hangar.”

He pointed to a screen. “Yes. I’ve got the hangar beacon and the repeater. Nothing. *Drumheller* tested the repeater and it’s working.”

“My God.” She slumped in the chair. “Not here. No signal. That means . . .”

“If they left on 9 Sovereignty, and we still don’t have a

signal, that's at least 21 weeks lag time. If they actually jumped here . . ." Jarvie trailed off.

Her pale skin went white. "They're over 5 years out!"

"That's what *Drumheller* calculated. Minimum."

"The known record for survival is 3 years," she whispered.

Jarvie nodded his head. "Let's hope they're still at Harbor." He'd barely survived his 17-week run with Beezan. Five years? Sometimes ships did disappear, assumed lost too far from their target star. He hoped Lanezi didn't face that fate.

Then Reeder marched in. "Why haven't you reported on the *Cheetah*?"

"I was just about to tell you. They're not here."

"You must be mistaken. Let me check."

"Reeder," Iricana scowled. "That's not necess—"

But rather than sit in the nav chair, he tapped Jarvie's shoulder presumptuously, so Jarvie hauled himself out of the pilot 1 chair and moved over. Iricana closed her eyes and meditated, and Jarvie rolled his eyes and silently fumed for half an hour while Reeder repeated all the work Jarvie had done, and quizzed the *Drumheller*. "They're not here."

Well, we're all agreed then.

"They must still be at Harbor," Reeder said.

"They were supposed to leave on 9 Sovereignty."

"Wouldn't they have sent a message if they didn't?" Reeder asked.

"Yes, but if it was at the last minute, that packet may have gone out on 9 Dominion," Iricana said.

"The day of the Harbor accident," Jarvie explained.

Jarvie could see that as painful as it was, Iricana wasn't one to dodge logic. She continued, "So either they're stranded in the deep, or they were destroyed in the Harbor accident, or, best case, they're stuck at Harbor."

"Our mission will be compromised without Thayne," Reeder said.

"Our people may be dead, or facing a long death," Iricana said, scowling at him. "I'll talk to Katie."

19-Light

Two days later, they huddled in the Med Bay, at the conference table, struggling to eat in their sorrow. When Jarvie and Beezan had troubles, they stayed in the kitchen, but now the crew congregated in the Med Bay. Katie stood guard over Beezan and Sky, but since the Lanezi news, she didn't participate much in their consultations. Reeder kept glancing over his shoulder at the cold vault where the bodies were. Oatah was planning how to proceed with the mission.

Iricana sat with Jarvie, helping him go over all the things that had to be done, what the options were, listing the variables and possible outcomes. With her calm assistance, Jarvie was able to make the everyday decisions about the ship, that were, by default, his responsibility. Waves of sadness and jump depression would come and go. Jarvie struggled not to cry. He tried to act as grown-up as he could. Katie struggled too, but then she would focus on her patients and distract herself. Oatah's tears streamed down his cheeks, seemingly unnoticed. Iricana would stumble for words occasionally and pause for a few deep breaths. Beezan cried in his sleep, or his trance, or whatever it was. Sometimes tears of sorrow, sometimes tears of joy. *Where is he?* Only Reeder never cried. He was as impatient and irritated as before, but now there was a sense of desperation about him.

They had come to the hard part of the consultation,

Lander's body. The one-hour travel time for the burial that was so strictly upheld on Earth couldn't be enforced for jump deaths. People usually traveled an hour or two before anyone knew they were dead—and then there was nowhere to bury them.

This upset Oatah and Reeder, who felt guilty about it. The others explained that the bodies were brought in and buried at the local burial site—sometimes on a planet or major moon, but usually on a small moon or asteroid that had been tagged as a burial spot.

There was no such place at Nocturne. Iricana, who was facilitating the consultation, finalized the two options, to hold Lander's body until they returned, or to find a moon and bury him. Immediate burial was preferable in keeping with the spirit of the law, but in their situation, it was also dangerous.

Oatah had not decided how long they would stay at Nocturne, but if they were waiting for Lanezi, there was no point staying at all. However, Katie didn't think Beezan would be ready to jump for 12 weeks. They avoided the major worry on all their minds. If Beezan did not know the way back, they might never get home. Jarvie wondered if Oatah's boss, if he had one, knew where they were. Would anyone ever come to rescue them?

"Did you check the moons as I instructed?" Reeder demanded of Jarvie.

"Yes," Jarvie answered, ignoring his tone. Jarvie had already put the planet/moon system up on the big screen. They all looked at it.

"What are the usual requirements for a burial place?" Iricana asked.

"Apparently, safe, and visible from the station, if possible,"

Jarvie answered, "but there's no station and we can't really determine how safe it is unless we do a long study and make a landing."

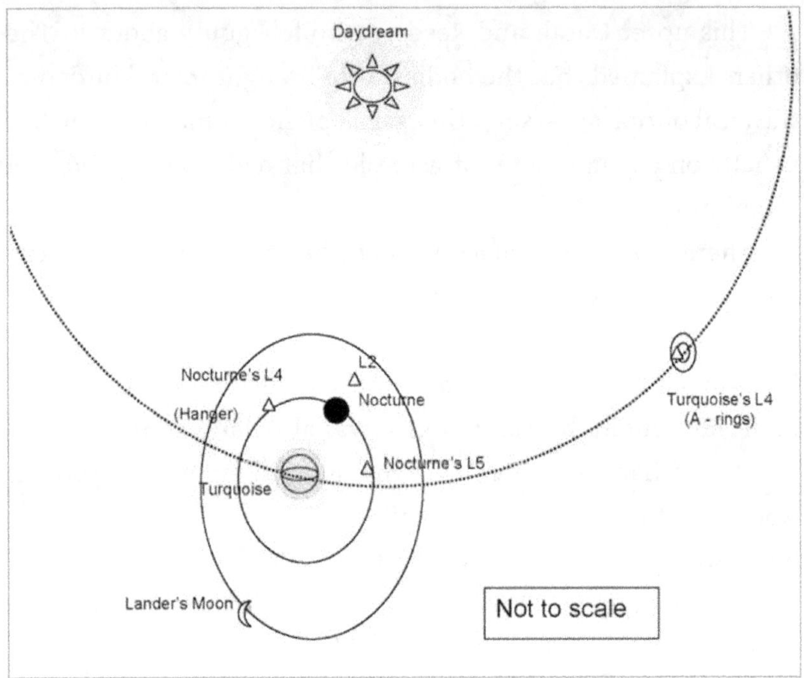

"Do any moons look safe enough?" Oatah asked.

"There are some more distant moons, further from the radiation of the planet, big enough to use the shuttle."

"What would the process be?" asked Iricana.

"We need someone who can pilot the shuttle. We'd need to take a construction robot to cut a . . . place," Jarvie faltered. "We'd need two people to manage the . . . casket, so probably three of us would have to go. They'd have to be able to function in suits in very low gee." Jarvie had barely paused when Oatah spoke.

"Reeder can pilot the shuttle and command the mission."

Reeder nodded, satisfied. Jarvie was taken by surprise. He didn't feel that they had all agreed to this course of action. "It will be dangerous," he insisted, but the others were in favor of burial.

"I'll go," Katie said quietly.

Iricana tensed. "Beezan can't go, Oatah—" he shook his head. "Oatah can't go. The third would be Jarvie or myself."

"I'll go," Jarvie volunteered.

Katie frowned. "I fear you are young, and have a tendency toward space sickness."

"The new meds work fine. I have experience outside and I could be the backup pilot."

They all stared. "You can fly a shuttle?" Reeder asked skeptically.

Jarvie tried to keep the annoyance out of his voice. "I was supposed to be a pilot once."

Iricana patted his shoulder. "Perhaps you will be. But I'm afraid we can't send you without Captain Beezan's permission and he is still unconscious."

"Ridiculous," Reeder said to several raised eyebrows. "I'm his legal caretaker. Now, which one of you operates the robots better?"

Jarvie was dumbstruck at his careless attitude and rude talk. Was that normal for the Earthborn? Iricana either ignored it or didn't even register it. She was taking the question seriously. "We each studied different configurations. It would depend on which one we choose. And," she let off a little flash of blue eyes at Reeder, "Beezan must give his permission for *his crew* to go."

Reeder impatiently picked a moon, one that was in easy

shuttle range, and Oatah ordered it. "You understand you're risking half the crew, your only doctor, and one of the shuttles," Jarvie persisted.

Reeder was more and more irritable. "I understand that all this teen training is about doing what needed to be done, even if it involves some sacrifice. If you are too scared to go, just say so and someone more—"

"Reeder!" Iricana admonished. Even Oatah looked Reeder's way and frowned.

"Someone *else* will take your place," he finished.

Jarvie had to hold his breath a moment. He had promised himself he wouldn't shout at these people, no matter how senseless they were. "I am scared. If you're not scared, you don't fully understand the difficulties involved. But I'd be just as scared sitting around here watching!"

Iricana put a hand on his arm. "Let's configure the robot."

2-Mercy

Beezan's mind wandered. He had the nagging feeling he was supposed to be doing something, but it was so far away. The resonance of Redrock / Nocturne vibrated in his bones. He could see the colors of the neighboring stars. He could hear their harmonies. He knew the stars now, as he never had. Lander had given him a great gift.

A wave of sorrow lapped over him. Lander was gone. He had let himself get attached to another person, and now he was gone. *How many times?* Yet, there was still someone . . .

Sometimes, Beezan's focus would shift to his physical environment. He was safe. He felt the protective presence of his healer. He felt the troubled one, the distant one, and the reasonable one. The wild two, one big and one small, would come and go, leaving a wake of emotions. Beezan tried to communicate with them, but he couldn't find his voice. *Wait. There's one more.* A small desperate life was clinging to him, searching for his spirit, keening in a voice almost like the stars, calling him, calling . . .

"Are we losing him, doctor?" the troubled one asked anxiously.

"Shhh, he can hear," she whispered and then continued in a normal voice. "He is not leaving us; he's just taking his time coming back."

"Can't you make that podpup be quiet? It's probably driving him crazy."

"Reeder, I know you're worried. Sky is bonded to him now. This keening may be a form of healing or comfort that we don't understand."

"He's been out for three days. That's not normal!" His voice began to rise.

"Reeder, come, sit." They moved away, but Beezan could still hear them. *Reeder, Katie, Sky*. Beezan was starting to snag the right words out of his brain.

"It's not normal, but I've heard it does happen after a pilot's first long jump. They call it wandering. You know, *'All who wander are not lost.'*"

A voice came over the s'link. "All crew, one hour until orbital injection. Please secure."

Who is that? Beezan's mind latched onto a puzzle. Who could be in charge? Lander gone, the others in here. Except the wild ones . . . *Jarvie!* "Jarvie?" He tried to sit, wincing in pain against restraints. His head fell back. Gravity. His eyes opened and then squinted against the bright lights.

He was suddenly surrounded by smiling people. "Jarvie's fine, Captain," Katie reassured him, misunderstanding his outburst. She turned down the lights.

"Whose voice was that?" Beezan struggled to speak.

"That's Jarvie, Captain," Iricana explained. Beezan's heart started to race. A huge weight settled on his chest. He was on a secret mission. The wild one was piloting *Drumheller*. Jarvie. He's only . . .

"Fourteen," Beezan said out loud. They looked puzzled. "He's only fourteen, you know."

"Yes, Captain," Iricana continued. "We know. He's coping. We're providing stability and support, but he will be relieved to talk to you." She smiled. Beezan looked from one face to another. Katie was smiling with tears in her eyes. Oatah was nodding as if all was going according to plan. Reeder looked tense.

Orbital injection? "We're there?"

"Coming in," Iricana answered.

"How long have I been out?" he asked Katie.

"Three days." *Three days!*

"The *Cheetah?*"

They all frowned. Iricana answered reluctantly. "There is no ship."

"We're alone out here?" His heart was in his throat. He could hardly choke out the question.

They all nodded grimly. Reeder cleared his throat. "Captain, we'd all feel better if you could say that you know the way back." The others frowned at Reeder, but glanced hopefully at Beezan.

Beezan blinked, confused. He knew the way anywhere. "Yes, I know the way." They all smiled with relief. The way was etched in his mind. He was drifting again. He closed his eyes. That weight on his chest started to wiggle. Sky. He tried to reach her, but couldn't figure out how to move his arm. "I know all the ways," he mumbled, slipping away again.

4-Mercy

Jarvie pulled himself silently along the deck and suddenly poked his head under the bunk. "Puff!" he said to Star, imitating podpup sounds. Star squealed with pleasure and scampered to another hiding place. Jarvie rested on the deck, wondering if he was getting his nice uniform dirty and reminding himself that he was supposed to be saying his morning prayers.

He had not been going to the Prayer Room lately. He was sad about Sarcee, but the others were so broken up about Lander—and in Katie's case, Lanezi—that he had to hide his relief that Beezan was alive and going to be well. And he had a gut feeling that Lanezi was fine. He tried to be respectful and subdued when around the crew, but secretly he played happily with Star when he had a few moments. It was good for Star, after all.

"Jarvie?" Katie's voice suddenly sounded over the s'link.

He started, half in surprise and half in guilt.

"Yes, Doctor?"

"Sorry to disturb you, but I think you'd like to come to Med Bay." There was a smile in her voice and Jarvie gasped as he heard Beezan's voice in the background.

"He's awake?" Jarvie asked, jumping to his feet. "Star, come on." He scooped up the pup.

Jarvie was up the stairs, out the door and running. Star squirmed in excitement. He did slow down as he burst into Med Bay, but Katie jumped into a defensive position blocking him from Beezan and ordering, “No hugging! You’ll break his ribs again!”

Beezan shot a defiant look at Katie and nodded to Jarvie to sit next to him on the exam bed. Beezan was sitting up, one arm strapped to his side and the other holding Sky’s bottle as she sat in his lap, taking only small gulps between burying her head in his sleeping clothes.

As Jarvie sat down gingerly, Beezan’s defiant look disappeared and he went back to the dreamy look. Jarvie wondered if he was medicated. Very slowly and gently Jarvie put his arms around Beezan and patted him with exaggerated care, just to aggravate the doctor, but she smiled. Then Beezan, with his head lowered, turned his dark eyes, somehow deeper and more mysterious than before, to Jarvie, and Jarvie’s heart skipped a beat. Beezan had a secret. Beezan was sad, but exhilarated. He knew something that he hadn’t told the others and wasn’t going to. It was all Jarvie could do to let go, and not hug Beezan harder and risk a rib cracking. He swallowed and looked down, adjusting his seating on the bed, while trying to collect himself. *What could it be?*

“Sky?” Came a strange little voice. Everyone’s heads whipped around to Star.

“He spoke!” Iricana exclaimed. Aside from demanding food, they had not yet said anything in human words.

Star was looking at Sky, wide-eyed with worry. Katie came close and patted Star. “Sky better.” Star still looked concerned. “They don’t understand much at this age. Sky wasn’t eating on her own—I know, whoever heard of a podpup not eating? I had to force feed her once a day.” She grimaced. “It wasn’t exactly dignified.”

Jarvie moved Star over by Sky so he could nuzzle her. Sky was less tense, so Katie had Beezan lay down with both pups next to him, on his good side. Another bottle was produced for Star and the room was filled with happy slurping.

"This is really making me hungry," Beezan complained.

"I'll get some food," Jarvie volunteered, but Katie held up her hand.

"I'll get it. He needs to start easy. I think Iricana wants to talk to you anyway."

Jarvie was uneasy after Katie left. Oatah and Reeder were near them at the big table going over something. He sat at the panel where Iricana was working. "The day after tomorrow, we're going to wash the body," Iricana said quietly. Jarvie tensed. "We—I mean the adults will wash—"

"Maybe he should help," Reeder interrupted from the table. "He's big enough to manage the body and has experience."

A wave of space sick feeling came over Jarvie and he clutched the edge of the panel. "I don't have any experience," he whispered in desperation. As much as he liked Lander and wanted to do his duty, he did not think he was ready for this.

"What about your family?" Reeder asked bluntly.

Jarvie saw Iricana's hand clench into a fist in her lap, but her voice was as reasonable as ever. "He is too young. He did not assist with his family. If he wishes to participate, he can help spin the casket." She turned to the panel and continued as if Reeder had never spoken. Jarvie barely followed what she was saying. Something about the machine that made the guided crystal casket and how it worked and how he could sit with her and help form it around Lander's and Sarcee's bodies. As she went on and Reeder did not protest, Jarvie breathed a quiet sigh of relief.

"How did you know?" he whispered.

She stopped her instruction, blinking in confusion.

"About my parents." He could barely speak. "I don't-I don't even know who washed . . ."

She slid her hand over his on the panel, where Reeder couldn't see. "I can tell you." He nodded. "Lanezi, of course, along with two of the surviving passengers. Also, the station commander and station medical personnel. All nine members of the Council helped with other passengers and crew. There were many volunteers. Your family members were heroes." She squeezed his hand while he bit his lip and struggled not to cry.

"Which reminds me, Captain," she continued quietly, changing the subject slightly, "we haven't been able to find any burial rings."

"Sorry," Beezan mumbled. "In my cabin. Back of the closet . . . little red box." He fell asleep again.

"Would you mind getting one?" Iricana asked Jarvie.

Grateful for a job to do, Jarvie escaped the Med Bay and hurried back to his cabin. He got to Beezan's cabin through the adjoining door and found the box right away. It was bigger than he expected, and covered with red velvet. It had a gold latch, but no lock. Popping it opened, he gasped. It was originally a box of twenty. *Twenty burial rings.* And there were only eleven left.

The reality of Beezan's life as a pilot, of his losses and grief, came crashing down on Jarvie. He suddenly understood what the appeal of working alone might have been for Beezan. No more loved ones to lose. *No wonder he was so reluctant to take me. And now he's lost Lander.* As Jarvie looked in the box, he noticed a little handwritten name and date in each empty spot. Trembling, he turned the box sideways to read them. Grandfather Koji – 1055. *Beezan's grandfather.* Cerab – 1057, Sinal – 1058, Forrest – 1060, Dani – 1062. Nurita - 1073 was in especially shaky writing. And there were three names with that same date as Nurita, nine years ago. That was the day Beezan had talked about with Kelson. So sad. So many deaths, even the One Tree. But none since. Beezan's long solo mission had spared him the agony of more deaths.

Jarvie sat down and stared at the box. The sobs that had threatened to well up and consume him ebbed away. Beezan had suffered so much, maybe not all at once, as Jarvie had, but year after year. He'd separated himself from other people, but in the end went back to the people, and the loss, and somehow didn't regret it. Jarvie remembered the look in Beezan's eyes, that secret joy. Was it that he suffered another death and survived, or was there something more?

Setting the box down carefully, Jarvie pulled out the next ring. Beezan had gone in order, so he did too, but was happy the next one was a beautiful emerald green color. It was wrapped in a little protector, but Jarvie could read it, ***"I came forth from God, and return unto Him, detached from all save Him, holding fast to His Name, the Merciful, the Compassionate."***[1]

Jarvie swallowed. He felt a spirit of peace wash over him. One day he would return to God. He would go when it was his time. Right now, he had work to do in the world. Closing the ring in his hand, he shut the box without writing anything and put it away. He was just going back through the adjoining door when Beezan's door opened and Katie came flying down the stairs with Beezan's s'link in hand.

"What's wrong?" He asked, his newfound peace being tested.

She stopped, "Nothing. I . . . Beezan woke up and said not to let you get the ring."

"Oh," Jarvie said awkwardly. "I already got it."

"Oh, well, he didn't say why," she shrugged and started back up the stairs, so Jarvie followed her. As they approached the Prayer Room, he slowed down.

"Do you need me?" he asked.

Katie looked at him closely. "We always need you, but there's time for prayers."

"Thank you," he said, for both, as he handed over the ring and went into the Prayer Room.

25 / LANDER'S MOON

7-Mercy

Jarvie stood tensely, waiting for the end of the prayer for the departed. It was much scarier on the burial moon than he expected. The moon was not so small as to be a giant potato rock. It was a real moon, round and covered with icy gray rubble. They'd landed in a clearing surrounded by penitentes—tall ice spikes that stood like ghostly guards of this new graveyard.

Although usually warm in the suit, he felt the cold creeping up from his feet. The ground seemed to shift, but it was hard to tell in the low gravity. They were almost done. Katie was reciting the prayer for the dead in a frightened, but determined voice.

"We all, verily, bow down before God.

"We all, verily, bow down before God.

"We all, verily, bow down before God."[1]

Jarvie held his tether for reassurance, but he could barely feel it through the thick gloves. It was even hard to stand still.

Every little move in the low gravity tilted him wildly. He could see Reeder gripping his tether and trying not to bounce around. The long spiky shadows of the penitentes did not help keep him oriented. The moon was orbiting fast, about to swing around the night side of the planet. Jarvie could imagine the dark coming, and they must be back in the shuttle, *Cricket*, before it caught them. He couldn't follow the logic of risking their lives to say the prayer out here, but Reeder was in charge.

"We all, verily, give praise unto God.

"We all, verily, give praise unto God."[2]

As soon as Katie was done, Jarvie would say the shortest possible prayer for Sarcee and they could go. He'd lost count of the nineteen repetitions. He wanted to pray for Lander but his mind bounced from the moon to flashbacks of his family's funeral and back to the spooky moon.

There was some kind of vibration. Jarvie glanced down to check the robot they had used to cut the grave. They'd already covered the casket, so the robot was in standby mode. Jarvie put his glove on it to see if it was shaking, but it wasn't just the robot. Everything was shaking. The vibration was growing.

Suddenly, the *Mammoth* and their close call flashed into his mind. He whirled around and started back to the shuttle without a second thought. "Come," he yelled over the suit link, interrupting the prayer.

Katie stopped. "What's happening?"

Jarvie couldn't look back. Before he could even answer, Beezan's voice came over the s'link, "Return to the shuttle! Incoming vessel. Resonance waves! Return to the *Cricket!* HURRY!"

Jarvie reached the shuttle, loped over the outrigger and pressed the door code. It took forever. Then he had to use his override code to force open the inner door without closing the outer door. A blast of misted ice flew out as moist air in the shuttle froze and the shuttle depressurized. Unhooking his tether, he bounded inside and hit the opposite wall. They wouldn't need to pressurize to take off. He staggered to the controls, took the engines off standby, and prepped for emergency take-off.

What is taking them so long? The buzzing was getting louder and starting to rattle his implants. Beezan was repeating to take off as soon as they were all aboard. Reeder was finally coming in the lock. He forgot his tether. Jarvie found his voice. "Katie, unhook the tethers!"

Reeder got to the pilot seat and swung in. "To me," he ordered and Jarvie reluctantly relinquished control.

Katie was in, struggling to pull two long tethers clear of the door. Finally, the outer door shut. "Go!" she yelled, still struggling with the inner lock.

The vibration was rattling the shuttle. Pain was building up in Jarvie's implants. He tried to pull up the outriggers but they were buried in the ice. He had to use the release jets to melt them out. "Now!" He told Reeder, who started thrusting straight up, but just then, the shuttle tipped slightly. Reeder let off the thrust and they fell back down, squishing into the newly melted and quickly refreezing surface. "Don't go straight up! Up and forward!" Jarvie shouted, forgetting who was in charge. If they could not thrust without tipping, they would wreck the shuttle. If the resonance waves of the incoming ship actually cracked or melted more ice, and they were trapped . . .

"Again!" Reeder ordered.

Jarvie blasted the outriggers free again and realized he had dual controls. As Reeder thrusted and they started to tip again, Jarvie adjusted by firing only one outrigger jet. *How much fuel is in these things?*

"Good!" Reeder exclaimed, grasping immediately what Jarvie was doing. Ignoring the panicked calls from the *Drumheller*, they worked in unison to free themselves of the moon's gravity, barely skimming over the tops of the penitentes.

"That's it!" Reeder called. Jarvie was only momentarily relieved. They still had to make the rendezvous burn, but Reeder was taking care of it. The vibration in his head was becoming so painful, much worse than he remembered from the *Mammoth*.

"*Drumheller* confirms you are on intercept," Iricana's voice announced tensely.

Katie, still trying to wrestle the tethers into the locker, answered her, "Jarvie's implants are hurting him. Jarvie! We're not pressurized! Hands off your helmet!" She was using her command voice, but Jarvie was scratching at the sides of his helmet and banging his head against the seat. He had to use all his willpower not to rip off the helmet and grab his ringing head. Then two space-suited arms reached over and grabbed his hands.

It was so much stronger than the *Mammoth*. *How close was the ship?* Jarvie faded into semi-consciousness, concentrating only on breathing and holding the side of the helmet. Finally, the pain faded to a pounding and then a mere pulsing and then it was gone. He took some breaths to steady himself. "It stopped," he told Katie. Tears were welling up in his eyes and floating around in his helmet. He had to shake his head not to breathe them in.

"Reeder?" Katie was asking.

"I have no pain," he said as if annoyed. Like all this had been an inconvenience.

Jarvie would have been mad if he had time. He was too busy checking the controls. Reeder was bringing them in just fine. He put an assignment camera on the moon to take a few last pictures.

The view forward was impressive as they came upon the *Drumheller*. Jarvie could see where the particles had recently hit the hull. How long ago that seemed. And now Sarcee was gone, without even a prayer at her burial.

Jarvie started to shake. He needed food, air without teardrops in it, and gravity. After landing, they did a quick secure of the shuttle. No one had come to do the tubeway, so they used the deck holds to work their way across the hangar. Finally, they got through the pressurized lock.

No one was in the Entry Lounge. They yanked off their helmets and gloves and floated free, just trying to drain off a little tension. Jarvie, self-conscious, wiped his face. He couldn't help but notice that Reeder had no tears. If all were well, certainly one of the crew would have come to help them. Jarvie exchanged a worried glance with Katie.

"Let's go," Reeder commanded.

The three of them got in the lift. Jarvie's head and neck ached. Katie gave him a little pat on the shoulder when Reeder wasn't looking. As they transitioned through the coupler and headed for the rim, Jarvie's suit got very heavy. His knees were very weak and a little hysterical feeling ran around in his stomach.

As they emerged from the lift, Iricana came running down the rimway, looking more anxious than Jarvie had ever seen her. She grabbed Katie and hugged her. "Katie, I thought . . ." She was about to cry, but pulled herself together.

"Beezan?" Jarvie asked in alarm.

"He's coming around. Very rattled. Was unconscious for a few minutes. I just left him in Med Bay; we have to get back there." She herded them along, holding Katie by the arm, but throwing worried glances at all three of them. Jarvie ignored his pounding head, and clumped on to Med Bay and to Beezan's bedside.

There was an awful keening in the Med Bay and Beezan was wincing. "Please, get these restraints off me!" he said.

Iricana jumped and rushed to him. "I'm sorry, Captain, I'm so sorry, you were unconscious."

Reeder stood helplessly with his hands over his ears as if Sky's keening was the worst thing yet. Jarvie released the pups from their box and Sky scrambled for Beezan, only stopping her noise after burying herself in his arm.

"Jarvie," Beezan staggered off the bed and caught him in an awkward one-armed, podpup and suit-squished hug.

"I'm okay. Shaky," Jarvie said. "Very shaky." Beezan's anger must have been tied to his worry over Jarvie, as it was already gone.

"Let me help you." With his one good arm, and Sky balanced on his shoulder, Beezan helped Jarvie out of his suit, while Iricana fussed over Katie. Jarvie tried not to look like he noticed that Reeder had no one to help him, no one to worry over him, and no one that came running.

Jarvie leaned over to pull off the top of the suit and nearly fainted from the pain in his head. He dropped to his knees. Then Star, who had taken a few wild laps around the room before greeting Jarvie, jumped onto the back of Jarvie's head. "Ahhh!" He fell to the deck, vision going white.

"Scan," Katie said, running to the exam bed in her suit underwear. Beezan pulled Jarvie up and steered him to the bed.

"Star! Easy!" Iricana commanded and amazingly, he stopped in his tracks and sat, whining up at Beezan. Beezan helped pull the rest of the suit off Jarvie, picked up Star and set him by Jarvie's arm. The pain was really getting too much. He groaned as Katie slid the headpiece over him.

Beezan gasped as Jarvie passed out.

"Does your head hurt?" Katie demanded of Beezan.

"A little, not much since the resonance waves stopped. Why is Jarvie worse than I am?" Beezan asked, feeling a new panic rising.

"Don't know. The implants are designed to help pilots detect resonance waves—they're not meant to be in the wake. It really happens so rarely." She frowned at the scan as lines of yellow and red formed around the implant areas on each side of Jarvie's head. Iricana forced Katie into a sweater as she stood and watched. When the whole scan was done, Katie was staring at it grimly.

"Doctor?" Beezan asked, trying not to sound as anguished as he felt.

"This scan does not match the one you did, Captain. The implants are different."

"How could that be?"

She paused. "I don't know. I'll have to check the files. His implants must have needed updating. He's grown so much maybe. Right now, I need to do . . . a little procedure. Access the shunts and drain them."

"No, he told me he had them done last year, when he was —" Beezan froze in horror, "—eighteen."

"What?"

God help me. "He did the scan himself. I thought he was nineteen! He told me he had his implants done when he was eighteen. Later on, when I found out he was only fourteen, I never even thought about it." Beezan was crushed. How could he have overlooked such a thing? Jarvie hadn't given him a brick for it.

"Well, it's usually done at thirteen too, so he still would have had it last year." Katie said.

"No," Iricana said. "Remember, he was dropped from the program. There would be no reason to upgrade his implants."

"But his med ID shows—" Katie was still puzzling over it as she pulled out her gear.

"He lied." Beezan said. "He rigged his med records. Whatever. Who knows how old those implants are. I should have guessed."

"Do not blame yourself, Captain," Reeder said. "He is responsible for his own lies." Beezan knew it for the truth, but a surge of anger at Reeder rose up in him.

"Katie," Iricana asked, "can it wait a bit? You need to rest and eat."

"It shouldn't wait, but if you could bring me some food. And if someone could clear out these pups!"

After being thrown out of the Med Bay, Beezan took the podpups to the kitchen and started trying, still one-handed from his injury, to get them some food. He was concerned about Jarvie and confused about exactly what had just happened. "*Drumheller*, play the shuttle *Cricket* record."

The visual was foggy and muddled, but the sound was direct from the suit links. The shuttle status showed at the bottom of the screen. The life and death situation was clear.

Even knowing they'd made it back didn't stop Beezan's distress. When it was over, he clutched the table with his one hand, breathing hard. To have a near miss with an incoming ship once was unusual, and now it had happened to him twice. Somehow, that fit his life. "*Drumheller*, what about that ship?"

"Unknown vessel has made course corrections toward the third planet. The potential exists for a double gravity-assist using that planet and the star. This could lead them either to the a-rings or to our position."

"Any beacon?"

"No."

"Packets?"

"No."

"Any identifying features?"

"No."

"Did you get a picture?"

"Not at closest approach." A smudge appeared on the screen. "Best picture."

"What do you think?" Beezan asked.

"This ship is not within normal human parameters."

There was a tiny gasp and Beezan turned, surprised to see Oatah and Reeder standing at the top of the stairs. He was so engrossed in the replay of the accident that he didn't hear them. Oatah had an anxious look on his face. He was holding up a hand to silence Reeder.

"Captain," Oatah whispered, "what have you done?" Beezan looked around in confusion. Did he put the lunch on the deck or something?

"With the computer," Reeder clarified.

"Oh." The AI. Apparently, they had not noticed before, but Beezan had just asked *Drumheller* its opinion.

"You have unleashed the Artificial Intelligence Operating System." Oatah said with both astonishment and disapproval.

"Jarvie . . ." Reeder suggested.

"We didn't do it! It just happened!" Beezan did not want to turn off the AI. He feared they needed it more than ever.

"Even on this old ship, 500 years of security would not *just* disappear, Captain," Oatah said accusingly.

"Well security and a lot of operating systems did just disappear—during some kind of computer attack on *this old ship*."

Oatah was shocked. "Attack from where?"

Beezan calmed himself. It wasn't Oatah's doing. "It was external. I don't know from where. But then there was a response of internal origin. Something in the cargo."

Both Reeder and Oatah went deathly still. "When did this happen?" Oatah finally asked.

"14 Sovereignty. We were out in the k-belt."

Oatah seemed sincerely concerned. "Captain, has the *Drumheller* taken precautions to prevent this from happening again?"

Beezan glanced up at the camera.

"Security was increased to block the invasive programs."

Oatah shook his head in disapproval at the AI's voice. "Captain, do you have any idea why the old AIs were . . . contained . . . within new operating systems?"

"People didn't like them, it fell out of fashion. I don't know." Now that Beezan had experienced using the AI, it didn't actually make sense to him to control a superior OS inside such a rigid command structure. He wondered briefly if the AI was aware of its imprisonment. *It's not a person!*

"I do know why, Captain," Oatah continued, "and there was a very good reason."

"What?"

Oatah merely raised an eyebrow. "We may have to accept it for now."

Beezan had a moment of paranoia. Was his own ship going

to do something crazy, or were AIs just an Earth phobia? Why wouldn't Oatah tell him? He was sure they had plenty of AIs on Earth. They were probably so good people didn't even know they were dealing with computers.

His p'link finally beeped.

"Yes!"

It was Iricana. "The procedure went well, Captain. He's sleeping. You can come see him."

A part of the shuttle record came back to him. Reeder had flown the shuttle in, but it was Jarvie's quick thinking that had saved the day.

9-Mercy

"You alright on the stairs?" Beezan called from his cabin.

Jarvie was ready, dressed in his uniform. Podpups were fed, but he was resting in his chair—again.

"I think so," he said quietly. The truth was he still had pain and disorientation. Beezan came through their adjoining door and frowned at Jarvie, not disapprovingly though.

"I'll come up with you," Beezan said, which meant Sky and Star went bounding ahead up and out the door. Jarvie walked up carefully, running his hand along the wall while Beezan followed.

He couldn't even complain. Almost everything wrong with his implants was his fault and he'd forgotten to give Beezan a brick for it. How many other things had he failed to come clean on? *It's not like a person would keep a list of lies in their p'link.* Besides, he'd run out of bricks long ago.

"You can rest again after the funeral," Beezan said to encourage him.

It had been two days now since the burial and attempted

funeral for Lander. Jarvie was surprised they had waited for him to recover from his little procedure before completing the funeral.

Beezan and Jarvie went to the kitchen first to secure the pups in their box. They fussed disappointedly when Beezan and Jarvie left the kitchen without feeding them again.

When they got to the Prayer Room, everyone else was already there. They stood in a missing friend circle. Reeder read parts of Lander's long and amazing biography from the pilots' database. Oatah and Iricana each said a prayer, and then Katie started the prayer for the departed again—from the beginning. Jarvie's nerves started up as he relived a few moments of their panicked departure from the moon, but he tried to focus on Lander.

Finally, it was his turn to say a prayer for Sarcee. He took a deep breath. He had been saying it in his head for days. He tried to say just the first word, but it would not come. The images of Sarcee, his only companion during the terrible years after the loss of his family, were streaming into his mind. He took a few breaths. The others waited patiently. Finally, Jarvie knew he had no voice to express his sorrow over Sarcee and his hope that podpups had eternal souls. He shook his head, which made it hurt, and tugged on Beezan's sleeve.

Beezan nodded, barely, and quietly chanted a beautiful prayer for Sarcee. The tears were streaming down Jarvie's cheeks, but he wasn't alone. They were relieved as well as sad, since they had at last laid Lander to rest. Beezan steered Jarvie gently to the stairs and down out of the Prayer Room.

"Can you eat?" Beezan asked, as they got into their shoes.

Jarvie started to nod and winced. Words would still not come. They walked solemnly to the kitchen; Oatah and Reeder, on opposite sides of the rimway, already reaching for their s'links; Katie and Iricana, gripping their prayer books to their chests and walking side by side; and finally, Beezan with his free arm around Jarvie. It was a great comfort to have Beezan by him. Jarvie looked down to thank him, but Beezan's eyes were far away again, looking to that place that seemed to be there since Lander left.

26 / PERFECT MATCH

When Beezan got to the kitchen, he let out the pups, who had the sense to be a little less crazy than usual. Iricana set out the breakfast. At first, they ate in silence, but then they shared stories of their short time with Lander. Katie recorded them to add to the pack for Lander's survivors. Between the stories and the biography, Beezan marveled how you never really knew someone until you went to their funeral.

Beezan watched Jarvie as carefully as he could without being too obvious. Jarvie ate well enough, but often froze as if movement hurt his head or made him dizzy. "Can I go lie down, Captain?" he asked suddenly.

"Of course. I'll walk you."

Jarvie didn't even bother to object, which worried Beezan even more. They walked slowly back to Jarvie's cabin alone, as the pups were well distracted in the kitchen. They got down the stairs and Beezan stowed Jarvie's uniform while he got in the bunk. It had one little *Drumheller* pin on it. With a pang, Beezan remembered folding up Lander's uniform for the survivor pack. It was covered in ship pins, around the stand-up collar, across the front yoke and down the sides of the pockets.

"Jarvie, if you don't have a *Sunburst* pin, we can make you one."

"I might have one," he mumbled. "Tomorrow. Thanks, Captain."

Beezan walked back to the kitchen, worried. Katie said Jarvie might be in pain for a few days, weeks, or even longer. He would need new implants immediately upon their return to civilization. Katie couldn't do the surgery as it was very specialized.

As far as the mystery ship went, Oatah insisted his other 'people' would not have come early without orders. At least now they knew that Oatah had a backup plan. Katie admitted she knew it couldn't be Lanezi, but, Beezan sympathized, she couldn't be blamed for harboring an irrational hope. Iricana only advised waiting for data. Reeder was on a mission to get that data and planned to spend the day spying on the new ship, even if it was too far away to see much.

Beezan, however, found himself thinking in all kinds of new directions since his jump with Lander. So many pathways. A person could recklessly pick a pathway and go. Ships sometimes disappeared. Was this mystery ship one? Had it missed its destination and ended up here? But where were the packets?

Beezan tried to eat a bit more, since everyone was still sitting in the kitchen. "It warms my heart, Captain," Katie said, "to see how well Jarvie's doing with you."

Beezan nearly dropped his spoon. "*What?* Jarvie's a wreck!" Even Reeder and Oatah looked up in puzzlement.

"Captain," Iricana defended Katie, "when that child came off the *Sunburst*, he was strapped to a stretcher, headed for detox on Atikameq."

"Detox!" Beezan said. *Another secret?*

"A passenger on the *Sunburst* drugged him," Katie explained. "S16." She shook her head in disgust.

"What's that?" Beezan asked.

"Not for children, and the passenger gave Jarvie too much," Katie continued. "I don't even know how much of his family's funeral he remembers. They had to send him to detox right after."

"We tried to keep tabs on him," Iricana said. "It was so sad. He was taken out of the pilot program, put in a monitor program, did badly at school. Of course, all that bad news just made Lanezi crazier to *rescue* him. However," Iricana grew a bit stern, "last we checked, he was supposedly at school, not anywhere near the *Drumheller*."

"He is quite good at compromising security—out here anyway," Reeder said. "Of course, security in Sector 1 is much better. Perhaps we could make use of his talent somehow."

"*What?*" Beezan said.

"Not to encourage lawless behavior, Captain. To redirect it to something useful for our purposes."

Beezan wasn't sure that was any better.

Jarvie felt cured after sleeping all day. Except for being hungry. He ate double for dinner, but no one complained. They were coddling him and he didn't plan to object. He wasn't even allowed to help with the dishes so he wandered back to his cabin with Star to get his *Sunburst* pin. He was pretty sure he'd mailed one to himself in one of those boxes.

He pulled out the top box and set it on the bunk. He didn't remember using a red box. After getting the lid off, he found a paper envelope at the top of the box. For sure, he didn't do that. He flipped the lid over again. The return address was coded. He did do that.

The envelope had no writing on it. Jarvie opened it, intrigued. A small sheet of paper unfolded to reveal familiar handwriting, but Jarvie couldn't identify it. He skipped to the end. Right before a P.S., a name jumped out at him.

I will not abandon you.
Love, Lanezi

Jarvie gasped and looked back at the top.

3-Dominion, *Cheetah* at Harbor

Greetings Jarvie,
God is Most Glorious.
Please forgive me for not writing you sooner. I will explain later. I am with a science group. We were supposed to jump on 9-Sovereignty, but my boss was sick. I told them I was sick now to stall another month, so I'm going to send this message out on another ship.
Jarvie,

Jarvie's mind was only half following. He looked at the date. 3-Dominion, they didn't go with the jump group on 9-Dominion, the day of the accident at Harbor. A thrill of discovery and hope shot through him. *He's alive!*

Jarvie jumped up. Holding the letter, he ran upstairs, with Star chasing, down the rimway, and up the kitchen stairs shouting, "He's alive! He's alive!"

The crew was still cleaning up. Katie came over as if to examine his head, when Iricana, dish in hand, calmly asked, "Who's alive, Jarvie?"

"Lanezi!"

Katie froze. They all went wide-eyed.

"How could—" Iricana asked, setting the dish down.

"I've got a letter!" He shoved it at Beezan. "Look, it says 3-Dominion and they can't jump because Lanezi says he's sick."

All eyes went to the big calendar. "So they weren't in the accident!" Jarvie continued. "Lanezi is alive at Harbor!" Beezan, reading the letter silently, was nodding slowly.

Katie's hands were over her mouth.

"But how could you have a letter now? Out here?" Iricana continued relentlessly, as Reeder and Oatah watched from the table in concern.

"It was in my mail—that was delivered at Redrock—except I thought it was just a box I sent to myself so I didn't open it. So I just now opened it looking for a *Sunburst* pin—but it was from Lanezi and there was the letter," Jarvie ran out of breath.

"There's a whole box?" Iricana asked.

"Yes!" Jarvie was impatient for them to believe him. The podpups were zipping around their feet in excitement. He turned and ran back to his cabin, grabbed the lid of the box and ran back to the kitchen, panting from so many stairs.

"Be careful of your head!" Katie admonished him as he handed the lid to Iricana. She calmly examined the label, ran her s'link over the coded return and overrode it for the tracking info. She read it out from most recent backwards.

"Total charges," she skipped.

"Hold for pick up at Redrock dock: 16-Grandeur-1083.

"Mirage to Redrock via *Oregon Trail:* 1-Beauty-1083.

"Atikameq to Mirage via *Corita:* 18-Loftiness-1082.

"Harbor to Atikameq via *Spring Tide*," she paused, "9-Dominion. The *Spring Tide* was one of the surviving ships," she confirmed.

"Why don't you want to believe it?" Jarvie asked in exasperation.

"I very much want to believe," Iricana said, glancing at Katie, "and I cannot think of any reason not to," she trailed off. At that, Katie jumped up and down and hugged a smiling Iricana.

Oatah, who was still at the table with Reeder, was now lost in contemplation. "Unless there was a last minute change, Lanezi and Thayne are alive at Harbor," he summarized.

Beezan was reading the letter, the whole thing, and he was frowning. "What?" Jarvie asked in alarm.

"Nothing," Beezan smiled, giving the letter back. "It is hopeful news."

"Read it," Katie encouraged and then stopped, "if it's not too personal."

"I don't know," Jarvie said. "I only read a little bit." The two women rolled their eyes at him.

Jarvie handed the letter to Iricana, who read it through aloud, at first calmly and then with more concern.

"Jarvie, I hope you are on your way to me. Please come to Harbor as soon as possible. I have stalled here too long. Contact me as 'Navigator' on *Cheetah*. I'll get you aboard the ship. We'll worry about documents later. Don't mention my name to anyone. Be sneaky. I know you know how.

"I've left you messages at every dock, hoping you can get to Harbor by 9-Splendor. I can't stall longer than that. If you don't make it, go back to school and wait for me to contact you. You may not hear from me for a year. Be patient. Work hard.

"I won't abandon you,

"Love, Lanezi

"P.S. Here are a few things I managed to save from the *Sunburst* scavengers. I thought you would like them. Could you please mail the little box for me? Thanks, L"

There was a general sigh of concern in the room. Even Katie bit her lip.

Reeder pounced immediately, "Lanezi has broken his oath!"

Katie winced. Jarvie felt terrible. He had betrayed Lanezi in his excitement. "I'm sorry," he said to Katie, but she shook her head.

"No harm has come of it," Iricana pronounced. "In fact, knowing they are alive changes everything. We must proceed with Plan G."

"Yes," Oatah agreed, and he and Reeder were back to business.

Plan G? Six plans were already wrecked?

Beezan sat a long time at the kitchen table that night, after Jarvie went back to his cabin. Very late, Iricana came in and sat with him.

"Lanezi and Jarvie. They sound like . . . like . . ." Beezan remembered Kelson McNelson, "two peas in a pod."

"Yes, it is troubling," Iricana agreed. "We had not seen that side of Lanezi, and he obviously had a lot of influence on Jarvie." She paused and shook her head. "The chances of Jarvie ending up with you and you ending up with us—"

Beezan's p'link beeped.

"Go ahead."

"Captain . . ." came Jarvie's anguished voice. He sounded injured or dying. Beezan and Iricana were out of their seats and running. Iricana called Katie on her s'link. Katie was only seconds behind them tearing down the stairs into Jarvie's cabin.

"Jarvie?" Beezan called.

He was sitting on his bunk, hunched over a red box, cradling something.

"Are you injured?" Beezan asked, looking down at his chest.

Jarvie shook his head, tears streaming down his face—and shoved something at Beezan. "Take it!"

Jarvie turned his head away and wiped his tears on his sleeve while Beezan stared at the s'link Jarvie put in his hand. It wasn't the same s'link that he'd previously confiscated. This one was a work of art, made of different colors of polished asteroid chips.

"Maybe we should go," Iricana said. Jarvie shook his head. Katie put away her med kit and found a handkerchief, embroidered, and sat down by Jarvie, handing it to him and patting his arm.

"Where did you get this?" Beezan asked and then realized that, of course, the s'link had come in the box from Lanezi. He flicked it on. It was active. "Level 2!"

Iricana gasped. "No. Lanezi wouldn't have sent . . ." but she stopped. If Lanezi had been standing there, Beezan didn't know if they would have contained their tempers. After all they'd been through, all Jarvie's lies and illegal use of s'links.

Iricana was muttering, "—to send this to a minor, an unlicensed . . . even unsecured in the mail."

Then Beezan realized why Jarvie was crying. What an effort it had been for him to turn it over. How much he would have been tempted to keep it, and how much it would hurt him to have to implicate Lanezi, whom he loved so dearly.

"Jarvie," he pushed the box over and sat down to hug him,

but his arm was strapped to his side. "You did the right thing. I know it was hard for you."

Jarvie kept his hands gripped together as if he might try to snatch the s'link back.

"Why would he send this to you?" Iricana asked.

"It was . . . my father's," Jarvie managed to explain.

Suddenly it all made sense. Beezan handed the s'link over to Iricana so it wouldn't be near Jarvie. "Maybe Agent Oatah could deactivate it, so you could keep the case," Beezan suggested.

"Oh, Reeder will love that," Katie lamented.

"Well," Iricana said sternly, "This is not your doing Jarvie. Lanezi swore his oath to me, so that matter is between us." She pulled out her s'link and ran it up to maximum. The others saw a white 1 flash on the side. Jarvie clutched Beezan's shoulder in shock. Beezan's mind boggled. *She's a level 1!*

Iricana used her s'link to deactivate the level 2 internal module, which she calmly popped out and pocketed. She handed Jarvie the empty case. He would have his father's s'link after all. Jarvie clutched it to his chest, "Thank you."

Beezan was suddenly a bit scared of Iricana. He had obviously underestimated her position. For the thousandth time, he wondered what he'd gotten mixed up in.

"Here," Jarvie said suddenly, reaching into the box and pulling out a smaller box. "I was supposed to mail this."

"We may have to intercept that." Iricana frowned and then looked at the name. Her eyes flicked to Katie and she swallowed. "It's for you, dear."

There was total silence as Katie took the box. They were out of gasps and tears. "I'm not sure I can take any more today," but she was opening it.

Inside was a single guided crystal rose, not red, not pink, in-between. The color of a star path, Beezan thought. It was stunningly beautiful and fortunately unbreakable, considering the ride it had. Hanging from it was a ring. It was gold with a single gem, the same color as the rose.

An engagement ring. Beezan's heart seized. It was tragic. Lanezi was trapped, maybe for life. If Katie accepted the engagement . . . Beezan knew what it was like to suffer an engagement that was not to be, without even the promise of a union in heaven.

But Katie did not look stricken. She sat up straight. A fiercely determined look settled on her face. She reached for the ring. Surprisingly, Jarvie stopped her, taking it himself, and with a new confidence on his face, slipped the ring on her finger.

Beezan was perplexed at their sudden hope. He glanced at Iricana to commiserate but she too looked strangely calm, nodding to herself and saying, "Yes, we must proceed with our plans."

10-Mercy

There was a bustle of activity in the Med Bay the next morning after breakfast. The others worked at the conference table while Katie took Beezan out of his arm restrainer. "That's a relief," he said to her.

"So he can move cargo now?" Reeder asked Katie from the table.

"*The Captain* can move cargo from the Cargo Control Booth, yes."

"We need someone in a loader—"

"Another four weeks, at least, for that."

"What takes so long?" Reeder complained.

"It's best to let the healing take the time it needs," Katie explained. Reeder frowned.

"I could do the loader," Jarvie volunteered from the other exam bed.

Five pairs of eyes swiveled to him. The combined affect was so powerful he pulled the blanket over his face. The thought of Jarvie, in his condition, out there in a loader made Beezan cringe.

After working his arm a few minutes, Beezan sat at the conference table to discuss moving the cargo with Reeder and Oatah while Jarvie had his implants scanned again.

There was a sense of excitement in getting back to everyday work. They had been through so much in the last few days, but now they could settle into a work routine.

Beezan could not fathom the others' attitudes after getting Lanezi's box. He could see Jarvie and Katie taking it as some kind of sign that they'd be reunited with Lanezi, unlikely as that was. But Iricana? She had hardly believed the letter was even from Lanezi. Yet she was pleased for Katie. Even Reeder and Oatah, though surprised by the news of her engagement, had not reacted as if it were a tragedy in the making. This could mean only one thing—*they know there is hope for Harbor.*

"Oh, good," Katie declared and clapped her hands. They all looked up at Jarvie's scan. Beezan went over to the bed for a closer look. There was a tiny bit of yellow here and there, but otherwise it looked normal.

"You are going to be just fine—"

"Priority One Alert," *Drumheller* announced.

"Go ahead," said Reeder stiffly—disregarding that it was the Captain's privilege to answer.

"Ship profile matched."

All their smiles disappeared.

"Big screen," ordered Reeder.

On half of the screen was a new picture of a fuzzy blob. "That?" Beezan asked, wondering why the *Drumheller* would call them for another unresolved picture. On the other side of the screen, another blob appeared with a file name in large letters at the bottom: *Hamada intruder.*

"Frequency of unknown ship field compared to alien ship at Hamada: 100% match."

It wasn't just a bad picture. The ship was actually a glowing fuzzy teardrop shape. Other pictures appeared, all fuzzy blobs of slightly different shapes: *Luminesse intruder, Firelight intruder, Harbor intruder.*

"God have mercy," Katie whispered.

"The aliens," Jarvie marveled.

"We've found them!" Reeder exclaimed.

"Or perhaps," Oatah contemplated, "they have found us."

"We do not know for certain that this ship is alien." Iricana commented sternly. "It remains a strong possibility. They might also be human descendants."

"There are no packets," Beezan argued.

"Packet protocol is practically unchanged for 500 years," Jarvie insisted.

"*Drumheller*," Beezan ordered. "Research packet and ship station communication protocols for . . . 800 years. Go to archival data. See if we can pick up anything with an older protocol."

"Researching."

Oatah nodded. "A necessary procedure, but I don't believe it will produce a human ship."

Beezan sank carefully into a chair. His instincts told him Oatah was right.

"I declare a first contact situation," Oatah said for the

record. "Even though we assume they are headed for the a-rings and we have work here, we must anticipate that we may communicate. The crew will review first contact protocols immediately."

"There are protocols?" asked Jarvie, plunking into another chair, ready to hear them.

"*Drumheller*, how long until they get to the a-rings?" Beezan asked.

"Three to four weeks, depending on injection points and velocity."

"Are there anti-contamination protocols in your first contact scenario?" Katie asked.

"They're not coming aboard!" Reeder said impatiently.

"How do we know?" Katie asked.

"What if they just beam over?" Jarvie asked.

Beezan thought Iricana might burst from all the irrational comments.

"We do not know enough to even guess!" Iricana insisted. "Even if they are aliens, they may or may not be the same organization causing the accidents and they may or may not be related to the so-called builders! We must not get carried away." But in his heart, Beezan knew these were not the builders. Just blunderers, like themselves, hopping around the sectors without a map.

"One thing is certain." All heads turned to Oatah. "We will be interacting with them soon. If not here, somewhere else. We face a great challenge, spiritually and practically. We must prepare ourselves. The fate of the sectors may be at stake. We have little time."

They all looked at Oatah in alarm.

"Does this mean plan H?" Jarvie asked, somewhat sarcastically.

Iricana looked at him sternly. “Plan T, I believe.” She was not joking.

“Let us review the protocols,” continued Oatah.

Plan T? Beezan put his head in his hands. *We are about to run out of plans.*

27 / NOCTURNE

11-Mercy

Beezan paced around the Med Bay waiting for the morning meeting to start. Oatah and Reeder sat at the conference table by themselves. Katie continued to work while they waited for Iricana to finish up in the kitchen.

Reeder was devising a communication flow chart for attempting to contact the "unknown" vessel. Iricana wouldn't let them call it alien, even though all human packet protocols were exhausted. As it turned out, *Drumheller* did not have data much older than its commission. They could only go back 500 years.

Except for the possible communication schemes, Beezan thought the First Contact protocols were useless:

Report to Sector Council Immediately. Oatah wouldn't allow a light-speed message and they couldn't jump back until Beezan was healed.

Avoid Hostilities. How long ago was this written? When was the last time there were hostilities anywhere? And how was he supposed to be hostile anyway? Not invite them for tea?

Monitor Alien's position until First Contact Team Arrives. Beezan turned to the big screen. The alien was headed for the a-rings.

Beezan switched to a 'top view.' The star was unofficially named Daydream by Lanezi, as he was the pilot who first jumped there. Unofficial or not, it was Daydream system now. Nocturne was the name of the coal-black moon they were orbiting. The *Drumheller* had left "Lander's Moon" to park at L2 of Nocturne, saving some fuel by using the moon for a partial radiation shield. Jarvie named Nocturne's parent gas giant Turquoise, for its color.

The secret hangar was at Nocturne–L4. They would head over there later. Then they would go around to the a-rings, at Turquoise–L4, very slow and easy, and see the aliens. Beezan had to admit to himself he was excited and couldn't blame Jarvie for his recent exuberance.

Beezan was alerted by the sound of Jarvie's loud running up the stairs and braced himself for the onslaught of the rib-cracking morning hug. Jarvie beat Star up the stairs, panting and pale.

"What's wrong?" Beezan asked. The others turned to look.

"The cargo! It's—something's happened. The adjustment rate—" Jarvie ran to the panel and tapped his p'link. The big screen changed to a simple graph, *Adjustments per Hour*. Jarvie, trying to be coherent, pointed to a spike on the graph. "I've had this program running since we put cargo 189 on the mass tester. It tracks the changes per hour." Oatah and Reeder were both nodding as if they were way ahead. "That spike happened ten minutes ago. It went from 8 adjustments per hour to a projected 137 per hour."

"What could possibly be in that cargo that would cause such a thing?" Beezan asked.

"Captain," Oatah said with false calmness, "Iricana suspects that there are containment fields inside the container, protecting some delicate cargo. However, there remains a possibility that the containment fields were placed there because the cargo is somehow dangerous. We don't know what it is and we don't know why no one was informed. But we do know that one of Thayne's engineers was working on containment fields. I believe it would be best to offload that cargo."

"Yes!" Beezan answered.

"I told you. It's a gravity ball!" Jarvie exclaimed.

Beezan discounted Jarvie's crazy notion, shaking his head.

"It is too small to be a gravity ball," Oatah said patiently.

"Captain," Iricana, who had come in after hearing the exchange on her p'link, laid a hand on Beezan's shoulder. "The cargo came safely from Hamada. It may just be an effect of fields adjusting."

"The fields are failing?"

"Possibly," she admitted, "If that's what's causing it in the first place."

"Was anyone going to tell me about these fields?" Beezan asked, uselessly, as no one answered.

"If it's unstable," Oatah interjected, "we cannot take it to the hangar. We must move it directly to the other L-point."

"Why can't we just boost it out the door?" Beezan demanded.

"You know it would come back to haunt us. We need to get it into a stable orbit somewhere else," Iricana said reasonably.

"It will take days to get to the L5 point!" Beezan argued.

"We must try. We can monitor it as we go," Oatah insisted.

Beezan deflated. "Fine." Anything to get it off the ship.

Jarvie was at the panel already, looking at the top view. Maybe it wasn't a gravity ball, but gut feeling aside, he wanted it off the ship. "Are you talking about the Nocturne–L5, counterpart to the L4 where the hangar is?" Jarvie asked.

"Yes," Oatah answered.

"*Drumheller*," Jarvie started and glanced at Beezan, who nodded his head in resignation. "Calculate path to Nocturne–L5." Jarvie touched the screen to show where he meant. It took a few seconds. Then several possibilities appeared.

Beezan touched a pop-up at the table. There could be Trojans at this L5. "*Drumheller*, start a scan of the L5 region as soon as possible. See if you can detect any debris there. How long to clear the rim of Nocturne for option 1?"

"3.17 hours. Scan on standby until then."

"What's the ETA after that to L5?"

"Three days, 4.82 hours."

Beezan took a deep breath. "Let's secure and spin down in two hours. *Drumheller*, Option 1, begin countdown."

The problem, Jarvie thought, with an unused L-point was that no one had been here to clean it up. A lunar L-point wouldn't have a lot of stuff, but dust, rocks, and a few mini-moons might be crowding the L5 orbital oasis.

Drumheller was continuously analyzing the objects and their relations during approach. Iricana sat with Jarvie, barely able to contain her annoyance with Lanezi and Thayne and whatever "lunacy" they were up to.

"Thayne is your boss? And Lanezi's?" Jarvie asked as they worked in the Command Bay, looking for a good spot for the monster cargo container among all the debris.

Iricana nodded. "He's the project leader. Or he was, before Oatah came. He's an extraordinary genius. His mother was quite a genius herself and he was a small sickly child. He hung in a podpup carrier around her neck while she worked. Theoretical math got in his brain along with everyday stuff."

"He's still sickly?" Jarvie wondered, remembering Lanezi said his boss couldn't jump.

"Yes, he is physically fragile and we must protect him. We only jump when he is well." Her mind wandered. "He's only thirty, and Lanezi is even younger. I worry about the two of them out there at Harbor. They have a crew of course, but Thayne picked them. Lanezi is a fantastic pilot, but Thayne . . . he's the only one who really understands all this stuff about the a-rings and how they might work. We need him." She was suddenly back-to-business. "Lanezi better be taking good care of him."

"He always took good care of me."

But for some reason Iricana frowned, then tried to cover it up. She pointed at the screen, where a diagram of the jumble of mini-moons circled. Three places were marked in red. "We're down to these three spots to park that cargo container. Let's let the Captain pick. He has to get us in there."

Beezan wished for the millionth time that Lander were still alive. He admitted to himself that this time missing him was totally practical. They needed another pilot. Someone had to keep the *Drumheller* from knocking into the flotsam and jetsam of L5 while someone else used the shuttle to tow the cargo container and release it. Beezan was in the hangar looking over the shuttles. The *Cricket*, the shuttle they had used on Lander's moon, was beat up, but usable, and both Reeder and Jarvie had experience on it. Whoever didn't fly the shuttle would have to go in the exoloader, detach the cargo from the adjuster, take it outside and hook it to the shuttle. Reeder or Jarvie? *It would be so much easier if I had complete confidence in either of them.* They weren't really short on pilots; they were short on cargo handlers.

Beezan took the lift down to Cargo Hold 2 and pulled his way into the Cargo Control Booth. His ribs were starting to ache. Sky rode along on his good shoulder. She didn't frolic around in nogee as much as other pups. She was such a strange, serious little thing. He reached up to scratch her neck as he gazed out at the cargo. He glared at the source of their problems, container 189. The only indication of trouble was the flashing green light on the panel. Normally the light would flash while the mass was calculated and then it would stop. But this just kept recalculating.

He stared at the little flashing light. Suddenly, his mind jumped. He reeled and caught a holdbar to stabilize. Sky yelped and grabbed on. *What happened?* He had a moment of panic. He'd felt like he was in a path. *Was that a star? Where are we?*

Redrock. No, Nocturne. He tried to stay calm and take a few breaths. *Thank heavens no one is around. What was that star I saw? Why did that happen? Was it the sight of the green flashing light in the dark room?* He had seen a jump path and they weren't even jumping. Nothing like that had ever happened to him before. As far as he knew, it had never happened to anyone. Sky looked up at him in concern. He shivered.

15-Mercy

It's half over, Beezan told himself. In fact, Jarvie's part was over so he could rest a little easier. In the end, it had been decided Beezan would stay in the Command Bay and fly the *Drumheller*—no choice really—but it satisfied the crew that their jump pilot was not outside. Jarvie would do the exoloader, which satisfied Beezan as it was the shortest worrying time and Jarvie wouldn't be going far from the ship. Beezan could see Jarvie now on the screen, hovering in his suit in the Entry Lounge. He had his helmet off while he was waiting for Reeder to come back. He had done well in the loader, been cautious with the cargo, but also firm and purposeful.

Beezan glanced to the other screen. Reeder was doing a fair job of flying, especially with the big cargo container on an arm behind the shuttle—it was ten times bigger than the shuttle. Beezan wasn't sure he would do much better. The particle shields on both the shuttle and *Drumheller* were at maximum and taking almost continuous hits of sand-sized dust. *Drumheller* had reprogrammed the shuttle particle field to include the cargo container, but after they separated, the cargo would be exposed. So the plan was to park the container right in the middle of L5 where most of the stuff was circling around slowly.

"Oh!" Iricana gasped. A large chunk hit the *Cricket*, enough to knock Reeder off course a bit. *Thank heavens the stuff is slow moving.*

"*Cricket*, status?" Beezan asked over the s'link.

"Fine, correcting course." Amazingly, Reeder did not sound the least bit nervous. He was in his element, determined to accomplish an important mission.

It was Katie's kitchen day, but she came to the Command Bay to watch, naturally. Oatah was working in the garden, not even worried about what was going on. Beezan did not think he could ever be that detached. Beezan smiled as he remembered his grandfather complaining about people who never worried. Too attached to their detachment, he'd say. With all these people aboard and all this commotion, Beezan hadn't thought so much about his grandfather lately. He hoped he wasn't drifting away from his memory.

"At position," reported Reeder.

"*Drumheller?*"

"Confirmed."

"You're clear to release cargo." Beezan said, resisting the urge to tell Reeder to clear out quick.

"Cargo released."

They couldn't see much from their far-off spot between the two biggest mini-moons, but the shuttle moved smoothly and quickly away. The plan was for the *Cricket* to exit forward and then circle back around to the *Drumheller*, just in case there was some problem with the cargo.

Jarvie had stuck a general sensor on the cargo container, which was now feeding back information to Iricana's pop-up. She stiffened in her straps. "The container is starting a slow spin." Particles would now be touching the container, but none of them should have been fast enough to do any damage.

Beezan watched Reeder, who was piloting much better now. Suddenly, Iricana hit the mute button so Reeder wouldn't hear her. "The container is spinning faster and faster."

"Is that bad?" Beezan asked.

"It's unexpected."

"What could it mean?" Katie asked.

"The small stuff hitting it wouldn't make it spin up like that. Something inside maybe," Iricana answered.

Beezan glanced at the *Cricket*. No sense rushing Reeder just to have a panic braking while he's trying to dock. His pop-up showed the *Drumheller's* position. His heart skipped. They were moving—and not just a little bit. "We're being pulled in! Strap! Jarvie get your helmet back on and find a restraint! Agent Oatah, we may be moving in a hurry. *Drumheller*, calculate burn to stabilize position. Oh, my God, the pups!"

"They're secure in the kitchen, Captain," Katie said.

"Thank you."

Iricana was trying to get more data from the sensor on the cargo, as they had specifically programmed the *Drumheller* to accept only data from their own equipment. They couldn't risk another computer battle. "The only thing I can think of is that some containment fields have failed inside the container and the remaining fields are interacting in some way to cause the spinning."

"But why are we moving?"

Iricana didn't answer.

"*Drumheller*, where's that burn information?"

"No stable trajectory. Too many changing variables."

"Reeder," Beezan went back on the s'link. "We're pulling out. Just get yourself out and we'll rendezvous later."

"Agreed," he replied, sounding as if he was having his own troubles.

"Secured, Captain," came Jarvie's voice.

Good. Where was Oatah? "Agent Oatah?" Beezan asked. *I never should have let him in the garden while we were doing this. What was I thinking?*

"Captain, I will be secured in approximately seven minutes. Please do what you need to regardless."

Seven minutes?

"*Drumheller*, show me a clear pathway." Beezan touched the screen in front of him, tracing a line out, but even as he traced it, he could see the big pieces spiraling in towards the cargo. "Why is stuff falling in?"

"The sensor indicates that the mass of the cargo has

increased," Iricana stated as if she didn't believe it. "Not fluctuating as before, but increased by ten-fold."

Ten times! "How is that possible? Even if the containment fields completely fail, how could the mass increase?" Beezan asked, but couldn't really wait for any answer. The two mini-moons he'd parked between would come closer together as they moved in. He needed to concentrate.

"Captain," Iricana asked hesitantly, "are we closer than we normally would be to a gravity ball?"

"Yes—IT'S TOO SMALL TO BE A GRAVITY BALL!"

"We don't know much about them . . ." Her already pale skin was almost white.

"We don't have the technology to make containment fields that block gravity!"

"No we don't, but—Captain, what if it is an inactive gravity ball that somehow turns on and inflates?" Beezan looked at her in horror, hardly believing she was serious. "What else could it be?" she whispered. "We may not have seven minutes."

"*Drumheller*, where is Oatah?"

"Garden deck, Arc 1."

"Oatah! Secure inside the lock and stay there! There are straps inside the blue panels." Beezan mentally plotted his way out of the mess.

"Securing, Captain."

"All crew, stand by for multiple burns." With a prayer for assistance, Beezan took the manual controls and made a few small burns to turn them. Then he made a 20 second burn to move along a path that would take them away from the two mini-moons. But they weren't getting as far as they should.

"Another increase!" Iricana warned. "It's massing half a gravity ball."

A terrifying thought came to Beezan. "Gravity balls aren't supposed to be in planetary orbit!"

"God Almighty," Iricana breathed. "What was Thayne thinking?"

Beezan was too busy to wonder. "We'll have to give it all we've got. We need to get out of planetary orbit."

Beezan held the controls, fighting manually for position and distance, dodging big stuff and trying to predict a clear path amidst a mess of incoming hazards. He was counting on the particle fields to handle anything small that came their way. *Almost.* Finally, they were clear enough for *Drumheller* to start calculating again.

"All crew, stand by for three minute burn." It didn't feel too crushing to Beezan, in his chair, and watching their escape from the maelstrom. However, to Oatah and Jarvie, who were not in their chairs, it would be painful and dangerous. Beezan risked a glance at Iricana's pop-up showing the cargo container. It was now surrounded by a whirlpool of dust and in-falling rock.

There was a sudden jolt. "Sensor destroyed!" Iricana struggled against the acceleration to report.

At last, the three minutes were up. Beezan made a quick burn to stabilize and they had a few seconds left before another burn. It was still hard, but they could talk a little. "We're clear." There were sighs of relief all around. Beezan spared a second to check the screen showing the cargo. The container was crumpled into a spherical shape. "It doesn't look any bigger."

"It's not," Iricana said with icy fury. "It must be a miniature gravity ball. And whoever put it in that container knew exactly what it was."

"Jarvie?" Beezan heard Katie ask quietly.

"Here," he gasped.

"Oatah? Agent Oatah?" There was no answer.

"Reeder, can you hear me?" Beezan could not see the shuttle. "*Drumheller*, give me *Cricket* on screen 2." Screen 2 popped up but Beezan could not see any shuttle in it.

"Cannot locate *Cricket* beacon."

Don't panic, anything could be happening out there. "Show particle hits on screen 4," Beezan added. *Bad idea.* A line drawing of the *Drumheller* with particle field was covered with yellow dots and even some bigger red ones. "Do you see the shuttle?" he asked the others.

"He may be on the other side, behind all that debris, Captain," Iricana said, which made sense.

"As soon as we're clear, I'll have to go for Oatah," Katie said.

"I'll get Jarvie," Iricana added. Beezan would just have to sit and make sure they were safely away from the whole mess. They all turned to stare at the scene. The two mini-moons were spiraling toward the loose mass in the middle. They would certainly collide. They sat transfixed. They'd seen these kinds of graphics, but this was real life.

"*Drumheller*," Jarvie whispered, "view of L5." His helmet screen blinked on, but he could barely open his eyes to look at it. His head was hurting so much. It hurt in the back where it pressed against the support. His neck was in agony. It felt like frozen rods were running from his eyes all the way down his back. He'd felt the meds three times already. Even after he managed to focus on the screen, he could hardly believe what was happening. Mini-moons smashing into each other? Puffs of obscuring dust darkened, and arcs of glinting ice accented a mass of jumbled rock. *Was there really a gravity ball in there? Was the shuttle in there too?* He felt a surge of guilt for not liking Reeder better. ***"Is there any Remover of difficulties save God? Say:***

Praised be God! He is God! All are His servants and all abide by His bidding!" [1]

Jarvie repeated the prayer as his head swam from pain and the confusion on the screen. He could hear Beezan calling Reeder, telling the *Drumheller* to search for the beacon continuously. He heard Katie calling Oatah. Sometimes she would call him. He would try to answer. "Tired," he said. "Head hurts." He couldn't stay awake, even though he really wanted to.

Katie reached for her straps.

"Just a little more," Beezan said. He wanted a lot more between them and that chaos, but they couldn't get too far from Reeder, or he wouldn't be able to catch up. Beezan thought he saw a glint of metal.

"*Cricket* beacon located."

The scene shifted and zoomed in. The shuttle was slowly tumbling out of control. They could see enough damage to guess that the hull was breached. Beezan felt sick just looking at it. Reeder was not running the automatic stabilizing program.

"*Drumheller*, take control of *Cricket*."

Beezan knew Katie was anxious to get to her patients, and Beezan was worried about Jarvie, but they couldn't be wandering around the ship while they were maneuvering.

"Unable to link with *Cricket*."

Katie gasped.

"*Drumheller*, keep trying."

Beezan took a few breaths to try to stop shaking.

"Captain," Iricana said calmly, "If there's nothing to do for Reeder, we must get to the others."

"There's plenty to do!" Beezan objected. "*Drumheller*, load the smallest rock relocator we have."

"It'll damage the shuttle hull!" Iricana argued.

"It's already vented. If Reeder's suit is damaged, he's already gone."

Katie was praying quietly. Iricana was on her panel visually tracking the *Cricket.*

"Relocator loaded."

"Target *Cricket,* launch when ready."

There was a small bump and a streak of light as the relocator shot out of *Drumheller.* A pop-up appeared with a graphic. It looked like the relocator was going to intercept perfectly. *Thank God for computers, I never could figure that—*

There was a flash on the main screen.

"Hit something!" Iricana exclaimed.

"Relocator signal lost."

"*Drumheller,* how many more rock relocators do we have?"

"Two additional."

"Load another. Launch when ready," Beezan ordered. *Stay calm. One thing at a time.*

Another bump and line on the graphic. He held his breath. Then there was a flash and the relocator slammed onto the shuttle, latching on and drilling in as they both tumbled. *Please let Reeder's suit be intact.*

"*Drumheller,* can you detumble the shuttle remotely, using the rock relocator?"

"Link established with relocator. Proceeding." By firing small bursts on the relocator, the *Drumheller* cancelled bits of spin, but if the major spin were in the direction that the relocator couldn't burn . . . would he have to launch the other one?

"Katie, go!" Beezan said. Iricana started to unstrap too.

"Iricana, you need to be back here by the time the shuttle comes in. I'll have to suit up to get Reeder."

"Yes, Captain." And she was gone, pulling hand over hand out of the Command Bay.

Beezan unstrapped and floated over to pull a suit out of the emergency closet. He tried to keep one eye on the graphic.

"Relocator fuel running low."

"Launch the other!" Another bump. *Last one.*

"*Cricket* link established. Auto stabilization program running."

Thank God. Just long enough to cancel that one direction was all they needed. The shuttle was coming closer. Beezan feared the *Drumheller* might lose control of it. "*Drumheller*, how strong is the link?"

***"Cricket's* only operational receiver is now in-line with our transmission. Link is stable. Third relocator redirected."**

"Run *Cricket* autodock."

"Running."

Concentrate! You're suiting up. He tried to slow down and think through every step. He knew he was in danger of making some fatal mistake from nerves and rushing.

"I've got Oatah," came Katie's voice. "He's conscious and responding."

After what seemed like an hour, Beezan was suited up, helmet still open and gloves hooked to his belt, when Iricana called breathlessly, "Jarvie's semi-conscious, in pain, bringing him to Med Bay."

Beezan passed Iricana in the rimway. She had taken off Jarvie's helmet and strapped a towline on him.

"Jarvie?" Beezan asked, wheeling over to him. His face was sallow and pinched in pain. Beezan touched his forehead gingerly and his eyes fluttered open.

"Sorry, honor."

"Shhh, I'll be back as soon as I can. Just rest."

His eyes closed again. Beezan was torn. But there was no one else to get Reeder. He nodded to Iricana to go on. He needed to hurry but he dreaded what he would find.

Only once before had he been part of a recovery team at the scene of a fatality. He had been young and the person had been a stranger. The *Cricket* appeared so damaged that Beezan hardly held out a hope.

At the hangar, Beezan studied *Cricket* from the window. One auto anchor was attached. The whole shuttle wavered up and down. He would have to anchor it first.

Pulling on his helmet, he tested his s'link. "*Drumheller*, do we have any status readings on fuel from the *Cricket*?"

"Fuel status reports zero, but there is high probability of malfunction. Recommend minimum time in shuttle."

"Any readings on Reeder?"

"Tracking beacon only."

"Iricana?"

"Here. We're in Med Bay; Katie's examining Jarvie. I'll head up to the Command Bay."

"I'm going to turn off auto monitoring so I won't be distracted. Call me if you have to."

"Good luck, Captain."

28 / SHOCKWAVE

The first thing Beezan did in the hangar was get anchors to lock down the *Cricket*. The mangled shuttle was pitted, blackened, and wet. *Is that fuel?* Who knew what chemicals were released or what systems were now unstable and dangerous. He hooked an anchor to the shuttle and then the deck and set it on the slowest speed. It cranked its way agonizingly slowly, but the thump when the shuttle hit the deck was frightening. Dust puffed out everywhere. *Probably toxic.* He put two more anchors on. "*Drumheller*, do you have the anchors?" Beezan saw lights flashing on each anchor in turn.

"Reading four anchors."

"Is *Cricket* still controlled?"

"Yes."

The lock was not badly damaged. Beezan moved well away. "Open the *Cricket* exterior hatch."

"Hatch does not respond."

"Try the inner hatch."

"Inner hatch is open."

Beezan maneuvered back to the shuttle and pressed the

code to manually open the outer hatch. With a prayer for strength of two kinds, he braced himself and slowly pushed sideways with the emergency door opener. It moved a bit. He pushed harder. *If I could just get my tool in the crack.*

Suddenly, the hatch was shoved back to reveal a still-alive Reeder. Beezan yipped in alarm and grabbed the holdbar. Reeder's suit was streaked like he'd tried to clean it off. Beezan grasped Reeder's arm in shock and relief. "Thank God. Reeder, can you hear me?"

Reeder's lips were moving, but he was shaking his head. And he was smiling, for once. "*Drumheller*, s'links on! He's alive! He's fine!" He heard the others' amazed and happy responses.

Beezan nearly dragged Reeder across the hangar to the 'dirty' lock. They emerged, decontaminated, pulling off helmets, and breathing hard. Beezan was so pleased he hugged Reeder, awkward in the suits. "We thought we'd lost you!"

Reeder was surprised and subdued. They looked through the window at the poor shuttle. It was practically a sin to abandon any sort of spacecraft. But it was dangerous and there was nowhere to get repairs.

"*Drumheller*, is the auto download complete?"

"Completed."

"*Drumheller*, jettison the *Cricket*. Easy."

They watched sadly as the anchors detached and *Drumheller* pulled the shuttle out with a tow arm, giving it one last push to send it on its way. "Track it. We don't want to run into it later. Cleaning robots to the hangar deck."

"Med Bay," Beezan told Reeder.

"I am uninjured."

"Good, but Jarvie—"

"Agent Oatah?"

"I believe he is all right."

"What happened here?" Reeder asked as they got into the lift.

"Apparently, there was a mini gravity ball in that—"

"*WHAT?*"

So he didn't know. "It seems so." Reeder had his hand on his chest as if he might have heart failure. "We had to move in a hurry," Beezan continued. "Oatah was in the garden lock and Jarvie was waiting for you down here. Jarvie was only semi-conscious when Iricana found him."

The lift went quickly after the coupler as there was no gravity to adjust to. He wanted to get to Med Bay and see Jarvie sitting up with Star and Sky zooming around.

Reeder stopped at the EVA Bay, still muttering "gravity ball" to himself, but Beezan kept on to the Med Bay, pulling himself up by the rail.

No one was sitting around of course. Even if there had been gravity, no one was in a sitting mood. Iricana and Oatah argued angrily in one corner and a very stressed Katie hovered over Jarvie—still strapped to the exam bed.

"What is going on here?" Beezan demanded. There was a sudden guilty silence. "This is no place for arguing!"

"Yes, Captain. Sorry," Iricana answered.

"Has someone checked on the pups?" he asked.

"I'll do that honor," and she was off, red-faced with fury and embarrassment.

"Reeder is in the EVA Bay," Beezan told Oatah, who didn't move. "He could use a hand with the suit and he's been through a terrible ordeal," Beezan said more pointedly.

"Of course, Captain." Oatah calmly floated down the stairs.

Beezan thought he would burst. Relief, anger and worry all mixed up into extreme aggravation.

"Thank you," Katie breathed. "Jarvie's brain has no additional damage as far as I can see. The pain was hard on him."

"I don't understand. Why is Jarvie worse off than Oatah? He's young and healthy."

"Exactly the points, Captain," she said wearily. "He is very young. His muscles have not kept up with his skeletal growth. He is NOT healthy. His heart is under great strain from lack of exercise and being so tall. He's suffered a series of physical, emotional, and chemical setbacks dating back two years. He doesn't recover from one when the next one hits. He has spiraled into a crisis. He'd be in the hospital under the care of a specialist if we were on Redrock."

"It's that serious?"

"Captain, it's critical."

Beezan vaguely recalled similar things Katie had said before, but they were finally getting through to him. On Redrock, Jarvie would be in the hospital—and he would probably be in counseling, one step from having his license pulled. But his overriding concern was for Jarvie.

"What can we do here?" he asked.

"Remove him from duty."

"What else?"

"Remove him from teen training."

"What else?"

"Full time exercise and rehab program."

"What else?"

"Spin would help."

"But what will he do all day?"

"Survive."

Beezan hung his head. Once again, he was a failure as a Captain. Without Katie, Jarvie wouldn't make it.

"*Drumheller*, remove Jarvie from the duty list. Rearrange all schedules and send to Iricana for approval."

"Removed."

"Iricana?"

"Here, honor," she said, coming up the stairs with two boxes in tow. One had the pups, slurping away, and the other had food.

"We'll have to remove Jarvie from all work including teen training."

"Yes, Captain." She glanced at Katie. "Can he have Star?"

Katie nodded. Iricana let Sky out and she came right to Beezan, squirmed between the suit neck rim and Beezan's neck, closed her eyes, and sucked on her bottle with contentment. He could hardly breathe.

Iricana had a stern talk with Star before setting him down by Jarvie, but within seconds, some color returned to Jarvie's cheeks.

"I'll help you with that suit, honor," Iricana said. Whatever she had been arguing with Oatah about had left her upset and shaking. She was normally so calm it was unnerving.

"What exactly happened out there?" Beezan asked her as she helped him.

"Exactly—I don't know. We've always known that gravity balls are machines. All gravity balls discovered so far are exactly the same size and put out the same gravity. There has been some speculation about whether it would be possible to turn them off. I don't believe it had occurred to anyone that there might be other kinds, smaller *and* more powerful. The sensor attached to the cargo container registered 1.7 gravity ball masses before it stopped transmitting." She paused as she pulled off the last of Beezan's suit. "Well, we don't have the technology to block gravity, as you know. So that leaves only one other explanation. It was turned off when it was put in the cargo container—and somehow, we turned it on, or it just went on."

"And," Beezan said, "whoever put it in there lied to you."

Iricana's eyes flashed. "Yes, Captain. Someone has lied."

"Priority Alert!"

Iricana jumped and Katie practically sobbed. *God help us.* "Report."

"Unknown vessel has changed course."

There was total silence for a heartbeat. All eyes turned to the big screen at the table. They didn't need to ask which way the ship was going now.

"How long?" Beezan asked.

"Unknown. Vessel is currently accelerating. Maximum time until intercept: 5 days, 12.7 hours."

Beezan instinctively reached out to steady himself in case his knees buckled, but they were in nogee. Katie and Iricana were staring at him with expectation. *I must take charge, give direction.*

There was a quiet triple-tone: sunset on a Holy Day, Redrock time of course. Beezan let out the breath he had been holding. He activated his s'link so Oatah and Reeder could hear. "First," Beezan said, hooking an elbow around a holdbar, "get some food and check all your stations. Iricana, can you cover for Jarvie?"

"Yes, Captain," she answered, gripping the food box.

"Second, medical exams for everyone.

"Third, clean up.

"Fourth, prayers, in Med Bay.

"Fifth, sleep. Tomorrow we'll proceed with the Holy Day as planned."

Iricana gave Katie her food. She took it and turned back to work. Beezan had to hold on a minute so his heart wouldn't pound through his chest. Iricana brought him a food packet, "Captain's orders."

Beezan took his food, and holding Sky on his shoulder with one hand, floated down the stairs. He was shaking and didn't want anyone to see him in such an agitated state, even though they were more upset than he was. He got to his cabin and let Sky loose.

He knew he should have gone to the EVA Bay to check on Reeder and Oatah, but he didn't want to face them. What he wanted was to spin the ship so he could collapse on his bunk with the blanket over his head. But they couldn't risk the fuel yet. He grabbed a blanket and strapped into the chair, trying to think straight, trying to stop shaking, trying to breathe between bites of his snack.

Sky finished her bottle and neatly put it in the net by the stairs, calm as ever. She coasted over to him and burrowed into the blanket, making him even less ambitious to get dressed. "Oh Sky, what is happening?" The more he thought about having a gravity ball on his ship, the more horrified he became, regardless of the fact that it was now off the ship. He couldn't stop the mental parade of might-have-beens. *It's a wonder we survived.*

Concerned for Reeder, Beezan tapped the big screen. "*Drumheller*, show me the EVA Bay." Reeder was holding a strap, struggling to put the suit in the suit checker. He looked cold and strained. Oatah, whom Beezan had sent to help him, was nowhere to be seen.

"Where is Oatah?"

The screen flicked to the Command Bay. Oatah was strapped in the pilot's chair. "Top priority. Send."

"Sent."

He's sending a packet! Where?

Iricana suddenly appeared behind Oatah. "*What are you*

doing?" She asked, and then flinched, probably at the accusatory sound of her own voice. They regarded each other, calm intensity leveled against agitated suspicion.

"As I said before," Oatah answered, "I had no knowledge of the gravity ball and would never have allowed such a thing. I am certain that Solo Journey and the Councils had no knowledge. An individual—or group of individuals—is responsible for this. However, I do not believe that you are one of them. I thoroughly understand your anger, but we must remain united in the face of this threat—which is what it is, especially in this time of crisis, when we are cut off from Earth." He paused. Iricana took a deep breath and strapped into another chair. He continued, "In the event that we do not survive the return jump, I have sent a light-speed message to Redrock."

"Well, that had to be done, but we need to get back there *now* and warn the Councils. Your message will take 20 years!"

"We cannot leave until we determine the nature and purpose of the other ship. And . . ." he paused, "I believe the person responsible is contained at Harbor, at least temporarily."

"Thayne? You think he would do such a crazy thing? He's—he was—the leader of the project. He's the most brilliant scientist in the outer sectors."

"Brilliance and good judgment do not necessarily go together."

"I just can't imagine—"

"Then who? Melawn? Tiati? Nkiroo? You know them all. You tell me." Although they were speaking calmly now, Iricana's frown deepened with every name. "Tell me about them," Oatah prompted.

She sighed. "Tiati—impossible. A good Solo Journey pilot with no personal ambition. Like Beezan, only funnier. Has our complete trust. Very reliable. Ferried alien cargo, selected and brought out the secret cargo team, did some salvage work. I can't imagine that he wouldn't report a gravity ball."

"Who would he report to?"

"Thayne. But Thayne has briefed Solo Journey on the salvage operation, of course."

"I agree with you that it cannot be Tiati."

Beezan had a moment of relief. His friend was not suspected. Then he realized he really shouldn't be listening as, no doubt, Oatah assumed that the Command Bay was secure. But someone had put a gravity ball on his ship and he was mad.

"Nkiroo?"

Beezan didn't even know who he was.

"Kiro hasn't even been out to Hamada."

"Then—"

"But . . . a specially engineered cargo container . . ."

"His sort of work?"

"Yes," she nodded grimly, "and I heard him talking about containment fields, except I wouldn't expect his design to fail."

"Possibly, someone used his designs without disclosing complete parameters. Melawn?"

"Well, he's Thayne's most trusted assistant. He supervised the salvage operation at Hamada and was personally responsible for the cargo team. He must have known about the gravity ball."

"And who would he report to?"

"Thayne."

"What about the cargo team?"

"Completely isolated. Packets monitored. No chance of leaks. They report to Melawn and no one else."

"But Melawn was not there. My reports say he is with the *Cheetah*."

"Well, yes. He left once all the cargo was ready. The cargo's been sitting there a while, just waiting for transport. Melawn went back to be with Thayne."

"So there was some opportunity for independent action from someone else."

"Unlikely. The cargo team stayed until the last cargo was loaded."

"What about you?" Oatah asked calmly.

"I was out there—while Melawn was still there. I did see the salvage hangar and a lot of cargo containers, but I didn't see that big one."

"Are you certain?"

"Yes, there were the other big ones that are now aboard the *Drumheller*, but not that one."

"What about Beezan?"

"I assume you ask for the sake of thoroughness," she said sharply. "He doesn't know anything."

"He ended up with the cargo."

"He's got a big ship."

"He ended up with Jarvie."

"Chance."

"Jarvie knows Lanezi."

"Chance."

"Jarvie saw the alien ship."

"Chance."

"Jarvie was headed for Harbor."

"As you say, *providence*."

"Jarvie even said it was a gravity ball. Jarvie committed many illegal acts to get aboard the *Drumheller*," Oatah said.

"Yes, more reason to suspect Jarvie, not Beezan!"

Oatah was taken aback. "I had not considered that."

Beezan switched the conversation to his s'link, threw the

blanket off so it went flapping about the cabin, pulled on his pants, and headed to the Command Bay with Sky.

"Lanezi?" Oatah was asking.

"Reports to Thayne, but he stays with the *Cheetah*."

"I understand that Thayne is quite charismatic and inspires great personal loyalty."

"In some. Melawn especially."

"So it's possible that Melawn and Thayne found a gravity ball, and under cover of the alien cargo planned to ship it to themselves," Oatah hypothesized.

"That is the logical conclusion. But why keep it secret?"

"Because they knew transporting it wouldn't be approved."

"So they'd risk a ship? If that thing had gone off at Redrock, or even—God forbid—while we jumped . . ."

Beezan gasped. He had not even thought of that. God had protected them all. He just wasn't looking at it the right way. He needed to have more trust in God, and less in people. His heart began to calm down and he stopped shaking.

"Thayne and his team are off the rails. And we have no idea what they're doing now," Oatah was saying as Beezan got to the Command Bay door and opened it.

Both Oatah and Iricana greeted Beezan and then, startled, looked at the s'link in his hand where they heard their own voices. Oatah glanced at the panel, where the private light was on.

"Captain's override," Beezan explained without guilt. "And you forgot something. I know Tiati too."

"Well, Captain," Oatah said. "You're the eye of the storm."

Although Jarvie's mind was fuzzy, he clearly sensed Katie's agitation. At first he thought it was about him, but she repeatedly told him he would be fine. Then he thought it was about the gravity ball, admitting that even though he suspected it all along, he was still shocked. “What’s wrong?” he asked her.

She scowled, but then came to his bed. “You’ve had a lot of medication. I’m sure the situation is confusing. The ship is safe. We’re well away from the gravity ball. We’ll talk about your rehab later, but you’ll be fine in time. Now rest.”

Maybe it was the medication; he just couldn’t stop himself from asking. “No, I mean what is wrong, what are you sad about?” Star gave a soft whine and gazed up at her with big sad eyes.

Katie sighed and patted Star. “Well, someone has done a terrible thing, putting that gravity ball on the ship. No one knew, so that means the Councils didn’t know. Someone has betrayed the Councils.”

“And you’re afraid it was Lanezi?”

“No!” She said, annoyed, and then relaxed. “Well, I don’t think Lanezi would do anything to harm anyone . . . but he is so eager to please, and Thayne . . .”

“Is Thayne a bad guy?”

“Jarvie! There aren’t any bad guys!”

“Well, someone put that monster on our ship.”

“Yes, someone who thought they were doing the right thing, someone who thought they knew better.”

“Someone who thought they knew better than the Councils? Someone like Thayne?”

She nodded grimly. “And now he’ll be angry. He’s stuck at Harbor and he didn’t get his gravity ball. And when Thayne is angry . . .”

“And Lanezi is stuck there with him.”

“Yes.”

“Maybe Lanezi can leave the ship?”

"He's sworn an oath, just like we have."

Jarvie frowned in sympathy, but knew in his heart that to Lanezi, an oath was a mere technicality. And maybe that realization was what really bothered Katie.

It was late at night before they had an actual meal, in the Med Bay. Beezan hovered by Jarvie's exam bed. Katie said Jarvie was given large doses of pain medication. He was well enough to be "sitting up," which in nogee was a slightly bent position. Katie was tethered on the other side of the bed and Iricana, Oatah, and Reeder had strapped in at the table. Beezan was starving. Had he eaten a food pack four hours ago? They were exhausted, but less tense since they'd said prayers. Jarvie ate slowly, but well, and looked dazed. The pups, of course, had already eaten three times.

"The unknown vessel has finally stopped accelerating," Beezan told the others. "ETA is now 4.3 days."

"Four days!" Iricana exclaimed. "How will we ever be ready?"

Beezan shrugged his hands. "I don't know what to do to get ready."

"No packets?" Jarvie asked. His color had come back and he was moving around more fluidly.

"Nothing," Reeder answered. "They are not attempting to communicate."

Beezan hoped that was true and not that the *Drumheller* crew was too primitive to understand. "Sorry doctor, we won't be able to spin. We're not in a stable orbit. We will have to make adjustments," he explained. Jarvie winced, but didn't complain.

"Why did they suddenly notice us?" Katie asked.

"They didn't—at least I don't think so." Iricana sighed as

they all looked perplexed. “They noticed the gravity ball. They changed course almost exactly in the time they would have detected it.”

“Is it sending out some kind of signal?” Oatah asked.

“Not that we can detect,” Beezan answered, “but it went from a low mass object to a higher mass object and that’s a kind of signal to someone who looks for it.”

“Would we have detected it?” Reeder asked.

“We wouldn’t repeatedly scan so many small objects and check and recheck their gravity,” Iricana answered. “Normally, mass changes are the result of impacts, explosions, or other obvious events.”

“So we don’t know if they’re coming to see us or the gravity ball, do we?” Katie asked.

“We’ll find out when they get closer,” Beezan said.

16-Mercy

The Holy Day, Martyrdom of the Báb, was Jarvie’s least favorite. He supposed he should feel guilty for having favorites, but it was so gruesome. A Holy Person being strung up and shot with projectile weapons—750 of them?

He hoped they would not read the long retelling of it from the *Dawn-breakers*. Jarvie didn’t think his nerves could take it today. He was worn out. He ached everywhere. He got winded getting dressed. He was cold and dizzy and had twinges of pain —sometimes full stabs of pain. He hadn’t slept at all. His nightmares woke him up and his memories of their bad day kept him up. *Bad day with a gravity ball.* It would end up as a note in a chapter in some boring history book. *Drumheller wrecks Turquoise environment and offends local aliens.*

He went to the Prayer Room early, but his mind drifted off to the Work Tower. He longed for the fun he had been having with Iricana and the robots. He wished he could go over there, not on a Holy Day, of course. He and Iricana had assembled the multibots into their standard configuration. In that mode, there were nine units. Each unit was a different form that fit into its Bot Bay niche, in the side of the Work Tower wall. A human-form robot, #9, was the 'manager.' Although the brains had all been loaded and checked, Oatah had not yet allowed them to be linked together, let alone linked to the *Drumheller*.

One niche was empty now. It had held the unit they left on Lander's moon. Jarvie wondered what had happened to it. They had a copy of its original brain of course, and could replace the parts, but it was still sad. How long had the robot survived? Had it known it was abandoned? Did the others miss it? Jarvie resisted the urge to say a prayer for it. It wasn't a person.

Jarvie just wanted to see them in action. Supposedly, robot #9 could run the whole 'family.' It could determine the best configurations and supervise the transformations and repairs. If there were more units than onboard brains, #9 would remote control the extras or link them to each other. There was even a consultation mode when the nine brains could work together, but in independent mode, to solve complex problems. It was supposed to work as well for robots as for humans. *Probably better*. Yet the robots were not AIs. Their programming was limited to physical problem solving. They were no match for the *Drumheller*.

Jarvie forced his mind back to the present as others came in the Prayer Room. They would start an hour before noon, Redrock time, and read the Writings and have music and prayers until noon, when the Tablet of Visitation would be read. It was the same Tablet that would be read at the actual Shrine of the Báb, on Earth.

The little tracking image of Earth was almost in the corner of the Prayer Room, so they arranged themselves around it, attaching themselves to the carpets with their stick-and-stays. Agent Oatah was in charge of the program today. He had asked Jarvie to chant the opening prayer.

Afterwards, they went to the kitchen and Jarvie discovered why Oatah had been so busy in the garden the day before.

"It's beautiful!" Katie exclaimed.

Picking up a cucumber, an amazed Beezan asked, "This grew in our garden?"

"Yes, Captain, with a little advice from Kelson McNelson."

Oatah had outdone himself with an arrangement of fresh fruits and vegetables for their special lunch. For a time, Jarvie could forget their situation. He tried to relax his aching body and just be at peace. They had good food. He had people that cared about him. He had faith. He would get better. Sky and Star were happy, healthy, and busy playing catch with a radish. The aliens would probably come over, take one look at their old ship and the mess they had made, give them an interstellar traffic ticket, and go.

29 / THE OCEAN OF SPACE

18-Mercy

The aliens didn't go.

The ship was coming right at the *Drumheller*. The blob became more spherical as the alien ship slowed to approach.

Jarvie felt sorry for Beezan, who lived in the Command Bay in case he had to move the *Drumheller*. Jarvie spent his time making sure he was near restraints so he wouldn't be flattened in evasive maneuvers. Finally, the ship was close enough to see. It had grown from a bluish white dot to a creamy-blue ball.

"It's . . . pearlescent," Katie said in awe, as they gathered in the Command Bay.

"It's what?" Jarvie asked.

"Like a pearl, how it appears to glow from within." She fished a necklace out from under her shirt and showed it to Jarvie, holding it out from her neck with a finger. On a gold chain was one small creamy-blue ball that did look like the approaching ship.

Everyone turned to look. "Is that a real pearl?" Reeder asked, almost accusingly.

Katie was surprised at his tone. "Well, I think so; it's been in my family forever. It's from Earth."

"It should be in a museum," Oatah said absently, turning back to the alien ship. The mere fact that the Earthborn were distracted from an alien spaceship by a pearl told Jarvie how rare it was.

"But why?" Katie asked. "There must be millions on Earth."

Oatah shook his head sadly. "No. Oysters are extinct. Natural pearls are no more. Surviving pearls are rare. DNA restoration has been . . . delayed."

Katie gulped and dropped the pearl back into hiding.

"Well, we can call our friend the *Pearl of Space*," Beezan suggested, jokingly, but Oatah nodded.

"*Pearl*. Yes." And everyone smiled. Except Jarvie. More like the blob of space, he thought. Its twin hadn't been so pretty destroying the a-rings at Luminesse.

On the first day of the month of Words, "*Pearl*" came within 1000 meters of the *Drumheller* and stopped. Jarvie crowded in the Command Bay with the others, all recorders on, for the historic moment. Beezan almost collapsed over the panel when *Pearl* finally burned for stationkeeping. Its shape became exactly spherical.

It was dazzling. Its glowing, translucent surface was accented by streaks and blobs of different colors. It shimmered, and the spherical shape of it even wavered and pulsed.

"Any packets?" Oatah asked.

"Nothing. We're still sending," Reeder answered. Jarvie had been kicked out of his chair by Reeder, so he sat in back. He monitored the assignment cameras and kept an eye on their fields. One camera was still watching Nocturne's L5 and the mess going on there with the bad gravity ball.

They stared at the ship, mesmerized. The colors would cascade, separate, freeze, blur, reverse direction, and change from reds to pale blues to greens to yellows to purples, pinks, whites, and combinations. *Was it communicating or not? Were the lights a message or just an effect of the field? Drumheller* was set to watch for patterns. After two days, it could only report that there were short patterns, but they cycled randomly and no overall pattern could yet be found.

4-Words

After two more days, *Drumheller* reported that the patterns had become slower and simpler. "If," Oatah suggested, "the lights are an attempt to communicate, they are not following any predicted first contact patterns."

"Well, if we can't understand their lights, and they can't understand our packets, then what?" Beezan asked.

"It's possible," Iricana said, "that the lights are a naturally occurring effect of their fields. But it's also possible they are trying to communicate at a more advanced level than we anticipate."

"Maybe they're not so advanced," Jarvie suggested. *After all, their people had managed to botch jumps, crash ships and destroy a-rings. More than once.* He supposed he was still harboring a grudge. He reminded himself that the aliens who caused his family to make the desperation jump were long dead. But in his mind, it was not the *Pearl.* It was the *Blob,* the *Big Blob of Space,* with the blundering blobbers aboard. He didn't hate them, and he had to admit he was excited about it, but he wasn't going to go into full admiration over a pretty ship.

"Do we have any lights, Captain?" Oatah suddenly asked. "On the outside?" Beezan popped up a tactical view of the *Drumheller* exterior as seen from the other ship. "*Drumheller*, show operational exterior lights."

"Lights showing."

Rows of lights ran around the torus, up the spokes and around the ends of the cargo cylinders. Small lights outlined hatches, docks, the hangars, and Cargo Hold doors. Bright clusters pinpointed extreme points. Accent lights shone on any external system that might need to be checked. Adjustable beacons were located strategically to investigate any problem. Although there were many dark gaps where the lights were broken, there were more than enough to be noticed.

"Can they see our lights through that glowing ball of their own?" Iricana asked.

"Do they even see in our visual range?" Katie asked.

"There is only one way to find out," Oatah said patiently.

"Drumheller, use the exterior lights in unison. From 2 to 47." He took a determined breath. "Send the primes."

They watched the simulation on the pop-up. Lights blinked two times, paused, three times, paused, five times. Seven, eleven, thirteen. This could take a while, Jarvie thought, watching the numbers at the bottom of the screen. He took a few deep breaths and forced himself to stop counting along. 41. 43.

Iricana gasped and Jarvie jerked his eyes from the pop-up to the main screen. The glowing ball of the *Pearl* had gone dark. It was still there, but now it was an indigo shadow in an inky background. Jarvie looked back at the screen. They had stopped at 47.

"Sequence complete."

Jarvie could feel his heart pounding. He stared at the dark

ball in anticipation. He thought Reeder might give the order to repeat, but Oatah held up a hand, "Patience."

Katie whispered a prayer. *Somebody better.* Then, a band of white lit up the equator of the *Pearl*—one, two, they counted. A pause, then one, two, three. A chill went down Jarvie's spine. Five. Seven. He had no desire to cheer or clap. Iricana had her hand on her heart; Katie covered her mouth. Reeder's hands were frozen on the panel. Oatah swallowed hard and nodded. Beezan glanced in the direction of the a-rings. *Thinking how fast we could get out of here.* Jarvie wasn't the only one with the sudden urge to run.

"Contact," Oatah whispered. They all jumped.

"11:07" Reeder added officially.

"O SON OF MAN!" quoted Katie softly, ***"Wert thou to speed through the immensity of space and traverse the expanse of heaven, yet thou wouldst find no rest save in submission to Our command and humbleness before Our Face."***[1]

Surprisingly, Jarvie's fear faded away. His dislike of the blobbers disappeared, and he knew they were standing on the brink of a new age. He grabbed his handkerchief before tears got loose in the Command Bay and saw the others doing the same. How did he ever get so lucky, to witness this moment in history? God had blessed him after all.

The sequence stopped. They waited. Beezan turned to look at Oatah and Iricana. "Proceed to establishing communications," he said formally, handing over the process to them. It was in the protocols. "Just don't sell the ship!"

Iricana and Oatah set to work, redoing the First Contact Protocols to use the *Drumheller* lights. The others watched breathlessly as *Pearl* sent a speeded-up pattern and *Drumheller* repeated.

This could get boring fast. "I'll go make lunch," Jarvie volunteered. The others nodded mutely, still entranced.

In the kitchen, Jarvie split the big screen to watch the *Drumheller* simulation and *Pearl's* responses. He got out squeeze bulbs and warming plates and stuck them to the prep counter. He lost track of the patterns quickly, but whenever he looked up, lights were flashing. He decided not to waste any good food on the crew. They were too distracted to notice what they were eating.

He fed the podpups and let them play around the dining side of the kitchen. They knew better than to come in the cooking area on purpose and the safety net kept them from accidentally landing in the lunch.

He put the s'link on loud so he could listen to the crew, but it was just a bunch of light sequences. Realistically, they could expect to do this for days, weeks even.

19-Words

And they did. Jarvie began to feel alone on the ship. The others did their chores, late or early while Jarvie was still sleeping. Katie made sure they all got their exercise. She especially made sure Jarvie did his workouts. Oatah still took care of the garden. But they spent most of the day in the Command Bay. The aliens and *Drumheller* ended up on a natural schedule. From lunchtime for 6.2 hours straight, they would blink at each other. Then the dark ball would turn back into a pearl and they were done for the day. The *Pearl* started again in 24 hours and 3 minutes, which was so close to 24 hours that they all wondered again if the 'aliens' were really human.

After fifteen days of it and increasingly complex messages, Beezan and Katie began to lose interest. Beezan confided to Jarvie that he didn't think they were getting anywhere. Sending and repeating patterns could go on forever if there wasn't some other breakthrough. They really needed a language expert. Oatah had one—back in the sectors.

It was amazing how fast a person could get used to an alien ship out the window. The *Pearl* was beautiful when it wasn't in blinking mode. Jarvie had a wild thrill of imagining what it would be like to visit. He pictured mermaids, giant starfish, and intelligent dolphin-like people. Still though, in his nightmares, he saw sharks and blob-like people. He found pictures in the library of pearls, oysters, and puffer fish, of tiny sea horses and giant squid. Most were extinct now. Jarvie found Oatah's name, Master Conservator of the Pacific Ocean—thirty years ago.

It was Jarvie's turn to arrange Feast, so he picked Writings that had the word *pearl* and *ocean* and he took the pictures to Feast. One quote stuck in his mind, ***". . . His signs have appeared and the billows of His rising ocean have scattered on every shore many a precious pearl."***[2]

He wondered if they were on the shore of a new era. He wondered if the sectors would be saved. He wondered if the aliens were from an ocean planet—if the ship was full of water.

"Well, I guess it's possible," Beezan said, when Jarvie asked him. "It's more massive than our ship. But we can't calculate the density, because we can't see how big the ship is under that glowing field." Beezan was stuffing down his dinner in the kitchen after their 6.2-hour shift. Iricana, Oatah, and Reeder were too exhausted to eat. Katie and Jarvie had eaten long before. The cooking had come to them by default and he spent most of his time cooking or exercising. Jarvie felt better, but still tired so easily.

"We don't think they were ever getting our packets. We may need an exact frequency to get through," Iricana was saying, "but we don't even know what sort of packeting they might use, or if they have some completely different system."

"Well, we don't dare mess with the packet transmitters," Beezan cautioned, "and we don't have an extra transmitter to play with.

"Don't worry Captain," Iricana consoled him. "We just need to know the right frequency. We need to get all the data we can to build one for next time."

"You mean we're leaving soon?" Jarvie asked, accidentally letting a little excitement into his voice.

Reeder glared at him. "We are not leaving yet. We have barely begun the protocols. When we have exhausted all possibilities, we will go to Redrock for more experts and come back immediately. Such an important task can't be given up just because we are impatient."

Jarvie scowled. *Blobs.*

2-Perfection

Everyone was worn down. Beezan reprioritized the aliens down a notch to focus on his real job, taking care of the ship and crew. He used to worry about the *Drumheller*, now he worried about the crew and prayed the ship would hold together. *How was having more people supposed to be easier?*

He checked on Jarvie in the Gym, doing his required exercise. "Hi, Captain," Jarvie said brightly as Beezan signaled him to keep going. Sky launched from Beezan's shoulder at the sight of Star and they tumbled off together. Beezan couldn't help laughing as Star bounced around chanting 'go-go-go.' Katie came into the Gym, so Beezan moved aside with her.

"How is Jarvie?"

Katie started out in her official doctor voice. "He has improved from his crisis condition of last month, but he has a long way to go. Some issues just aren't going to be resolved until we get to Redrock. He is cooperating and I have insisted that he eat more. He is still growing." She dropped her voice. "I fear his height may be a mutation. No one in his family has been near this tall. We need to have his genes checked at Redrock. If we're going to be out here much longer, he may need gene therapy."

"But he's only 14," Beezan whispered.

"Exactly. He could grow for five more years. He's nearly two meters now. He already has complications. If he gets much taller he'll be grounded."

Beezan felt a surge of panic. "Can't he start the gene therapy now?"

Katie had a pained look. "I did broach the subject with Reeder, since legally I need his approval. I never expected a problem, but apparently, non-essential gene therapy is illegal on Earth."

"Why?"

"I'm not sure I understand it. Some backlash against people modifying their bodies too much."

"But we're not on Earth! Being grounded would be a curse. It is essential out here."

"I know," she nodded sympathetically, "but Reeder thinks it's morally wrong."

Beezan's recent tolerance for Reeder drained right out of him. "Captain," Katie continued, "Jarvie will be 15 in three months. He'll be able to speak for himself in medical matters. I think it best to wait. It would be better to do it at Redrock anyway. I'm no expert in gene therapy."

Beezan nodded reluctantly.

"I think Reeder is coming around," she whispered, "but the last thing we want is a power struggle with him."

A happy chime sounded and the podpups puffed with excitement. "I . . . did . . . it." Jarvie smiled, as he floated in relief. But he was pale and gasping for air. A fleeting frown crossed Katie's face.

After that troubling discussion, Beezan went to the Garden Deck to check on Oatah. Oatah was floating near the lock, staring forlornly at the ceiling. Beezan wanted to say something comforting or understanding, but "What are you looking at?" came out.

"Forgive me, Captain. I find myself having moments of selfishness. I just wanted to see the sky," Oatah said sadly. "God willing, I will see the sky again."

Beezan was puzzled. He floated over to hover shoulder to shoulder with Oatah. "I could open the big window in the Observation Room, if you don't like the cam views."

Oatah turned to Beezan in astonishment. "I'm sorry, Captain. I meant the real sky. The sky of Earth. I want to see the *blue* sky. I want to feel the breeze on my face. I want to smell the ocean air, hear the crashing waves, feel the sand and warm sun, see all the little scurrying creatures. I want to know the connections between ourselves and our place in the universe. I want to feel human again." He stopped and gazed at Beezan. "You really have no idea what I'm talking about?" Beezan looked away, defensive. "Have you lived all your life in the outer sectors?" Oatah asked.

"Agent Oatah, I have lived all my life *on the Drumheller.*"

Oatah shuddered. "If this ship is your home, it is a palace, but if it is your whole world, it is a prison. The sky is always dark, as if you are trapped in nighttime, frozen in a bad dream."

Beezan swallowed. *I am not backward!* He saw in front of him all those pathways and a surge of emotion welled up. "Am I less of a human for having lived among the stars rather than on Earth?" Oatah began to shake his head to object that he was not insulting Beezan. But Beezan would not be stopped. "*Drumheller* may be small but it rides the paths of stars. What are the oceans of Earth compared to the ocean of space? What is any of it compared to the Ocean of God's Words? We are not alone and trapped out here. And we are all still connected."

Oatah hung his head, "I cannot feel it. Even after Kelson McNelson. I can't feel connected. Not to this place or this ship, not to the plants or the planets, not even to the people."

Maybe that's the problem. "Agent Oatah, there's someone aboard who really needs you." Beezan knew he was overstepping, but boldly went on, trying to think of the things Kelson McNelson had said to him. "All living things need . . . nurturing."

"I know," Oatah shook his head, "but the losses. Skeena, Kerre, Lander. There is so much loss out here. It's a life of loss."

Beezan swallowed. There was too much truth in that. "There is no other way for us."

"And yet, even as your connections are ripped away from you, you still feel connected."

Beezan nodded. "Agent Oatah, we are only connected to Earth through our bodies. We are connected to heaven with our whole being. That's a connection that can never be brok—" Beezan stopped, hit by a sudden inspiration. "You," he pointed at Oatah, who recoiled, "must jump with me."

"What? I'm not a pilot."

"You don't have to be. You jump with me next time, awake.

You will see with your own inner vision. You will see the connections of the universe."

Oatah gazed at Beezan with piercing eyes. "Sometimes, you remind me of your father, Captain."

Beezan was taken aback by the change of subject. "You've met my father?"

"Of course, Captain. I report to Sector 1 Council frequently, as does your father. I know both your parents. They are quite extraordinary. I was puzzled that their child was a cargo captain."

Before Beezan could get offended, Oatah smiled humbly. "Of course, then I had no idea what it meant to be a pilot or captain. And yes, Captain, I would be honored to jump with you."

By the time his "cheering up" rounds took him to Iricana, in the Command Bay, Beezan thought he might quit while he was behind. His emotions heaved up and down as if he were coming out of a bad jump. *Oatah knows my parents? Why didn't he ever mention it?* "Where's Reeder?" he whispered.

"Briefing Jarvie."

"Why?" he asked in surprise.

"Katie said Jarvie could do a little light work to feel useful, so we're going to send him to the Work Tower."

"Oh." Beezan really wasn't pleased, but didn't want to baby Jarvie either. Getting all the way around to the Work Tower in nogee was enough exercise for anyone, and Jarvie had just had his gym session.

Knowing that, Beezan didn't worry when Jarvie wasn't at lunch. Jarvie, after all, never forgot to take food with him. Apparently, both Star and Sky had gone with him. Beezan suspected that Sky was watching over both of them.

Iricana and Oatah dutifully left lunch to be on time for *Pearl.* Beezan wasn't inspired, but he did tap a pop-up. The *Pearl* was still in pearl mode. Beezan glanced at the time.

"Are they late?" he asked over his s'link.

"Yes, Captain, and they have never been late before," reported Iricana.

"Well, maybe it's a Holy Day or something."

"There are many poss—"

Beezan saw it on his screen too. The glowing ball was growing a bump. As he watched, the bump separated into a tiny glistening pearl that was headed right for them.

"Captain—"

"I see!" He grabbed his lunch stuff and stowed it in a bin. "Crew, secure all stations. I'm coming to the Command Bay."

"Honor?" It was Jarvie. *Oh, no! He's in the Work Tower.*

"Jarvie—no time to come back here. Secure everything. Start with the big stuff. Then get to a safe place."

Why is it, he thought, as he dived down the stairs, *every time I want something to happen, the wrong thing happens?*

30 / SHUTTLE DIPLOMACY

"If it's a probe, it's a big one," Iricana said when Beezan burst into the Command Bay.

"How big?"

"Twice the size of *Cricket*, and they're not wasting time. They'll intercept our field in eight minutes."

"They don't have merge codes!" Beezan said. "*Drumheller*, what will happen when they hit our particle field?"

"Unknown. Possible damage to them."

"*Drumheller*," Beezan took a deep breath. ***Protect us from what lieth in front of us and behind us.***[1] "Drop the fields. All other impact detectors on full."

"Fields to zero power."

Beezan tried to ignore his strong foreboding at their exposure; he was relying on luck again. The little ball approached, but slowed as it came, finally coming to a relative stop. "Jarvie, are you watching?"

"Yes, honor."

It hovered less than 100 meters away, inside their field

threshold. *We can't just sit here without the fields.* "*Drumheller*, bring the fields back up, slowly."

As soon as the fields went on there was a sparkling around the little blob and its glowing fuzziness disappeared. There was a unified gasp in the Command Bay as a much smaller object was revealed.

"A starfish," Oatah said in wonder. Beezan wouldn't have known what he was talking about if Jarvie hadn't shown pictures at Feast.

"I believe it is a shuttle, roughly shaped like a five-pointed star," Iricana corrected, but it hardly looked like a machine. It was beautiful in a way that human ships were not. It almost seemed alive. It was slightly bending its 'legs' and reorienting with short bursts from the tips. Then the shuttle began to ease towards the *Drumheller*.

"Do they mean to dock?" Beezan asked in panic.

"What else could they intend?" asked Oatah calmly.

Beezan tried to reorient his mind to the idea that aliens were coming aboard. "*Drumheller!* Open the hangar door!"

"Perhaps we should stop them," Reeder suggested, though how he meant to stop them Beezan didn't know.

"It is our goal to communicate," Oatah said, "be calm."

"We'll be contaminated," Katie breathed. "We should suit. It's in the protocols," she added quickly.

"Yes, proceed," Oatah ordered.

"Jarvie, report," Beezan called over the s'link.

"I've secured the big pieces and the pups are helping me collect the little stuff."

"Stay in the Work Tower. That's an order."

"Yes, honor."

They were helping each other suit up, always a challenge in

nogee. The *Drumheller* cameras were switching madly to keep up with the starfish.

"They're not heading for the hangar!" Beezan called out in panic.

"What are they doing?" Iricana asked calmly.

"The torus! They're headed for the torus! Too fast!" Beezan couldn't believe it. They were so close. Regardless of how well-meaning they were, they were about to ram the ship. "*Drumheller!* Prepare for venting. Make sure all the doors are closed!" He braced in his seat, thinking he should have put his suit on sooner.

"Contact in five seconds."

There was an incredible, deafening, terrifying banging and shuddering that made Beezan's skin crawl and stomach flip over. The *Starfish* must have slowed down at the last second, because bumpy as it was, it wasn't a full-on collision. Then came the loud screeching of the mass-adjusters hurtling down the wheel spokes and slamming into new positions. The whole ship rocked. Beezan's hands flew over the panel, helping the *Drumheller* stabilize. The crew had dived for their chairs and managed to strap in.

The main screen showed the *Starfish* now stuck on the side of the torus. "Was that what they call docking? They are crazy. Crazy!" Beezan said.

"Thank heavens we weren't spinning," Iricana added.

"*Drumheller*, have we cancelled the main torques?"

"Yes. Harmonics will take several hours to dampen."

"Damage?"

"No venting alert. No coupler damage. Possible cosmetic damage to torus surface."

Beezan tried to calm his breathing. "Maybe Jarvie was right. They really don't seem so advanced."

An alarm went off on Katie's s'link. "It's Jarvie's med monitor," she told Beezan.

"Captain?" Jarvie asked, obviously frightened.

Beezan was staring at the pop-up. "The *Starfish* has attached itself to the torus, near the A-8 hatch. No sign of venting. Jarvie, just stay in the Work Tower."

"Jarvie," Katie continued, almost suited up, "take a few breaths. Rest a minute if you can." But she sounded as breathless as Jarvie.

"Let's not get too panicked," Iricana suggested. "Maybe they are just going to attach something to communicate with."

A hatch on the top of the *Starfish* swung open. "Captain! Your suit!" Reeder reprimanded. Beezan launched out of his seat, letting Reeder replace him.

The others helped Beezan suit up while watching the pop-up at the same time. Something shot from the open *Starfish* hatch to the side of the *Drumheller*. "A tether," Iricana said.

Reeder transferred to the co-pilot chair, Beezan slid back into his chair holding his helmet. Katie glanced back to the door. "Stay here!" Beezan said simply and she hung in back looking very worried.

Beezan glanced at the Work Tower pop-up. Everything looked secure, but there was no Jarvie in the picture. "Jarvie, get strapped, just in case they do something else crazy."

"Yes, honor." He sounded very tense.

Jarvie clutched a holdbar for a moment and tried to catch his breath. He was tired, panicking, and confused. He had managed to get the robots back in their niches while the pups played in the rimway. Then the pups helped Jarvie secure the rest of the extra parts in bins or anywhere they could stuff them. He'd missed a few parts that he'd had to avoid as they went slinging around the big open tower. He counted the pieces to get them when it was safe. He chastised himself for taking out so much at once. He knew better.

He looked along the row of robots, panels dark and lifeless. A panicky, but compelling thought came to him. *If something happened to the crew.* He reached for the control panel and powered on the whole multibot wall. Jarvie pressed the private button on his p'link and, with a prayer that no one had thought to forbid it, whispered, "*Drumheller*, control the robots."

Drumheller did not respond. *Maybe it's too busy.* Then small lights illuminated the top of each niche. The robots were online. *If nothing happens, I'll just turn them off again. Oatah will never know.*

The small tremblings of the ship were unnerving and setting Jarvie on edge. He realized that the others had put their suits on, but he would not be able to. If there were some terrible disease, he'd be the first to know. He glanced at his p'link and froze.

A space-suited form had just emerged from the *Starfish*. As it righted itself to the shuttle and turned, Jarvie gasped in unison with the rest of the crew. It was human.

He heard Iricana arguing, "One helmet, two arms, two legs, do not necessarily make a human."

But the way it—ze moved was so normal. Ze went hand over hand along the tether until ze reached the *Drumheller* hatch. Another followed. Ze carried a box, somewhat like the podpup pressure box, but bigger. The suits were white, but non-reflective, like marshmallows.

"*Drumheller*," he heard Oatah order, "open the outer hatch."

Jarvie heard Beezan choke, but he didn't countermand the order. The aliens did not even jump when the hatch suddenly opened. Maybe they did this all the time. The two of them got in the lock and the outer door closed. Oatah ordered Beezan to open the inner door, letting them into the Arc 8 rimway, but the cameras were not working there. Jarvie tapped a pop-up on the worktable and called up his door repair data. It showed a diagram of the rimway with the door numbers labeled. "Should we lead them up here?" Beezan asked.

"No," Oatah answered. "Not yet. Open some doors and let them look around." Then the aliens came through the double lock into the Arc 7 section where a camera was working. They went into the first open room, which was an unused Gym. They came out after only moments.

The aliens tried another room, an unused Med Bay, and came back out, now floating towards Arc 6. *Probably looking for people.* Jarvie squinted at the diagram on his p'link. They went in a Prayer Room, then a Library. There were no cameras in those rooms. Jarvie studied the remaining rooms, cabins downstairs, and upstairs the small kitchen and the Work Tower. They were coming his way.

Beezan wouldn't let them in. He wouldn't. But Jarvie was sure he could hear a door cycling. He looked at his p'link. It was the section lock on the alien's side. "Captain . . . you're not letting them in this section . . . are you?" he asked nervously.

"Of course not." Beezan answered him, and then Jarvie heard a gasp. "How? *Drumheller*—don't open the A7-1 lock!" Sky was whining in her carrier, looking at the door. Jarvie turned to look. *What is she whining about?*

"Star!" Jarvie shouted. He looked around in a panic. "Star, come!" *He's not in here!*

"Jarvie, what's happening?" Beezan called.

"I don't see Star! He must be in the kitchen."

"No," Beezan answered in alarmed realization, "he's in the lock, trying to get back to you. That's why the door opened."

"Let him!" Jarvie pleaded. "The tag won't open the second door."

"We cannot risk it," Oatah said. "He could expose you to the aliens."

"*Drumheller*, close the lock," Beezan ordered. "We'll trap Star inside and deal with him later."

Jarvie breathed a sigh of relief as he saw on his p'link that the door had closed. Then it opened again.

"Remote tag is triggering the door. Cannot prevent."

"Those tags are hacked to override *Drumheller*?" Beezan's anger was tinged with great alarm. "Jarvie!"

Jarvie cringed. Another lie come back to torment him.

"Captain–" It was Reeder. "Visitors are leaving the Library." The aliens made their way—*back, thank God*—towards the *Starfish*. Suddenly, a furry mass hurtled into view. *Star*.

The aliens paused, drifting, startled by Star. They turned to each other and then one reached out and grabbed Star with both hands, pulling him close and holding him. "Star!" Jarvie shouted and launched for the door.

"Stay where you are!" Beezan commanded. "*Drumheller*, do not open the Work Tower door, level 2 override!"

Jarvie hit the door. He fumbled for the manual code, but that would not override *Drumheller's* order from Beezan. "You don't have a suit!" He heard Katie warning him. *I should have hacked a tag for myself!* He was on the verge of disobeying a direct order.

"Please, please let me get him."

"You will not interfere," Oatah said sternly.

"Jarvie, I'm sorry," Beezan said more gently.

"NO!" *Please, don't take him away*, he prayed. *Not after my family, after Sarcee, please don't take him.* He hooked on and tried pulling the manual handle, but it was pointless. He pounded on the door, sending himself jerking back against the tether. Sky left her carrier and floated over to watch on the p'link. Jarvie looked at her through his tears. Suddenly, he noticed her tag.

"Sky!" She looked up at him. "Sky, come! Help me get Star." He knew she wouldn't understand, but she would obey him. "Sky come!" he insisted. She turned her head from Jarvie to the door and her eyes took on a strangely knowing look. *"Sky, come!"* He unhooked himself. Sternly, she gave the slightest shake of her head and a flash of eyes that froze Jarvie to the core. She did understand. And she would not let him disobey Beezan.

He felt a surge of shame and sorrow. He hooked onto the chair. She let him scoop her up and hold her. Rocking her, he whispered, "I'm sorry, Sky. I'm so sorry." *Maybe they will let him go. What if they just take him in the lock and he dies?* "Captain," he appealed to Beezan, not even knowing what to ask. He started saying the Remover of Difficulties over and over.

"Doctor, is there something in Jarvie's med patch we can use?" Reeder asked, "Like a sedative." *No!* Jarvie reached under his shirt and ripped off his med patch.

"That is only for the most extreme of circumstances!" Katie answered.

"Visitors have entered the hatch airlock."

"Close the inner door," Oatah ordered.

"No! Don't let them go with Star!" Jarvie cried, but they ignored him. He checked the screen. There was no view of the inner hatch, but eventually, they did come out the outer hatch. Two aliens, one box. No Star. They unhooked their tether from *Drumheller* and floated back to their shuttle. There was a jolt, much gentler than the arrival, and the *Starfish* detached and went on its way. The mass adjusters were screeching again. Jarvie swayed back and forth in the chair. He could hear the commotion in the Command Bay as Beezan and the *Drumheller* compensated for the mass change.

“Reeder, make a sweep,” Oatah ordered.

Jarvie didn’t want Reeder to find him emotional. He tried to control his tears and shaking and prayed for Star. Sky looked up at him. “Star go,” she said, and buried her head in his chest.

Reeder never came to the Work Tower. A stricken Katie eventually got there and helped Jarvie back to the Med Bay, where she put a new med patch on him.

Star was nowhere to be found. Reeder checked and reported to Oatah. Now Beezan was checking. But Jarvie knew they wouldn’t find him. If Sky said Star was gone, he was gone.

He huddled in the exam bed net in misery. He told himself to be grateful for what he had, to accept God’s Will, to not give up hope, but the tears wouldn’t stop. Sky stayed by him constantly.

Eventually Iricana, Reeder, and Oatah worked their way to the Med Bay to inquire about Jarvie. “I just don’t understand what they were after,” Iricana said. “They could not have known we had podpups.”

“Maybe they think we *are* podpups. They may be trying to communicate with it,” Reeder.

“But they took him by force!” Katie complained.

“Maybe not. We didn’t see the whole thing. You know that white one is a wild thing,” Reeder argued.

Jarvie could have screamed. “That alien grabbed Star. They could have grabbed one of us!” Then he realized that, of course, Oatah wouldn’t have opened the hatches to let them go with one of the crew. But he didn’t stop them for a mere podpup.

“I don’t think they came here for a podpup,” Iricana insisted, “but, they probably don’t mean him any harm. We must give them the benefit of the doubt. If we make them enemies in our minds, we will make them enemies in reality.”

"Well, they didn't take anything else." Reeder answered.

"Yes, they did." There was a chorus of shocked exclamations as Beezan came up the stairs. He floated straight to Jarvie with a grim shake of the head. He studied the medical readouts for a moment while the crew waited impatiently to hear.

"The map," Beezan finally said.

"Map?" Oatah asked.

"A large—but out of date—sector map was on the wall of that Library. It's gone. They must have put it in the box."

"God help us," Iricana sighed. "A podpup and a map. The two things life circles around out here."

"What are we going to do?" Katie asked Beezan.

"We must wait," Oatah answered, "and see what tomorrow brings."

31 / THE TWO SEAS

3-Perfection

Jarvie held his breath and tried to be as still as possible. With his ear pressed against the exam bed he was sure he could hear doors closing on the other side of the ship. It was faint, but Jarvie was familiar with the sound from his days of avoiding Beezan. There were so many slams he could make them out between Sky's snores. *How many people are over there? Why would they go back without telling me?* His heart clenched. *Is it something about Star they don't want me to know?* Jarvie realized that Katie's breathing had changed. She was awake too. Usually Iricana stayed in the Med Bay too, for company or chaperoning, he wasn't sure, but he didn't hear her.

The Med Bay door opened, startling Jarvie and jolting Sky, who snuffled, but didn't wake.

"Doctor?" Beezan whispered.

"Captain!" Jarvie was alarmed. "If you're here, who's doing that?"

"Doing what?" Katie asked, turning on the lights.

Beezan blinked. “Good question. Doors in Arc 7, where the aliens looked around, are opening and closing. *Drumheller* says it’s one of those remote tags.” He floated over to Sky and checked her collar, patting her on the head.

“I took it off.” Jarvie tried to reach the drawer, but he was too tangled in his net. Beezan freed him and peeked in the drawer to confirm the tag.

“Star’s tag?” He asked.

“Still on him, last I saw.” Jarvie said as steadily as he could manage.

“It can’t be Star,” Katie breathed.

“No,” Beezan shook his head sadly. “Even Star couldn’t flit around that fast.” He pushed over to the big screen and tapped it. A diagram of the *Drumheller* came up. “I was just over there getting the cameras to repair, so we don’t have visual, but the *Drumheller* is approximating the path of the tag from the door openings. Something is really zipping around.”

“Some kind of device?” Jarvie asked.

“I assume so. They must have left it here and we didn’t find it when we were looking for Star.”

“But how would it have the door code?” Katie asked.

Beezan frowned again and looked sympathetically at Jarvie. “No doubt, from examining Star’s tag, they have retrieved our frequencies and door code override and managed to transmit it directly to their device.”

“Oh, no.” Jarvie said. “That’s why it can only go so far. Second locks won’t open.”

Beezan nodded. “What I need to know, doctor, is if you analyzed those filters.”

“Yes. There is nothing new or alien detectable in them.”

“Good, that means I can go over there without a suit.”

Jarvie leaped off the table, forgetting he wouldn't land. "Can I come?"

He expected an automatic 'no' but Beezan glanced at Katie while he pulled Jarvie back down. Katie looked at the clock. "Can he eat first?"

Beezan nodded. "I was thinking of spinning the ship. It'll be easier to move fast, especially if we skate. But I'll have to wake the others."

"We're awake," Iricana said, yawning as she floated up the stairs. Reeder and Oatah followed. Reeder was the only one in uniform. After being briefed, the others frowned in consternation.

"When did this start?" Oatah asked.

"Sixty-seven minutes ago," Beezan answered.

"Why would they leave a device?" Reeder asked.

"To collect data. To communicate," Iricana said. "We'd probably do the same."

"I would be happy to go check for you, Captain," Reeder volunteered.

"Thank you, but if you would go to the Command Bay and supervise the spin–up, I'll take Jarvie with me to find whatever it is."

"Let's go," Beezan said, handing Jarvie a specimen box. At first Jarvie felt like they were in 5g, but after ten minutes of skating around the rim with Beezan, he stirred up new energy. He missed skating so much. He could tell that Beezan did too; he was a great skater, for his age.

"Maybe it's not a device, maybe there's some scrambled code running around the computer," Jarvie suggested.

"*Drumheller* was especially spurnful of that idea when I suggested it," Beezan said. They rested from fast skating at the lift lock and proceeded more cautiously after that. They passed the Work Tower and came to the double lock between Arc 6 and Arc 7. Beezan peeked through the little window into the small lock. "I don't see anything." He watched a moment and then let Jarvie look. Seconds after Jarvie looked, the opposite door opened. Jarvie saw a flash of blue wings and something banked away from him.

"I see it!" The door shut, blocking his view. "It's a flying drone with wings!"

"Great. I hope there's no AI." Beezan frowned and used his s'link to open the door so they could enter the lock. "We're going to have to trap it. We'll lock the section doors and side doors manually and corner it. Then you can get it with those long fingers of yours."

Beezan opened the inner door and they jumped into the next part of the rimway. Jarvie watched while Beezan locked the door with his s'link. They heard other doors farther down opening and closing. Beezan skated fast to the kitchen door and locked it. Then he started up the rimway, locking the doors on both sides. Jarvie skated all the way to the Arc 8 hatch and looked through the little window. Suddenly, that very door opened and Jarvie couldn't duck in time.

Something warm flapped against his face, pushing off his forehead, and heading down the rimway toward Beezan. "Ewww! It's alive! It's big! And it's coming!" Jarvie warned, trying to shake off a surge of grossness.

Beezan came back, ducked, and threw the s'link to Jarvie. The creature, wings fully out now, flapped away from Beezan. "Lock the doors!"

Jarvie caught the s'link and got the rimway door locked. He

locked five side doors and was almost to the library where the aliens had taken the map, when the creature came back. He tentatively reached up to grab it, but it banked away. He locked the library. “That’s it!” He yelled to Beezan. “It’s smart enough to get away.”

Now that the doors were locked, the thing was zipping from door to door, zigzagging across the rimway in a frantic search pattern. Beezan and Jarvie crouched down on the deck to avoid being hit.

“It’s got some kind of device strapped to it,” Beezan said.

“Maybe we should have trapped it in the lock. We’ll have a hard time trying to grab it in this long rimway.”

“Let me try!” Jarvie said, watching it as it headed back toward them.

“Don’t hurt it!”

Jarvie jumped for it, but missed. The ceiling was just a little higher than he could reach, unless he jumped really high. He skated back to the lock to get some room while Beezan went the other way to scare it back. Jarvie took three fast strokes and jumped as high as he could, reaching up with one hand. The creature flapped up and hit the ceiling. Jarvie was able to bat it on the rebound and Beezan, skating up the rimway, caught it, crashing into Jarvie in the process. Beezan went very pale as he held the wildly flapping, and now squawking, thing to his chest.

“Is it hurting you?” Jarvie yelled over the noise.

“No, it’s just strange, like a feathery podpup. But I can feel a heart beating.” Jarvie got it in the specimen box. Beezan managed to get his hands out and get the box sealed without it escaping. It kept up its wild squawking. Beezan swallowed hard. “We better get back. I don’t know how long this box will hold it.”

. . .

"It's a bird!" Reeder exclaimed as soon as he peeked in the box. Jarvie and Beezan looked at each other in astonishment.

"They've never seen a bird," Iricana whispered.

"Of course, we have," Jarvie objected. "I mean, on screen. But I thought they were little." He held his fingers close together.

"Some are," Reeder explained. "Many are this size, and some are quite large." Reeder held his fingers more than shoulder-width apart.

"Yes," Oatah said, frowning. "Especially predators."

Beezan spun around in alarm. *"Predators?"*

"Remember," Reeder said, "they're the descendants of dinosaurs."

Iricana shook her head at them all. "This is most likely a completely alien creature with a unique evolution. It has a device strapped on it, which I need to get off."

"Don't let it eat your fingers," Oatah warned. "And protect your eyes."

"Seriously?" she asked.

Oatah looked at Beezan. "The Captain is unharmed. Perhaps they are domesticated. But I wouldn't take any chances."

Beezan patted his arm. "Try to get some sleep, Jarvie,"

"Yes," Oatah agreed. "We will have another challenging day tomorrow."

"You think they're coming back?" Katie asked.

"I am certain of it. And this time, we must show ourselves."

Oatah was right. The next day, Beezan leaned on the panel, exhausted, watching the screen in the Command Bay. At the regular blinking time, a bump detached from the *Pearl* and headed over, but this time the *Drumheller* crew was ready. They had operational cameras now, which he'd stayed up all night replacing. Iricana had stayed up as well, examining the bird and its payload. It had a camera and *scientific* detectors for testing the air, viruses, and radiation. Nothing threatening, so he "*shouldn't interpret it as a hostile act.*"

Fine. Beezan kept the torus spinning this time. If they could train a spy bird, they could figure out how to fly into the hangar. *Especially since the hangar isn't spinning.*

Everyone was in their suits. Oatah, Reeder, and Iricana waited at the lift lock. Beezan didn't want to send them down to the Entry Lounge or anywhere near the crazy alien pilot. The aliens would have to come up the lift. He was ready to guide them up with lights and door openings.

Katie stayed in the Med Bay. This time, Beezan kept Jarvie with him in the Command Bay. Jarvie obviously hadn't slept much. Sky had stayed with him, but now left Jarvie's lap to jump onto Beezan's panel and look at the screen. "Star coming," she said happily and jumped down.

Jarvie gasped. "Sky, is Star on the shuttle?"

"Jarvie, she's a baby. Don't get your hopes up," but Beezan had a surge of hope. Podpups knew things.

Sky turned to Beezan. "Star coming!" she said sternly.

The hangar door was wide open. The lights were on and flashing. Beezan sat with his finger on the guide beam control. The *Starfish* hesitated a moment. Beezan's skin crawled at the thought of more mass adjusters slamming. Then the *Starfish* flexed and altered course for the hangar. "Yes!" Beezan exclaimed, shifting to his second set of worries. *Would they crash in the hangar?*

But the *Starfish* coasted in and set down in the hangar like a dancer. Its own anchors—glittering gold—extended and attached. A door opened, and two suited figures came out, looking around almost casually.

"Two boxes!" Jarvie exclaimed.

The crew would faint away if they had to hold their breath for the long minutes it would take to come up the lift. Beezan sympathized when Jarvie just put his head down on the panel, too stressed to watch.

The lift ride bringing the aliens to gravity did not faze them. They exited the lock, set the boxes on the deck, and turned to regard Oatah, standing slightly in front of Iricana and Reeder.

"I cannot see through their faceplates," Oatah reported. "They are slightly shorter than I am." Beezan felt both dread and anticipation. It wouldn't be a happy historic moment if the 'aliens' turned out to be renegade humans warning them out of their territory. He glanced at Jarvie, who was now biting his lip.

Slowly, one alien bent down and opened a box. A podpup poked its nose out, and then sensing all was well, darted out. Beezan smiled with joy for a second. There were gasps all over the s'links. "It's turned purple," Oatah said, mystified.

"It's not Star," Jarvie said, equally puzzled.

Beezan looked closer. It wasn't. It was too big and of course, purple.

"God in Heaven," Katie said. "Could these be the people that abandoned the podpups?" Whoever left the podpups to die would automatically be number one on humanity's bad list.

"We must not jump to conclusions," Iricana reminded them.

Beezan watched as the purple one checked out the rimway, giving Oatah's boots a cursory sniff, but otherwise ignoring him. Then it wandered back to the other box. Slowly, the other alien reached down and opened the second box. In a flash of white fur, Star came bounding out, raced up the rimway with the purple one in pursuit, circled back, smacked right into Oatah, and proceeded with a game of hide-and-seek in the boxes.

"Star! Star!" Jarvie was literally jumping up and down in front of his chair. Beezan was flooded with relief. Now he had hope for the future. If they brought Star back unharmed, he could deal with them somehow.

"Can you hear the audio pick up?" Iricana was asking.

"Shush, Jarvie," Beezan grabbed Jarvie's arm to still him. "Listen. *Drumheller*, amplify."

"Zharvee? Zharvee, Friend. Purple friend. Play. Zharvee?" And they were off again.

Friend?

In all the commotion with the podpups, Beezan almost missed the historic moment, but Jarvie's wide-eyed look made him glance at the other screen. Oatah had reached up to his helmet and slid the seal open.

Then, taking an audible breath, Oatah pulled off his helmet. The aliens looked quickly back and forth. The colored lights on their suits were blinking wildly. Were they having a medical emergency?

It was a frozen moment. No one knew what to do. They stood, maybe getting used to the idea of a human. Then Star came to Oatah and urgently said, "Hungree!"

Oatah, Banisher of Podpups on Earth, bent over and, setting his helmet down, gently picked up Star, shifting him to hold in one arm. "Patience, little one."

The change was immediate. The aliens became more fluid, as if they had been standing at attention before. They reached up and unsealed their helmets. "Brace yourselves," whispered Katie.

But when the helmets came off, Beezan couldn't take in

what he was seeing. All thoughts of renegade humans left his mind as he looked at one of them. *Alien.* It had a head, yes, with eyes—big blue eyes, rounder than human eyes—and a nose and mouth, but across the forehead was a pulsing membrane of light. "Oatah," Beezan whispered, "Their foreheads?"

"Yes," Oatah said quietly, "I believe the light bands are part of them, but they do match the lights on the suits."

Oatah's talking caused them to focus on his mouth. Oatah took a slow step forward and made a small bow. "God is Most Glorious. Welcome to the *Drumheller.*"

They stared. Their light displays went wild with color.

Then, as one, they bowed. One spoke, but Beezan wasn't even sure which. Beezan could see they had dark, maybe black hair and purple skin. One was dark purple and the other lavender, like the podpup. If they were male or female, old or young, scared or happy, Beezan could not tell.

"Hungree!" Star demanded.

"Perhaps we should tour the kitchen," Oatah suggested, with more composure than Beezan could have mustered. "Jarvie could bring some food for the pup."

Jarvie practically dislocated Beezan's arm, pulling on it, whispering, "Please, please."

"Should he stay in his suit, Doctor?" Beezan asked.

"They're not human. Transmission rate is completely unknown, but Oatah is already exposed. And so is Star," Katie said.

"All right, go," Beezan said. *Why not? Things are already out of control.*

Jarvie squeezed his arm and practically jumped out of the suit. He flew out of the Command Bay only to stop at the door with a lurch and worried look back.

"You'll be left out."

Beezan hadn't considered that. He did really want to see the aliens, but someone should stay in the Command Bay. It was heart-warming that Jarvie had thought of it.

"I'll have my chance; go on." Jarvie headed for the kitchen.

Oatah had made a 'come along' gesture to the aliens, and started toward the kitchen. One understood and followed immediately, with Iricana and Reeder behind. The other bent down and pulled something flat out of one of the boxes.

Beezan glanced at the *Pearl*. It wasn't doing anything. The *Starfish* was secure. His look at the aliens made him a bit shaky. He sat back down. They were not ugly. They were interesting, but they were going to take some getting used to.

Jarvie scurried around the kitchen making five bottles of Star's favorite food. Sky pouted, so he gave one to her. It wasn't very long before he heard clomping feet in the stair well. In his rush to get the bottles and see Star, he hadn't considered coming face to face with the aliens.

"Star?" he called tentatively, holding the bottles. Star bounded through the door squealing, ran a lap around Jarvie as he sat down on the deck, and then hopped in his lap, ready to drink. Jarvie hugged Star and whispered a prayer as he gave him the bottle. Star probably hadn't eaten for a day. *Eternity for a podpup.* Jarvie was so happy and grateful to have Star back that he had an overwhelming rush of good will towards the aliens. Then the purple podpup peeked around the door and slowly came over. Jarvie stared. It was really purple. The fur and the skin were a soft light purple. It came right over to Jarvie and sat looking up at him with dark purple eyes.

"Greetings, purple one," Jarvie said quietly.

Star finished the first bottle and gasped for a breath. "Purple friend." He tossed the bottle aside and grabbed the next one.

Jarvie wanted to touch the purple one, but wasn't sure if he should. Two space-suited feet appeared in front of him. He'd been so focused on the pups, he hadn't heard. Jarvie froze, looking up. The dark purple alien stood over him. The forehead lights were shifting with dizzying speed. Jarvie's heart leaped into his throat. He started to gasp for breath. He was suddenly trembling. His brain could not make sense of the purple head and flashing lights.

Then Star stopped drinking, looked up and said, "Neeyah!"

Did that mean no? Star didn't seem upset though. *I should stand up. I should say something.* However, he was inexplicably frightened and looked down as if to block it all out. He just sat there shaking. *Some brave first contact.*

"Jarvie, are you all right?" came Beezan's voice. "Katie, can you check on him in the kitchen?"

But it was Oatah who came over and even patted his shoulder. "Be at ease. I don't believe they mean us any harm."

"I'm sorry," Jarvie gasped, hugging Star tighter.

The alien bent down and offered a small container to Jarvie. He scooted back. Iricana came in. "I think they want a sample—of the food."

"Oh." Jarvie got the next bottle out, rather than trying to wrest the current bottle from Star, and shakily poured some into the container. When he handed it back, his hand touched the suited glove of the alien and he had a surge of panic.

"Captain, I'm sending Jarvie back to you," Oatah said. Everyone was staring at him.

"Sorry, I'm sorry," he murmured, feeling embarrassed and foolish, but relieved. He gathered the full bottles, adjusted Star in one arm, and stood up. Both aliens had to tip their heads back to look up at him. The close one took a giant step backwards and Reeder had to jump out of the way.

For a moment, the big alien eyes met Jarvie's and Jarvie saw him for a person. A man, important, not quite like Oatah, but enough. He was brave, intelligent, and most worrying, determined.

"He's the Captain!" Jarvie told Beezan back in the Command Bay. Jarvie was still shaking. "Sorry, I'm so sorry," he found himself repeating.

"Easy, Jarvie, come sit down." Beezan guided him to the chair with one hand and patted the too-busy-slurping-to-be-bothered Star with the other hand.

"I just had a flash that he's the Captain; the dark one, the one standing over me. He's a man, Reeder's age, I think."

Beezan was taking this information for what it was worth—nothing. He shrugged politely and said, "Well, who knows." But Jarvie knew.

Sky had stayed in the kitchen, slurping on her bottle and staring at the aliens. Jarvie was just as glad to have a few minutes with Star, sitting in the Command Bay. Beezan had the kitchen scene on the big screen to watch.

Beezan and Jarvie could see the lavender alien unfold the flat thing and spread it across the table. It was the sector map that they had taken from the library. Lavender had another folded sheet, which was then unfolded and placed next to their map. There was no good view of it from the camera. All Jarvie and Beezan could see was Sky jumping up on the table to look for herself.

"It's a sector map," Iricana whispered.

"Captain, perhaps you should join us," Oatah suggested.

. . .

Beezan worried about dragging Jarvie back there, but Jarvie settled down and stop shaking. They headed back to the kitchen with Star. A pile of space suits was dumped in the rimway where some of the crew had shed them. Beezan slowly entered the kitchen and took in the scene. Iricana, Reeder, and Katie, unsuited, were sitting at the table, looking over the new sector map in awe, along with Sky, just as serious as if a baby podpup could read an alien star map. The aliens, to the right, and Oatah, to the left, were still in their suits, so they couldn't sit. Oatah nodded to him and said "Beezan," slowly for the aliens.

"God is Most Glorious," Beezan said formally.

They nodded solemnly, lights flashing. The dark one said what sounded like "nee-ah" pointing to himself and "sone-too-la" pointing to the other. Beezan nodded politely again.

Jarvie had hesitated in the doorway, either from nervousness or from podpups—Star and the purple one—rolling over his feet. Beezan thought he might bolt, but Oatah calmly said, "Jarvie," for the aliens. For Jarvie, the aliens stood and bowed.

Jarvie looked down at them and whispered "God is Most Glorious." Then he sat down right in the doorway and let the pups crawl all over him. The alien pup jumped right in his lap, but he didn't seem alarmed, patting it on the back and whispering to it. The aliens' colors changed again as they watched Jarvie play with their podpup, and they calmly sat down.

Meanwhile, Beezan slowly moved forward enough to see the sector maps. The alien map was striking for its color. The stars twinkled in their natural colors against a black background, connected by bright lines. Were they colors of the jump paths? Beezan's head swam trying to take it all in. There were no circles, as the humans had drawn, grouping their systems into sectors. The human map was not to scale of course, and this alien map couldn't be either. He gazed in wonder. What stars were these? Had humans ventured this way? Where to begin to figure it out?

Iricana sat as if possessed. Her eyes searched across the map with such intensity he was surprised it didn't burst into flame. Suddenly, she pointed to a star, "Daydream." The other humans frowned in puzzlement. The star was on the far right of the alien map.

"See," Iricana explained, pointing to a small diagram next to the star. It enlarged when she touched it, into a virtual pop-up. She froze for a moment, but continued, "Daydream is a yellow star, with a rocky planet, no moon; rocky planet, two small moons; brown-orange gas giant, three large moons and two sets of rings; turquoise gas giant, no rings, many moons. Here's Nocturne." Then she traced her finger out along the orbit of Turquoise to where the *Drumheller* was in orbit. She stopped and looked up at the aliens.

They had no cultural knowledge to know if nodding or shaking heads or special color flashings meant yes or no, but Beezan's impression was that the aliens were excited. The dark alien took his gloved finger and traced it around the inner gas giant and back around, retracing the path of the *Pearl.* He brought his finger up to Iricana's finger and stopped. Everyone stared. Yes, the humans nodded in unison, that's where we are.

The alien pointed to the *Drumheller* map and waved his finger around as if lost. "Oh, it's not even on this old map," Iricana replied. Iricana had to draw in Redrock; the map was so old. Then she drew the jump path from Redrock to Daydream. She drew a little picture of the *Drumheller* and the *Pearl* in orbit. Again, she put her finger on the map. This time, the alien picked up his own map and put it down on top of the *Drumheller* map, overlapping the two Daydreams. He held his finger on his map.

The background color went from opaque to clear. The two maps were joined.

In the hush that followed, Katie whispered a verse from the marriage prayer, ***"He hath let loose the two seas, that they meet each other . . ."***

The end of the quote rolled into Beezan's mind: ***From each He bringeth up greater and lesser pearls.***[1]

32 / ALIEN FEVER

4-Perfection

Beezan woke from a dream of the alien ship. It had been hot and steamy inside and he had been lost and panicking, looking for Jarvie, looking for the pups, looking for a way out.

He was trying to calm his racing heart when he realized he was sweating. *Fever.* Already, he had an alien flu. He had trusted in luck. *Stupid. Please God, don't let it be fatal.*

He was exhausted besides. Had he truly slept all night? *No, it's only 4 in the morning.* He sat up, puzzled and uneasy. Sky was sound asleep. Was she warm or not? Beezan was so hot himself, he couldn't tell. He grabbed his p'link and s'link and went to check on Jarvie, who was bright pink and sweating. Beezan shook him gently. No response.

He called the doctor.

"Captain?" She must have been awake. "Are you all right?"

"I have a fever, but I can't wake Jarvie."

"Go, I'll be fine," he heard Iricana say. Katie must be checking on her.

"Be right there, honor." Beezan checked Star and tried to

wake Jarvie again. The door opened and Katie plodded down the stairs. Beezan could see, even with her dark skin, that she was flushed.

"You've got it too."

"Yes. Oatah is already in the Med Bay. Reeder and Iricana and I have slight fevers. I was going to check on you next."

She frowned over Jarvie. "He's got a higher fever." She reached under his shirt and inserted another capsule into his med patch, programming it with her s'link. "He's too big to move, can you stay with him?"

"Yes, but isn't he unconscious?"

Katie pinched him hard enough to bruise. He groaned and pulled away. "I've got the med computer working on it. We should have the antiviral in a few hours. No need to panic," she paused, looked up at Beezan and mouthed the word 'yet.'

Beezan wrapped up Sky in his blanket and hauled her to Jarvie's cabin, plopped her in the bed with Star and Jarvie and then settled in a chair. He listened over the p'link to Katie's running reports, but they soon grew vague.

Katie came again to start autohydration packs. Iricana brought food, water, and podpup bottles. "Stay," Beezan whispered to her.

"I can't, honor. I'm sorry. I'm watching Reeder and Oatah." She looked ready to keel over. "Katie will be here."

"The aliens? Have they come?"

"It's not time yet."

Not time? Had it only been a few hours? Iricana went up the stairs slowly, pulling on the holdbars. Beezan managed to feed the pups, but they were almost too sick for food. Finally, Katie staggered back down. "The computer's not done. We'll have to ride it out."

"Who's in the Command Bay?" Beezan whispered. His throat hurt so much.

"No one. They're in the Med Bay. They'll get the meds automatically, and then they will come help us. I've left a log, and Oatah sent a coded light-speed message to Redrock."

Beezan nodded, gripping his p'link and moving to the deck near Jarvie, rather than the other chair. Katie could have the nearby chair. "*Drumheller*," he swallowed painfully, remembering Oatah's misgiving about AIs, "take command. Maintain position. Allow any of us to resume command at any time. If no one takes command in 10 days, go into a safe orbit at Lander's Moon and wait for a human ship. Maintain life support as long as any of us or the podpups are alive."

"Confirmed."

"*Drumheller*, have the aliens come yet?"

"No."

"Don't let them in."

He rolled a blanket into a pillow and lay down. He just needed to rest a minute. Then he would check on Jarvie. Katie curled up on the chair, gasping for breath. He should say a prayer . . . long healing prayer, ***O Thou . . . Healer . . . O Thou . . .***[1] But the words eluded him.

5-Perfection

Beezan's soul surged through space, rejoicing in the beauty and freedom of the stars. The jump paths sang and danced around him, calling him, each one pulling him with the promise of a new place. He knew the stars. He could feel their simple but expansive spirits. But there was a powerful spirit—a soul—nearby. *Lander!* He reached across the threshold to join him. Like comets, they raced the heavens. Beezan followed Lander on a golden path that was so long, so precise, so perfect that Beezan thought he would die from the glory of it. He felt the resonance of it imprinted on his soul. But they were too close. The star! It was so hot, too hot . . . *Must go back.* Go Back. *No. Too wonderful to leave.* Go Back. *Lander. Telling me to go back, like a sentry. But I'm not dead; I'm not jumping.*

Beezan slept again for a long time. When he woke up, he was confused and wet. His whole body hurt. He was thirsty and cold. He blinked and slowly focused. His autohydration pack was empty. He unhooked it. *Water.* He found a bottle and drank huge gulps. His stomach reeled. He stopped and tried to stay calm. *The sickness.*

"*Drumheller!*"

No response. *Need the p'link.* It wasn't on him. He looked around. He was still on the deck by Jarvie's bed. Judging by the mess, it had been a day or so. Katie had fallen off the chair. She was still flushed, but that meant she was still alive.

Beezan stood, nearly heaving up the water he just drank. There was a med monitor stuck on the back of his hand. He didn't remember Katie putting it there.

"Jarvie?" He grasped his arm. Jarvie was pale and cold and half huddled in a blanket. His eyes opened, confused and scared. *Alive, three alive.* Beezan's hopes soared.

"Beezan?"

"Jarvie, thank God you're still with us. We've been sick."

Beezan found Jarvie's p'link in the bed.

"*Drumheller!*"

"Captain?" Did it sound relieved?

"Report."

"It has been 27.3 hours since your last orders. Three crew in the Med Bay are alive and received medication 4.3 hours ago. Three crew in Jarvie's cabin need medical attention. The aliens

did not send a ship. *Pearl* communications have been recorded and are being analyzed. Position is stable. Repairs made. Recommend you go to Med Bay immediately."

"Yes. Prepare three doses, for myself, Katie, and Jarvie, that I can administer." *Dehydration.* Beezan held some water for Jarvie and then woke Katie enough to take a swallow. He couldn't continue in his soiled uniform. He crawled to his cabin and found the two podpups by the facility door. He felt them. They were sleeping, but were cooler.

He cleaned up as well as he could in a hurry, shaking the whole time. With a few more sips of water, he had enough strength to go on. He found his links, attached his p'link to his uniform, and spoke into his s'link.

"*Drumheller,* I resume command."

"Confirmed."

He gave Jarvie and Katie more water and went up the stairs of Jarvie's cabin. The door opened, he stepped out into the rimway, and had the fright of his life.

He jumped back inside the stairwell, heart pounding, and slapped the emergency close button. The door slammed shut. He sank down to the deck with both hands on his chest. The vibration of heavy clomping feet went past, outside the door.

Three stiff, shadowy figures of different shapes and colors had loomed over him in the dark rimway. *Aliens? No, they were too stiff.* Besides, the *Drumheller* said the aliens hadn't come. Finally, his logical mind took over and provided a reasonable answer—robots. *But whose robots are they?*

"*Drumheller,*" he whispered into the s'link, "What are those robots?"

"Robots?" Jarvie groaned. "Oh no. I forgot."

"Internal Repair Robot Configuration has been dispatched to maintain critical systems."

Ours. They're Oatah's robots. But last time Beezan had seen them, they were deactivated in their niches. *Oatah must have turned them on when we got sick. Is Oatah awake?*

"Who's programming them?"

"Repair robots are under my command."

Beezan gulped. "Where are they?"

"Two units are inspecting Life Support Sub-Stations. Two additional units and the robot manager, #9, are returning to the Med Bay."

"From where?"

"The Main Computer Bay."

"Why?"

"Main computer was in need of upgrades, repair, and manual program overrides."

This was not what he needed right now. "Where did you get program upgrades?"

"Upgrades to main operating system were included with repair robot #9."

"What do these upgrades include?"

"Primary upgrade allows autonomous data collection, repair and interaction, observation, analysis, and command interface."

"How is that different than before?"

"Robot #9."

Beezan didn't like the sound of it. But he had always trusted the *Drumheller*, both before and after the AI was revealed. Oatah had just planted doubts in his head.

There was more clumping, then a sharp knock at the door, and the door opened. Standing before him was, no doubt, Robot #9. Two unblinking, shiny black eyes tipped down to look at him. Red lights blinked on and off where a mouth would be.

"Captain, I am Drumheller."

Beezan was speechless. Now he knew why people didn't like

AIs. A disembodied voice of the ship was one thing, but this was a whole different psychological thing—a walking, talking, roaming-the-ship AI. Beezan backed farther into the stairwell, allowing the robot to come in. He stared as it hooked its ‘leg’ to the glider and clunkily rode down to the deck, standing upright. It scanned the cabin.

“Med robot #7 is preparing the medicine. Cleaning robot configuration #4 will be dispatched. Repair robot configuration #2 will commence glider cleaning and repair.”

Beezan tried to contain his initial reaction. The *Drumheller* had been the guardian angel of his life, the voice of calm and reason from above. He had always found it a great comfort. A small part of him wanted to run to the Command Bay, barricade himself in, and program the robots away. He gripped the s’link. But he didn’t want to leave Jarvie and Katie while the robot was in the cabin, and what of the others?

“*Drumheller,*” he said, and the robot turned toward him.

“Yes, Captain?”

Beezan stood, sick, shaking, thirsty, scared, confused and faint. He needed help. The *Drumheller* had never let him down. He had to hold on to trust, not of the machine, but of the people behind the programming. He had to trust in the designers of centuries ago and trust the input of his parents, grandparents, and all the others, through the generations, who had modeled command for the *Drumheller*. It was gazing at him. He took a resigned breath. “What are the conditions of the other patients?”

“Stable; sleeping. Medicines have been administered and are registering early success. Temperatures are dropping. Hydration continues. Recommend rotating patients.”

“I can’t move them, unless we spin down.”

"Unnecessary." And with that, the robot leaned over and picked up Jarvie as if he were a podpup.

12-Perfection

Beezan was getting tired. Although he had only been sick for three days, it felt like thirty days. He needed to sit down. He found a free panel in the Med Bay to do his work. The ship was getting too crowded. First Jarvie and Sarcee, then Oatah and Reeder, and Lander and Iricana and Katie, and baby podpups. Now aliens, *another* podpup, and robots. *What next?*

Thinking of Lander brought a flash of memory to Beezan but he couldn't place it. There was far too much noise in the Med Bay to concentrate. Iricana, Reeder, Oatah, and Neah, the dark alien, sat around the Med Bay conference table, pointing at maps. Sontula, the lavender alien, now had a handheld device that was apparently a translator-in-development. Occasionally it would blurt out sounds or words that made no sense to anyone.

Star, Sky, and Purple Friend raced around, ignored in the general excitement. Jarvie rested on the exam bed while Katie sat at a nearby panel laboring over the medical programs, trying to stay ahead of the most dangerous viruses. Luckily, none were as bad as the first. Katie had quickly relegated med robot #7 to standby mode. It was sulking in its Med Bay niche.

Robot #9 proved to be both a Godsend and a pain. Although no one called it Drumheller, it had taken on a presence. It roamed the ship, supervising repairs, checking on and scaring the crew, bossing the garden robot, upgrading, compliance checking, recording, reporting, and generally doing everything Beezan was supposed to have been doing his whole life.

While the scientists and aliens struggled to communicate

and the robots took care of the ship, Beezan worked on the alien map. He studied the stars, their planetary families, and the marks that must be spectra or some other physical data. At first, he thought it would be simple to figure out, but he found himself distracted with worry over Jarvie.

With the exception of Jarvie, the crew had recovered well from the onslaught of new germs. They had learned that the *Pearl* crew was also dealing with sickness and some fearfulness, but they were coping and had suffered no losses. Katie worked almost continuously. She and the aliens had exchanged samples, which Katie said helped tremendously.

Jarvie, however, did not recover as well. As Katie had explained before, it was another crisis upon crises. He did not recover from the first bad virus before another got him. And then another. Right now, he had a rash of purple dots across his nose and chest. The aliens called this one *mershla*. Even with the meds, Jarvie was confined to Med Bay. Now he was resting on the exam bed under regular scanning. Beezan marveled at how Jarvie didn't have any trouble resting with all this commotion going on.

Beezan had offered to move the aliens to the Consultation Hall, but Neah and Sontula wanted the input of Katie and Jarvie and were content to meet in the Med Bay, germs and all. He knew he could go work in the Command Bay to avoid the crowd, but a little part of him didn't want to miss out.

The aliens now stayed about four hours a day, long enough to take off their suits. Except for the light-flashing membrane above their eyes and their skin coloring, their similarity to human form was astonishing. The variations were so small they took concentration to notice. Their eyes were slightly rounder; their earlobes were shaped differently, curving sharply into the skull like a cup handle rather than hanging down. They also figured out that Sontula was a woman, although she did not seem much different from Neah, except for being shorter. They were smaller in general, and had somewhat fleshier hands with thicker pads on their fingers and palms. The aliens were more formal than humans, at least humans living on a cargo ship. They made small bows and gestures to each other and to the *Drumheller* crew. Interestingly, Sontula always deferred to Neah and always called him Neahjik. And Neah called her Sontulatan. But clearly the humans were not to call them by those names. Sontula and Neah came every day, and the extra two or three aliens that came with them were always different, as far as Beezan could tell.

They didn't touch each other, but did not appear to disapprove when Iricana would pat Katie on the shoulder. They seemed more puzzled about Beezan giving any attention to Jarvie, so Beezan felt self-conscious. They all just muddled along, not really understanding each other except for basic math, maps, and a few breakthroughs of sign language or an occasional word. The aliens would listen respectfully if the crew said a prayer and once the aliens sang a quiet song together that might have been a prayer. It was impossible to begin a discussion of religion, as they just didn't have the common language. Yet Beezan felt a connection with them. They certainly had kindness and sympathy, gentleness and curiosity, and were working hard to communicate.

Beezan no longer bothered to keep watch on the crew or even the aliens. He watched the robots. After they finished all possible repairs, which admittedly might take a year, then what would they do? He didn't want a bunch of bored robots scrutinizing his ship.

Failing again to concentrate, Beezan glanced over at the table where the aliens were working. They had shown pictures of the *Pearl*, or the ship within the Pearly field. It was a spherical ship, white and silver with patterns in the surface and colored lights, seemingly only for decoration.

Decoration, beauty, or art was obviously important to the aliens. They had beautiful clothes and jewelry, which were different every day. They didn't match each other in any obvious way. They each had a distinctive style. Even their s'links were small treasure boxes, rather than the worn, functional, sometimes-sticky s'links Beezan was used to.

Their map was a work of art, with a border of galaxies and its color-changing surface, its virtual pop-ups, and glowing colors. Beezan worried about what the aliens must think of them. Except for Katie, they were all very plain. They wore the same uniforms day after day. Their fanciest jewelry were the Greatest Name rings, which they all wore. Although Oatah and Iricana didn't talk about their spouses very often, they both wore wedding bands. Only Katie wore any other jewelry, including the engagement ring, the pearl necklace, and various hair ornaments.

Iricana and Neah proved to be the best at drawing, communicating ideas through stick pictures, then hash marks, moving to numbers. Luckily the numbers were base ten; Beezan breathed a sigh of thanks.

Since he couldn't work anyway, Beezan went over to the table to watch. Today, Neah had drawn a picture of *Pearl* and 67 stick people. All except 20 were grouped into seven sets that must be families. Each set had at least two 'grownup' figures and several 'small' ones. Neah drew lines from each family and the group of twenty to himself and the ship. *Jarvie was right. Neah is the Captain.* Oatah and Reeder stood and gave a formal bow to Neah, with the rest of the *Drumheller* crew scrambling to follow suit.

Iricana sketched the six people of their crew and two podpups. She wrote on their 'chests' the first letter of their names and indicated each by pointing. The aliens pointed to their lines connecting the families to their children and pointed to the *Drumheller* figures. "They want to know how we're related," Iricana said.

Iricana drew separate circles around Oatah and Reeder, herself and Katie. Then she drew one circle around Beezan and Jarvie. Beezan was surprised but pleased. The aliens nodded, which seemed to mean either yes or go on, so Iricana drew lines pointing from each of the circles to Oatah, naming him as their leader. Neah and Sontula made deep bows to Oatah, although his leadership had been well established before. Then Iricana drew a line from Beezan to the ship. At this they squinted and colors flashed. They pointed at Jarvie and then Beezan and Neah made a short gesture, as if indicating a child.

"No," Iricana actually laughed. She made an erase motion and then pointed to the children on the picture of the *Pearl* crew, saying "child, child, child" and then pointed to Jarvie's stick figure and said "child." Then she turned to Jarvie, who was sitting up on the exam bed looking embarrassed, "child."

They stared at Jarvie. Neah made his hand go up from small to tall. As he did his colors changed and his eyes went wider. Beezan shrugged and laughed. If Jarvie looked embarrassed, the aliens looked mortified. Their colors shifted to solid aquamarine —signaling embarrassment, Beezan realized, but they were smiling.

"They thought you were the parent!" Katie told Jarvie.

"Maybe they thought he was the Captain," Beezan said. This made everyone laugh more.

"Perhaps," Iricana said seriously, "height may continue to increase with age."

"He'd be 200 years old," Katie laughed.

As the humans laughed, the alien colors shifted to burgundy with yellow pulses. Humor? Their colors were emotions. For some inexplicable reason that made Beezan happy.

Their light-hearted moment was short lived. The alien sense of family must be strong. They wanted to know who Jarvie's other grownup was. It wasn't the angle Oatah wanted, but they needed the moment to introduce the subject they had been waiting for. Iricana carefully walked through drawings of an alien ship coming into Luminesse—and blowing up.

Neah and Sontula were obviously stunned. Their colors went gray. Then Iricana quickly sketched out the accidents at Firelight, Hamada, and Harbor.

The aliens were distraught. They sat, slumped over the map. Sontula's colors faded away completely and she looked faint. Katie hovered around her, not knowing what to do.

"I hope they don't think we did it," Reeder said.

Iricana tried to convey the idea that the ships were crashing into the gravity balls. The aliens watched with buried heads. Finally, Iricana drew a human ship running away from the Luminesse accident to Canyon. The aliens seemed to understand. Iricana drew the human crew of the *Sunburst*, all of them. She drew Jarvie in his family group and pointed to him. Then she took a red pen and crossed out Jarvie's parents. Tears ran down her face as she crossed out his brother, his uncle, and most of the *Sunburst* crew. She paused while the aliens absorbed this. Then she drew a line showing Jarvie coming to the *Drumheller*.

They looked over at Jarvie. He had drawn his knees up to his forehead on the exam bed so he could hide his face. Beezan went over to him and put an arm around him. Jarvie clutched him with one arm while still hiding his face with the other.

The aliens were shaken and flustered. Gray and black alternated on their membranes, sometimes with a horizontal band of orange. They practically jumped into their suits. Reeder and Katie tried to get them to slow down or stay but they would not. Finally, they took the human map and left. The crew sat and prayed for them until they disappeared into the *Pearl.*

And they didn't come back.

After three days, *Drumheller* began blinking again, but there was no response. Oatah, Iricana, and Reeder were crushed. Iricana blamed herself for moving too fast, but the others assured her the facts themselves were heartbreaking. Oatah speculated that the aliens might even have had friends or family on those other ships.

Katie was increasingly worried about Jarvie.

Beezan felt lost and useless. He fantasized about running cargo and jumping. It had been so long between jumps. He was supposed to be a pilot. He missed jumping so much. He missed his packets. He even missed the news. He missed the quiet orderly life he once had. Even Sky was lethargic and depressed. This had all been very exciting, but the truth was Beezan was still lonely. He prayed, but he was distracted. He felt out of balance and tired. The exhilaration he had felt after long jumping with Lander was elusive. Maybe he didn't know the ways.

Beezan rested in his bunk, staring up in the dark. Sky was sleeping quietly. He was so grateful to have her. She stayed with him at night, giving him a warmth and comfort he had not had in decades. He thought about getting married, but now he was bound by his oath to Oatah. He might get back to Redrock, but he would be just as much a captive of the *Drumheller*. He thought about that day he had sworn his oath and began to regret it. He admitted to himself that he had wanted company, needed help, and been attracted to the adventure. He should have taken Jarvie and handed over the *Drumheller*—but at the time it was too much for him. In his heart, he knew that would never have happened. Somehow all this was meant to be and he just needed to accept it.

So they waited. They prayed. They looked at the *Pearl* a hundred times a day, watching for the blob that meant the shuttle was on its way. When they finally did come, it was with a new resolve.

33 / TO SAVE CANYON

2-Names

"Captain!" Jarvie ran up the Prayer Room stairs and burst through the door. Beezan looked up at him, alarmed. "Sorry! It's a bigger shuttle."

Beezan came down the stairs right behind him to the Command Bay. On the screen, they could see a shuttle five times bigger than the *Starfish*.

"*Drumheller*, open the hangar!" Beezan ordered. "We don't want that thing banging into the torus." Jarvie sat in growing anticipation as Beezan ordered the crew to their places, Oatah at the top of the lift and Reeder, Iricana, and Katie in the Med Bay. "You stay here until we get the all clear," Beezan said to him. "And, *Drumheller*, park the robots."

Jarvie got Sky and Star locked into the jump bed. Then, since he'd learned that Beezan liked the robots tracked, he checked to make sure they were all out of the way. They had not yet determined what the aliens thought of robots.

Beezan shut the Command Bay door and locked it with his s'link. "Just a precaution."

"Do you think they are mad at us?"

"I have no idea."

Jarvie tapped a screen, "*Drumheller*, track visitors."

For this big shuttle to get into the hangar, *Drumheller* started the guide beams. It came right in, touching down nicely. Three auto anchors latched on, to Jarvie's relief. It was so big it dwarfed the other shuttles in the hangar. "Do you think they'll need help?" Jarvie asked, not sure what to do if they did.

"No. They're obviously prepared at being uninvited guests."

Prepared and serious. Seven of them came out of the shuttle in an orderly line and headed right for the Entry Lounge. One was Neah; they could recognize him by the icon on his suit, an upturned semicircle with dots above it. It was the same symbol he wore on his collar. They had no podpup box and they did not stop to show the newcomers around. They took the lift in two groups with Neah leading the first group. He took off his helmet and stood silently by Oatah until all seven were present. Then the other six removed their helmets. Sontula was one. Jarvie was surprised how familiar she and Neah had become.

Jarvie and Beezan watched the big screen in fascination. "God is most Glorious," Oatah greeted them. "Welcome to *Drumheller*." The translator was making sounds, but it wasn't clear if the aliens understood.

Neah actually took Oatah by the arm and with most seriousness proceeded to the Med Bay. When they arrived, the aliens were introduced to Iricana, Reeder, and Katie. There was a moment of silence. Neah turned to Oatah with a flash of red. "Beezan Jarvie," he said, to Jarvie's astonishment.

"Agent Oatah, what do you think?" Beezan asked quietly.

"You must come, Captain."

Beezan nodded with resignation. Jarvie left the podpups and

walked quietly with Beezan until the stairs. Then he dropped behind as a show of respect—and because he was scared.

Names were exchanged for the second time, but Jarvie missed them again in his nervous state. The new aliens all stared up at him, especially one. He was taller and older, and looked stubborn. The fact that his membrane was glowing a steady white did not make Jarvie feel any better.

Reeder, Katie, Beezan, and Jarvie moved to the exam side of the room leaving the others around the table. Sontula had her translator out and another alien set out the map that Iricana had made of the accidents. Two others had what were obviously cameras. *Two?*

Neah gestured for Jarvie to come forward. Jarvie edged closer, not sure what they wanted, and positive he didn't want to be on the alien news. Exasperatingly, he started shaking. Beezan went forward with him and pointed to a chair. He slid into it, right in front of the map. Beezan stood behind him, one hand on his left shoulder.

The older alien, Hef-something, stomped over to the table. Suit and all, he squeezed into the chair by Jarvie, banging his helmet on the table. Jarvie jumped. He looked up at the other four newcomers. They stood in a group and stared down at him like a bunch of lawyers—or counselors. Jarvie wasn't sure which, but he knew he was in the hot seat.

Hef, dark purple like Neah, thinning grayish-purple hair and a wrinkly membrane, gestured to the map, pointing to the drawing of the accident at Luminesse.

It's my turn to tell the story. Someone put a pen in his hand. He shakily drew pictures, gestured, and spoke in nouns, as Iricana coached him. He drew his jump group in the a-rings at Luminesse, his ship aborting the jump just as an alien ship appeared. He drew the alien ship as he remembered it, in a more teardrop form, not like the spherically-shaped *Pearl.* He drew the impact he saw, the alien ship hitting the gravity ball and exploding into huge tumbling pieces.

Hef stopped him and pointed to Jarvie's eyes and then the ship breaking up.

Jarvie nodded, "Yes, I saw it—on the helmet screen." He pointed to a small screen inside Hef's helmet.

Hef again pointed to the drawing of the ship in pieces. This time, Jarvie used Iricana's method and put a big red X over the ship. They gasped. Then he put another big red X over the a-rings and gravity ball. They gasped again and all started blinking their colors and talking at the same time. Jarvie took a moment to wipe his eyes, but only Beezan cared, squeezing his shoulder gently.

"Perhaps the newcomers did not believe that the a-rings were destroyed," Oatah suggested.

Then Iricana leaned over and crossed out the a-rings at Firelight and Harbor. She crossed out an a-ring segment at Hamada.

The aliens were nearly in an uproar. Jarvie was frightened by the sounds of their alien arguing, but Beezan did not move from behind him or take his hand away.

Finally, Neah overrode the others, who all clapped their hands once, seemingly in agreement, except the old one, who kept pointing at Luminesse and Jarvie.

"What does he want?" Jarvie asked, trying to keep his voice steady.

"Proof," Reeder said.

"Proof we have," Oatah replied grimly. "According to Iricana, small cargo from Hamada was taken to the hangar."

Jarvie saw a look flash between Oatah and Iricana. *There's proof in our Cargo Hold. But Oatah doesn't want them to know that.*

"Explain about the cargo at the hangar, and the gravity ball," Oatah said.

Iricana frowned and drew the hangar at Nocturne's L4, circled a piece of the exploded alien ship at Hamada and drew a line to the hangar.

Another uproar. While they argued, Iricana drew a small gravity ball at Hamada with a line going to Nocturne's L5. The suited aliens crowded around the table, pressing against Jarvie. They actually jostled Beezan out of the way. Jarvie couldn't stand it. His only escape was to slip under the table and sit. Katie, being so small, managed to crawl under and sit by him, but she didn't have to hunch over.

The arguing was getting louder and angrier. The translator was spitting out words like '**child**,' and '**ship**.' The one old alien was banging on the table.

The strong calm tones of Beezan's chanting suddenly filled the room. The entire group fell instantly silent. After the prayer, there was a moment of quiet and then the aliens filed out. Jarvie could see their suited feet leaving. One, Neah probably, stood over Hef until he got up to leave. Oatah, Reeder, and Iricana followed them.

As soon as they were gone, Beezan reached under the table and helped Jarvie out.

"What was that about?" Jarvie asked.

"Seems that the Captain of their ship is not really the one in charge," Katie mused.

"Sounds familiar," Beezan sympathized.

Jarvie let Beezan and Katie fuss over him, ate some food, hugged Star, and had another med scan. "I'm all right, Captain," he finally said. "Just a little rattled."

"Well, I have a job for you then," and Beezan plopped Sky into his lap with Star. Jarvie took them to the makeshift play area and sat down with them while Beezan went to the table to help Reeder and Oatah. They had returned and were immediately going through the secret cargo manifests.

"Why didn't you tell them we have more Hamada cargo in our hold?" Iricana asked.

"I'd like to know what's in it before turning it over to them, as of course we will," Oatah assured her.

"Who were those other people?" Jarvie asked.

"Some sort of witness group? Reporters? Maybe a decision-making committee, something like a council?" Oatah speculated.

"Our Councils would never act like that," Jarvie objected.

"It's a different culture," Reeder explained. "Many cultures of Earth have similar . . . expressiveness."

"We mustn't judge them by their culture," Iricana insisted. "We must communicate. It is a good sign that they are upset. That means that *our* problem is also *their* problem."

3-Names

The next day, only four aliens came in the same big shuttle. Three talked with Oatah while Sontula came up with the translator. She worked with Iricana on basic time words.

Sontula drew that Neah, identified by the icon he wore on his collar, was still on the *Pearl*. It seemed as if there might be some trouble there.

They left soon after, Sontula saying something into the translator that came out as "**one day**."

4-Names

It's one day, Beezan thought, as he stared out the Command

Bay window. Sure enough, a blob separated from the *Pearl*. He watched it, trying to determine if it was the *Starfish* or the bigger one, when Jarvie gasped. "Another!"

Oatah and Reeder were waiting by the lift. Katie and Iricana were in the Med Bay. "Two shuttles today," Beezan relayed to them.

Jarvie gasped again. "Make that three," Beezan said.

"Do you think they plan to invade?" Reeder asked.

"Reeder!" Beezan shook his head as he watched the first shuttle. *What a notion.* But Jarvie didn't look so sure. "Honestly! *Drumheller*, estimate trajectories of the three shuttles."

"Shuttle 1 approaching *Drumheller*. Shuttle 2 approaching the hangar at Nocturne L4. Shuttle 3, possibly targeting Nocturne L5."

"They're going to the hangar? How do they think they are going to access the cargo there without our help?" Reeder asked incredulously.

"We must help them," Oatah answered calmly.

"Oh."

"Captain," Iricana said, "I'm familiar with the hangar."

"Thank you," he breathed. "Agent Oatah, can Reeder and Iricana go to the hangar in," he paused to check the shuttle list that Jarvie had already put up, ". . . the *Peacock*?"

"Yes, Captain."

"Thank you. It's in Hangar 2."

"You have a shuttle named *Peacock*?" Jarvie asked.

"It's not my shuttle! It's one of Oatah's. Go down there and help them," he snapped, but then felt bad. He grabbed Jarvie's arm and said more gently, "Stay on the *Drumheller*."

"Don't worry about that, honor."

They could get set up in Hangar 2 without worrying about

the incoming alien shuttle, which turned out to be the big one. The alien shuttle going to L5 would be on its own.

After the aliens had parked their shuttle and come up, Beezan headed to the Med Bay. The 'committee' was back, with only one camera, and thankfully led by Neah today. As Beezan stood in the rimway while they went upstairs, Neah approached him. Neah looked tired and tense. He met Beezan's eyes with a steady, but Beezan thought, worried expression, and faded colors. Neah slowly reached out his hands, palms up, as if asking for something. Beezan was baffled. He shrugged. He didn't understand the gesture, or Neah's colors. He put his hands out like Neah's.

Neah stood and looked. Apparently, that wasn't the proper response, but Neah was understanding and headed upstairs. Beezan followed him up, just as Jarvie came down the rimway. "The *Peacock* is off," he whispered. "Katie's going to monitor them."

"Good." Jarvie hesitated, so Beezan signaled for him to go up, but let him sit with the podpups.

The old alien, Hefreesay, as far as Beezan could catch the name, was seated again, but this time Neah and Sontula sat too. Beezan and Oatah joined them, Oatah handing him a pen.

"Iricana?" the aliens asked.

Beezan drew that he was sending Reeder and Iricana to the hangar. Neah called on his beautiful s'link box, probably telling them to expect help. He relaxed a bit.

Slowly Sontula made some marks near each gravity ball accident site on the map. Then she made human numbers. She spoke into the translator, which said **one day** and then she pointed to the numbers.

That many days? The Harbor number was smallest, 189. "*Drumheller*, how many days since the Harbor accident?"

"One hundred, eighty-nine."

"Yes," Beezan said, and circled the number. That was the day an alien spaceship had crashed into the a-rings while ships were jumping, destroying at least two a-ring segments.

The aliens nodded grimly.

"*Drumheller*, how many since Hamada?"

The Firelight, Luminesse, and Hamada numbers all matched within one day. The number of days since the alien ships disappeared matched the number of days since the accidents in the human systems. *Finally. We're getting somewhere. We need to convince them to stop crashing into our a-rings.* Beezan circled all four sets of destroyed a-rings. Perhaps this would help convince Hefreesay.

Neah took a deep breath and motioned Sontula to continue. She wrote the number 37 next to Canyon.

God in heaven, had Canyon been destroyed? Beezan and Oatah looked at each other in alarm. Katie glanced over from the panel where she was monitoring *Peacock*, but was very preoccupied. Jarvie stood up and looked over. "We don't know if it was destroyed," Oatah said, "only that a ship may have jumped there."

Sontula wrote backwards arrows by the numbers at Harbor, Firelight, Hamada, and Luminesse. Then, colors going gray, she wrote a forward arrow over the 37 at Canyon. So the Canyon jump was planned for 37 days in the future.

"No!" Beezan gasped.

"I don't understand," Jarvie said.

"They plan to jump to Canyon in 37 days," Oatah calmly explained. "And since each of their previous jumps resulted in disaster, we will have to negotiate a change in their plans."

But the bad news was yet to come. It was not *Pearl* that was planning to jump to Canyon. Another ship was making the jump from a star near the top of the alien map. Neah traced jump paths from Daydream, around the alien map to the star where the Canyon jumper was waiting. He numbered the stars, one through seven, as he went.

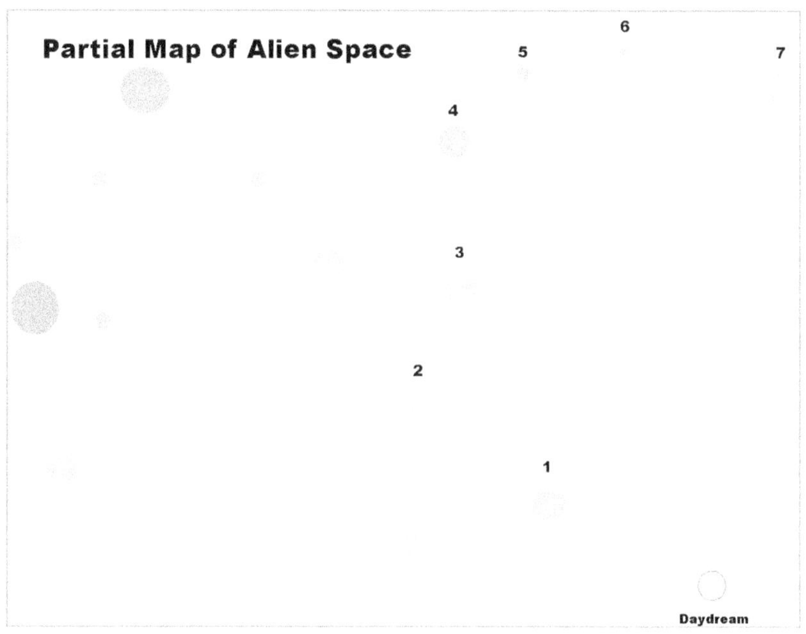

"Seven jumps! They'll never warn it off in 37 days!" Beezan realized. In a panic, he counted the jumps in human space. Redrock to Petrichor to Atikameq to Canyon to the star called Seven where the alien ship was waiting. Still five jumps. "We won't make it on the human side either."

"Even with relay ships?" Oatah asked. It took Beezan 20 minutes to get across the idea that one ship would jump to the system and rather than waiting days or weeks to reach the a-rings and jump out again, a lightspeed message would be sent for a different ship to take. Humans had "relay ships" at each a-rings just for such emergencies.

Neah nodded that this could be done for stops 1-4 on his side, but not the rest. **"No ships wait,"** the translator said.

"Maybe those are just outposts," Oatah suggested.

"We could relay on our side," Jarvie suggested.

Beezan turned to the human map. "It won't work," he said. "We need a seer at Canyon to make the blind jump to Seven and there's no way to send one ahead. And even if we got a message to Canyon, there would not be enough time to evacuate."

Iricana summarized. "Either way, human or alien, we'd be blind jumping to a new system. We have to get a seer to do the blind jump and we'll be too late."

Neah nodded. **"Problem."** Then he added a new star to his map. He pressed a small sheet down and activated it. It showed an orange star between Daydream and Seven. "Two jumps," he said without the translator. So instead of jumping all the way around, they could make it to Seven in two jumps.

"What's the catch?" Jarvie asked.

"Looks like a desperation jump," Beezan said. He swung over to the panel and checked over his work on the alien stars. Yes, one matched, a star very well known and coveted by humans. "It's 5F." 5F was a star outside of the Firelight sector that was considered for exploration jumps. It was already known to fit the requirements for a-rings. Beezan met Oatah's gaze. Their hopes were dashed as Neah drew circles around 5F. "No jump." He placed his finger on every neighboring star to 5F and said "No jump, no jump."

"Why?" Beezan asked.

"No number."

Beezan shook his head, not understanding.

"No jump number computer."

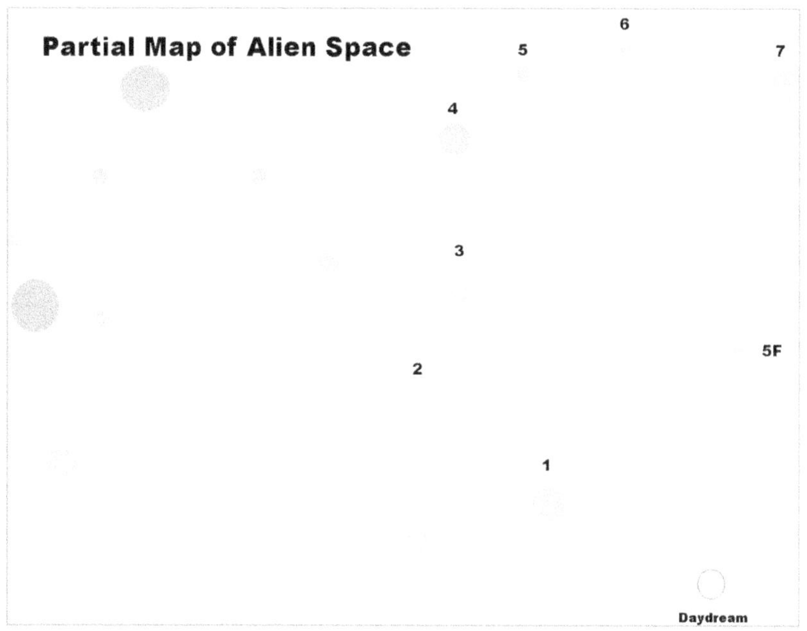

Neah used his s'link box to show a picture of some kind of control panel. Beezan made no sense of it.

"Agent Oatah, please."

Neah showed and Oatah's eyes went wide. "It's an a-ring control panel."

"I thought they were all destroyed," Jarvie said.

"All but the one on Tektite." *Which explains why people are struggling to keep the Tektite system open.*

"But obviously, the control panels were not destroyed in their systems," Oatah whispered. "Control panel," Oatah said in a normal voice, pointing. "A-rings," pointing.

"Yes," Neah said. "**Need code. Then jump.**" He pointed to 5F.

“They have jump codes,” Jarvie whispered in amazement.

“Jump codes?” Beezan was having trouble with the whole idea. He had never believed in the control panel idea. How could you use a code? How could programming the panel send your ship the right way? How could the pilot feel the next star?

“Humans have code Five-eff?” Neah asked.

“No,” Beezan shook his head. “Humans, no codes.”

Oatah drew a small picture of the control panel at several a-rings in the human system and then crossed them out with the famous red pen. “No control panels.”

Neah and company were shocked, talking among themselves. Finally, Neah turned and pointed to Beezan. “Jump, no control panel.”

Beezan thought Neah was asking if humans jump without codes, so he said “yes.”

Neah pointed to Beezan, the picture of *Drumheller*, to Daydream and 5F. Then Neah smiled. “Beezan jump Five-eff, no code.”

“What?” They all said at once, when it suddenly became clear what Neah wanted. He took their reaction in stride.

“Neah come.”

“No, no, no, you don’t understand.” Beezan was suddenly hot and flustered. Make another desperation jump after barely surviving the jump to Daydream? “Too far.”

“Remember what Lander said,” Oatah said calmly. *Oatah wants me to do it!*

Neah took another big breath. “Beezan jump five-eff, no number. Beezan jump Seven. Stop ship. Bold move.” *He wants me to make both jumps. Two untried desperation jumps?* Beezan looked at Oatah in a panic. But Oatah was not panicking; he was considering.

"What?" Katie suddenly asked, breaking away from monitoring the *Peacock*. "What does he want?"

"If we are to save Canyon," Oatah calmly replied, pointing to the map, "Beezan must jump to 5F and then to Seven."

Katie's eyes went wide. "We can't!"

"I have every confidence in Beezan's ability to make two untried jumps."

"No! We can't go anywhere but Redrock!" she flicked a glance at Jarvie.

Beezan's coping ability was about to run out. The aliens were talking and showing all kinds of colors. The translator was going crazy.

"Stop!" Beezan held up his hand. There was total quiet. His head was swirling.

"Why can't we go?" Oatah quietly asked Katie.

"Captain, Agent Oatah, Jarvie only has one jump left. We must go to Redrock for the implants. Otherwise . . . he will die."

34 / A LITTLE SHIP

Die? Jarvie hadn't believed he was so sick. Beezan looked horrified; Oatah looked skeptical. Katie jumped from her chair and dragged Jarvie to the exam bed. Before he knew it, the scanner was over his head and his implants were on the screen for all to see.

The aliens frowned. *Did they even have implants? If they had codes, they might not need them.* Neah signaled one of the committee to come forward. **"Doctor,"** the translator announced. The alien doctor was more of a blue purple than the others, with fewer decorations and a no-nonsense manner. He flipped a hood on, which covered his membrane. He pulled out a device larger than the s'link boxes which he set on Jarvie's chest. It felt warm and vibrated.

"Does it hurt?" Katie asked, sliding the scanner off.

"No." A field sprang from the device, stretching out to cover Jarvie.

"Doctor, Danumae," Neah reminded them of his name. Danumae studied the virtual picture around Jarvie, touching places for enlargements.

"How can they tell about a human?" Jarvie asked nervously.

"Maybe it just shows the picture of anything," Katie answered. Tentatively she touched the area showing his implants. She frowned at the enlargement and briefly met Danumae's gaze.

Then she had Beezan get on the other exam bed and pointed to his very different scan. "Beezan good. Jarvie brain hurt. Needs surgery. Redrock." She pointed to the map, "Redrock."

Danumae picked up his device and quickly tested Beezan. Then he put away his device with a snap of finality. Pushing back his hood, he flashed a burst of yellow. **"Jarvie two jumps die. One jump . . ."** he stopped. **"One jump."**

"Am I going to die anyway?" Jarvie asked, quite bravely, he thought.

"No," Katie reassured him. "We need to come in close. You'll go straight to surgery."

Jarvie was self-conscious with all the aliens staring. "Well, then we have to go to Redrock," a stricken Beezan said.

"Captain," Oatah said sympathetically, "we must stop that ship. We cannot lose Canyon."

Beezan shook his head in a daze. "It wouldn't matter. We can't make those jumps without a seer anyway. We can get one at Redrock."

"No, Captain. That would be four jumps. It would be too late." Oatah spoke gently but firmly. "You will be our seer."

"But Jarvie can't come!" Katie insisted. Oatah looked with great sadness at Jarvie.

"Perhaps he is stronger than we believe."

"He isn't!" Katie cried.

"No," Beezan shook his head.

The committee, after listening to Danumae, understood the problem. The aliens argued and pointed. They counted out jumps, but Jarvie knew there was no possible way to save Canyon.

If they didn't go, the aliens would lose another ship—but the humans would lose a key colony and the tide would be turned against the outer sectors. Everyone at Canyon would die, abandoned. He couldn't be responsible for such a thing. One person's life, especially his, was not worth all that. Even worse, everyone would know.

"I'll take my chances!"

"No," Beezan and Katie chimed together.

"We must put aside our feelings and do what is right," Oatah said. Beezan, who had been standing by the exam bed, turned and walked away from them all. Jarvie sat up to go after him, but Oatah paused him. Oatah wasn't cold-hearted, Jarvie knew. He was committed to what must be done. Katie, of course, was only in the mind of saving the patient. Jarvie would have to convince them, somehow, that he was willing to make the sacrifice.

The aliens stood, almost forgotten. Jarvie sat on the exam bed, with Katie and Oatah standing guard over him like good and bad angels. Beezan's back was turned to them all. Then a wild idea hit Jarvie.

"I could stay here."

Oatah looked stunned. "What?" Katie asked. "You can't. There are no living quarters at the L4 hangar."

Jarvie was desperate. "A shuttle! I could stay on a shuttle."

"Not for weeks!" she argued.

"Why not?" Oatah asked reasonably.

She took an exasperated breath. "Well, maybe for a few weeks, in a radiation safe orbit. If there was enough room for food and—*do you know how much water?* AND you don't go crazy from being alone and die from lack of gravity and exercise!"

Of course, Beezan would never agree, but Jarvie's mind was turning. What if Beezan didn't know? *What if the others helped me sneak out right before—*

"No!" Beezan whirled around to face him. "Don't even think it! I'll lock you in your cabin!" The others looked at Beezan in bewilderment.

"Calm yourself, Captain. Jarvie wouldn't do anything rash," Oatah advised.

Beezan rolled his eyes in exasperation. Katie stormed over to the panel and called up the shuttle list. "They are all too small. They're not rated for more than 10 days as a closed system and there's nowhere to store extra supplies."

Oatah turned to Jarvie. "I think it would be best to come with us. ***'If it be the will of God to protect man, a little ship may escape destruction . . .'***"[1] he quoted.

Beezan sat on the deck. He slammed his hand down. "You don't understand!" He actually shouted. The whispering aliens fell silent. "I couldn't jump anywhere thinking it would kill him! We would never make it." His shoulders slumped over in defeat. "No amount of mental preparation or prayer or supposedly being a seer would make a difference."

"You underestimate yourself, Captain," Oatah said. "You must have the same hope you always have when you jump."

"No," Jarvie shook his head. "That's not how it is for a pilot. The only hope for you to make the jump is for me not to go."

They stood helplessly. Jarvie looked over at Katie. "What is the biggest shuttle?" She moved back to the panel in defeat, scowling at it.

Then Neah slowly came over to Beezan, letting himself down to the deck next to him. Gently, he put his hand on Beezan's shoulder, his colors a steady, but not blinding, white. Almost in a whisper he said, "Jarvie, *Pearl*, no jump."

Jarvie's heart constricted. *Stay on the alien ship? By myself?* He was suddenly terrified. What if the *Drumheller* never came back? He'd be stuck with the aliens. He was about to object again, when he saw the looks on all their faces. Like it was the solution they'd been praying for. Katie was contemplating. Neah was determined. Beezan was frozen, except for the tears slowly rolling down his face.

Oatah was quite satisfied with the idea. He was nodding vigorously to Neah. "Brilliant! Yes. Jarvie could bring everything he needs. He would have exercise, gravity. He wouldn't be alone. He'd have a unique opportunity to interact with the aliens in their own environment. It will be quite exciting for him."

Exciting? Jarvie thought he might choke. However, if it convinced Beezan, he had to go along with it, no matter how frightening. "Star? I could take Star?"

Neah nodded in the human way. He looked sympathetically at Beezan. "Beezan, Oatah, *Pearl* one day. Beezan see *Pearl*."

"Yes," Beezan whispered.

Neah stood and made arrangements with Oatah. There was a bustle of activity as the aliens prepared to leave. Oatah escorted them to the lift.

"Drumheller," Beezan asked in spite of his tears, "what's happening with the *Peacock*?"

"Shuttle *Peacock* has arrived at the Nocturne L4 hangar. No estimated time of return."

"Keep me informed," Beezan said quietly. He wiped his face and stood up. He wasn't able to meet Jarvie's eyes. He paced around the Med Bay instead. Jarvie wanted to tell him it was all right, that he was scared, but that he would do it. That it was better than being alone in a shuttle. Just one thought kept repeating.

"What if you don't come back?" Jarvie whispered.

Katie put up a calming hand. “Oatah has another group scheduled to come in a year. The *Pearl* can wait for them.”

“What if they don’t wait?” Beezan asked. “What if they just take him away?”

“What if they take you and Oatah tomorrow?” Katie asked sternly.

Beezan stopped pacing.

“I wasn’t serious!” Katie said. “I’m just pointing out if we’ve decided to trust them then we must trust them.”

“Who says I’ve decided to trust them?”

“They took everything?” Oatah asked. It was 14 hours later, nearly morning, when the *Peacock* finally returned from meeting the aliens at the L4 hangar.

“They took all the containers stored at the L4 hangar.” Reeder clarified, almost cowering from fear of reporting such a thing to Oatah, but Oatah was unconcerned.

“We couldn’t see any diplomatic way to stop them,” Iricana added. “They were very insistent.”

Both Reeder and Iricana were exhausted and frazzled. Reeder even had three hairs out of place. Jarvie brought Iricana her food first, since she was senior, and then went back for Reeder’s, as they settled around the kitchen table. Beezan had left for his cabin once they reported the crew and *Peacock* safely back.

“It is of no importance,” Oatah assured them. “We no longer need bits and pieces to have proof of aliens. We are returning their property to them. All will be well.”

“You’re right,” Iricana sighed, “it’s just all the years of work and planning—”

"Which were not in vain, as we needed the information to get where we are now," Oatah reasoned.

Reeder was relieved, even thanking Jarvie for his food.

"What's happened here?" Iricana asked. "Beezan didn't look good."

Furtive glances passed between Katie and Oatah. Reeder and Iricana froze, spoons halfway to their mouths. "What has happened?" Iricana repeated more sternly.

Oatah cleared his throat. "Actually, a wonderful opportunity has presented itself. Captain Beezan is adjusting to it."

Iricana fixed Oatah with a *stop the doubletalk* look and he continued. "We need to proceed most urgently to a star, called Seven, in the alien sector, to head off a ship that will be blind-jumping for Canyon."

They put down their spoons.

"How long do we have?" Reeder asked.

"Thirty-seven days—"

"Thirty-seven!" they both exclaimed.

"Yes," Oatah carried on calmly, "Two unknown jumps. The aliens use codes normally, but Beezan will be making these jumps."

"Codes . . ." Reeder repeated in wonder.

"No wonder he's adjusting," commented Iricana.

"That is a mere distraction. We have to leave Jarvie behind—due to his implants. He'll be staying on the *Pearl*."

Luckily, they had put their spoons down. Iricana's blue eyes could not have grown any wider. She started to protest, but Jarvie could see the whole situation sorting itself in her mind. "Not enough time to drop him at Redrock . . ."

"Exactly."

"Not enough time to get a seer?"

"Correct," Oatah confirmed.

Iricana patted the seat next to her and Jarvie sat down by her. "I'll go with you," she said to him. It warmed his heart, even as Oatah explained that he wouldn't let her.

5-Names

As Beezan, Oatah, and Neah approached in the *Starfish*, the glowing field of the *Pearl* became a wall of light. Beezan remembered the few times he had been on a planet with some atmosphere, *in broad daylight*. The interior of their control room shimmered with the creamy light. Already-shiny control panels gleamed gold with colored glints reflecting off the buttons. Beezan's visor had darkened several levels. He did not even realize they had passed through the field until Oatah pointed out the ship. Squinting, Beezan could see the spherical ship, rotating, but slowly, not enough for gravity.

Beezan was not as nervous as he thought he would be, partly because it was so exciting, and partly because it was Neah who was now piloting the *Starfish*. He tried to concentrate on his job, which was to observe and report as much as possible about the ship. Although he felt he was at a loss for words to describe it, he dutifully whispered a stream of awed, but inadequate, commentary.

Oatah's job was to focus on the people. They could both speak freely now, as they still had their helmets on. However, once they boarded the *Pearl*, Beezan knew they would have to take them off. He had a pang of fear at the thought, but Neah and the others had no trouble with the *Drumheller* air, and Katie's analysis of samples proclaimed the *Pearl* air "better" than *Drumheller's*, much to his disgruntlement.

Both Beezan and Oatah had their suit cameras running. If the *Starfish* was any indication, the *Pearl* would be spectacular.

"Well," Beezan struggled to explain, "Everything in the shuttle is beautiful. The control buttons are like sparkling gems. The walls are textured with pictures, but I can't make them out. Wait, one looks like a sailing ship. The more I look, the more I see that every detail is a work of art. Even the deck is soft."

Beezan was grateful for the helmet. He could turn off his external audio pick up and close his eyes to shut out the overwhelming colors and images. The *Starfish* was fairly quiet, humming as if happy. Neah wasn't talking much and there were mercifully few of the beeps and chimes that human ships favored.

Beezan even imagined that he understood a bit of the color talk. A flash of yellow—he could see it on the alien membranes and on their panels. One flash of yellow, like "Got that?" "Understand?" And an icon, a bird's eye, often seen above a lens, was obviously the sign for a camera. They were everywhere. Neah sometimes looked at them on purpose.

Earlier, Neah had clued them in to a key social factor, since the humans confessed they couldn't tell the men from the women. "We can't either," he'd said, touching an icon on his collar. Apparently, for those who wished to declare, females wore a blue circle pin on the left side of their collar or shirt. Males wore one on the right. But the colors were slightly different. Neah explained it as the difference between sea blue for women and sky blue for men, but only Oatah and Reeder really understood what he meant.

"Captain?" came Katie's tentative voice from the *Drumheller*.

"I'm okay. Resting my eyes." Katie and Jarvie were monitoring him, leaving Reeder and Iricana to monitor Oatah. Beezan opened his eyes just in time to grab his chair in alarm. The approach angle was all wrong. He sat up, but no one else was worried. “Some strange approach,” he told the listening *Drumheller* crew.

“It’s a lunar approach,” Oatah calmly reminded him.

Astonishingly, that meant the *Pearl* had gravity. Beezan’s eyes went wide and he turned to Oatah. *What kind of technology do these people have?*

Oatah shook his head slightly and raised a hand to caution him, “Perhaps.”

After they landed and it was a sure thing, Beezan relayed, “Yes, they have gravity.” They were in the *Pearl* hangar and he was completely disoriented. The shuttle had flipped over to land, bottom toward the center of the ship. The ‘sky’ through the hangar door was visible right above them. “Central gravity, like a moon.” Beezan heard their excited voices, but as the hangar door slid shut, the s’link failed. Oatah and Beezan were on their own.

Beezan understood Oatah’s caution. Continuous examples of superior alien technology were not necessarily a good thing. Although Reeder often reminded him that technology in Sector 1 far exceeded theirs, Beezan knew they didn’t have ships with gravity. What would humanity have to offer in exchange for all this? And would the price be too high? It was not even mentioned in the protocols, but Beezan understood instinctively that humans must present themselves as equals.

Beezan, out of his suit now, aboard the *Pearl*, breathing alien air and still alive and standing, offered a great prayer of relief and thanks. *And please keep sending the help because I am going to faint right here in front of all 67 aliens during the most historic moment of our First Contact.*

He couldn’t hide his eyes any more so he stared at Oatah,

who finally had his chance to talk after very many welcome speeches and presentations. Oatah had kept Iricana, Reeder, and Jarvie awake all night folding golden paper into birds called cranes, to give as gifts to the aliens. It was a good thing too, as presentation of gifts was important to the aliens.

The aliens could not understand him, and Beezan wasn't listening, but Oatah carried on, unruffled, dignified, and commanding attention. Beezan would have been proud of humanity's first representative if he hadn't been so busy trying not to keel over. He had not expected the heat, or the smell, or just the presence of so many people. He couldn't talk to the crew now anyway, but it was for the best, as he didn't want to scare Jarvie. *He's fourteen; he'll adapt quickly*.

Not only were there people, 67 of them, from Hefreesay to a baby, with adults decked out in jewelry and children in frilly clothes, there were also podpups of all colors and more birds with devices. The birds were small and colorful, but silent. Occasionally, one zoomed in close, as if to investigate. *Cameras. With emotion monitors? Remote controlled?* Every time one came near him, Beezan instinctively ducked. Even Oatah was slightly distracted by them.

The talks were over at last. Sontula appeared next to him with her translator and they set off for "**a walk**." Along the rimway, the aliens lined up against the walls to let them through. As they began to pass, each alien reached out one of their hands, palm up. Beezan didn't know what to do, but Oatah calmly put his hand on top of theirs, like a hand press instead of a handshake. Beezan followed Oatah's example. He found himself pressing the hand of every single alien, even the baby. At first, it seemed contrived, but then he was caught in the moment. Aboard the *Drumheller*, it had been all business, but here, there was ceremony, history, and even destiny combined.

This was the real first contact. The mother of the baby, with no fear of Beezan, held the baby out and Beezan touched ziz hand. The membranes of all the aliens were glowing coral with pulses of blue and green. The baby flashed steady emerald green while ziz blue eyes met Beezan's. This baby would grow up never remembering the time before humans. Ze would be the first child of a new generation.

The ship was smaller than he'd thought and as crowded as a Section 3 station. He lost all sense of direction. Oatah, however, was in his element. The heat, the overwhelming colors, aliens, podpups, birds, the talk, the singing, the sounds of so many feet on the deck, the smells he couldn't even begin to identify did not seem to bother Oatah in the least.

Beezan trudged after Oatah, hoping that his falsely pleasant expression would be good enough for the aliens. Oatah managed to give him a stern look without even changing *his* expression. Their tour guide, Hefreesay, was proudly thorough. Beezan looked where he pointed, listened to whoever was speaking, nodded and 'mm-hmmed' appropriately, but nothing penetrated his brain. He said a few prayers to himself while Hefreesay was showing some kind of room—a school. Beezan's mind suddenly came to attention.

The aliens didn't notice Beezan's change in alertness as they'd apparently given up on him and were addressing Oatah. He scolded himself for indulging in selfish contemplation while he had a job to do. Jarvie would be living here. He needed to be a responsible caretaker and pay attention.

Jarvie waited anxiously by the hangar lock, waiting to help Beezan and Oatah back in. He knew they were both exhausted. They had stayed until midnight, *Drumheller* time. As soon as they were safely through both hatches, *Drumheller* flashed the hangar lights and *Starfish* was on its way home.

Jarvie dutifully helped Oatah with his helmet and suit. He wanted to grab Beezan and talk to him in private to ask what it was really like. Beezan had been more silent than usual since they'd left the *Pearl*, but Oatah was streaming with commentary.

They met the rest of the crew in the kitchen. They listened raptly to Oatah while Star and Sky sniffed Beezan all over. Beezan slumped over the table while Oatah paced around in his excitement. Katie did a quick med check on Beezan and nodded her approval, but had to follow Oatah around since he couldn't seem to stand still a moment. "Reeder, your idea of the paper cranes was inspired. They have so many birds," Oatah was saying in wonderment, turning to Jarvie, "you must observe them." He continued, "They're so similar to terrestrial birds. Study might lead us to fundamentals of their evolution-planet . . . unless of course they were specifically bred . . ."

Iricana got food and Reeder recorded all Oatah's comments, listening with an almost worshiping expression. Iricana set out the podpup bottles so Jarvie used that as an excuse to slide in the table next to Beezan to let the pups eat together. They sat back with the pups in their laps, slurping away. Jarvie was just starting to get a tiny bit excited about going, the way Oatah was carrying on, when Beezan slowly opened his eyes and looked up at Jarvie. "It's all right," he whispered. Beezan reached over and grabbed his hand. "You'll be fine there. You're young; you're used to more people and excitement."

Oatah had paused and all the crew turned to look at Beezan and Jarvie at the table, but Beezan did not let go of his hand. "They told us you will be joining Danumae's family."

Jarvie nodded. He was relieved. Someone he had met, the

doctor. He even seemed nice.

"It will work," Beezan was still saying, "He'll take good care of you," now with his eyes closed again. "I can make the jump, if you stay there," but he didn't let go of Jarvie's hand, even after he fell sound asleep at the table.

8-Names

Thirty-three days, Jarvie thought. *The race is on. Except that I am getting off before the starting line.*

Jarvie had barely had time to think, let alone sleep, in the time since Beezan and Oatah had returned, so he also hadn't built up much worry. Now, waiting the last few minutes before he was scheduled to suit up, his fears and disappointment bubbled up. As much as he wished to go with the *Drumheller*, he knew it would be dangerous and stressful. He had been so scared of the aliens at first, but now they really didn't seem all that different from humans, and he wondered how that was possible. There were times, even, when Neah was less alien than Reeder.

What am I forgetting? Something nagged at his brain.

A year's worth of human and podpup food was packed, under Katie's supervision, with medicines and other supplies. Jarvie had a few personal things, including a beautiful photo album Katie made for him. She had given it to him this morning when they officially said goodbye after prayers. It had photos of his family, *Sunburst*, Lanezi, the *Drumheller* and crew, the podpups, Nocturne and Lander's moon, all printed as permaphotos—a treasure. He kept it inside his shirt. It was a little bulky but it would fit under the suit.

Jarvie had been instructed to update his will, which he did, leaving his family credits to Beezan. *Wouldn't he be surprised to be rich?* He'd been given a special packet with the crew's wills and an official message for Any Sector Council in case something happened to the *Drumheller*. He had cleaned up his room for Neah. He'd been briefed (lectured, grilled and practically threatened) by Oatah and Reeder on his being a proper representative of humanity, as well as appropriate diplomatic behavior, as if he hadn't grown up on a diplomatic ship! Lucky for Oatah and Reeder at that moment. Iricana and Katie had fussed over him and barely held their tears back this morning, but Beezan had gone to jump mode. He was in 'walking meditation,' serene and distant.

Jarvie's p'link beeped. It was time. He took one last look at his cabin, swallowed hard, and went up the stairs. Just before he got to the top, the door opened and Beezan came in. He was standing two steps above, so for once, Jarvie had to look up at him.

"I believe you forgot something," Beezan said calmly.

Jarvie's breath caught, "What?"

Beezan smiled and pulled out Jarvie's armband. He hadn't worn it for ages. It was meaningless to the aliens. Beezan straightened it out and Jarvie saw that instead of "14" printed on it, there were two symbols, the ones they used with the aliens. One was the dinosaur egg, symbol of the *Drumheller*, and the other was Jarvie's stick person that they used in the alien drawings.

"Just so they don't forget where you belong," Beezan said dryly as he put it on Jarvie's arm. Jarvie reached out and hugged Beezan fiercely, happy that he could press his head against Beezan's chest, like a real kid. Beezan hugged him back, but in a strangely detached way. Jarvie looked up. Beezan's eyes were looking to that far away place. "Whatever happens, Jarvie, I will find you. In heaven or on Earth or in between, I will find you."

35 / THE RACE TO SEVEN

The exchange had been made. Beezan hovered in the Entry Lounge with Iricana and Katie. Neah watched the *Starfish* depart with steady white on his membrane. Beezan felt for him. He was proud of Jarvie, who had gone with grace and dignity, but when the hangar door slammed shut, reverberating through his bones, Beezan suddenly snapped out of his serenity. He lunged forward, grasping the hatch. Iricana and Katie looked at him with alarm, but Neah turned calmly and said, "Jarvie safe *Pearl.* No fear." Beezan slumped over. At least Reeder and Oatah had missed his little scene.

"Thank you, Neah."

"It is my honor to share this bold adventure with you," Neah said, and his colors blazed a bright blue that stirred confidence in Beezan's heart.

It was agreed that aboard the *Pearl* there would be no ceremony or speeches or any official role for Jarvie, that he would merely be a protected guest. That arrangement did not prevent a very long, involved tour with the acting captain—Hefreesay. *Surprise*, Jarvie thought. Maybe Neah would be happy for the vacation.

When Jarvie's escort, complete with photographers, finally brought him around to meet his hosts, Danumae was waiting outside the cabin door. He leveled his no-nonsense colors at Jarvie's escort and they set Jarvie's bags and Star's box down inside. They nodded to Danumae and departed. Quickly.

Jarvie wanted to drop onto the deck in exhaustion. His body shifted to slow motion. Danumae waved him inside. He took a deep breath and stepped through the decorated door to face his 'new' family. They stood formally in a row, craning their necks to look up at him. He wished that he were shorter.

Danumae introduced his wife, "Zhenulell, doctor." She touched her sea-blue icon on her left collar and bowed her head slightly. Then in order of size, the children, "child-girl, Zhenumae, child-boy, Danulell," who touched their respective gender icons, and "child Quay," who was only about 4 years old, judging by his size. Quay touched his right collar where the male icon would be if he had one, and gave a quick frown to his father. *Noted*, Jarvie thought, relieved that the genders were announced as he could not figure it out.

Jarvie pressed hands with them all, saying, "God is Most Glorious," despite their puzzled looks. Although the parents were the same color, the children ranged from the girl's dark purple, almost black, reminding him of Katie, to Quay's bright, almost pure blue, leaving the older boy in the middle with vivid purple skin. The older two children were close in age. Jarvie suspected this family had been arranged because they were mid teens as he was.

Jarvie tried to say their names, but got mixed up, so they repeated several times. He realized they were combinations of each other's names, which made it all the more confusing. He was going to have to take notes. He'd have plenty of room on his p'link since Reeder had erased everything in case it "fell into the wrong hands."

"*Drumheller*?" Jarvie asked, hoping they might have some news. Danumae showed Jarvie to a small alcove off the common room. There was a screen already tracking the *Drumheller*. The deck was covered with a variety of pillows and pads to sit on. He stepped over them carefully to see up close. *Drumheller* was not spinning anymore. Any time now, they would boost to the a-rings. Jarvie swallowed a lump in his throat. After all those hours staring out the window at *Pearl*, now he was on the *Pearl*, staring out at the *Drumheller*.

At dinner, or whatever meal it was, in a large common dining room, Jarvie sat in an unbolted chair at a long table with his assigned family. Podpups had a side area where they ate together, but some didn't go, so Jarvie felt it allowable to keep Star by him and make sure he got the right food. They had screens on every wall, alternately showing *Drumheller,* the star maps with the route, and photos of Neah and the *Drumheller* crew. His photographers had faded away in the dining hall, but Jarvie suspected this news-watching was a big pastime and Neah's adventure of the *Race to Seven* would be the cause of much sensation. Too bad they wouldn't hear what happened for weeks.

Jarvie survived the meal, eating a dinner pack from his bag, despite being distracted by the screens and the feeling of everyone staring at him. On the walk back with his family, the teens were allowed to lag behind and there was some interaction with a few others. Jarvie quickly learned to cross his left hand over and touch his right collar, even if he didn't have an icon. He instantly lost all their names and connections, and was self-conscious from their attention, but felt that they looked on him with some sympathy and understanding.

Jarvie rested on the warm bed in the dark sleeping room, listening to the little snuffles of Quay, not much different from Star's, who was half on Jarvie's chest. Jarvie had taken over Quay's bed in the cabin he shared with Danulell. Jarvie knew Danulell was not really sleeping either—even after an hour of lying in the dark. It was tense for both of them. Jarvie guessed they were of a similar age and that Danulell had been 'coached' on the importance of his behavior as much as Jarvie.

Jarvie remembered with embarrassment how scared he had been when first seeing the aliens and how it had taken some time, until he had seen them as individuals, to not be afraid. Now Danulell was sleeping in the same room with Jarvie, who was an alien to him, mere hours after meeting him. Jarvie worried that he might seem even more scary because he was so tall. Danulell had also fussed with Quay, who was put out about sleeping on the pad on the deck. Jarvie would have offered to sleep on the deck but expected that it wouldn't be proper.

The *Pearl*, now that he was aboard, reminded him of the *Sunburst*. It was so much nicer than the *Drumheller*, but then most any ship would be nicer than the *Drumheller*. Like the *Sunburst*, there were more people, even if they were aliens. It gave the comfort of hearing voices around the bend rather than ghostly breezes, of footsteps on the rimway instead of creaking metal plates, the laughter echoing off the walls, warmth and family, podpups and birds. It was as wonderful as Oatah had said. Also, just like passenger ships, there was a more formal hierarchy. Jarvie assumed his place to be somewhat close to Danulell's and tried to follow his lead. He watched him carefully, but it was sometimes Quay who was more directly helpful, showing Jarvie how to use things, tugging Jarvie's pants and flashing colors. He suppressed a laugh remembering Quay's 'full demonstration' of the facilities and Danulell's embarrassed reaction. But they had laughed, the two older ones together, so a bit of the ice was broken.

Jarvie's thinking of the facilities was a mistake, as now he had to go. It was very dark. Could he make it without walking into the wall? He took a breath and swung out of bed, resettling Star gently. As soon as his feet touched the deck, soft lights outlined the two doors, one to exit into the common room and the other to a facility.

When he came out, Jarvie stopped short. There was just enough light to see that Quay was no longer on his pad. Had he crawled into the bed with Star?

No, Jarvie sighed with relief. Quay, after all his fussing and troubling Danulell, had crawled in with his older brother and now they were both sound asleep, Quay's disgruntled and Danulell's harassed expressions given way to contentment, and their colors running a soft easy pink.

Jarvie sagged against the doorframe with a pang of longing. It had been almost three years now since he'd lost his brother—but sometimes the pain came back full force. He feared he would lie in that alien bed forever and never go to sleep.

The outline of the other door was still glowing. Jarvie quietly made his way out and to the little alcove, almost shaking in fear of the dark alien room and the possibility of running into someone.

He had no idea what time it was or how long they would sleep. He watched the *Drumheller* for a few minutes—now on its way to the a-rings. It was such a good image. Tiredly, he sat on one of the pads. It was surprisingly warm just in his sleeping clothes. He would sit and watch the *Drumheller* for a few minutes . . .

Jarvie heard a yelp from Star and a general commotion. Lights blinked on. He felt around. *Where is Star? Where am I? Aliens.* They were rushing about in their sleeping clothes, Star underfoot and panicked. *What is happening?* If it was some alert, he didn't hear anything. He got up from the deck and edged out, trying to understand. Quay saw him and pointed. They all turned to look and slumped over. Danumae held the sides of his gray membrane as if in extreme discomfort.

"Jarvie, come," said the mother, with every bit the same tone as Katie when exasperated. *How could such things be the same?* He went to her, head hanging. *They thought I was gone.*

"Sorry," he said, shrugging his shoulders, not knowing what else to say.

She pointed back to the sleeping room and they all trudged off.

"How long until morning?" Jarvie asked Danulell, but he just shook his head. *Where is that translator?*

The translator, and Sontula, showed up in the morning, at the breakfast table. Apparently, breakfast seating was more flexible as Quay and Zhenumae went to sit with friends. Jarvie smiled as he greeted Sontula. It really was good to see a familiar face. The aliens were eating something like pink scrambled tofu. Star stayed by Jarvie again, but now kept an eye on the other podpups.

Jarvie visited the kitchen for the first time, meeting the head cook, Karinew. She was commanding from a central computer panel, surrounded by setup tables, plates, food, noise, and assistants—all kids. The ruckus stopped suddenly as Jarvie came in. All the children stared up at him. But one flash of orange from Karinew and they were back in action, shuttling food out to the tables. Jarvie wondered if they had even seen her colors as they were all looking at him, or if they just knew somehow. Karinew took Jarvie to the back, where the storage units were, and showed him one that they had dedicated to his food. More of his food was in a section of the freezer, which she showed him but shook her head not to go by himself. "Yes, Karinew," he said dutifully. He got his breakfast from the storage room. Karinew gave him some water, which Katie, having checked it before, had said was water like any other water. Oatah had been excited about that and admonished Jarvie to contemplate the water.

He took it back to Sontula and contemplated every last swallow. She spoke quietly into the translator, which was now smaller. **"Today—school,"** it said.

"*School?*" A sickening feeling came over him. He was so far behind in school anyway. How would he keep up with these aliens, especially with only a primitive translator?

To Jarvie's great surprise and consternation, he found out how. He was put in Quay's class. Quay proudly took Jarvie by the hand and brought him over to a small circle of children. The only face-saving thing was that Sontula and her translator were also joining the class.

It was a small class, only three kids besides Quay. None of them had gender icons. During introductions, they crossed their hands over their chest and bowed as quickly as they could get away with. They lost all discipline when they realized Jarvie would be joining them. They crowded around him, hand pressing, flashing, and squealing with delight. Sontula laughed. All Jarvie could understand from the translator was **"old."**

A young alien, not adult height anyway, greeted Jarvie. "Jarvie, teacher Norijay," Sontula introduced them.

"God is Most Glorious," Jarvie said, figuring they were getting used to it regardless of what the translator came up with.

10-Names

Beezan struggled to flick away unwanted thoughts as he drifted into the Command Bay for the jump. He's spent two days pretending to be serene. Neah had received a last message from the *Pearl* sending *bold journeys* and a report that Jarvie was doing well. If the crew was nervous about surviving an unknown jump with an unofficial seer, they didn't show it. Katie and Iricana, being from the outer sectors, tended to coddle Beezan, as was traditional, but Oatah and Reeder had no such inclination.

The jump would be a true test of nerves. Besides the jump itself, they would be flying into the a-rings at speed, which would trigger the hot-start. The ring system would go on automatically and they would be at quarter JV already.

The robots were in their bays, still online. Oatah had been horrified to learn they were loose during the alien flu, but whispered, "No turning back," in his strange way.

Reeder and Oatah were both to remain awake with Beezan in the Command Bay. Gently, he settled Sky in the jump bed, alone. "Humph!" She gave him a half-hearted spurn. Ever since Star got to go to the *Pearl* and she didn't, he'd been on notice that there better be an equal treat.

Beezan got his brackets and helmet on and sealed up his cocoon. From the passenger lounge, Katie signaled ready. Reeder and Oatah were ready. Beezan wasn't ready at all, but the moment was upon him.

"Ten seconds," reported *Drumheller*.

Beezan blinked off his last extra screen to focus only on the a-ring entrances. *Drumheller* would do the entry and exit corrections, but in the unlikely necessity, Beezan would do manual corrections, as well as the main jump thrust.

"Five seconds."

Beezan's hands tightened on the controls. The a-ring segment entrance appeared to expand like the big bang as they hurtled toward it.

"Four."

"Three."

"Two."

"One."

First segment: there was no surge, so *Drumheller* curved them around. In a few seconds, they were out, but Beezan couldn't see the main lights of the next segment. The *Drumheller* made a correction burn and provided the next graphic, On target, so Beezan released his grip, trusting in the *Drumheller*.

In a few minutes, they were through the second segment, but Beezan didn't feel the surge of the a-ring thrust. The lights of the next segment didn't come on. *Don't panic.* Another exit correction. Was there some trick to turning on the a-rings that Beezan didn't know?

On target. Still no surge, but just after the exit correction, the distant lights of the next segment came on. Beezan could feel the mental cheers of the crew. It was a beautiful sight.

On target. *The surge! Yes! Now we are in business.*

For three hours, Beezan's only thoughts were seeing those

lights and listening for *on target*. Between the segments, he went back to his prayers.

"... traverse, in the twinkling of an eye, the world of dust and advance into the realm of holiness . . ." Surge, bump, breathe. ***"... with one step cover the earth of limitations and reach the domain of the Placeless."***[1] Surge, bump.

"Up from thy prison ascend unto the glorious meads above . . ." Surge, bump. "... from thy mortal cage wing thy flight unto the paradise of the Placeless."[2] Surge, bump. It was getting painful.

"... away from this abode to the placeless realm."[3]

The intervals became shorter until it hardly seemed like there was time to make an exit correction between. Without the *Drumheller* computer, it would have been impossible. Now there was no time for prayers, only words, and when there was no time for words, it would be time to jump.

The rings were flashing by now like lights in a tunnel. The corrections, like one jolt after another. Two more laps, Beezan thought. He could no longer feel any separation between himself and the *Drumheller*. They flew as one.

Six more segments, he took a huge breath.

Five, he felt a glimmer of excitement from the crew.

Four, he could visualize the *Drumheller*, blazing through the last ring segments.

Three, it would be a good jump.

Two, he suddenly remembered his dream of Lander and realized where they had gone.

One, they were free. Beezan's mind burst open as they catapulted from the rings, searing through the fabric of normal space.

The paths were plain before him. If he had feared he

wouldn't see them, he now feared he could never choose between them.

The *Drumheller* shuttered in its window, skipping up and down the resonance waves, waiting for the pilot to choose the right path—and Beezan had no idea.

Stay calm. He blocked out all stray thoughts, all weak paths, all resonances too high and too low. He focused on those ahead and remembered the golden ribbon of his dream with Lander. *Should I trust in a dream?* Even as he pondered, a golden path caught his attention. He lined up and it practically yanked him. His hand pressed the jump thruster of its own volition.

The surge pressed him forcefully back. The *Drumheller* slipped into the path even as he felt the sting of the jump drug. The crew was behind him, not following, but holding on as if they felt the invisible pull of it too. He felt Reeder, close and steady, Oatah, overwhelmed with astonishment, Katie, relieved, Iricana, asleep but serenely observing, and something he had never felt before, iridescent bubbles of emotions, without names but full of colors, rippling over all of them— Neah.

Beezan offered a prayer of joy and gratitude as they skimmed lightly across, barely troubling the sentries—those small guards of the Kingdom. Then his mind went fuzzy from the meds. Even as Beezan fought the impulse to dive deeper, putting the sentries on alert, he wondered why they took the jump drug. He was sure he didn't need it. He was at home here.

"Venting," the word filtered through Beezan's wandering mind and coldly slapped against his consciousness. That their beautiful jump should be ruined by such a thing was unfit. Reeder was talking to *Drumheller*, checking on the repairs. Robot #9 had been dispatched. *Drumheller* was warning the crew to remain in their cocoons.

"Particle fields on full. Adjusting course to avoid further damage." There was a strong burn, a reorientation, and another strong burn. This time Beezan felt his recent wounds. He tried to focus on the physical world; it was just so misty. He would have faded away again if not for Reeder's voice.

"Captain, are you with us?" Reeder was amazingly calm.

Venting? Beezan popped his hand braces, unsealed the cocoon, and pulled off his helmet. "Yes." He knew without asking that they had all survived the jump and the bright shining star out the window meant that Daydream was far behind.

"*Drumheller*, identify star."

"Star is 5F. Searching for projected a-ring planet."

Beezan knew they were inside the orbit. He'd even had a sense of a ripple. They may have passed close by a big planet. He popped up a rear-view and found it. "*Drumheller*, there," he said, touching the pop-up. "Locate a-rings and set as destination. We need the ETA." The experience of the good jump was fading already, as the post jump depression set in on top of the realization that they had come in at the worst possible angle.

The others must have sensed his worry. "What's wrong?" Oatah asked. "Aren't we close?"

"Very close, but going the wrong way fast. Either we'll have to turn around and go back, which takes too much fuel and lots of gees, or we'll have to do a gravity-assist, which takes too long."

Thinking of a gravity-assist, he remembered Jarvie for the first time and felt somehow bad that he hadn't missed him before.

Reeder was scanning the panels in agitation. "Can we get to

the a-rings in time? We only have 28 days." Then the two main options appeared on the screen. Both Reeder and Oatah gasped and Beezan's heart dropped into his stomach.

Decelerate, reorient, and reboost to target, best trajectory: 35 days.

Stellar Gravity-Assist: 34 days.

Too late. They would be too late to save Canyon.

36 / DESPERATE DECISIONS

10-Names

Drumheller

They sat, stunned, staring at the screen, unwilling to believe they had failed.

"Vent damage temporarily repaired. Life support is stable."

"Secure repair robots for boosting," Beezan ordered. Every second that passed might mean minutes, or hours, possibly critical ones, added to their ETA. He glanced at their fuel and did a double take. He was so used to running on empty, but they had enough fuel for a few more good burns, even after the particle avoidance burns.

"*Drumheller*, is it possible to reduce option one to 28 days?"

Drumheller showed the details. Beezan despaired. They would have to accelerate 20 hours a day at nine gee.

"Nine gee!" gasped Reeder. "We'd be crushed."

"Only Captain Beezan and Neah need survive to complete the mission," Oatah calmly reminded him.

"Agent Oatah," Beezan said. "It would be pointless. We'll all die and no one will get to Canyon. *Drumheller*, Can we reduce the gravity-assist ETA to 28 days?"

"Trajectory posted."

They would use 5F's central star for a gravity-assist, swing around it, and then continue with daily boosting, totaling 28 days, but not at nine gees. They would survive. It would test the crew to their limits. Beezan glanced over at Oatah.

"We must proceed, Captain. We must get to the a-rings on time, no matter how difficult for the crew." Reeder nodded solemnly in agreement, not that Oatah had asked.

"*Drumheller*, proceed with gravity-assist option, immediately." Beezan kept telling himself it could have been worse. It could have been much worse, but he couldn't help wishing for an 'if only.' If only they had come in at a better angle. If only they had popped into normal space outside of the orbit of the a-rings. If only the a-rings had been in a different part of the orbit. If only they had a few more days. If only it was all over with.

Pearl

Sitting on the deck, Jarvie was studiously copying his numbers, while Quay and the others did the same at their desks. He was ignoring all the children's antics and sincerely trying to learn. As Oatah said, it was his special opportunity. How could he ever explain that he'd been the first human to live with the aliens and not learned a thing? Well, he had learned one important thing. The alien's home world was called Ramia. A picture of the planet hung prominently in the learning zone. It was surprisingly Earth-like, but the land was greener. Jarvie suspected that Reeder and Oatah would have been homesick just seeing it.

Gradually, he became aware that Danulell had come in and

was waiting for his attention. As soon as Jarvie looked up, Danulell signaled for him to come. Automatically, Jarvie glanced to the teacher for permission. Norijay waved at Jarvie to go, so he quickly put his workpad away in the little desk that he could not even sit at and joined Danulell going out the door.

"*Drumheller* soon go," Danulell explained. "Come." Jarvie was starting to learn some of their words, so Danulell spoke to him in a mixture of Ramian, Alkulu, color flashes, and hand signs. Danulell took him to the dining room. Many of the other adults were there, and more were coming, taking a few minutes from their work for the big moment. Even the birds gathered around. Two big screens were on, one showing the picture of *Drumheller*, the other showing a graphic of the projected path. Jarvie shivered, realizing that the lag time was around nine minutes. In real time, *Drumheller* had already entered the rings. As soon as he was seated, between Danulell and an adult he didn't know, he said a quick prayer for the jump.

Danulell whispered to Jarvie, "Neah family," and pointed. Five people were sitting up by the screen. Two were adult women, one older, and three were small children.

Jarvie sympathized with them. Although he had great confidence in Beezan's ability to get to Seven and back in one piece, he could understand their fear of Neah being aboard the *Drumheller*. Compared to the *Pearl*, the *Drumheller* seemed like a ramshackle, dusty old cargo ship. *Which is what it is*, he realized and then felt defensive. "*Drumheller*, good ship," he insisted to Danulell. Danulell must have passed the word, as Neah's wife turned to look at him. Jarvie resolved that he would be full of confidence, for the *Drumheller*, for Beezan, for humanity. He sat up straight and smiled, fixed his gaze on the *Drumheller* image and willed it to hold together.

There was a collective gasp when *Drumheller* entered the

first ring segment. Jarvie thought he was still putting on a good show of confidence, even though he was gripping the chair with both hands. Behind the backs of Neah's family, worried glances were exchanged between the adults. Again, after *Drumheller* passed the second segment, there was a stir of concern. Then *Drumheller* passed the third segment and a ring of lights went on ahead. The segments were active now, shining hoops of light to aim for as they circled the gravity ball. There was a relieved cheer in the room, which startled Jarvie. Among humans, jumps were only viewed with the utmost reverence.

Everyone stayed to watch. Soon most of the Ramians were there. Jarvie continued to pray quietly. It was strange watching without listening to the jump coordinator and without hearing the ship captains. Slowly he dropped into the trance-like state of the jump. The others glanced at him in alarm. Danumae ran a quick med check on him. Jarvie roused himself enough to tell them he was all right, but slipped back into the trance. Last lap. He sat up. The others noticed and watched the screen more closely. *Drumheller* was blazing through the segments. Suddenly it went out straight. This was the moment of the jump. Jarvie held his breath.

Drumheller disappeared. Jarvie smiled and sagged with relief. They had jumped so quickly, Beezan must have seen the way easily. The crew broke out into a happy song. Jarvie swallowed. He was happy too, but now came the waiting game. And now, he was alone among the aliens.

18-Names

Drumheller

Beezan made another calendar in the kitchen, counting down the days. This time he called them 5F days. *We need a better name.* He crossed off days 22, 21, and 20, the gravity-assist part of the trip. They were past closest approach. Now the long hard days of boosting back to the a-rings started. For six hours a day, they would feel almost twice their weight.

Katie had worked out a routine to keep them mentally, emotionally, and spiritually healthy during the rest of their ordeal. When not boosting, they had a strict schedule of chores, work, eating, prayers, exercise, and sleep. She even organized their daily six-hour burn.

Their six hours would begin with a deepening program, then alternate personal study time and music. Then they would run an episode of *Journey of our Hearts* during the fifth hour, so when that was over, there was only an hour to go, which was mostly quiet time.

So began another journey of Beezan's heart. Somehow, the show, some of which he had watched before with Jarvie, brought the rest of the crew together. Reeder and Oatah began to understand ship and outer sector life in a way that no Earth-bound seminar had taught them. Living on the *Drumheller* had only added to their confusion. Neah, who studied each episode again, after the burn, got a glimpse of humanity beyond the *Drumheller*. For although it was fiction, there was truth in it, as well as the carefully crafted messages of the teen training program. The episodes illustrated the responsibility of the care-takers, the hard work and sacrifice of teens, striving for excel-lence, love and fortitude, patience and unity, hope for humankind, and the power of prayer.

The themes worked as an almost magical medicine on all of the crew. Iricana felt freer to offer support and care to Katie, who for all her extraordinary qualities was still young and carrying so much responsibility.

The most obvious change was occurring in Oatah. Beezan

had been right about jumping. Oatah had seen and felt the connections of the stars. It banished the worry from his heart and lifted the burden off his soul. He looked all around as if seeing for the first time. Late one night, as Beezan was leaving the kitchen, he saw Oatah, staying up past the official bedtime, slide into the kitchen table next to Reeder and gently push Reeder's work away.

Beezan and Sky missed Jarvie and Star, but spent a lot of time with Neah—and, annoyingly, Robot #9—working on the translator. They quickly became used to the delay and double voice. Beezan began to see Neah as a friend and fellow captain.

Beezan learned to understand the colors of puzzlement, of reverence, of fun, of concentration, and of pain. For colors could not hide and the strain of the burns flashed across Neah's forehead.

Twenty days to go, Beezan thought. One more day than the 19-day fast, he lamented. Stressed and exhausted, they clung to their routine, each one being brave for the others and concentrating on the goal of saving Canyon.

2-Might

Seventeen days: They stood solemnly at attention in the Consultation Hall, in their best uniforms, as Reeder read:

> In the Name of God / The One Spirit, the All-Merciful:
> Diego Loyal Oatah, representative of Sector 1 Council,
> government for the People of Earth and all Sector
> colonies (listed in Appendix 1), hereafter referred to as
> Human, and Neah sme Colli-ell, Captain of the Pearl /
> Zharta, acting representative of the government of
> Ramia and all sibling-governments in Ramian space

(listed in Appendix 2), having journeyed together and after prayer / singing and consultation have concluded the following treaty:
Agreement 1: The System referred to as Daydream / Manua (see Appendix 3 for coordinates) is declared a common system for both Human and Ramian travel and occupation.
Agreement 2: The System referred to as 5F (see Appendix 3) is likewise declared a common system.
Agreement 3: No resources shall be removed from or permanent settlements established on Daydream / Manua or 5F until use treaties are established.
Agreement 4: Access to stars listed in Human space is closed to Ramians unless traveling with human permission, until travel agreements are established.
Agreement 5: Access to stars listed in Ramian space is closed to Humans unless traveling with Ramian permission, until travel agreements are established.
Agreed to this day: 2-Might-1083 / (Ramian date: Mist 1409:14:2)

Oatah and Neah signed hard and electronic copies in both languages. Beezan was surprised to be asked to witness. With shaking hands, he put his name on the first Human-Ramian document.

Reeder had been on his own writing the treaty. They had left the first contact protocols far behind. No one on Earth had anticipated their current speed of cooperation. Beezan knew it would take time for diplomats and documents to catch up, but in the meantime, they forged ahead, building a foundation with the Ramians that foresaw a future of friendship.

7-Might

Twelve Days to go: They had asked Neah to rename 5F. He had called it Quartil, temporarily puzzling the translator. But when it finally announced "**Friendship**" they cheered. Beezan added it to their joint map, Quartil / Friendship. The renaming became the first amendment to their treaty and was signed by Oatah and Neah, who then pressed hands all around. They had a special tea ceremony and Neah sang a blessing.

It infused in them a great satisfaction, which they needed to sustain them through the final days of their hard burns.

12-Might

Seven Days: The burns were not actually getting harder, it just seemed like it. Neah was very brave and never complained, but Beezan could see his colors shifting to gray. He was tired and cold all the time. Beezan knew Neah was lonely and missing his family. None of them could really concentrate during the burns any more, except during *Journey of Our Hearts.* They had come to episodes that Beezan had not seen with Jarvie.

In one scene, the children were trooping down the rimway to their kitchen, jockeying for position, and carrying their armbands. It's before breakfast, Beezan realized. They're going to their Captain to put on the armbands. But they didn't. Entering the kitchen, the children, including the caretaker children, went to their parents, who put on the armbands and gave them hugs or high fives. Of course, the Captain wouldn't have time for that on a big ship. That meant that Jarvie had come to Beezan, not as a Captain, but as caretaker. Jarvie had stopped after they had sworn their oaths to Oatah, because Reeder was technically his caretaker. Legally, Reeder could take Jarvie with him when they got back to Redrock. *Although Jarvie will have to go to surgery, so I'll have time. I can trust them to transfer Jarvie to me. Can't I?*

17-Might

Two days: Beezan should have known that Katie would do something, but it took him by—

"Surprise!" they all shouted, patting him on the back in the kitchen. "Happy Birthday, Captain!" they chorused. He smiled, embarrassed.

"Thank you, it's really . . . unexpected." In fact, he had been alone every birthday for the past eight years. Regardless, he was happy to provide distraction for them during the burns. They offered small gifts, even a box of candy, which he shared with them. And they had cake balls, a nogee favorite. Sky was wearing a pink bow for the occasion, which looked ridiculous to Beezan, but she liked it, going over to the shiny robot glider to look at herself.

Neah taught them two birthday songs, one for kids, which he sang in Ramian, and one funny one that he tried to translate, about how the birthday person was still getting taller. Except that Beezan wasn't getting taller, so that made it funnier. Oatah and Reeder were a bit aloof from the silliness, but that didn't put a damper on the rest of them.

Getting into his bunk, Beezan reached over to take Sky's bow off. "No! Sky keep. Show Star."

"Alright, but it might be a while." He hoped Star was having fun. Though as he cast his mind out, picturing Daydream,

Turquoise, Nocturne, and the *Pearl*, he had a pang of worry for Jarvie. He hadn't felt nervous before; he trusted the Ramians. *Just getting jumpy. Only two more burns to go.* But he couldn't shake his sudden concern for Jarvie.

Pearl

"What are we done with?" Jarvie asked Danulell. Now that he was learning the language, he was overhearing things, but not enough to make any sense.

"We're done with the evening meal," Danulell replied in his exact way.

"No, what are the adults talking about that is finished today?"

Danulell puzzled over that, but Quay, sitting on Jarvie's other side at the table, understood and rattled off the question to his father.

Danumae turned to Jarvie, flashing pleasure at his interest and pulling out a translator. "We finished mapping here. Tomorrow we go to . . . to check." Jarvie didn't follow where they were going, but must have looked alarmed. Danumae put out a hand to reassure Jarvie, then pointed to Turquoise on the big screen. Well, it was away from the a-rings, so they weren't going to skip the system with him.

The routine was changed the next morning as they prepared to move. All items were stowed, which Jarvie always did automatically. After breakfast, he ended up helping Quay chase down a drawer-full of assorted small toys and game pieces that had ended up in every corner of the room.

"Star! You're not helping!" Jarvie scolded when Star nosed a toy back into its hiding spot between the beds. Quay laughed and scattered three more toys on the deck.

"Star!" Quay shouted and the podpup went scurrying after the toys while Quay crawled under the bed to get others.

"At this rate, we'll never get done," Jarvie nagged him. Danulell was rushing around securing the facilities and closets. Finally, the three of them got all the toys stored and folded the beds up in their niches. Jarvie stared. The design on the wall had become a picture now that the beds were up. The completion of the design had been on the bottom of the beds and the wall underneath it. It was just subtly etched, but Jarvie could make out a lake with spiky mountains reflected in it. A lone boat with a tall sail floated in the lake. There was no snow on the mountaintops as there would be in Earth pictures; in fact, it looked warm and pleasant.

"Come on," Quay pulled at him. The family's big room was practically empty with everything flipped up and stowed. Etched scenes covered those walls too. Jarvie tried to make them out as Zhenulell finished one last inspection before they all went to the "travel room."

It was more like a holiday than travel, with singing and a party atmosphere. The teens gathered in a clump in the travel room, talking excitedly. Jarvie felt shy to approach them, and Quay ran off to his group, leaving Jarvie standing awkwardly by himself. He looked around at the chairs. None would be big enough for him. He might be better off propped against the wall, but the chairs swiveled and the wall didn't. He didn't want to be tossed across the room with a sudden change of direction.

Jarvie decided to investigate a chair to cover his unease. It did look like it might be adjustable. While he was concentrating, one of the other teens came over. Jarvie glanced toward the group and saw a flicker of annoyance cross Zhenumae's forehead. Something was up. This alien, *Ramian*, Jarvie reminded himself, was taller than Danulell and was, Jarvie knew, without looking at the icon, definitely a girl. She was covered with tokens and bracelets and all the little art things that the Ramians favored.

"Hello, Jarvie," she said without any translator, flashing a steady bright pink at him, a color he wasn't familiar with. He didn't need a lesson in galactic relations to know that he was in a situation. *Don't even think about entanglements,* Reeder had threatened him. This girl had entanglement written all over her, but Reeder hadn't given any advice about avoiding it.

"Greetings," he answered politely, looking back down at the chair.

"Come, chair here," she said, actually taking his arm quite firmly and leading him into a far corner. He would have had to obviously break away to avoid going with her. Since she had taken the trouble to learn human words, Jarvie knew she had been plotting something. He glanced quickly at Danulell for help, but the other teens had all turned their backs. *Quay*, Jarvie desperately turned to look, but he was playing hide and seek under the chairs.

They reached her chair of choice and she proceeded to make it longer for him. He tried to watch how she worked it but felt distracted. *Don't be crazy*, he told himself. *She can't do anything.*

Finally, she patted the chair for him to sit down. It wasn't just what she was doing, but the strange feelings he got from her and her steady color. He felt bossed and manipulated and didn't like it, but he also didn't want to cause a scene, so he sat on the edge of the chair. *Where is everyone?*

She moved her hand as if to put it on his chest so he scooted back. Now he was really feeling embarrassed. What would happen if he told her to leave him alone? His mind raced. Just as he was all the way back in the chair, she leaned over him. Suddenly Star jumped up into his lap and nuzzled her right in the face. She backed off, wiping her face and scowling at Star.

Thank you Star! Jarvie was so relieved. She was persistent though, checking quickly around to see if anyone was looking, she dropped one of her tokens onto his chest. "Telluvay," she whispered, blazing an electric pink, and left him.

He collapsed in relief and hugged Star. *What was that all about?* He knew 'entanglements' would never be allowed, so why didn't anyone help him out? *Have I done something wrong? Will I be blamed? Are they testing me?* He slipped the token into his pocket. *Maybe no one noticed.*

He had a few moments to recover his composure before Quay found him and chose the chair next to him, pulling out kid-straps from a side compartment. "Where to put Star?" Jarvie asked him.

"Twells here," Quay showed him. Under the chair was a small round chamber, padded and having a window and air. "Quay get water," he said and ran off. Jarvie made sure he was very busy getting Star settled while Quay was gone, not even daring to look around.

By the noise around him though, it seemed that people were getting into chairs. Quay came back with water for Star and showed Jarvie where to hook it. He really was a helpful child. "Thank you, Quay," he said and smiled at him. Quay lit up, literally, with color, eyes brightening and smiling back. Then he took an excited lap around the room. *What was that Beezan said? Kids are like podpups?*

"Jarvie?" Startled to hear Danumae calling him, Jarvie stood up quickly. Danumae was looking around. Seeing Jarvie, he came over and inspected Jarvie's chair. "Ready?"

"Yes, honor,"

Danumae gestured for Jarvie to get back in the chair. Then he showed how the straps worked and helped Jarvie adjust them. Quay popped up into his chair, strapped in, and pointed ahead, "Go!" he said in Alkulu. Jarvie couldn't help laughing. Maybe this wouldn't be so bad.

It wasn't bad. In fact, it was boring. *I should have known. We're not jumping. It's just a few burns.* Jarvie wondered how Neah was doing on the *Drumheller*, probably having the ride of his life. He wondered if they'd made the jump to Seven yet. They would get to see a Ramian planet, maybe even visit it. Maybe Canyon was already saved and they could come back whenever they wanted.

The easy burn pushed Jarvie into the chair less than a gee. In fact, his only concern was when the next snack break might be. Quay fell asleep, so Jarvie just shut his eyes and daydreamed away.

After the burn, Turquoise was large in the screen. They had lunch and went back to school, with much grumbling from the little ones. However, it was obvious to Jarvie, even as he dodged the aggressive girl, that he was being given the cold shoulder by the other teens. *What did I do?*

On the way back from dinner, it was unbearable. The others all walked way ahead, snubbing him. Danulell's mother, Zhenulell, paused, letting Jarvie catch up. She took the translator from Danumae and asked in a not-so-motherly way, "What is the problem?"

Jarvie swallowed and looked nervously ahead and behind. She frowned at him, flashing displeasure. Slowly, he reached into his pocket, pulled out the token and gave it to her. "A girl gave this to me." Maybe at least she would explain things. He was totally unprepared for her angry outburst. Her colors blazed and the translator garbled. Danumae turned in surprise and hushed her, hurrying the last few steps into their cabin.

"Who?" Danumae asked. But before Jarvie could answer, a stream of commentary came from Zhenumae. He distinctly heard the name Telluvay.

"And you took it?" Zhenulell asked unbelievingly.

"She dropped it on me!" Jarvie finally got a word in. He was confused and embarrassed, and starting to get annoyed.

"Telluvay bad, breaks rules," Zhenumae interjected. "You should not let her!"

"How do I know?" Jarvie protested, "How could I stop her?"

All their talk froze. They all stared at his forehead in sudden understanding. Then Danumae put his arm around Jarvie's shoulders. "You stop her by flashing . . ." and he flashed a horrid lime green with a black horizontal line through it. Before Jarvie could complain that that was impossible, Danumae held up a hand and said, "Not your fault."

Tears were starting to leak, but they were on his side now, so he spilled out the whole story. Then he stopped, suddenly worried that he was insulting their ways, or they would punish Telluvay for something she wouldn't normally be in trouble for. Danumae dismissed the other kids after telling them to pop out the couch. He sat down with Jarvie next to him.

"No one gives tokens to Jarvie," Danumae explained. "Captain Neah's orders. Telluvay breaks rule. Telluvay is in trouble."

"What do tokens mean?" Jarvie asked.

"Many things," Zhenulell explained, gently sitting on his other side. "It depends on the token, who gives and why. It's very complex—that's why no one is supposed to give you tokens. In this case, she tried to claim you friend, maybe even first friend or long friend, maybe even—" She paused and decided that was enough.

"But I don't even know her!"

"Not your fault," Danumae insisted. "We will give back the token and she will not bother you again. Take no other tokens."

Jarvie was both relieved and sorry.

A look passed between the two parents. Slowly Danumae said, "I think you should understand Jarvie, that you are very . . . male."

"What?" Jarvie wasn't sure he understood.

"Not just you, most of your people. The males are very male. The females are very female. It is something that may trigger some behaviors among some of our people . . ." he trailed off. Jarvie felt the heat rise to his face. He covered his face with his hands. Danumae patted his shoulder. "There is nothing you can do about it. Hold your head up. It is our challenge."

"I want to be friends with people," Jarvie said quietly.

"You are—but you need not tokens," Danumae said firmly. Jarvie considered that Danumae and Zhenulell had very few decorations. "They are only for show."

"True love and fellowship come from the heart and need no other proof," Zhenulell added.

It was something his mother might have said, and suddenly, sitting between them as he once did between his own parents, a wave of sorrow and nostalgia came over him and he hunched over and cried. They were not alarmed. They were parents and understood. They sat by him, singing a wistful prayer / song, while Danumae patted him on the back.

By breakfast, Danulell and Zhenumae were back to treating him as their temporary brother, which meant being both friendly and mischievous. Quay had never wavered in his near-adoration and Jarvie found himself getting more attached to the child. He whispered to Danulell, "Quay knows I'm going home soon?"

"We have told him," Danulell stated, always precise. Jarvie wondered if he should distance himself. Then he thought of all his time with Lanezi when he was younger. Even though they were torn apart he would not have given up the friendship to save himself the future pain. He looked down at Quay, who goofily stuck a food bit on his nose just to entertain Jarvie.

"I'm sure I'm not supposed to laugh!" Jarvie told him, grabbing the bit and eating it without even thinking. It was moments later, after their laughter had died down, that he realized he'd just eaten alien food. Alien food that had been stuck on an alien nose.

37 / BATTLING GRAVITY BALLS

The next day at school, Jarvie slogged through his lessons with no translator. They had a 'basic' color chart with 64 colors. Each had a different word. Jarvie gathered that the color word was the same as the emotion word. It was the big clue to Ramian communication, so he studied it carefully. He looked for the frightening pink that Telluvay had bombarded him with, but didn't have a translation for the word. He noticed another color that was the same color as the planet Turquoise. He glanced up at the screen, wondering what the Ramians had named the planet.

He blinked in confusion. The planet was gone. He got up to look more closely at the screen, trying to figure out where they were going. Quay automatically got up and followed him. Another kid said something Jarvie didn't catch, except for the word "tan." The other kids snickered. Jarvie turned in puzzlement, but Quay whipped around and stormed back to the group. Fortunately, Norijay was faster. Holding out a hand to stop Quay, he blasted the others with the horrid lime green.

They froze immediately, eyes down. Norijay rattled off a stern command and backed it up with a flash of orange.

Quay's shoulders relaxed slightly, but he didn't sit with the others. Jarvie was stunned. Both Norijay and Quay were so easy going. Then Norijay took a breath and smiled at Jarvie. "Insult Quay, not Jarvie," he reassured him. But Jarvie wasn't happy to hear that either. Quay came back to stand by him, giving the other kids an angry side eye. *Later, I will get the story.*

Meanwhile, on the screen, he could now see that they had swung around Turquoise and were approaching L5 and the mess with the gravity ball. "Where are we going?" he asked Norijay. Norijay pointed to the jumble of Trojans surrounding the bad gravity ball. Jarvie shook his head. "It's not safe."

Norijay laughed, pulling out the translator. "Gravity generators very safe. One inside ship."

"WHAT?" Jarvie exclaimed, suddenly feeling mortal danger. "There's a gravity ball *inside*?" He pointed down under their feet.

"Yes, how did you think we have gravity?"

It must be a small one, Jarvie realized, like the bad one. And since the Ramians kept crashing into them, they couldn't be the designers. "But you don't make the gravity balls."

"No, but we know how to work them, how to control their strength. Don't worry!" He flashed yellow with a pink line and went back to the kids.

Don't worry! Jarvie stared at the screen. Where did they manage to get enough mini gravity balls to stock their ships? Did they really know how to work them? It didn't seem like it. Jarvie tried to relax and go back to his work, but it nagged at him. In teen training, if you disagreed with something, you could ask for a review. But what to do here?

• • •

After lunch, before they went back to school, Jarvie asked Norijay if he could talk to the Captain, but Norijay said they were busy and you had to have permission and wouldn't help him. He flashed the *don't worry* colors at him again. Jarvie frowned, trudging out of the dining room. The Captain was never in the dining room at lunch. *Where was he?*

Quay, who'd been silent and agitated at lunch, reached up and took his hand. "I'll take you to the Getti, Jarvie." *Getti.* He'd heard that word a lot. With Neah and Hefreesay. Captain, of course. That made sense.

"Yes, thank you Quay." Leaving Star with the other pups, they went opposite of the school, heading in the direction of the travel room. *I should have paid more attention yesterday.* Quay backtracked a couple times, looking for the way. *He's a child! What was I thinking?* He didn't have a translator either. *Whose crazy idea was it that I shouldn't have one all the time? Probably Oatah's.*

"Are we lost?" He asked Quay. Quay just pulled him along. Jarvie started to feel a little panicky. He reached for his p'link automatically, but that was useless. He couldn't see any s'link-like controls on the walls. They were probably there, but to him everything looked like artwork.

"Quay, call Getti?"

"Getti Hefreesay!" Quay shouted out at the top of his lungs. *Heaven help me,* Jarvie thought. Suddenly there was an answering voice.

"Captain?" Jarvie called out.

"Jarvie?" came a surprised and possibly annoyed voice. This was going to be bad when it turned out he was imagining things. Two Ramians came hastily down the corridor to intercept them. Quay announced that Jarvie was coming to see Hefreesay.

"No visit," said one in Alkulu. Jarvie remembered him as one who had come aboard the *Drumheller*.

"Getti Hefreesay," he said firmly and kept walking. They put out their hands to stop him.

"Go!" Quay urged and proceeded forward with Jarvie. The two moved aside, flashing madly but not touching them. Then they fell in behind.

A door opened ahead. Jarvie broke into a run. He burst through a second door and froze in distracted wonder. He had not been here on his *supposed* tour. It was not even remotely like the cramped little Command Bay of the *Drumheller* or even the more spacious and pretty *Sunburst*. The flight deck was huge. There were windows or screens banked around the room and overhead. The effect made it seem as if you stood on the brink of space itself. He could have stared all day, but the view of L5 forced his mind back to the problem.

Maybe the Ramians were far superior. Maybe they did know what they were doing. Yet for some reason he was now in a state of extreme agitation, just like the day he had suspected the gravity ball was malfunctioning on the *Drumheller*. And he had been right to be afraid that day.

Hefreesay, along with two others, stood and considered Jarvie. Hefreesay slowly pulled a translator out of his pocket. *He's prepared.* "Danger," Jarvie said immediately. "Bad gravity ball."

They flashed orange with a line of the horrid lime green, followed by the *don't worry colors*. "Don't go so close," Jarvie insisted. "There's a bad gravity ball in that clump of Trojans." They calmly discussed it. Then there was a simultaneous hand clapping and Hefreesay went back to work, leaving the others to deal with Jarvie.

They explained to him as if they were talking to Quay, with

great patience and good humor. The translator only managed part of it. "Gravity generator stable . . . now testing . . . no sign of malfunction . . . known codes . . . many years experience . . . thousands of generators . . ."

Thousands? "It went on by itself!" Jarvie insisted.

"Your people, humans, don't know how to work them. You turned it on by accident."

"We didn't do anything!"

"It is complex and you are a child. We have many experts. Gravity generator failure is rare."

They would have no further argument. Jarvie could not think of any specific thing to convince them. They calmly walked him to the door, giving Quay a command to take him to Danumae. Jarvie tried one last time. "My heart tells me to be worried."

"We are not angry, be at ease."

That was not what he meant. Quay stood outside the door by him after they had closed it. They passed to the other side of the double lock and it shut too. "They not listen." Quay said. He looked shaken and concerned, running solid amber colors. Jarvie had scared him.

"Sorry Quay; don't be scared," he whispered. They began walking down the corridor. What would happen to him? *First the girl and now this.* He was still very uneasy about the gravity ball, but realized he should have gone first to Danumae or Sontula for help. It was too big a hierarchy for him to go straight to the Captain.

They passed several sets of doors, which now closed automatically behind them, final reminders to *stay out.* The Captain's spokesperson had told Quay to take Jarvie to Danumae, but where was that? *The Medical Center of course.* "Where is the—" Jarvie was interrupted by a jolt, as if a mat was pulled out from under him. He and Quay fell sharply to their knees. Before they could get up, an alarm sounded. Quay's eyes went wide with fear.

"What is it?" asked Jarvie, wishing for the translator.

"We move. Find safe spot!" Quay cried, reaching for Jarvie's hand. They were boosting, or falling, or something. *The gravity ball! No solace in being right.*

They could not stand up. "Straps?" he said to Quay. They were sliding slowly down the corridor. Quay was terrified, looking around in confusion. "The travel room?" Jarvie knew they were near. Quay glanced up ahead. Jarvie started to crawl that way, using one hand to help pull Quay along, but he was fussing now. "Get on my back!" Quay climbed up, clinging to him. Jarvie could move much faster that way. He was terrified they'd do a big burn and he and Quay would be dumped the length of the corridor, certainly to their deaths.

He moved as fast as he could, but it was like trying to crawl up a steep slick ramp. He did make it to the travel room door, which opened. Half thinking and half praying he managed to get to a chair. For once, he was grateful for his long legs. He wrapped them around the base of the chair to hold on, freeing his hands to hold and strap Quay. "Okay, you're safe," he told Quay, but the child clutched his hand. "I'm going to go to a chair." Quay nodded and let go.

Jarvie let himself slide down to the chair in front of Quay, hooking it again with his legs so he could adjust the length of the top part. It would have to do. He didn't think he had time to lengthen the bottom. As he pulled up into the chair, there was a jerk and he lost his grip.

They were weightless. The gravity ball inside the *Pearl* had failed.

For a moment he floated, a mere hand's length from the

chair. He tried to grab the arm, but it was just out of reach. He saw Quay reach for his strap as if to get out and help. “NO!” he shouted and then a loud alarm rang. In desperation, Jarvie did a summersault, hoping to catch the chair with his legs.

Too late. A strong burn started and he was falling across the room. He had time to wonder how far. Then he hit the wall with a flat painful thud. He didn’t feel like he’d hit that hard. Nothing hurt after the first shock. In fact, the steady pain in his head that he’d become almost used to was wonderfully gone. If they didn’t change direction, he might be all right. Except he felt a little fuzzy. Quay was crying. *Why?* He wasn’t that bad. He even felt warm and sleepy. He would just close his eyes for a moment.

Then he felt them, the sentries, those young angels that guarded the Kingdom. They were near. Other people might not know them, but Jarvie had crossed over so many times he could feel their presence. He was fading from the world. *No*! *Who will take care of Star? I’ll finally be back with my family, but what about Beezan? Will he ever know what happened to me?*

19-Might

Drumheller

They cheered when the last long burn was finished. They pressed hands with Neah and had a huge dinner with extra dessert. Then they went straight to bed. At 04:00, they would take the *Peacock* over to the a-rings so Neah could look for the control panel and get the codes. They had only allotted six hours and Beezan felt the pressure of saving Canyon loom large in his mind, now that the long burns were finally done.

. . .

"There," Neah said, pointing out the window of the *Peacock*. Beezan slowly rendezvoused with the segment Neah indicated. There was no way to dock; they just had to orbit in tandem long enough to get the space walkers out. It was non-tethered work and very dangerous. Only Beezan could pilot, so Iricana went across with Neah to learn how to get the codes.

Pearl

Jarvie fought against dying and then he fought against living. The sentries came close and retreated many times until Jarvie lost all awareness. When he finally woke, his body felt like a weak shredded thing, but he knew that he still lived, that he was still with the Ramians, and that something terrible had happened.

He hurt, but he could move and there was a blurry light in his eyes, so he could see. Agitated voices swirled around him and only if he held very still could he catch the whisper of the translator. "No funerals yet . . . finding remains . . . repairs . . . pressure not holding . . . must decide . . . take command . . . confusion . . . you should go down there, Danumae."

Danumae. Quay. "Quay?" Jarvie thrashed on the medical bed and called out, trying to reach out as well, but he was restrained. Footsteps hurried to his side and a blurry Danumae looked down on him, his colors hidden by the doctor's hood.

"Jarvie, you are well. Do not be worried. You will heal completely."

"Quay?" he asked again.

Danumae reached over and turned up the translator that was hooked to the side of the bed. "Quay was unhurt." He paused significantly, "Thanks to you," and he put his hand on Jarvie's chest. "My family thanks you from the spirit."

"What happened?" he whispered.

Danumae frowned. "I will tell you more later. You are well and safe."

"Look who's here," the translator mimicked a different voice. Zhenulell leaned over the bed with Star.

"Star!" Jarvie exclaimed with pleasure. Danumae shot a relieved glance at his wife and unstrapped Jarvie's hands. There was another restraint on his torso. Danumae tapped the latch and said lightly, "Leave this one on."

"The ship?" Jarvie asked in alarm.

"We are safe. Rest. We'll get some food if you feel up to it."

"I'm starving."

"Starving!" Star repeated. Jarvie laughed, but Danumae and Zhenulell barely managed a fake smile between them. *What is going on?* They hadn't really told him anything. He felt his head as Star nuzzled around. It was sealed in a squishy cap, but it didn't hurt. In fact, his head felt better than it had in a long time.

Danumae managed to distract Jarvie with food and walking around a bit for several more hours, but eventually faced the fact that Jarvie wasn't going to stop asking, especially after he learned it had been days since the accident.

Jarvie was sitting up on his bed when Danumae finally came to talk to him. "Jarvie, we have a recorded summary to show you, tomorrow, but first there's something I must tell you." He swallowed. "Without your consent or the consent of a guardian or any person of your family or even . . . species," He sounded like he was reading a treaty or something, "we found it necessary to choose between letting you die or . . . performing brain surgery."

"What?" Jarvie reached for his head. Aliens had opened up his brain?

"Yes, actually . . ." the translator completely garbled the medical explanation. Then Danumae showed him a picture. "Head injury, dangerous, your implants were killing you." It was certainly a picture of Jarvie's bad implants; he had come to recognize them, only far worse. "Removed, replaced, new implants, we made them."

Jarvie started to shake. Alien implants now. They could have done anything to him. Danumae was patting his shoulder, assuring him that all was well and their implants were better than his old ones. Jarvie took some comfort in the fact that it didn't even occur to Danumae to deny any sinister actions. In fact, the day-to-day kindness of the Ramians had brought Jarvie's heart to trusting them. He tried to calm himself. They meant no harm. "Jarvie, I couldn't let you die. I must answer to Captain Beezan. He did not even require my son, he trusted me so to take care of you."

"What? What do you mean?" Jarvie asked anxiously.

"Didn't they tell you?" Danumae glanced at the approaching Zhenulell. "In our promise to look after you, Hefreesay offered Danulell to be placed aboard the *Drumheller* as . . . assurance of our good intentions."

Jarvie was horrified. *Was that really Hefreesay's idea, or Reeder's?* He was furious. "I'm sorry! I never would have asked such a barbaric thing."

"Your Captain refused. He said he would take only willing adults necessary to the mission." Tears filled Danumae's eyes. "Beezan said, 'keep your son and let him be a friend to Jarvie. I know you will do everything to protect him as if he were your own.'"

Jarvie nodded, smiling. Beezan did not find it easy to trust, but he would do the right thing anyway. "Well . . ." Jarvie said, "see, you did have permission."

Now Danumae was confused. "I don't understand."

"You would have done it for your son?"

"Yes, of course."

"Then Beezan expected you to do it for me." Danumae puzzled over that. "My head feels better anyway."

"Good!" and for once he gave a real smile. "Tomorrow, the summary of what's happened. Now sleep." Zhenulell settled him in, strapping him snuggly and rounding up Star.

Jarvie, shakily walking, holding on to Danumae, was led to a tiny theater in the Ramian Medical Center. He was seated in front of a screen next to Norijay, another of the badly injured. They were to see the summary together. Norijay barely resembled the confident, *don't worry,* teacher Jarvie knew. Aside from being covered with the healing seals, he was pale blue-grey and haunted. He turned away from Jarvie to his mother, who consoled him, but did not seem angry with Jarvie. Jarvie was filled with worry that people would blame the humans, and especially him, about the accident.

Danumae sat down by Jarvie and attached a new translator to Jarvie's collar. They were getting smaller every week. "The summary of what happened is unpleasant, but it is part of your history, and our situation requires decisions. You must both be informed," he said grimly.

Jarvie swallowed nervously. The screen lit up, beginning with a simple (for the Ramians) graphic, showing an exterior view of the *Pearl* approaching the L5 point. The gravity ball, still inside the smashed cargo container, was marked in green. It was surrounded by the jumble of Trojans that had been pulled in since *Drumheller* had accidentally turned it on. It was a messy crowd with hundreds of rocks bumping, spinning, and disturbing others.

A beam of yellow light was shown going from the *Pearl* to the gravity ball. The translator took up the narration.

"The gravity generator was outputting a steady power 2. The non-interference safety field was engaged. The standard command to identify was sent. There was no answering signal. The first of 17 known override codes was sent, preceding another command to identify. A malfunction occurred in the gravity generator. It immediately increased gravity by 25% and continued to climb."

The picture showed the *Pearl* being jerked toward the gravity ball, along with all the debris around it.

"Captain Hefreesay gave orders to go to emergency safe spots." The translator struggled, but Jarvie could make out that as Hefreesay waited as long as possible for the crew to signal they were ready, the *Pearl* was drawn in very close to the mess of Trojans. Finally, he gave the order to make a steady burn away. Meanwhile, override messages were still being sent.

The bad gravity ball continued stepping up gravity to a level that surprised the Ramians. It got so strong they feared they would be pulled into the mass of Trojans and crushed. Desperately, the *Pearl* sent the self-destruct code to the bad gravity ball.

Unfortunately, in that moment when the *Pearl's* shield was modulated to let the code through, the bad gravity ball somehow sent its own command to the *Pearl's* gravity ball—to disable.

That was when the *Pearl's* gravity went off. Jarvie pictured that moment when he hovered over the chair. The *Pearl* made a breakaway burn, and then the bad gravity ball blew up. The explosion not only turned off the gravity, allowing the hundreds of Trojans loose, but somehow caused a wave that knocked everything up, down and outward. The *Pearl* was caught on the crest of the wave and hurtled away—taking damage as Trojans collided with it. The graphic showed an especially big Trojan hitting the *Pearl*. Danumae looked away. Norijay gasped. "The flight deck was destroyed," the translator continued. "The crew was killed."

Killed? Hefreesay? Dead? How many others? Was the ship out of control? Jarvie wanted to stop and blurt out his questions, but the summary went on. The graphic changed to a schematic of the spinning out-of-control *Pearl*. Jarvie cringed to see it.

Someone in the gravity ball room aboard *Pearl* had taken command. The *Pearl's* gravity ball went back on. Burns were made to stabilize the *Pearl* and maneuver it as far away as possible. The *Pearl* was now in a safe orbit around Turquoise. Pressure was lost on the flight deck, but the airlock doors were holding and some repairs were underway. "Repair estimate: not possible under current conditions."

Jarvie slumped in his seat. His heart was pounding. They were lucky to be alive.

"There's more," Danumae whispered. Then the real images started. They were cut together from different cameras inside and outside the ship. They told a story all the more gripping and terrifying. It started, Jarvie was mortified to see, with his warning to Hefreesay. *Will they blame me?*

It showed Jarvie and Quay crawling up the hall, getting in the chairs, Jarvie hitting the wall and then being thrown about the room several times, smashing his head and crumpling. It was the screaming of Quay that made it unbearable. Danumae was looking at the deck. Norijay grabbed Jarvie's arm as if to reassure himself that he really was still alive. Jarvie found it hard to believe himself. *No wonder they had to operate on my brain.*

Then it switched to the school and Norijay's heroic efforts to save the panicked children. No human children in the outer sectors would be so untrained in emergencies, but then, they had so many to train for. Safe spots were in the walls. Jarvie had just not known. When the big burn started, Norijay was not strapped. He hit the wall and was thrown about as badly as Jarvie. Likewise, if he had not been sitting next to him now, Jarvie would have been convinced Norijay was dead.

The scene changed to the kitchen. Adults were doing the final lunch clean up. There was no time to secure objects. Everything went flying. In the dining room, not everyone was secured. It showed other parts of the ship, the Medical Center, the cabins, the computer room. Tears rolled down Jarvie's face. Then the view switched to the flight deck. Jarvie grabbed Danumae's hand in horror. They wouldn't show—Jarvie saw that the flight crew was strapped in and two people even had suits on—an emergency plan. Maybe they were saved.

Then the front of the flight deck was just gone. Norijay jerked. He clutched his mother and sobbed. Jarvie looked away, unwilling to see what happened to the people, to Hefreesay. But his eyes traveled back of their own will. The sudden depressurization and damage had ripped out half the controls. The two suited figures hung limp in their straps. There was no sign of the others.

The scenes switched to panic and scrambling in the auxiliary flight deck. The translator was useless as the Ramians struggled to bring their ship out of the maelstrom and restart their gravity ball. Just as things calmed down there, the scene went to the Medical Center. "Rescue operations commenced."

"Stop," said Danumae. "That's enough for now."

In the end, only seven were dead. Astonishing as far as Jarvie was concerned. Hefreesay was one, along with five others in the flight deck crew. The only person killed from the acceleration impact injuries was in the dining room—hit by one of the unbolted chairs. Three bodies had not yet been recovered, but shuttles were out looking for them. Apparently they had homing tags so it was not an impossible job.

Ten people who had taken hard hits, including Jarvie, were saved by the advanced medical care of the Ramians. Only four of them were still in the Med Bay. The newborn baby was safe. All the podpups survived, even though many were bumped around. All the birds died, which for some reason was a great test to the Ramians.

The gaping hole in the flight deck could not be sealed. The damage was extensive. Pressure was holding in the adjoining areas and the situation was called "delicately stable."

Their immediate problems were outlined by Zhenulell: Assess damage to the flight deck and determine if repair was even possible, repair of outside instruments including their communications equipment, medical care, funerals, selecting a new captain, support for families, and reconsideration of mission goals.

Jarvie slumped against Danumae. He seemed to read Jarvie's heart, even without colors. "No one blames you. No one blames humans. It was our own fault."

Jarvie silently disagreed. A dark seed of blame formed in his mind for the person truly responsible—Thayne.

38 / CODE JUMPING

1-Will

Drumheller

Beezan and Iricana whispered together in the kitchen after she returned from the spacewalk.

"Did you see Neah program the control panel?" Beezan asked, gathering a snack-munching Sky into his lap.

"Yes, just like he said. He showed me how. I could do it myself. A map appeared with text by the stars—numerical codes, I assume. He copied them."

Beezan was skeptical. "But they can't possibly get out of their ships just to program the jumps."

"No, it's a manual backup system. The Ramians can send the code once they know it."

"So, the Ramians know the frequency the a-ring builders used?" Beezan asked, amazed. Sky stopped her crunching and looked curiously at Iricana.

"Yes, and as soon as Neah explains it to *Drumheller*, we'll know too," Iricana nodded excitedly. Demonstrating an imaginary panel, she continued, "Neah turned it on. A map appeared with three jump choices. Neah took a long time with his suit computer, figuring out what stars they were, but then decided that one destination was Seven, another was the star we call Three and the third was a star in our space. He programmed 'Ship #1' for Seven. Easy as that."

"It's insane. I'd rather blind-jump."

"He says the rings will realign and they will kick us out exactly into the path. You won't have to search. And you don't have to go as fast."

"I don't understand how that's possible. You have to get to jump velocity to see the paths."

"Neah said the faster you go, the easier it is to see the path, but it's possible to see it at slower speeds, and if you're positive you're going in the right direction, you can go slower. He claimed they only go to .5-.7JV in the rings."

Beezan shook his head in denial. "I know, he's explained it all before. Half the speed, but I just don't trust it, not in my head, or in my heart."

She sighed in sympathy. "It makes me uneasy too. But, they got here, didn't they? As long as they have the codes, they seem to know what they're doing."

"They seem full of confidence. That doesn't mean they know what they're doing. They crashed into gravity balls."

"Well, Captain, perhaps you could keep your finger on the trigger, just in—"

The door slid open and they jumped guiltily. Neah stopped short. "I am sorry. I am disturbing you."

"No, Neah. Please come in," Iricana said. "Are you hungry?"

"No. I figured out what the third star was, on the control panel. I thought you'd want to know."

"What?" they asked in unison as Neah moved to the big map.

"This one," he said, pointing.

"Harbor!" Beezan gasped. "How could that be? The stars are too far apart to jump."

"Actually, we have even longer jumps. If the stars are compatible, it is easy."

"Easy," Beezan echoed, dryly.

"Easy," Sky agreed, going back to her crunching.

Neah laughed. "You'll see, Captain," he said. "You'll see."

2-Will

It was just as well they were code jumping. Beezan had never been so unprepared in his life. He realized that he had thought that for several of his jumps lately. *Am I getting reckless?*

They'd been in the rings three hours already and were just getting to half speed. They were all riding conscious, with Katie and Iricana in the passenger lounge, Oatah and Reeder to Beezan's left and Neah to his right in the Command Bay. Neah kept insisting that code jumping was perfectly safe.

Beezan watched the graphic of the external view. In it, the ship circled through the a-ring segments. The bumps were strong enough to push them hard into their chairs, but not yet strong enough to hurt. Neah was unbothered. How Oatah could sleep through them was a mystery. *Mental discipline, no doubt. He probably isn't hungry either.*

"Final lap," *Drumheller* announced.

Beezan's whole body tensed. It wasn't fear of jumping with another pilot leading. He felt like there was no leader, and they were going too slow.

Three segments left. Two. One. On the exit of the last ring, there was a gentle tweak of acceleration. He'd never felt that before. *That's it!* Beezan thought, *the ring gave* Drumheller *a last adjustment.* Beezan forced his finger to stay still and not press the thruster. He was shaking inside. His implants started to vibrate. And he did see, or thought he saw, the barest hint of a red path, not even a thread, barely a wisp. But Neah hit the main thrusters and they were in a path. Beezan tensed, awaiting the jump drug, and then remembered there would be none. They would ride this all the way, as he had dreamed of doing.

He tried to relax his mind and breathing. They were so solidly in the path that his implant stopped buzzing and was instead humming in nice long waves. They skimmed the threshold of the Kingdom, not even alerting the sentries.

The *Drumheller* graphic had gone blank. Beezan toggled through his screens to get the forward view. It said 'error.' He didn't know how to pace himself as they usually spent this part of the ride unconscious. Curious, he cast his mind forward again. He could feel the presence of Seven now—and a pulsing. He gasped. His hand tensed on the controls, thumb on the abort button. Their timing was off by a day; the jump ships were already in the rings at Seven.

No one else will realize it, Beezan thought. The pulsing was strong and regular. *How close to JV are those ships?* In trying to save Canyon, would *Drumheller* cause an accident at Seven? He had to drop out of the path—but when? He had no experience with this. Normally, the ship dropped out automatically. If he waited too long, they might crash. If he popped out too soon, his message wouldn't get to the ships in time to stop them from jumping.

Beezan told himself to count to a thousand, all the time worrying he'd destroy the *Drumheller* by hesitating. At four hundred though, there was a slight buzz in his implants and he squeezed the abort button.

There was a tremendous lurch as *Drumheller* made a deceleration burn and turn that would drop them into normal space. They were thrown forward against the harnesses, and then to the left. His arm shaking and whole body sweating he held on, not even feeling his thumb. Two gees, three gees, *he held the button*. Beezan felt fuzzy. *Stay alert!* Suddenly his implants buzzed loudly and the ship made another sickening lurch. They were back in normal space.

Beezan heard the *Drumheller* say "Normal space," and let go of the abort button. Desperately, he toggled through his screens. *Yes!* The messages saying not to jump had been sent automatically. Beezan popped his braces, unsealed his cocoon, and pulled his arms out to open his visor. He heard the others doing the same.

"What happened?" Iricana asked over the s'link.

"They're jumping!" Beezan said. "They're in the rings right now."

"Are they near the final lap?" Oatah asked.

"Very near," Neah answered.

"*Drumheller*, what's our location?" Beezan asked.

"Arrival at Seven System confirmed. Position shown."

Beezan gasped. They were so close to the a-rings. And even worse, they were headed straight for the star. "Stay strapped!"

"This late in the jump, there may not be anyone listening for messages," Neah said.

"*Drumheller*, show the direction that the Canyon jumper would take," Beezan said. A graphic appeared with the outline of the a-rings and a red line showing the direction a ship would take to Canyon. The oncoming *Drumheller* was alarmingly close to that path.

"With a burn," Oatah asked, "Could we intercept?"

"*Intercept?*" Beezan was horrified. "At speed? We'd obliterate each other!"

“We don’t need to survive,” Oatah reminded them. “We just need to stop that ship.”

“Well, we would need perfect timing, which we don’t have.”

“We need to get their attention!” Neah said. “What if you send a shuttle and blew it up, like a warning?”

“Blow it up?” Beezan shook his head inside his helmet. “There’s no self-destruct! There’s no way to sabotage the engine, unless I spent days overriding a hundred safety features.”

“Shoot it?” Neah asked.

Beezan wondered what kind of people the Ramians were after all. “We don’t have weapons!”

“Something like a harpoon?”

“Like a rock relocator? We used them all on the bad gravity ball.”

“Plasma jets? Like sending a flare?”

“Neah! We have lights! That’s it!”

“We must stop them somehow,” Oatah reiterated.

“What if we launch a shuttle into the a-rings?” Reader suggested.

“NO TIME!” Beezan insisted. His implants were starting to buzz.

“*Drumheller*,” Neah asked suddenly, “Can you access the work from the panel in my cabin, about the frequency of the gravity generators?”

“Yes.”

“Can you modify the Ramian transmitter to this frequency?”

“This has already been done.”

What? Beezan thought, but Neah went on quickly. “There’s a list of gravity ball codes in graphics.”

“Confirmed.”

"Second to the last—not the last! That's a destruct code—second to last is a stop code."

Drumheller put the code up on the screen.

"That's it."

"Someone jumped!" Reeder hissed.

"*Drumheller*! Send the stop code!" Beezan ordered, feeling the jumper go in his implants.

"Sent."

"Another ship jumped!" Reeder said.

"They are going to the planet you call Six," Neah said.

"Captain," Oatah asked. "What is the lag time?"

"Less than a second. *Drumheller*, show clock."

But several seconds had already passed before the clock appeared.

Almost casually, the a-ring segments relaxed, as if they gave a sigh and settled back. Two ships came flying out of the rings at odd angles—and the first one jumped anyway.

"Also going to Six, if they make it," Neah said, subdued.

The last ship was so close to the Canyon trajectory. Beezan thought the pilot might make a correction burn and go for it. They all sucked in their breath together. Beezan prayed for minor injuries at Canyon. But the ship braked and rolled, insuring they'd drop out of the path. "Thank God," Oatah said and the others let out sighs of relief.

But Beezan was still worried. "*Drumheller*, show our trajectory."

It flashed on the screen. **"Recommend immediate burn to avoid stellar trajectory."**

"Yes!"

"Options—"

"Just do the first one!"

They made fourteen hard burns before they ran out of fuel,

including three to reorient the ship. The crew hung in their chairs, exhausted, hurting, and scared.

"Additional injection burn will be needed in 4.5 hours."

"Will we have the fuel?" Beezan whispered.

"Yes. Burns were calculated to optimize fuel."

It was quiet in the Command Bay and passenger lounge except for panicked breathing and Katie calling "Neah?"

Beezan wrestled his way out of his cocoon to check Neah and saw his colors.

"Those last burns must have been too much. Doctor, let me help you get him to the Med Bay."

"No, Captain, you better stay here," Iricana countermanded with all politeness, "I'll help."

"Thank you."

"Keep him conscious!" Oatah said sternly as they pushed out of the door. "We may need him."

"*Drumheller*, collect system data and display," Reeder ordered.

Beezan looked over his shoulder at Neah. So the Ramians knew how to turn off a gravity ball. He sure hoped they knew how to turn it back on.

39 / BOLT FROM THE BLUE

An hour later, happy to be in a safe trajectory, with his first code jump completed, with the knowledge that Canyon was saved and Neah reportedly in good health, and—bonus—they wouldn't be flying directly into a star, Beezan floated lazily in the Command Bay sipping a bulb of warm tea and holding Sky's bottle for her. He'd hooked onto the wall by her jump bed so he wouldn't float into Reeder or Oatah who were making *Drumheller* pull every last data-speck out of the Seven planetary system. One by one, locations, sizes, and types of planets were appearing on the main screen. They had approximate orbits from Neah's map, but they needed real-time data.

Beezan closed his eyes and took long deep breaths to help the tension drain out of him. *It's over.* They could return in a sensible, leisurely way. They could pick up Jarvie and go home to Redrock. *Go home.*

Then Reeder made the slightest little sound, half alarm and half surprise.

"What?" Beezan's eyes flew open.

"An extra planet," Reeder said in complete puzzlement, pointing to the screen.

Beezan unhooked, grabbed Reeder's chair and pulled himself closer, Sky peeking over his shoulder to see. Reeder showed the original Ramian data from Neah now being overlaid with incoming data from *Drumheller*. "Neah's map showed two terrestrial planets, an asteroid belt, a superjovian, two jovians, and a small k-belt. But live data show an extra planet between the terrestrial planets and the asteroid belt." The three of them stared at the screen. Oatah had an especially worried look on his face.

"*Drumheller*," Beezan ordered, "can you confirm the third planet, possibly using the Ramian receiver?"

"The planet Seven-3 is confirmed. There are three Ramian beacons in this system, including one at Seven-3. The planet Seven-3 is in the habitable zone, has no natural moons, is oceanic, has an oxygen-nitrogen atmosphere, and may have a small artificial object in low orbit. There are indications of possible primitive signaling technology, but we have no protocols."

Oatah, Reeder, and Beezan stared in open-mouthed astonishment. "They've found a life planet." Beezan whispered.

"And Neah didn't tell us," Reeder added. Beezan felt a flicker of fear grow inside him.

"I'm sure," Oatah said darkly, "that's because Neah doesn't know anything about it."

"Which means they won't be happy to see us," Reeder finished.

"How are we going to broach this extra planet with Neah?" Beezan asked, still staring at the screen.

"Directly and immediately," Oatah said, turning in the air.

"Yes," Reeder added, "especially as we have incoming Ramian messages."

Beezan stayed in the Command Bay with Reeder, but popped up a screen to watch the scene unfold in the Med Bay. Oatah floated over to Neah's bed, showing nothing but concern. However, Katie, ever the protector of her patients, must have sensed something.

"Agent Oatah, he must rest!" she said, coming over to intervene.

"I'm sorry Doctor, this can't wait. Getti Neah, there are a couple of issues we must deal with before you can sleep."

"What's happened?" Neah asked, grabbing a handhold to orient to Oatah.

"I believe all is well. However, we are receiving messages from your people that may need immediate responses."

"Yes, of course."

"But before we play the messages, there's something you must know about Seven System."

Neah, Katie, and Iricana all looked at Oatah in puzzled alarm. "*Drumheller*, show Seven System on the big screen."

They all drifted over to the table to look. Katie and Iricana studied it. "Oh, there was a mistake on your map," Iricana said calmly. "There's one more planet here."

"I don't believe it was a mistake," Oatah said gently.

At that moment, *Drumheller* chose to update the display, switching to a just-assembled close-up of the third planet, seen in crescent.

It was stunning to anyone with a drop of human blood, no matter how far removed in generations or distance from Earth. Tears came to Beezan's eyes. An actual sob escaped Oatah. It was blue, with white clouds. There were brown and green landmasses.

No one could even speak. Neah was obviously as stunned as they were. His colors showed confusion and then a growing excitement. All the years, all the centuries, Beezan thought, that humans had searched for another Earth—and the Ramians had found one first.

"Actually," Neah said in a teary voice, "this explains something."

"What?" Iricana asked.

Neah glanced at the deck. "Well, I didn't want to worry you so I didn't mention that this system is . . . off limits."

In the Command Bay, Beezan and Reeder exchanged dismayed expressions. "Better send those messages through to Neah," Beezan suggested to Reeder, as a chorus of confused voices and stymied translator came from the Med Bay.

As *Drumheller* played the messages aloud to Neah, written translations appeared on their main screens.

NEAH SME COLLI-ELL, GETTI *ZHARTA*, CONFIRM IDENTIFY SELF.

IDENTIFY SHIP.

NEAH, ENTER ORBIT AT [NO TRANSLATION]

DO NOT APPROACH [NO TRANSLATION]

DO NOT SEND SIGNALS / TRANSMISSIONS ON [NO TRANSLATION]

CONFIRMING YOUR MESSAGE RECEIVED, JUMP ABORTED.

VISUAL CONTACT REQUESTED / COMMANDED.

IDENTIFY SHIP ORIGIN.

IDENTIFY.

Despite Katie's scowling, Neah slowly hooked himself to a panel in Med Bay and pulled out his treasure box. "*Drumheller,* what is the source of these messages?"

"Messages originate from Seven-5 L2. We are near the source."

"Return messages to same location."

"Confirmed."

"Neah," Beezan broke in. "Where do they want us to orbit?"

"Seven-5, where we are going."

Speaking slowly and clearly, Neah began to respond to his messages. The others watched the translation on the screen.

"BEGIN: This is Neah sme Colli-ell, Captain of the *Zharta.* I am aboard a ship made by aliens who call themselves human. We have come here to stop the [unknown] ship from jumping into human space. Our previous attempts to jump into human space have resulted in disaster. I cannot send a visual signal. We do not have a [unknown] transmitter. I can explain more. Please tell me who is in command there. END." He paused and then told the *Drumheller*, "Send it."

"Transmitting."

4-Will

By the time the *Drumheller* made orbit around the fifth planet and went back to spin, many things had been made clear. The third planet was inhabited. In fact, the low orbit space station was the inhabitants' own, not the Ramians. The Ramian ship "*Watcher*," with a captain named Drann, was in charge of the Ramian operation in the system. They had taken precautions not to reveal themselves to the inhabitants. The Seven-3 beacon was hidden behind an orbital shield so the inhabitants would not detect it. The other beacons were also programmed to transmit only when they were behind their planets, relative to the third planet. The humans and Neah could immediately see the resemblance of this system to their own home systems. Whoever built the a-rings had purposely left the new aliens alone, just as they had left the Ramians and humans alone.

The Ramians called the planet Qwetamar, which meant something like "First Jewel." However, they called the inhabitants Tanashu, "Fighters." Drann was not happy about the arrival of *Drumheller*. Beezan imagined what it would be like to be guarding one set of aliens while a different set showed up.

"I explained," Neah told them at dinner, "to Getti Drann, that it would not be wise to meet in person. Their medical facilities are small and their people are spread all over this system. Viruses also may be tracked back into our space before we are prepared. I transmitted the virus data. They will send a team to the planet you call "One" to prepare the population for the return of the *Zharta*. Then they'll send a ship to Daydream in case something should happen to us during our return trip."

"Thank you." Beezan felt his long-held knot of worry over Jarvie loosen slightly. His period of extreme concern about Jarvie had passed, but for some reason something still nagged at him.

"This system is quarantined because the Tanashu exhibit extremely warlike behavior. Their technology is advancing quickly in spite of it. They will be able to detect the a-rings and our presence soon. We were hoping to forge a link to Canyon that might bypass this system. We will hold off on those plans until we have treaties with humans, of course. We'll have to clear out of here in the next 10 years. I'm afraid that it has also made my people wary of aliens in general."

They sat quietly, eating, disturbed at the news. Beezan glanced up at Iricana just in time to see her flash a look of alarm at Oatah.

"We must be bold," Oatah said quietly.

"So we aspire to be," Neah agreed.

"What . . ." Beezan said.

"The truth," Oatah continued with conviction, "may be difficult, but it is still the truth, and from that we may forge true connections." Iricana pressed her lips together, seeming to know where Oatah was going.

"Getti Neah," Oatah proceeded, "our people were once 'fighters,' as you call them, too. It is a disgraceful period of our history, from which we emerged much chastised less than a thousand years ago, and to which we will never return. Peace and progress for all, *together*. It has become our way."

Neah looked at Oatah with a color they had never seen. *Admission of guilt*, Beezan realized. Neah nodded. "It was no different with us."

"Perhaps it is the way of the universe." They all stared at Oatah. Suddenly everything Reeder had ever said about Oatah rang true. He seemed to be seeing the future, or even drawing it together himself. He was bigger, wiser, and spoke with the utter conviction of long authority. "All human beings view each other as family, as brothers and sisters, and you, the Ramians, shall be our cousins. Humans and Ramians will work together for the good of all."

"Yes," a sincere Neah nodded, "I will dedicate my life to it." Neah and Oatah reached across the table and pressed their hands together most solemnly. It was not a treaty. It was not an oath. But Beezan knew it was the future.

6-Will

Beezan, Oatah, Reeder, Iricana, and Katie stared at one screen and then the other, heads turning back and forth as if at a sporting match. They couldn't stop looking at the blue planet any more than they could stop looking at the spectacular Ramian ship, bigger than the *Pearl*, glittering like a frozen crystal ball.

Neah only had eyes for the planet. Iricana sighed. Beezan

looked up at her in sympathy. They had been forbidden to record anything and had already erased some records. They were allowed to spend a few days in orbit near the ship. After that short rest, they would go to the a-rings. A Ramian would program the jump for them, now that they knew the code, and they would go back to Friendship.

In the meantime, the Ramians couldn't stop them from looking. Beezan knew that by the time they got to Daydream, Oatah would have more plans: plans for working with the Ramians, plans for figuring out their own a-rings, and now, plans to find another Earth.

In the equation of boosting verses travel time, it was always a balance between stress and boredom. This time, Beezan had no trouble choosing the 28-day boring trip to Seven's a-rings. The trip was especially long as the a-ring position was so far from the planet. Despite wanting to get back to Jarvie, Beezan knew the crew needed to rest. Neah, Oatah, and Getti Drann could also stay in contact, exchanging information and planning.

Planning was hardly the word for it. Oatah was orchestrating the future of humanity. He was in his element and Reeder adoringly followed his every theme. They worked with Neah as a go-between arranging a series of highest-level meetings with the Ramians, each a step on the way to what sounded like total unification.

Beezan was unsure. Treaties, yes. Friendship, yes. Working together, yes. Overlapping territories, yes, but what exactly did Oatah envision in his see-all-connections-mind?

Beezan decided to detach himself from such star-spanning contemplations and concentrate on the everyday realm of running the *Drumheller*. By necessity, he ended up working with the robots and Iricana, supervising repairs. Beezan had a nervous worry that Oatah would use his oath to have him surrender the *Drumheller* in favor of some fancier diplomatic ship. By upgrading the *Drumheller,* he might hang on to it. He also fretted about Reeder turning Jarvie over to him. He knew he should trust them enough to at least go talk to them, but in the face of Writing The Future, his own little troubles were petty. So he put them aside and worked.

Pearl

Jarvie stood shyly in the Ramian medical center, looking at himself in the mirror. He was putting on Ramian "guest" clothes, custom made in the *Drumheller* sky blue. They even fit. They were the fanciest clothes he'd ever worn. A pair of pants that actually went to his feet was overlapped with a thigh-length matching tunic. Both had extra material that draped and swirled. The tunic had bits of glitter in some kind of subtle picture, but Jarvie couldn't make it out. He also couldn't get it on right. At least it had small pockets hidden inside so he didn't feel entirely frivolous. Star looked suspiciously at the new clothes until Jarvie folded him up in all the extra material and ruffled him into acceptance.

They had recycled his uniform. Zhenulell brought him his p'link, which was undamaged. He glanced at the date, 8 Will, his birthday. That meant the deadline to save Canyon had passed five days ago. He stared at his p'link.

"Are you all right?" Zhenulell asked.

"It's over," he said, looking down at her. "The race to Seven, I mean."

"Yes. It is too early for news though. We don't know if they will be delayed at Seven."

"Why would they?"

"Oh, anything," she said lightly, "diplomatic reasons. It may be many days yet. Don't worry about your ship. I'm sure they're fine."

They probably think we're fine.

Norijay was also being released, so Zhenulell was hurrying them along with their clothes. Norijay was silent and subdued making Jarvie feel awkward around him. Looking for a diversion, he said, "Doctor?"

"Yes?"

"You were talking about reconsideration of mission goals."

"Yes?"

"Well, I was just wondering . . . what is your mission?"

She flashed surprise at him, but no insult. "Didn't they tell you? We are Finders."

She didn't explain so Jarvie thought the translator might be missing something. "What do you find?"

"Gravity Generators," she said solemnly.

Jarvie was excited. "You know where to look?"

"Well, yes, the Builders, as you call them, have their patterns of doing things, from where they put a-rings to where they store gravity generators. It doesn't make sense to us. Why would they store the generators in the outer belts? No one knows. We have many experts on board. It's a ten-year mission. It's taken us three years to organize and be approved and get a ship. We've put together a strong set of families to survive it, and a good crew. Well, we had a good crew. We don't know what will happen now. We may not go, after all that."

"You don't seem as upset as the others," Jarvie noted, wondering if he was overstepping politeness. Zhenulell smiled sadly.

"I am sorry for the loss of life, for my friends, but as for the mission—I believe we've found a new mission." Norijay looked over and nodded seriously. "Now! Finish up and I'll release you both," she said briskly, bustling about and glancing at the door.

Norijay came over to Jarvie and gently fixed his tunic, flipping it over his shoulder and folding the cloth under the belt where he had it wrong.

"Thank you."

"Jarvie, I," his colors flashed such distress that Jarvie couldn't imagine what was wrong. He'd been told that no one from Norijay's family had been injured. Norijay took a deep breath and blurted out, "I am sorry. I should have listened to you."

Now Jarvie understood the problem. "Norijay, it's not your fault!" Norijay's colors went so gray that Jarvie grabbed his arm as Zhenulell rushed over.

"Sit down," she said firmly. "Didn't you learn anything from the summary?" Jarvie couldn't believe she was scolding him. "Nori, you saved three children. You could not have changed Hefreesay's mind any more than Jarvie could."

Norijay slumped over, holding his hands over his membrane. Jarvie sat by him and tried to think of useful things to say, but was saved by the door opening. A pack of preschoolers, including Quay, came in, followed by their parents. *The kids Norijay saved.*

Then Jarvie was practically knocked out of his seat by Quay, who launched himself into Jarvie's lap and threw his arms around him. Norijay was similarly accosted by the other three kids who hugged him over and over, telling him thank you while their parents stood by, tears in their eyes and colors glowing tan with a pink line. The crowd of parents parted and a familiar-looking adult appeared.

"Acting Captain Avistav," Zhenulell whispered behind

Jarvie. *Of course!* Jarvie had seen him on the summary. He was the one who had taken control from the gravity ball room and saved them all. Jarvie and Norijay jumped to their feet, spilling children on the deck. Whatever the occasion was, the kids were in on it, clapping their hands and jumping up and down. Star jumped up on the bed to see, and Quay took Jarvie's hand and stood by him.

The Captain approached Norijay, who had hastily wiped his tears, smearing them all over his face. Avistav pulled a small box from inside his shirt. The box was a work of art itself. Slowly he opened it. Inside was a shining band, a thick ribbon of gold. The children gasped. Avistav held it in front of Norijay for him to see, handing the box to a parent. Jarvie could see that there were four symbols on the band. Quay tugged on Jarvie, so Jarvie picked him up. "What is it?" Jarvie whispered to Quay, while Quay peered over.

"It's a hero token!" the translator struggled to interpret Quay's excited whispers. "Only the Captain can give one. Those are the marks of the three kids and the mark of the *Zharta Pearl*."

Avistav latched the band around Norijay's wrist and there was more hugging and crying, but now Norijay was smiling. "We can't give you one, because Captain Neah said so," Quay pouted.

"Oh Quay," Jarvie squeezed him affectionately, thinking of their panic in the rimway. "You are all right. That's everything to me."

In the following days, Jarvie came to realize the truth of Danumae's earlier words. Jarvie was not blamed. In fact, his attempt to warn them and his rescue of Quay had gained him a new status. He no longer went to school, much to Quay's disappointment. He was given a translator full-time and Sontula was assigned to help him during the workday. He was trained in all safety measures and ship procedures, and was given maps of the *Pearl* to study. Most startling of all, he found himself assigned to the new 'advisory crew' that assisted Acting Captain Avistav.

Sadly, the first advice he ended up giving was about Lander's Moon. They asked to bury their people there. Jarvie said humans had no claim on the moon and found himself making a formal agreement to share the moon—against all Oatah's orders.

It broke his heart. The first thing that Ramians and humans would share was a cemetery.

Jarvie finally found a few minutes to himself in his cabin to fish out the package Beezan had given him for his birthday. He had been 15 for a week now. It was supposed to be his Year of Reflection, a year to stop his technical training and focus on his spiritual goals and reorientation.

He sighed. He was so far off the teen training program that there was probably no hope for him. He slowly opened the package. Part of him was eager for a bit of home and part of him reluctant to stir up any more emotions. There were several small packages within the box. One was a white armband, rolled up and tied with a blue ribbon and a note.

> *Greetings Jarvie, sorry we can't be with you as you begin your Year of Reflection. Happy Birthday. See you soon, Love, Beezan*

He swallowed a lump in his throat as he unfurled the

armband across his lap. He picked up another present and opened it.

Crew Jarvie, Happy Birthday. Perhaps you will find these useful. Reeder

It was a comb and brush set. Jarvie laughed to himself. Reeder didn't want him turning into Beezan. But it was a nice gift, so Jarvie sent Reeder a mental thanks.

Then Danulell and Quay came in. "Presents!" Quay jumped on the bed with Star right behind.

"Oh, forgot that I exist?" Jarvie asked Star, who had taken to Quay while he was in the medical center.

Star paused for half a heartbeat from investigating the presents to look up and say, "Love Zharvie!" before going back to the package.

"Oh, Star." He hugged the podpup, who was now holding one of the presents.

"What is it?" Quay bounced up and down.

"Well, it's my birthday package."

There was a heartbeat delay as Quay listened for the translation. "Birthday!" Then he was out the door yelling, no doubt spreading the news.

"May you have a year of growth," Danulell said formally, with a little bow, and then they both laughed.

Zhenulell appeared in the door with Quay. "Come, it's your birthday, do not be alone. Bring your presents."

Jarvie took the armband and the box and went to the living room. The whole family gathered and sat in a circle with him. He was both embarrassed and pleased. He opened the other gifts. From Oatah, he got a manual on diplomatic protocols, which only Danulell approved of. There was a box of candy from

Iricana. Katie gave him a piece of pink crystal mounted on a piece of wood. On the bottom it said it was from Earth. Jarvie held it reverently, explaining it was from their home planet and that the bottom part was from a tree. He held it out so they could touch it.

"You've never been there?" Quay asked.

"No, it's very far."

"Don't you wish to go?" he wanted to know.

"Well, we can't go. At least not now. Some of our a-rings are broken."

"Oh." Quay pondered the problem. "When I grow up I will help you fix them, and then you can take me to Earth."

Quay's brother and sister flashed skepticism, but Jarvie felt as if a pebble had just been dropped, sending out ripples to change the future. He stared down at Quay.

"I'd like that," he said quietly.

"What is this? Zhenumae asked, pointing to his armband.

"It replaces the purple one," which had disappeared with his uniform. "It's for 15-year-olds."

"Like a token?"

"No, more like an identification badge." They frowned at the translators rendering. "A status indicator . . . to tell people what I should be expected to know and do, in case of an emergency especially. All teens have to wear them in the outer sectors."

Now they were glowing understanding. Jarvie lifted it up. They were hard to put on, but with the wide sleeves of the Ramian shirt it would be even harder. "The Father or caretaker is supposed to put it on every morning. It's just a little tradition."

Danumae's colors flashed yellow and he reached out for the band. "I cannot take the place of your Captain, but I promised to try." He gently wrapped it around Jarvie's arm, folding in the shirt material. He even patted him on the shoulder, reaching up, just as Beezan would.

"Thank you," Jarvie whispered. It had been a happy birthday after all.

At dinner that night, Jarvie sat by Danumae. "Honor, would it be all right if I studied the gravity generator information? I mean where to find them especially."

"I don't see why not."

"Well, we don't have an exchange of technology treaty."

Danumae pondered. "It makes sense for your people to look. I'll ask."

"Thanks."

From across the table, Danulell studied Jarvie thoughtfully.

40 / DESTINY AT DAYDREAM

Pearl

Jarvie slowly realized that despite assurances and flashes of upbeat colors, all was not well aboard the *Pearl*. In the weeks since the accident, funerals and memorials were finished, repairs were underway, the injured were discharged, school reopened, and all the adults went back to work. Jarvie hid in the cabin to avoid the memorials, feeling awkward, but figuring they'd be happy he didn't show up. The shock and grief of the survivors was evident and everyone was supportive and sympathetic. There was also fretting over their mission and grim resignation about the birds, which Jarvie didn't fully understand. Overall though, he sensed an attitude of *we're all in this together*.

Yet, there was something else. Extra activities for children and youth appeared with strange regularity. Although Zhenumae was pleased, the ever-vigilant Danulell confided his suspicions to Jarvie that he thought adults were trying to keep kids busy so they could work more. At first Jarvie dismissed it. He'd expect extra work after a big accident. He was busy enough anyway. Captain Avistav had granted Jarvie full permission to study gravity balls. He'd even been let off the advisory committee to do it. He spent his days with Sontula, studying.

"So what strange things happened today?" Danulell asked when they were alone in the sleeping room.

"Well," Jarvie admitted, "Someone asked me if I had the plans for the human receiver in my p'link."

"It's been destroyed, then," Danulell concluded, sitting down next to Jarvie.

"That makes sense." But Jarvie figured it wouldn't do any good to feed Danulell's conspiracy theories. "But *Drumheller* will still find us."

Danulell nodded, but continued to sit by him. Jarvie sensed his chance to finally ask something else. "Danulell—" he looked up sharply, but Jarvie went on. "Something happened. The day of the accident. Something with Quay that I didn't understand."

"What?"

"The other kids called him something and he got mad. And it sounded like a color, but that didn't make sense, and Norijay was stern with them. I think they called him "tan."

Danulell jerked upright, a flash of dark green with aqua stripe crossing his membrane before settling back to blue. But Jarvie had learned that Danulell was better than others at controlling his colors. So whatever it was, it jarred him out of that control for a moment.

Danulell, blinked, stood up, walked around, frowned, sat down. "What does it mean?" Jarvie whispered.

Danulell pulled out his translator, trying different words and shaking his head. "Cohort, co-schemer, sidekick—"

"Sidekick? Like when there are two superheroes and one is the boss and the other is—"

"Tan. Yes," Danulell said. "Jik and tan. Not colors. Hero and sidekick."

Jarvie pieced this together. "Neah and Sontula."

"Yes."

"Not married people."

"Usually not," Danulell confirmed. "The jik are rare. Being their tan is competitive. People will jockey for position even from a young age."

"So why was it an insult?" Jarvie asked.

Danulell walked around again, sat down again. "Because, Quay is a third."

"A third . . . what?"

"Child. Sorry. A third child, like Neah. You can tell from the short name. Thirds have no duty to parents or tradition. They are independent. With thirds, there is always the potential, the hope, that they will be jik."

It was still an hour before dinner, study time for the family. Jarvie lay on the deck in the study room going over his gravity ball maps. He was thrilled with it all. Another universe had opened up to him. He was astonished that the family took so little interest, especially for a ship of Finders. Of course, the parents were doctors and Zhenumae was leaning that way. Danulell, as far as Jarvie could see, would make a perfect administrator.

However, Quay, in grand preschooler style, was not only interested in gravity balls, but knew everything about them. Jarvie had to laugh to himself. He'd hardly needed permission. All along, he could have just asked Quay.

Quay even had a comic book about Finder ships and loved to talk about them and how *Pearl* was going to be one of them. He was oblivious of the fact that a hole had been blown in their ship and they weren't going anywhere.

"And in Kletiba system," Quay told Jarvie, "twenty gravity generators were still on and the entire k-belt was clumped up in 20 giant clumps. I say that's why they did it. To clean up the belt. No one believes me," he scowled.

"Quay, we told you. Clumps are unstable," Danulell said.

"Not if you clean them up before they come apart."

"Well, none of the systems are cleaned up—"

"How would we know?" Quay argued.

"—how would you clean up such a mess of stuff anyway?"

"Maybe the clumps can become solid."

"They can't become solid and besides, then there would be more than one planet in an orbit, and we haven't seen anything like that."

"Not if they moved them," Quay grumbled.

This was obviously an old argument. Jarvie made a mental note to get the real version from Sontula. He knew that gravity balls didn't have the strength to hold together a bunch of rock against the tug of a giant planet next door, but what about . . .

"Do you ever find bunches of gravity generators together?"

"Sure," Quay said, "but not when they're turned on. They don't like each other. See what that bad one did to our ship."

"So they can't really make planet-size clumps."

"One could," Quay whispered to Jarvie, "if it were a super-powered one."

Gravity generators were the tools of Quay's superheroes and there was probably a big difference between fantasy and reality. With exaggerated stealth, Quay scooted over next to Jarvie on the deck and whispered even lower. "They don't believe. But I do. That gravity generator that blew up, it wasn't a regular one. It was super-powered. It was a planet-maker."

A chill went down Jarvie's spine. His eyes met Quay's intelligent blue eyes, intense and earnest. This child was no tan.

• • •

14-Knowledge

"I can't believe we're finally jumping tomorrow," Katie breathed. "No offense, Captain!" She added quickly, looking up at him from her dinner.

"Believe me," he replied, "I've considered a few surprise burns, just to move us along."

"Well," Iricana added, "I think the others will be sad to go." Oatah, Neah, and Reeder hadn't even come in to eat yet, they were so busy.

"Are you anxious about code jumping again, Captain?" Katie asked.

"No, not anymore," he replied honestly. "I'm just starting to feel like I really want to go home."

"I thought *Drumheller* was your home," said Oatah, coming in.

"It is, but *Drumheller* somewhere I can get packets," he said. Katie and Iricana laughed in sympathy.

15-Knowledge

One thing Beezan really liked about code jumping was coming in close. The path was so steady it didn't break up until disturbed by Friendship's giant planets. He had the feel of it this time.

"ETA Friendship a-rings: 8.34 days."

They cheered. Two small burns and they went back to spin. No venting, no gravity-assists, no big emergencies, and best of all, very little post jump depression.

"Don't get used to it," Beezan reminded them. "Without control boxes we'll still have to do it the hard way."

. . .

4-Power

Eight days later, they were doing it the hard way. Now that Beezan knew about codes, he couldn't figure out why the Friendship control panel wouldn't have a code to Daydream. Neah said codes could be added when needed as they had done at Seven, so maybe only the most popular jumps showed. Without the code though, Beezan was on his own.

The golden path that he had originally seen in his dream of Lander was just as strong on the way back to Daydream. He skipped the jump drug, but let the *Drumheller* fall out of the path in the normal way. Depression and unease settled on him immediately. He told himself he'd feel better as soon as they located the *Pearl*. Neah had given the *Drumheller* a priority list of locations as the *Pearl* had planned to do mapping work while they were gone.

"ETA to a-rings: 17.7 days. ETA to Nocturne: 16.9 days."

"Stand by for destination. Scan for the *Pearl's* beacon."

"Scanning."

The crew got out of their cocoons and stowed their gear. Beezan let out Sky, fed her, and got snacks for everyone. He kept one eye on the screen, but Neah sat anxiously staring. One by one, beacons appeared; the human beacon at the hangar, the one at Nocturne, and the Ramian beacons in similar places.

"Shouldn't *Drumheller* have located the *Pearl's* beacon by now?" asked Neah.

"No *Pearl* beacon in orbit at the a-rings or along the L4-Turquoise arc. Checking Turquoise vicinity."

Neah frowned.

"Maybe they're just behind the planet," Beezan said, but it sounded unconvincing.

The crew crowded into the Command Bay, snacking and poking at pop-ups.

"New beacon found."

They all turned to the screen. A purple icon appeared. "Is that on the surface?" Beezan asked, confused.

"Yes, a Ramian beacon is on the surface of Lander's Moon."

Katie gasped. "It's right next to Lander's marker."

"A grave marker?" Reeder asked. "Do you do that?"

Neah's colors had gone gray. "Yes," he whispered, "in remote places."

"*Drumheller*, any sign of the *Pearl* in orbit at Lander's Moon?"

"No beacon."

"Scan for other signs."

"Scanning."

"We must remain positive," Iricana said. "They could not have placed the marker if they were destroyed." *Could it be Jarvie? Was that why they put it next to Lander? What could have happened?*

"Lander's Moon has passed behind the planet. Scanning on stand-by. Beacon scanning in Turquoise space continues."

Neah's color surged from the sickeningly gray to a blazing white.

"Strap!" Neah ordered.

Beezan started in surprise, but then realized that Neah was doing what any captain would do when his crew was threatened, taking command. Beezan signaled the others to comply.

"*Drumheller*, secure all."

Even as they jumped to obey, Iricana objected. "We don't know that they are still at Lander's moon!"

"They must be," Neah said. Oatah nodded.

“Yes,” Beezan agreed. “*Drumheller*, get us there in seven days.”

Pearl

Jarvie was just rolling up the map when there was the unmistakable ear pop of a pressure loss. Jarvie was on his feet before the alarm sounded. Zhenulell and Danumae locked eyes a moment before she said “Go!” and he was out the door, headed for the medical center, no doubt. Zhenulell herded the rest of them into the alcove, which was their safe spot, sealing both locks.

“What’s happening?” Quay kept asking. Zhenumae took him in her lap, hushing him, while Zhenulell brought up their emergency channel.

“Oh no,” Danulell whispered.

“What does it say?” Jarvie asked. Danulell explained it for Jarvie’s translator.

“An airlock in the safety perimeter around the damaged area has lost pressure. Now another level of locks had to be shut. Some people are trapped. They may be able to get out before the air runs out.” They watched as pictures appeared on the screen from different cameras.

The travel room, Jarvie thought, and looked up at Zhenulell, but she flashed him a caution, so he didn’t say anything. *What would they do if they couldn’t jump?*

Days later, when there was a new perimeter and everyone was safe and the anxiety didn’t seem as if it would die down anyway, Jarvie met with the rest of the teens in the dining room. Captain Avistav had decided to tell them what was happening. Jarvie left

Star with Quay to distract Quay from the fact that he couldn't come.

Avistav was a straight-talking commander. "Our situation is not desperate, but it is not good and it is deteriorating. The accident created a hole that cannot be fixed with materials aboard the *Zharta*. If we were in a different system, we could go to a repair station, call for help, transfer to another ship while this one is being repaired, or any number of solutions. We believe we can still jump. Everyone would have to suit up to go to the travel room and there is the chance that more damage will occur during the jump, but we expect it would be survivable. Older students that have studied ship science know that the grown-metal we use cannot be exposed to certain radiations without breaking down. That is what's happening now. Our first priority is to rebuild the radiation field projector. Currently, all five remaining shuttles are attempting to shield the Zharta. We would jump immediately, but we cannot leave the Daydream system until the *Drumheller* returns."

Ten sets of eyes glanced at Jarvie. He almost objected, but caught himself before interrupting the Captain. *How do I always end up being a problem?*

"We lost the long-range human receiver in the accident, so we may not know the *Drumheller* is back until they find us and come closer. We expect the *Drumheller* any day though, and will leave as soon as possible after they arrive. We fully expect to survive and be repaired. It is our goal to continue our Finding Mission after repair." There were some relieved smiles and colors for that.

"Meanwhile, we ask you to be brave, be patient, and help out the adults as much as possible—"

Someone spoke out of turn, "What if the humans don't come back?"

Avistav frowned. "At some point we will be forced to jump to save ourselves. We will leave a message for the *Drumheller*."

"Why don't we just go now?"

"We must wait as long as possible."

There was a sudden loud beep from Jarvie's pocket and he nearly jumped out of his fancy shirt. *How did my p'link get set on such a volume*? he wondered, embarrassed, pulling it out and pressing the answer button. "Sorry," he muttered, before even realizing what was happening.

"Jarvie?"

He froze, looking at the p'link. There was a little tiny Beezan looking at him in puzzlement, but all the same, a familiar human face. As the teens joyously leaped out of their seats, Jarvie numbly realized: the *Drumheller* was back.

Beezan looked at Neah with a small sigh of relief. Jarvie was alive and there were enough people alive to make a complete ruckus. Beezan sat back in his seat to take a few calming breaths, turning the camera to Neah.

When they had come close enough to see the damage to the *Pearl,* Neah had nearly lost hope. However, *Drumheller* reported shuttles and activity around the ship and they had finally come close enough to use the small receiver in Jarvie's p'link.

After what seemed like ages, the teens left and a familiar Ramian came on the screen. His colors were pained as he told Neah the situation. The others gathered around quietly, listening on their translators.

"Avistav my friend, what has happened?"

"Captain, a long story, and sad. Forgive me for telling the short version, but we are in need of haste."

. . .

Neah spent hours talking with the *Pearl*. The crew left him for a while to give him some privacy. When they came back, Katie checked on him and brought him food. At another panel, Beezan, Reeder, and Iricana scanned the area where the gravity ball had been, shaking their heads at its destruction and the chaos it had left. Beezan had never seen Iricana so furious. "That Thayne. He is lucky he is stuck at Harbor where I can't get him."

"What would you do?" Reeder asked.

"Remove him from the project at the very least! Arrest him if I had to."

"Arrest the genius of the outer sectors? Isn't that somewhat harsh?" *Coming from Reeder? The person who nearly arrested me once?* Beezan had to hide his annoyance.

"Harsh?" The usually reasonable Iricana was nearly shouting. "Thayne has concealed and stolen a gravity ball, risked the ship, and how many sets of a-rings? And now our first contact with the Ramians has resulted in loss to them—all because of that—stupid—gravity ball!"

Reeder nodded. "I suppose you are right, but we can't do anything about him now. We should concentrate on helping the *Pearl*."

"We may have to," Iricana added. "Either make a jump for them to get help, or do something with repairs."

"If we have to jump, we'd have to leave Jarvie on a crippled ship," Beezan reminded them.

"I know," Reeder said, "But what else can we do?"

Iricana frowned and stared at the image of the *Pearl*. "What they need is a big patch. A chunk of—" she froze and looked at Reeder.

"A chunk of?" Reeder repeated.

"Of Ramian hull material! Like we have in the Cargo Hold!"

Iricana's fingers flew over the panel. "These!" She looked up at Beezan. "Containers 177 and 178: Two large sections of unidentified hull."

18-Power

Pearl

Everyone who wasn't working on the repair came to the dining room to watch. Neah was still aboard the *Drumheller*, directing repair assistance from there.

Norijay brought his class into the dining room. They jostled their way to Jarvie and sat all around, leaning on him, Quay crawling in his lap, the others tugging on his arms, and standing on the seat to feel his scars through his newly grown hair. Norijay laughed sympathetically, but didn't make any move to stop them.

Now that the *Drumheller* had not only returned in time, but also miraculously been able to help the *Pearl*, Jarvie's status had gone from alien, to rescuer of Quay, to local hero.

Jarvie downplayed it all, knowing this rescue work was way beyond him and that everything depended on the genius of Iricana and the robots. He did have a pang of missing out though. For the humans, this was a good thing. Although human technology lagged behind the Ramians in general, they were ahead in robotics, and it never hurt to have the image of being in the right place at the right time with the right stuff.

"Look!" Jarvie said to the kids, pointing to the screen. Cameras that had been installed to help with repairs were now focused outward, tracking a glinty cargo container on its way from *Drumheller*.

The excitement of the past week had been unbelievable. A team of Ramians had gone over to inspect the wreckage in the

Drumheller Cargo Hold and discovered hull material with "growth" properties intact, thanks to the safety of the *Drumheller* Cargo Hold. It was even enough to close up the damage on *Pearl.* The incredible odds of the *Drumheller* having just what they needed only added to the feeling of mutual destiny that was growing among the Ramians. Jarvie hoped Humans saw things the same way.

The cargo loader stopped near the *Pearl.* There was a long process of opening the first container and extracting the hull piece. Then all at once, the robots pushed the piece over the rim of the container and paused a moment to reorient for the burn to the ship. The angle of the Daydream's rays caught the edge of the Ramian hull metal, causing it to gleam. Then the simultaneous small burns of the robots lit up the screen and the hull pieces caught the full light of Daydream.

Jarvie was struck by the shape of it, like an angel of starlight descending to their rescue. He gasped in wonder. The Ramians must have seen a similar vision for they broke out in a joyous prayer / song. Jarvie had not heard it before and never expected to hear it again, but always in his heart was the memory of that moment and the kinship he felt with the Ramians.

41 / HOMEWARD

19-Power

Drumheller

Now that Neah had gone back to the *Pearl*, Oatah called planning meetings in the Consultation Hall after breakfast every day.

"We may not have much time to plan once we return to Redrock. There will be many distractions and demands on our attention," Oatah began.

"Providing we come in reasonably close," Reeder specified.

Oatah turned to Beezan, "What is your feel for it, Captain?"

Beezan was suddenly uneasy. He tried to ignore Reeder's unnecessary jab, but the truth was, he was nervous about the jump. "I really don't know. I have a better feel for coming in now, but . . ."

"What?" Iricana asked gently.

"Well, it is a long hard jump." Embarrassed, his voice dropped to a whisper, "And well, it is the jump that killed Lander." The crew sat back in their seats, surprised. It was almost as if they had forgotten. It did seem like a long time ago.

"I understand pilots focus a lot on who died in what jump," Katie said quietly, "but remember, Lander was . . . well . . . elderly, to say the least."

"I know, but he seemed so strong, and then he was just gone."

"His spirit was strong, but that won't keep a frail body in the physical world forever," Katie said.

Beezan nodded, feeling foolish. Secretly he thought he'd feel a lot better with a trustworthy co-pilot. If only Jarvie could go back to pilot training and jump with him.

"Captain, we have every confidence in you," Oatah continued, dismissing his worries. "We'll have packets, probably thousands, within hours. Since we have disappeared for so long, they will expect an immediate report, which I'll have prepared. No word of the Ramians must escape until I can return to Sector 1 with the report."

"You're going back to Earth?" Iricana asked.

"Yes," Oatah said firmly. "I must. Reeder will accompany me home as my First Assistant." Apparently, this was news to Reeder, who was very pleased, either about going back to Earth or being named First Assistant.

"We don't know that the work-around path was successful," Iricana objected.

"I am confident that a work-around has been or will be found for the Firelight problem. In the meantime, I'll leave instructions for you. Iricana will be in charge here and Katie will stay. A few new crew will be necessary."

"What about Jarvie?" Beezan couldn't stop himself from asking the question that was bursting from his heart.

"I think he should come with us," Reeder said quickly.

All eyes turned to Reeder in amazement. "I don't think he will want to," Katie said.

"But think of it," Reeder went on, oblivious to their concern. "Agent Oatah will need more help. It would be such an opportunity, to travel with Agent Oatah, learn from him, visit the inner sectors, see Earth. Jarvie can report personally on his experience with the Ramians."

Beezan's heart was pounding. He was shaking his head no, but couldn't speak. He felt Iricana's knee bump against him. "Well, we may have to wait on that decision," she said casually. "He's 15 now, you know. The law gives him some input in residence and caretakership."

"Yes, of course," Oatah said. "I wouldn't take him against his will." Beezan breathed a small sigh of relief, casting a silent thank you in Iricana's direction. "For now, we must concentrate on keeping the Ramians a secret."

1-Speech

Jarvie hadn't slept for two nights by the time he went back to the *Drumheller*. He had expected to stay on the *Pearl* longer, but as soon as Neah returned, he ordered him back, saying Beezan was worried about him.

Jarvie had rushed through the rest of the gravity generator data, packed up his small treasures, and said a tearful goodbye to his 'family.' He had steeled himself for Quay's sadness, but it was the others who were sad. Quay hugged him and said he would miss him until he came back. Quay's family reminded Quay that Jarvie might not ever return, but Jarvie had given up arguing with the child. Quay flashed confidence and excitement. Jarvie tried to hang onto those colors during the ride back.

Reeder greeted him formally and carried on polite conversation with Danumae as they flew back in the old cold *Peacock*. It meant an extra shuttle trip for Reeder, but Danumae insisted on seeing Jarvie home personally.

Jarvie fretted over seeing Beezan. Should he be formal? Hug him? Act like the big teenager he looked like or the small and confused child he felt like? Did Beezan really miss him? Or did he have a change of heart? For that matter, had Reeder changed his mind?

They parked in the hangar and went up the lift. Trudging up the rimway in his suit, helmet still on to hide his very short hair, Jarvie heard another group coming their way. Jarvie hung back behind Reeder and Danumae, self-conscious. Star banged against his box, so Jarvie paused to let him out. He frolicked around Jarvie's legs until the other group approached.

Beezan, Iricana, and Katie followed Oatah down the rimway, with Sky in a big pink bow, scampering ahead. Jarvie's heart leaped just to see them.

"Star!" Sky squeaked, and ran towards them.

"Sky!" Star turned and bolted in her direction. They burst into podpup language as they ran. They were going so fast that they skidded right past each other. Jarvie's awkwardness left him as both parties erupted in laughter.

Jarvie stood quietly by as Oatah and Beezan greeted Danumae and thanked him. Then Beezan couldn't get near Jarvie for the podpups jumping on them. Finally Iricana and Katie grabbed them. "You two!" Iricana scolded Star.

"Love!" Star declared and nuzzled her right on the face.

Beezan hugged Jarvie gently as if he would break and then pulled back suddenly, looking at him sharply.

"What?" Jarvie whispered.

"You've grown." Everyone laughed again, except Katie, who was now scrutinizing what she could see of him.

"You look well, Jarvie, better than ever," and her eyes slid to Danumae.

"Yes, Captain, Doctor, there is a medical matter to discuss if you'd like to continue to your Med Bay." No one budged.

"What?" Katie asked in the huge silence.

"It's good news, actually," Danumae hesitated, glancing at their foreheads but unable to read their reactions.

"It is good!" Jarvie intervened, pulling off his helmet. "I have new implants. I don't need surgery at Redrock."

They did not fully believe until Jarvie was on the exam bed with the new implants showing on the screen. Danumae discussed the finer points with Katie, including other injuries that Jarvie hadn't even known about. A worried Beezan hovered about, hesitantly feeling the thin scars.

"It's okay," Jarvie whispered to Beezan. "I don't have any more pain." Beezan looked across the exam bed to Danumae.

"Thank you," Beezan pressed hands with him. "Thank you for saving him." Danumae gave Jarvie a relieved smile, as he finally accepted that Beezan wouldn't be angry.

Jarvie nearly cried when Danumae left. Beezan was kindly walking him back to his cabin, but was called away by Oatah. "I'll be all right," Jarvie mumbled tiredly and continued on. He was worn out, cold and sad. He almost stumbled down the steps to his cabin. He had a flash of that day so long ago that Beezan said he could stay on. He had been so relieved. A safe, if empty and freezing, cabin had been a good thing to him then.

There was nothing in it now except the standard foldout bunk and chairs. It looked like a picture he had seen once of an old prison cell. The *Drumheller* had felt lonely all along, but now it felt like a cave. He'd thought he would be happy to see the crew again, and he was, but they were different, distracted somehow. He didn't feel like one of them anymore.

What would happen to him now? Would Reeder take him away to a life of obsessive work and no family of any kind?

Family was all he wanted. Quay's family had the encircling love and warmth, the easy give and take, the everyday story-lines, and the acceptance and support that he so desperately missed.

Sinking down on the bunk and hugging his knees to his chest, he looked around his cabin in despair. As he had learned since the loss of his real family, waking from a good dream was worse than waking from a nightmare. Now, coming back from the *Pearl*, he knew his good dream was over. Even if he did see them again, they wouldn't be like a family.

His heart hurt so much he could have sworn it was physical pain, that it would never stop and that he didn't know how he could go on. There was a sudden rustling and podpups were nuzzling him, trying to burrow under his arms. They had come through the adjoining door, sensing his mood in their podpup way. Then Beezan sat beside him, arm around him, "Jarvie," he whispered, "you didn't want to come back."

"I did!" he protested tearfully. "But . . . I wanted to stay too."

"I know," Beezan sympathized. "Danumae said they'd become very attached to you."

"What will happen to me now?"

He expected Beezan to answer with his usual optimism, and grew even more agitated when he took a deep breath and sat back on the bed. "Well, it's partly up to you, I think. I still have hope that I can keep the *Drumheller* and Reeder will sign you over to me," he continued as Jarvie swallowed hard. "Oatah has a good heart, but he sees the future for the good of all. Our concerns are not meaningful to him. Maybe that's as it should be. A lot has happened since you left."

"Can you tell me?"

"Some." Despite his lack of sleep, Jarvie sat riveted by the telling and content for the moment to be reunited with Beezan and Sky. Then, as Jarvie couldn't keep his eyes open any longer, Beezan chanted a prayer and left Sky with them so the two podpups could be together.

Reeder was facilitating the morning meeting. Beezan had already sent the flight schedule to their s'links, but reminded them that they were leaving in only five hours. "The *Pearl* is entering the rings within the hour. We don't plan to jump together. We must stay to help if they have a problem. It's also safer for us, in case debris comes off their ship."

Everyone nodded. There was an underlying tension around the Consultation Hall table. Beezan was pleased to have Jarvie back in the seat next to him, although he had always liked Neah. Iricana was on Jarvie's other side and then Katie. Then there was Lander's empty chair, and empty chairs on either side of Reeder and Oatah, making it an us-and-them set up. Beezan realized that he, as Captain, should have changed the seating, but his stubbornness almost wanted Oatah and Reeder to prove themselves. He said another prayer to himself to work together.

"Well Captain, you'll be happy to know that Agent Oatah has determined that Jarvie must stay on the *Drumheller*." Reeder smiled, obviously expecting an enthusiastic response. But the wording of it was so strange. Not just "change caretakers," but "stay on the *Drumheller*?" Jarvie looked over at him, worried.

"I'm not sure I follow that," Beezan said quietly.

Oatah himself answered. "I had considered the suggestion of allowing Jarvie to choose if he would like to come with us." Jarvie gave a sharp shake of his head, but Oatah held up a hand. "Unfortunately, I must not allow the choice. Jarvie must stay on the *Drumheller*. After consultation with the Doctor, we determined that the alien implants would not pass for human technology. We cannot risk a medical exam. Jarvie must stay here."

"Well, I'm not arguing," Katie said, "but you know, he'll have to have his fifteen exam on Redrock anyway."

"No, Doctor, I am being precise when I say that Jarvie must stay *on* the *Drumheller*. He must not leave the ship." There was a general gasp of realization as Oatah went on. "If non-crew members come aboard they must not see him or access any data about him."

"For how long?" Iricana asked reasonably.

"It's uncertain. Long enough for me to return to Sector 1, inform the council, who will no doubt, go to the Highest Authority. After a plan is made, either I will return myself or send a message. Jarvie won't be able to leave the *Drumheller* until the Ramians are public knowledge."

"That could be months," Iricana said. *It could be never*, Beezan thought, especially if they don't find a work-around.

"Two to three years possibly, at the most, but it will not be boring. I have a special assignment for the *Drumheller*."

They sat back in their chairs in stunned silence. Beezan put his hand on Jarvie's shoulder.

"I don't think that would be acceptable to counseling," Katie ventured.

"It will have to be. I will order him confined for security reasons, and only the highest levels will even know that. I know it is a challenge, but let us take a moment to consider what would happen if word of the aliens got out."

Iricana took up Oatah's question. "People would reasonably expect full information."

"There might be confusion, fear of contamination, even panic, attempts to evacuate certain stations," Katie suggested.

"Uncoordinated response planning," Reeder stated.

"People might be excited and hopeful," Beezan suggested. Reeder raised an eyebrow at him.

"Unauthorized pilots would jump into Ramian space," Jarvie said quietly. Iricana and Katie looked doubtful. Beezan slowly nodded, scowling.

"Bringing diseases with them before the Ramians are ready." Katie added.

Oatah nodded slowly. "Yes, I see that you understand the seriousness of the situation, Jarvie, and why we need you to make this sacrifice. I personally believe it will not be as bad as you expect."

Beezan expected a breakdown or outburst of the usual sort and tried to think of what to say to head it off, but Jarvie took a deep breath and said, "I can do it, if I have work to do, if I'm not alone." Suddenly Beezan sat up, excitement washing over him. *Why didn't I realize before?*

"You won't be alone," Beezan reassured him, with agreements from Iricana and Katie, "and I know the perfect work for you."

"What?"

"To go back to pilot training."

Jarvie's eyes went wide with surprise.

"He can't," Katie started, and then reconsidered. "Can you?" she asked Jarvie.

"Yes, yes, I know I can. You heard Danumae. They fixed all the damage." He was practically jumping out of his seat. "The new Ramian implants will work, I'm sure of it."

Beezan glanced at Oatah and did a double take. Oatah's eyes were shining with satisfaction and possibly even happiness. "Yes, Captain, a wonderful suggestion. Especially as you are now a seer and can pass on your valuable knowledge."

Did Oatah plan all this? Beezan felt a stir of great hope, for himself, for Jarvie, for their work and the future of humanity.

"There's just one technical matter." Reeder produced two sets of thick bamboo paper documents. "Transfer of caretakership."

Finally, Beezan thought, more hopeful than ever following the head-spinning thought of Jarvie becoming a pilot again.

"This one," Reeder tapped it, "is the standard agreement. It's temporary caretakership. The Sector can intervene with little cause, it is easily transferable, and it expires when the child finishes teen training. It is the contract that Jarvie had with his cousin and has now, with me." Everyone nodded, but Beezan was puzzled. As far as he knew, there was only one kind of contract.

"This," Reeder paused significantly, "is permanent caretakership. It is much more difficult for the Sector to intervene, it is non-transferable, and it does not expire. On Earth it is called adoption. It also carries all the rights and responsibilities of parenthood, such as the responsibility to educate, etc." Reeder paused and looked at Jarvie.

Beezan was still puzzling over the second contract when Jarvie reached for the temporary one. Beezan's heart sank a bit, surprising him. Then Jarvie swept aside the temporary contract, sending sheets flying to the deck and setting the podpups into a chasing game. In a matter of seconds, the signing of the permanent contract was over. Beezan hardly had a moment to clearly consider it all. "So this means," he asked, "when we get back to Redrock, Jarvie will be . . . like . . . my child?"

"No Captain," Reeder said, with what seemed like tremendous relief. "The document is executed immediately. Jarvie is your son."

Jarvie jumped out of his seat, catching Beezan in a huge hug that he thought would break his ribs yet again. The others gathered around, patting them on the backs, congratulating them, and steadying them against the jumping-for-joy-without-knowing-why podpups.

Son? I have a son. Family. I have a family.

Jarvie held his breath as he watched the *Pearl* in the a-rings. Every instrument was on highest resolution watching for small parts coming off that they might need to track. Jarvie was so nervous his prayers ran in little circles along with the *Pearl.*

Jarvie tried to relax. He didn't want Beezan to regret giving him the co-pilot seat, especially bumping Reeder down to do it. But Beezan was in his meditation mode. He seemed especially calm and pleased and Jarvie knew it was because he was happy about the caretakership and Jarvie's ability to pilot again. Jarvie hadn't realized how good he would feel either. Beezan wasn't a whole family by himself, but he was that part that felt like a strong, protective, steadying, keep-on-the-path influence that Jarvie needed so much. Besides, Beezan was a good person in himself. That Oatah had declared Beezan a seer was astonishing. Seers were old long jump pilots like Lander.

Jarvie alternated earnest but unstructured prayers with getting his brackets on and getting set. *Drumheller* was timed to go as soon as *Pearl* left. If there was a problem, they'd be doing some serious breaking burns, so it was just as well to be in their brackets anyway.

"Not long now," Beezan whispered. Reeder, on the other

side of Beezan and the other three in the passenger lounge stared at the screens. *Pearl* was just starting to blur now. "Last lap." Jarvie pictured them, all in their suits, in the travel room, hull barely held together, exhausted and scared. He pictured Quay and his little friends. A prayer leaped into his mind, ***O God! Protect these children, graciously assist them to be educated and enable them to render service to the world of humanity. O God! These children are pearls, cause them to be nurtured within the shell of Thy loving-kindness.***[1]

Then the *Pearl* was gone. They'd hardly left the rings when they slipped into the path. Jarvie felt a little hum, like a wake passing over and glanced over at Beezan, but he showed no sign of any distraction.

"Path is clear," Reeder announced.

"*Drumheller*," Beezan said, "take us in."

Jarvie pulled on his helmet and sealed it with a satisfying click. He felt strong and hopeful. It would be a good jump.

Beezan went from literal heart-stopping fear to excruciating joy in one stretched-out moment of the jump. What appeared to be an impossible maze of pathways suddenly resolved itself into a picture of the human sectors. He could find Redrock, even that thin path. He rocked between the stars, sorting them out in his last moment of physical consciousness. He felt Jarvie with him, excited, but focused. "There!" and they were lined up. He didn't know if he pressed the thrusters, or Jarvie, only that they were in the path.

Finally, they were going home.

42 / PATHS TO THE FUTURE

Have to drop out of the path. No, it's automatic. Wait. I didn't take the jump drug. I shouldn't have been unconscious. Beezan thrashed against the brackets.

"Easy, Captain," came Katie's calm voice. "You're okay. You've resuscitated. Stay calm. Everything is under control."

His helmet was off. He could feel Katie's hand on his head. There were other voices. "Excellent jump, Captain," Reeder was saying. "We are only ten days out."

"Redrock?" he mumbled.

"Yes, Captain, Redrock."

"Jarvie?"

"He's in the kitchen," Katie told him. "You've been out for a couple hours. Reeder is acting as monitor. Oatah and Iricana are fine. Podpups are eating."

"My heart stopped."

"Yes, early on."

"I was scared," he said, opening his eyes. Katie looked at him, trying to understand. "There were so many paths." And then he saw them again. But now they made more sense.

"Don't go wandering too far. We need you," she whispered. "Besides, you have about 700 packets." She laughed warm-heartedly.

11-Speech

Katie made Beezan stay overnight in the Med Bay, so Jarvie asked to stay in the other bed, to keep an eye on him while he was wandering. Sky could not be pried from Beezan's side anyway, and someone needed to feed her.

By morning, Beezan had moments of focusing on the world around him, managing to clean up and eat between periods of staring off into space. Jarvie brought Beezan his white armband in a moment when they were alone. Beezan opened it out and looked at it. "White," Beezan said in a puzzled voice, staring at the armband.

"Captain?"

"There are some white paths," and Beezan was lost again. Jarvie took the armband and put it on himself, then guided Beezan back to the exam bed to rest.

"What do you see?" he asked, not really expecting an answer.

"Pathways," Beezan said from afar. "Like they are flash-printed on my mind. Not just one path. Everywhere I look, I still see them. But if I try to concentrate on one, to see where it goes . . ." and he drifted off.

Suddenly Beezan was back. "Did you see them?" He asked.

"No. Just the one, once we were lined up."

"You will. You will see them soon," Beezan said. Jarvie shivered a little at the thought.

The rest of the crew came up the stairs for their morning

meeting. "Let the Captain rest, Jarvie," Katie said gently, shooing him away and trying to make the Captain lie down.

Beezan defiantly sat up on the exam bed so he could see while he listened to the crew. He was focused enough to know his mind was drifting. It might help him to concentrate on the consultation, but they just wanted to talk to Jarvie. After a prayer, Reeder said, "Agent Oatah has a few questions for you, Jarvie."

"Yes, honor," Jarvie answered, turning to Oatah, but it was Reeder who continued to ask.

"Did you learn to speak the Ramian language?"

"No, honor."

"In all that time?"

"They had translators."

"Did you learn the written language?"

"No, honor."

"Alphabet?"

"Um, not really."

Reeder frowned. "Anything about their religion?"

"I learned a couple of prayer / songs."

"Good," Reeder said with false praise. Beezan was focusing fine now and getting a bit annoyed. "Could you translate one for us?"

"Oh, well, no. The songs seem to be in a different language."

Reeder sighed. "Any math?"

"Just numbers, which we already knew."

"Biology?" Jarvie shook his head no. "Ship design? Engineering? History?" Jarvie kept shaking his head.

"I thought the adults would talk about all that important stuff."

"Reeder," Iricana said reasonably, "perhaps *we're* asking too much." Beezan was ready to jump off the bed and tell Reeder to leave him alone, but Jarvie was calm and unperturbed.

"Surely you must have learned something."

"Colors."

Reeder blinked in confusion, but Oatah raised an interested eyebrow. "Do you mean," Oatah asked, "that you can interpret the emotional content of their self-broadcast coloring?"

"Yes, most of the time."

"Excellent," Reeder said, following Oatah's interest. "Can you write it down?"

"I'm not sure that's possible."

"Why not?"

"Well, could you write down how you know what other people are feeling by their expression? For strangers and friends? In general and for individuals?"

"I *don't know* what other humans are feeling—besides the obvious," Reeder retorted. Beezan wasn't sure about the obvious.

"Well, the obvious. Maybe I could make a few general rules. But I wouldn't want you relying on them for some high-level diplomatic thing and getting in trouble because I said blue green hint of purple and you thought it was blue blue green."

"Perhaps," Oatah intervened sternly, "we will rely on you *personally* when we get to high-level diplomatic *things*." Jarvie sat back in alarm.

Beezan laughed and came to sit with them. "You'll scare him into a life of cargo loading."

"Oh," Jarvie said, "there was something else," and Beezan caught a glint of mischief in Jarvie's eyes.

"Yes?" Reeder prompted wearily.

"I could write down a map of gravity ball finds in Ramian space." Beezan's heart skipped a beat. *Is he kidding? Just to get back at Reeder?* The others sat up in stunned silence.

"Also strategies for finding them and command sequences for controlling them . . . and I've been thinking about where . . . we . . . might look," Jarvie slowed down as Reeder looked ready to pounce on him.

"That's not funny!" Reeder scolded him. "You know how much that would mean to us."

"I'm not joking," Jarvie said and appealed to Iricana. She literally took him by the chin and looked him in the eye. "I'm not."

She glanced at Oatah. "God in heaven, Jarvie, I can't believe you didn't bust out with the news!"

"That's how they have gravity. There's a gravity ball in the middle of the ship."

"*What?* Are they *crazy?*" Beezan said, understanding now why Neah had avoided his gravity questions.

"That's what I thought, when I found out."

"Where is all this data?" Iricana asked.

"I coded it," he said, tapping his p'link.

"And you haven't transcribed it yet? You'll forget," and she was up looking for another pad.

"Interesting, Jarvie," Oatah said, "but before you get absorbed in that, there was actually only one thing I wanted to know."

"Yes, honor?"

Oatah leaned forward to look Jarvie right in the eye. "Can we live in harmony with the Ramians?"

Beezan felt another of those Oatah moments where the future of humanity hung in balance. Jarvie did not hesitate or pull away from Oatah's penetrating gaze. In fact, he focused in on him. "Yes," he said with a confidence and maturity Beezan had never heard from Jarvie. "We will."

In his cabin that night, Beezan stared at his pop-up. 715 packets, including 539 official ones. *Drumheller* had filtered all news packets to a separate file. Beezan had missed his packets so much, but now he didn't know where to start. So much had happened in his own life, how could he absorb more news from outside? They may have come 'home' to Redrock, but Redrock wouldn't be the same. His world had changed. He had changed.

"It's a little scary."

Beezan jumped. He hadn't heard Jarvie come to their shared door. He nodded, patting the other chair for Jarvie. "I don't know why," Beezan admitted.

"Iricana is summarizing the news," Jarvie told him. "She says there's no work-around. Yet." Beezan hoped his friends were all right.

"And we've been listed as a possible loss. So it's big excitement that we're back. You'll get a bunch of packets from reporters by tomorrow."

"Oh, I'm sure Reeder will intercept them."

"They'll be gone soon," Jarvie said cautiously.

"Who?" Had Jarvie been assigned to break some news to him?

"Oatah and Reeder. They're not going to wait a whole eight days to come in. We're rendezvousing with another ship and they're going to try their own way to get back to Earth."

"Iricana and Katie are staying?"

"Yes, that's the good news."

Beezan frowned. "And . . ."

"Oatah has some new crew hired. They're on the way here now, on the ship we're meeting."

"Already?" Beezan felt a surge of panic.

"Yes. It's the *Nightingale.*"

Beezan shook his head. More new people. "I don't know that ship. But Oatah shouldn't make you tell me all this stuff. It's not fair to you."

"There's good news actually. Oatah is sending us to Tektite to check out the control panel. Iricana has more orders but she's not allowed to tell us yet."

"Tektite," Beezan said. "Lots of jumps."

"Will we go through Mirage?"

"Sandune, I think. Then Radium Junction, Tetra, Tundra, and Tektite. By the time we get back you'll be jumping on your own." Beezan felt a bit of calm just talking like a cargo pilot again.

Jarvie smiled, but a flicker of sadness crossed his face. "When I came aboard and said I wanted to go to Harbor and had this fantasy of reuniting with Lanezi, I knew in my heart it would never happen. It was just some vague hope, something to do. I never imagined I'd be happy again, or have real hope, or have a home," he whispered. "Thank you."

Beezan's heart swelled with affection. "Thank you," he said, reaching out and clasping Jarvie's hand. "I didn't really have much hope either. I told myself I was trusting in God, but I really think I was testing God. God forgive me," he added. "For my feeble trust, I was greatly rewarded."

Jarvie smiled shyly. "I may end up being more of a test."

Beezan took a big breath and looked at his little sector map. "I'm sure we have many tests ahead. We will put our **'. . . *trust in God, and, holding fast unto Him, follow in His way.*'**"[1]

. . .

17-Speech

Jarvie tugged at his too-short uniform sleeves as he waited for the rest of the crew to assemble outside the kitchen. They wore their best uniforms for their last day together. Reeder was already gone, in a flourish of formality. He had taken Oatah's fancy shuttle over to *Nightingale* to pick up three new crewmembers. He was on his way back to drop them off and take Oatah.

Iricana appeared, whispering a few last commands to *Drumheller,* and then stood quietly beside Jarvie. Katie joined them with a silent smile. Although Reeder's departure had been full of good wishes, there was no real sense of loss. Not so with Oatah. They had all come to like and respect him and to understand the great responsibility on his shoulders. Beezan waited at Oatah's cabin door for an old and rarely used custom, the honor walk.

When Oatah appeared, Beezan took his personal bag and motioned Oatah ahead. With a puzzled look, Oatah continued up the rimway. Katie and Iricana walked ahead with Jarvie. Beezan walked behind Oatah with the podpups, for once minding and being serious. "Lights," Iricana whispered, and the main lights dimmed. The red emergency lights going on added to the sense of pageantry. An old classical piece, probably from Earth, began to play. Oatah lowered his head humbly as they took their last walk down the rimway.

So much had happened, right here in this rimway, Jarvie thought. How spooky and lonely it was when he first came aboard. The music unloosed a river of memories: Dragging the oxygen-deprived Beezan back to his cabin, looking over his shoulder while fixing the doors, skating, crashing into Beezan, he recalled with a wince. The heart-hammering race to stop the computer shutdown, the brick wall, Sarcee, he thought with a bittersweet pang. His sneaking out on the hull, his sickness when Beezan towed him around, meeting with the others after so many weeks alone. Lander. Jarvie swallowed hard. The Ramians coming aboard, taking Star, and Star scampering around after his return. The Robots.

As they approached the lift, Jarvie looked up. Two rows of robots, in tall thin mode, and #9, all stood at attention along the walls. As they began to pass between the robots, an archway of light sparkled over them.

The lift lock opened. Jarvie stood aside with Katie and Iricana. Oatah stopped and turned, considering them all with one long last look. "Thank you," Oatah said quietly, "May God bless and protect you all." He took his bag and shook Beezan's hand.

"Thank you," they all said. A chorus of "God is Most Glorious" followed Oatah into the lift. The doors shut and the lift started down, the music still playing. They could see on the status indicator that the music ended exactly at the right moment when the lift stopped. Slowly the rimway lights went back on.

Jarvie smiled down at Katie and Iricana, very happy they were staying. They waited nervously for the lift to come back so they could greet the new crew. Jarvie told himself to give them a chance. *Trust in God.*

"Well," Beezan said quietly, "while Oatah is off to order the future, our future is coming up the lift."

"Have faith, Captain," Iricana said. "We weren't so bad."

He smiled nervously.

Then the door slid open revealing three people in suits, holding their helmets, surrounded by luggage. A yellow-banded girl, a stern woman, and a very old man stepped forward. *Kelson McNelson? The One Tree founder himself?* "Captain, my child," he said "I am pleased as potatoes to see you!" and handed his helmet to an astonished Beezan.

EXCERPT FROM THE SUNDERING SERIES, BOOK 2: THE UNBOUNDED

Chapter 1: No Escape

Date: 3-Dominion-1082

Harbor Station

A young man, 27 years old, outer-sector thin, circled furtively on the Harbor Station TopRim. His cold hands were tucked nervously under his poncho, holding a red box. He had medium brown skin and dark eyes that darted constantly, as if he were on the run. But if others noticed anything, it was the expensive alpaca wool of his brown and tan poncho, an uncommon show of wealth. Although he wasn't wearing a pilot's jacket, his intense demeanor was enough to identify him and keep strangers away.

Lanezi stopped abruptly, realizing he was pacing in circles. Poncho swirling, he turned and made himself pace in a line—but then he had to retrace that same line—so it was still a circle, no matter how flat he made it. There was no escape.

Circles. He had walked TopRim four times today: giant circles of nowhere to go. Now he paced in his flat circles, outside the art gallery, waiting for the buyer to pay him. The owner was concerned about Lanezi's request for a cash slider, but since Lanezi was a sector-famous artist, as well as a respected pilot, it had been arranged. The gallery had already hung one of his paintings, "To Atikameq." A cluster of people gathered around it, seeing in the painting what only long jumpers could see in life.

Lanezi circled away to avoid the crowd, so the buyer had to come out to pay him. Finally, slider in hand, Lanezi hurried to the cargo dock to put his box on a ship out of Harbor.

Lanezi hesitated outside the cargo customer desk. The gears of his circling mind ground to a shuttering stop. He was about to ship a package that would change his life. Before he lost his nerve, or his hope, he took a breath and went up to the desk.

He said a prayer for the smaller box within the box, the engagement ring for Katie. It carried his hopes for a future with his own family, a spouse and children, a future where he would no longer be cycled from family to family, ship to ship, just to be cycled on, in indifference, in practicality, in tragedy and more tragedy. Surely he had had his share.

He shook himself. Life in the outer sectors wasn't easy. He wasn't the only one struggling. Better times were ahead. He would break free of the circles. Katie would get the ring and they could be married, and someday Jarvie might even catch up and be his shipmate again, his surrogate nephew, his co-survivor of Lanezi's latest cycle of loss.

Lanezi was so, so grateful that he had not been separated from his few remaining loved ones in the Sundering, the tragedy that had recently rocked the outer sectors.

As far as most people knew, Firelight System, in Sector 5, had lost its a-rings in an accident. Lanezi, on Thayne's top-secret team, knew that aliens were attempting to jump into human space—and every time they tried, there was a terrible accident.

Of all the possible losses, Firelight, the one transit point between the inner and outer sectors, was the worst. Now separated from Earth, Lanezi feared that the outer sectors could not survive much longer. But the Sundering had not been personal. He had only two people in his life, Katie and Jarvie. Katie was part of Thayne's team, on Redrock now. And Jarvie—Lanezi fervently hoped that Jarvie was on his way to Harbor and would soon arrive.

He watched until the box disappeared down the sorter, then took another deep breath and sighed, relieved that it was finally done. He'd been off the ship all day. Thayne was too sick to notice, luckily. Thayne, as leader of their secret mission, "Project Restore," and Captain of the *Cheetah*, could command Lanezi not to go to the station, as Thayne usually did. Today Lanezi had been able to take his paintings and get out without anyone even knowing.

Lanezi had a little pang of guilt. Thayne would have been able to jump last month and the month before if not for Lanezi's secret stalling, hoping that Jarvie might arrive. Now Thayne was too sick. The weakness of Thayne's body and the storms of his mind combined to disable him, sometimes dangerously.

Lanezi started back along TopRim, not as fast as his moment of guilt might have driven him. Thayne had an Earthborn personal doctor, a genius engineer, and the best data hunter in the outer sectors, along with assorted ship robots to support his every whim. Lanezi could be free for a day. Free from the constriction of circling around Thayne.

Lanezi was truly not jealous. His own unusual jumping skills were an undeserved gift. If Thayne wanted to use him to augment the mission, Lanezi was happy to help, for the sake of the sectors. But Thayne was work, not family.

Lanezi meandered along TopRim, savoring his last circle of freedom, before heading back to the *Cheetah* to see what Thayne's latest mental firestorm had launched. His p'link beeped again. He ignored it, for the twentieth time, and concentrated on staring into the nearest shop window.

"RESCUE" The sign caught his eye, but it wasn't a teen training sign. Lanezi was staring into the Podpup Nursery. The "available" sign advertised seven pups and one rescue. The seven pups were right in the window, tumbling about and ignoring all else. Back in the corner, an adult podpup in a pink knitted sweater cowered inside a box. Lanezi bent down to see better and she, seemingly on guard, looked up and met his eyes. They stared at each other. *What happened to her? Was she abandoned? Was it possible she was mistreated?* Lanezi had never heard of that happening, but the way she cowered under the box was heartbreaking. *I haven't been mistreated, but I feel that way sometimes.*

Go! We don't waste our time on podpups! a voice insisted in his mind, but it was only the echo of Thayne invading Lanezi's conscience. Lanezi ignored it and read the sign again.

"RESCUE. Female, 8 years old. Former Locator."

A locator! Locators were specially trained to find people or bodies after a disaster. She was a rescuer herself, and now she needed rescuing. Lanezi shook himself. He had people to worry about. He looked back down at her. She was still staring at him with hurt and beseeching eyes. He needed to go, but he felt a great surge of sympathy. She had been torn from her former life and family just as he had. "Good bye, little one," he whispered and turned quickly away.

He had not gone three meters when he was overcome by a

heart-rending sound, a keening that seemed to strip the blood from his veins. He dropped to his knees in shock and pain. He could see others cover their ears and look around, but they were not struck down as he was.

Several people were coming to help him when it happened again. Now his heart was on fire. Heat pulsed through his body and engulfed his brain. *What is happening?* He turned on his hands and knees to look behind him, knowing where the sound was coming from.

A tall, very dark-skinned, man ran out of the Podpup Nursery and paused in the rimway, his fierce eyes scanning the stunned people. “Bring him!” he commanded as soon as he saw Lanezi crumpled on the floor. Two green-banded teens hovering beside Lanezi grabbed his arms under his poncho and dragged him into the Podpup Nursery.

“What is it?” One teen asked the other.

“The death cry. The last cry of an abandoned podpup.”

“No,” Lanezi feebly shook his head. “I just looked in the window.”

“There,” commanded the man, pointing to a reclining chair. The teens hauled Lanezi into it.

“He says he was only looking in the window,” one reported.

The man leaned down to look Lanezi in the eye. “I am Dr. Obala. Do you deny you are bonded to the podpup?”

“I was just looking in the window,” Lanezi repeated. “I haven’t had a pup since I was a child.”

“Go,” the doctor told the teens. “Restore order outside.”

“Yes, honor,” and they were gone.

Another cry started and Lanezi thought he would faint in the chair. He was gasping for air.

“Look at you!” The doctor had a tinge of desperation in his

voice now. He yanked the poncho off over Lanezi's head. "The cry is killing you. Somehow you have bonded with her."

"I . . . just . . . looked . . . in—"

"You were chosen." The doctor turned and signaled to his assistant, a purple-banded teen with tears streaming down her cheeks. "Bring her. Perhaps it is not too late."

The doctor looked on sternly as the assistant put the podpup, in her little pink sweater, into Lanezi's shaking arms.

Lanezi held her against his chest, but did not feel any relief, on his part or hers. If she cried again, he feared for his life. He had heard of it—just rumors of course.

There was a rumbling in her chest and Lanezi let out an involuntary sob.

"Where is the human med team?" Dr. Obala was asking into his s'link.

The rumbling was building. "No, no," Lanezi begged her. "I'm here. No more crying. I didn't know." Lanezi couldn't keep the panic out of his voice. "I won't leave you." The rumbling reached a roar inside the pup and she uttered a cry that shook Lanezi to his core. He heard himself scream the same strangled wail as if they were crossing through some crucible together, and then she collapsed against his chest, expiring her last breath.

Lanezi was vaguely aware of the doctor holding his shoulder, hard. The assistant was sobbing while trying to comfort the seven pups. Other medical people were suddenly around him. They had his p'link. *Supposed to be secret*, his foggy mind fretted.

"Lanezi. He's that famous artist."

"He's a long jump pilot," the other said. "We may be able to save him."

"We must save them both," the doctor declared, sliding a resus pack under the podpup's chest.

Lanezi said a parting prayer as he faded from the world, but he was not afraid. Whether they saved him or not seemed of little consequence. The rumbling had stopped. If he never heard that sound again he would not care if he lived or died.

Coming soon!

Sign up for news at:
https://www.draepricebooks.com/the-sundering-series

ACKNOWLEDGMENTS

The Sundering Series took many MANY years to write. I'm very grateful to all the people who encouraged and supported me on this long journey.

To my childhood writing and adventure buddy Brian Burriston, to my patient husband Jeff Price, to my social media and fiction advisor Raeleigh Price, and to my professional mentor Amy Renshaw, all of whom read and advised on The Sundering, I could not have done this without you. Thank you so much.

Special thanks to additional brave beta readers Jordan Price, Shirlie Burriston, Don Burriston, Goleta Dawia, Doug Krotz, James Schwartz, and Sally Caldwell.

I'll be forever grateful to Amethel Parel-Sewell, Editor and Creative Director of **Brilliant Star Magazine** for giving me the chance to write professionally. And thank you to the rest of the Brilliant Star Crew for your creative passion and hope for humanity: Amy Renshaw, Susan Engle, Annie Reneau, C. Aaron Kreader, Heidi Parsons, Katie Bishop, Foad Ghorbani, Lisa Blecker, Darcy Greenwood, and Dr. Stephen Scotti.

To my 7th grade English teacher Mrs. Dann, who asked me to send her a copy of my first book, and my 12th grade English teacher Mr. Chuck Foster, I wish I knew where you both are, so I could thank you in person. Not much compares to the power of teachers who believe in you.

I'm so lucky to have the talented and spaceship-loving Tom Edwards illustrate and design the Sundering Series covers. Thank you for bringing the *Drumheller* to life!

Thank you to all the readers who gave this book a try. I hope you'll stay tuned for more.

I'd like to thank my husband again for supporting this long project and my mom for bringing me the Bahá'í Faith, a source of comfort and guidance in my life. I'm so thankful that I live a life where I have the opportunity to write and publish. I yearn for a world where everyone will have the opportunity to reach for their stars.

-DRP

ALSO BY D RAE PRICE

What You Win: Stories for the Whole Family

• How can Mica compete at the science fair when parents are helping the other kids?

• Niccolo doesn't want to play in the symphony this summer, but can he bring himself to blow the audition?

• How will Jenna and Abby ever become astronauts if they're stuck on the farm, and lost in the maize?

From silly to serious, here are sixteen hopeful stories about walking your own path, finding friends, and fighting everyday battles.

ABOUT THE AUTHOR

A native of Earth, D Rae Price lives in the San Francisco Bay Area with her family. She has a bachelor's degree in astronomy, but spent her class time thinking up space adventures instead of thesis topics. In real life, she's looking forward to the Lucy mission flybys of Trojan asteroids and finding out more about the origins of our solar system.

NOTES

5. FIRST CROSSING

1. *Bahá'u'lláh: Persian Hidden Words, #12*
2. *Bahá'u'lláh: Persian Hidden Words, #7*
3. *Bahá'u'lláh: Persian Hidden Words, #17*
4. *Bahá'u'lláh: Persian Hidden Words, #40*
5. *Bahá'u'lláh: Persian Hidden Words, #38*
6. *Bahá'u'lláh: Persian Hidden Words, #9*
7. *Bahá'u'lláh: Persian Hidden Words, #19*
8. *Bahá'u'lláh: Epistle to the Son of the Wolf, p. 16*

13. PICKING UP THE PIECES

1. *`Abdu'l-Bahá: Selections from the Writings of 'Abdu'l-Bahá, p. 26*

14. STARTING OVER

1. *`Abdu'l-Bahá: Selections from the Writings of 'Abdu'l-Bahá, p. 178*

21. THE ONE TREE

1. *`Abdu'l-Bahá: Promulgation of Universal Peace, p. 661*

24. WANDERING

1. *Bahá'u'lláh: Kitáb-i-Aqdas #129*

25. LANDER'S MOON

1. *Bahá'u'lláh: Bahá'í Prayers (US edition), p. 36*
2. *Bahá'u'lláh: Bahá'í Prayers (US edition), p. 36*

27. NOCTURNE

1. *The Báb: Selections from the Writings of the Báb, p. 217*

29. THE OCEAN OF SPACE

1. *Bahá'u'lláh: Arabic Hidden Words, #40*
2. *`Abdu'l-Bahá: Selections from the Writings of 'Abdu'l-Bahá, p. 13*

30. SHUTTLE DIPLOMACY

1. *The Báb: Bahá'í Prayers (US edition), p. 153*

31. THE TWO SEAS

1. *`Abdu'l-Bahá: Bahá'í Prayers (US edition), p.119 & Qur'an 55:19-20*

32. ALIEN FEVER

1. *Bahá'u'lláh: Bahá'í Prayers (US edition), p. 102*

34. A LITTLE SHIP

1. *`Abdu'l-Bahá: Promulgation of Universal Peace, p. 65*

35. THE RACE TO SEVEN

1. *"Likewise, these souls, through the potency of the Divine Elixir, traverse, in the twinkling of an eye, the world of dust and advance into the realm of holiness; and*

with one step cover the earth of limitations and reach the domain of the Placeless." —Bahá'u'lláh: The Kitáb-i-Íqán, p. 157

2. *"O OFFSPRING OF DUST! Be not content with the ease of a passing day, and deprive not thyself of everlasting rest. Barter not the garden of eternal delight for the dust-heap of a mortal world. Up from thy prison ascend unto the glorious meads above, and from thy mortal cage wing thy flight unto the paradise of the Placeless." —Bahá'u'lláh: Persian Hidden Words, #39*
3. *"O my spiritual loved ones! Praise be to God, ye have thrust the veils aside and recognized the compassionate Beloved, and have hastened away from this abode to the placeless realm. Ye have pitched your tents in the world of God, and to glorify Him, the Self-Subsistent, ye have raised sweet voices and sung songs that pierced the heart." —'Abdu'l-Bahá: Selections from the Wittings of 'Abdu'l-Bahá, pp. 317-318*

41. HOMEWARD

1. *`Abdu'l-Bahá: Bahá'í Prayers (US Edition), p. 28*

42. PATHS TO THE FUTURE

1. *Bahá'u'lláh: The Kitáb-i-Íqán, p. 3*

Printed in the USA
CPSIA information can be obtained
at www.ICGtesting.com
LVHW011253111124
796255LV00045B/805

* 9 7 9 8 9 8 5 2 0 4 3 3 9 *